Under The

Grapevine

S. LEE FISHER

THE WOMEN OF CAMPBELL COUNTY BOOK 2

Cover Design by 100 Covers
Editing by Wandering Words Media
Beta Reading by Nola Li Barr and Inghild Okland
Formatting by Tapioca Press

Print ISBN: 978-1-7367526-3-0
Ebook ISBN: 978-1-7367526-2-3

To Ralph, my rock, with love.

SWEET DREAMS

CAMPBELLSVILLE, AUGUST 1925

*T*wenty-four-year-old Olive screamed, thrashing from side to side, arms waving as if to ward off an attack. The sound woke the tiny infant—who was sleeping in a woven basket laying at the bottom of the bed—as well as her husband, Tobias Bailey, who stirred, wiped his eyes, then sprang to attention.

"Darling," Tabs' arms encircled his wife, whose cotton nightgown clung to her sweat-drenched body. "Darling, it's okay. I'm here. You had another nightmare."

Thunder rumbled, the storm raging outside as Olive trembled, slowly gaining awareness of her surroundings. She was safe, warm in her bed, her loving husband beside her. She pulled away from Tabs as she reached for her neck, resting her shaking hands on her throbbing chest.

"Let go; you're smothering me," she said. "I need some air."

Tabs released his grip. Sliding out from under the quilt, he lifted the tiny boy and rubbed his back. "Shush, little man, all is well. Mama had a bad dream." He bounced the baby gently as he motioned to the two girls peeking in the doorway. "Shhh, now, go back to sleep, all of you. It's all right. Papa will keep you safe."

The baby relaxed. Within moments he was sound asleep, wrapped in his father's loving arms.

Tabs lay Albert back into the basket as a bolt of lightning lit up the room. Olive's face paled as she jumped. Looking at his wife, he creased his brow.

"Olive, this makes three nights this week. Please, won't you tell me what is so upsetting?"

Running her hands through her long blonde curls, Olive turned her head away from Tabs. She wiped her forehead with the hem of her nightgown. "I'm not reliving it. It's bad enough that I suffer from the dream so often, especially during a storm. If we had better weather, I wouldn't dream. Let it go. Please, Tabs, let it go."

SUMMER RAINS

CAMPBELLSVILLE, SUMMER 1929

*T*he clap of thunder startled her. Olive Bailey's apron tie caught in the mangle crank as she faced the direction of the noise.

"Blasted storm."

Turning the mangle crank in reverse, she escaped her entrapment. Darting out of the kitchen into the yard, she rushed, pulling wet laundry off the clothesline before the sky opened.

"Esther, hurry. I need help," Olive called to her oldest, ten-year-old daughter. "June, keep an eye on Alice. And Albert, for goodness' sake, sit yourself down on a kitchen chair and stay there."

Summer storms in western Pennsylvania appeared quickly, often with little warning. Olive shivered as the dark clouds moved over the hilltops and down into the valley, settling over the river. The air hung close and damp on her skin as the squall raced toward her. She calculated five, maybe six minutes before a complete deluge.

Esther and Olive scrambled with their baskets of wet sheets, towels, Tabs' dungarees, and Olive's aprons as the wind increased, whipping the laundry up and over the clothesline. A bolt of lightning cracked, both mother and daughter jumped.

"Mother, that was close. Look!" Esther pointed to a puff of smoke spiraling from the river, now shrouded in fog. The Conemaugh flowed through the middle of the town, separating Campbellsville into two sections. "I think it hit close to the foundry. I hope Papa is okay."

"Don't worry about him. Grab your basket; up to the attic, you go. This makes three Mondays this month with rain. Wretched weather," Olive grumbled. "I hate when my work schedule is disrupted."

Then to herself, *I hate it more when it storms all through the night.* She brushed her neck as if shooing a bug.

Tabs and Olive Bailey lived in a prominent corner house in Campbellsville, Pennsylvania, amidst rolling hills and lush green valleys. The borough was laid out in a grid formation of four-acre blocks, and sported large houses on every half-acre corner lot. Four smaller company houses filled in between, completing the tree-lined streets. Olive's pride and joy, the eight-room three-story brick structure was much smaller than the massive Georgian-style farm mansion in which she was raised.

Olive clomped through the kitchen, sliding on the linoleum floor. Stopping to drop the wet clothes, she regained her balance. Monday was wash day, followed by Tuesday for ironing. Wednesday and Thursday were designated for mending and sewing, leaving Friday to shop, Saturday to house clean, and Sunday for church, then rest. The Baileys omitted the church part.

"Esther, when you are finished rehanging that first load, come get this other pile." Olive spun on her heel, attacking the barrel tumbler clothes washer. She whirled the hand crank. "Son of a...!" she screamed as she carelessly touched the crank lever that squeezed water from the wet clothing. "I burned my finger!"

Wearing a hand-me-down gingham sundress, three-and-a-half-year-old Alice toddled toward her mother. "I kiss it, Mommy. Make finger better."

"No. Alice, move. Go with June. Stay out of my way. I have too much work to finish."

The door opened as Olive shunned the toddler. A boom of thunder and a second lightning strike filled the sky. The smell of burning wood filtered through the threshold.

"Papa!" Eight-year-old June, four-and-a-half-year-old Albert, and Alice ran to embrace their father, who dripped wet with rainwater.

"Come here, darlings." Tabs kissed and hugged each child in greeting. "Where is Esther?" he asked, looking around the kitchen.

"In the attic, hanging clothes, *again*. Why are you home?" Olive glanced at Tabs. "Wipe your feet. For God's sake, strip out of those wet clothes before you track water through my entire house."

Tabs lifted Alice into one arm as Albert jumped into the other, his muscles quickly bearing their weight. June clung to his work trousers, which were covered in patches and grease. "Good afternoon, children. Are you helping Mama?" Tabs asked as Olive rolled her eyes.

"For goodness' sake, Tabs. Now the children are wet and dirty," Olive grumbled. "I have enough work already today."

Tabs nuzzled his offspring, "Find a towel, June, let's dry off."

He tickled their bellies and rubbed their hair; his children squealed in delight.

"Okay, now over to the corner. Stay out of Mama's way." Tabs shooed the trio. Walking up behind Olive, he grabbed her around the waist and hugged her. Kissing her neck, he said, "Hello, beautiful Wife."

Olive swatted his face with the back of a soapy hand. "Leave me alone; I'm working," she said smiling.

Dressed in a housecoat-like apron, her curly blonde hair pulled off her face with a bandana, Olive's attractive and shapely appearance paled only slightly in comparison to the beauty she had when Tabs had first met her. The birth of four children did little to diminish the youthful vitality of the woman, who was only twenty-seven years old.

"You didn't answer. Why are you home in the middle of the day?" Olive furrowed her brow as she dumped the clothes into the rinse tub. "Speak, man."

"The foundry was struck by lightning. We can't work until tomorrow." Tabs bent over; lifting the wet clothes, he guided them through the mangle as Olive turned the crank. "I have a crew working to repair our equipment."

"Shouldn't you be helping them?" questioned Olive. "Will your wages be docked? We already live week to week."

"Do not worry, Wife. You sound like we are destitute. Don't forget that I am salaried as a shift supervisor." Tabs leaned in to steal a kiss. Olive pushed him away.

"I liked it better when you pulled extra shifts for over-time." The crank stopped as a lump of fabric lodged between the rollers. "Blasted," Olive repeated as she tugged and pulled at the mass.

"Allow me." Tabs' muscled arms easily dislodged the bundle. He leaned in toward Olive, attempting another kiss.

"Stop this tomfoolery. Help with the laundry, if you wish, but leave me alone." Olive's hand swatted Tabs on the side of the head. The children giggled as Tabs retaliated, tickling his wife and pulling her to the floor. Soon, all five were rolling on the wet linoleum, with Olive laughing.

Hearing the commotion from the attic, Esther hurried down the two flights of stairs.

"Wait for me!" she said as she jumped on the pile of humanity.

"Ah, there's my beautiful firstborn." Tabs welcomed her to the fun and games. Esther shared her father's diminutive stature, while the other children grew tall and lean like their mother. Olive, at five-seven, towered over Tabs by at least two inches, despite his thick, brown, billowing mane.

After several minutes of tumbling, Olive glimpsed her stack of laundry. She regained control. "Enough, Tobias Bailey! I swear, you are a bad influence on me." Her mercurial mood and expression hardened.

"But Olive, you no longer need to mop the floor. It's done." Tabs waved at their clothing.

"Strip, all of you! I now have an extra load of washing," Olive ordered as everyone, including Tabs, shimmied down to their skivvies. Olive gathered the bundle of wet items, threw them into the barrel, and began cranking again, frowning all the while.

Wearing only his long john's and T-shirt, Tabs gently nudged her away. Taking the crank, he offered, "May I, darling Wife? I promise you, my services are not needed at the foundry today. Allow me to complete your chores." Olive's face softened.

She kissed Tabs on the cheek before asking, "Who wants homemade noodles and chicken for dinner?"

"Yummy!" Six hands (Alice raised both) flew into the air as Olive moved to the Hoosier and opened the flour bin to make their evening meal. While she possessed a multitude of talents, cooking was not one of Olive's proficient skills. Her childhood was spent on a prosperous farm that employed a full-time cook; Olive learned to can and preserve the harvest, but never to prepare the daily meal.

"Did you kill one of our birds?" Tabs asked as Olive kneaded the dough. Small puffs of white filled the air like ash from a spewing volcano.

"No. Lupinetti's had a sale on chicken last week. I had one delivered with my Friday order." Olive motioned to Esther. "Are all the clothes hung in the attic?"

"Yes, Mother." Esther stood at attention, her thin petticoat covering a slowly changing body, awaiting her next command.

"Then you may coat the chicken and begin frying," Olive said without looking in Esther's direction.

"Papa, will you stoke the stove? I'm not tall enough to reach the back, even with a poker."

"Certainly, Daughter dear." Tabs abandoned the laundry to load the wood into the burning box of the cast iron coal burning stove and oven. The fire flared, and the chicken crackled.

Esther dredged the meat in flour and plopped a scoop of lard into the iron frying pan to heat. Dipping each piece in egg and dredging with a coating of crushed corn flakes, she gently laid each piece in the skillet to begin sizzling.

"Olive," Tabs said. "Perhaps we should consider purchasing a gas stove?"

"Absolutely not! They are too dangerous. I'll not risk blowing up *my* house for convenience's sake." Olive shook her head disapprovingly. "Don't talk nonsense. This stove is perfectly fine. We stock plenty of coal and wood."

"Always the practical one. Of course, any expenditure is your decision." Tabs deferred household finances to Olive, his budgetary whiz.

3

THE ARBOR

*A*lthough the house boasted a large dining room reserved for special occasions, the family always ate their meals in the kitchen. The square center table, painted white, served as the main workstation. Two adults, two adolescents, and two toddlers in highchairs crowded around it in cozy family comfort.

"Delicious. Thank you, dear Wife and Daughter, for this meal." Tabs kissed both on the cheek, repeating his evening ritual. "Olive, now that the rain has slowed, I need to tend the garden. Will you join me on the porch for a cup of tea later?"

"Esther, June, clean up. Yes, Tabs, I'll be out in five minutes."

Tabs slipped his feet into a pair of rubber Wellies, a souvenir of the war.

At the top of the property, the garden adjacent to the alley camouflaged the chicken coop from the rest of the yard. Many of Campbellsville's residents maintained small vegetable gardens, chickens, and even a pig or two. The Bailey's property also featured several flower gardens for display and cutting, terraced in the sloping backyard. Tart red apples, sour plums, and juicy peaches from the tiny orchard provided fresh fruit for eating and canning. The property's main feature, a large arbor covered with grapevines, offered shade, a place of solitude, and many jars of jelly. Olive and Tabs duplicated the massive Westchester Farm as best as they could on the half-acre lot.

Olive carried a tray and a drying cloth to the four Adirondack chairs under the grape arbor. A favorite spot for relaxation and conversation, the site was usually occupied when weather permitted.

She placed the cups on the chair arm, then wiped the seat with a rag. "Tabs, your tea is ready," Olive called as Tabs carefully picked his path down the slippery yard.

"Is Esther tending to the little ones?" Knowing the answer already, he continued, "Ahh. This is the life." Taking the cup, he sipped the sweetened liquid. "Honey instead of sugar?"

"Yes. Ingrid is selling it at Lupinetti's. It's tasty, reminds me of the farm."

Tabs lit a cigarette, then a candle as Olive silently reminisced. Her mind drifted to the many candlelit parties in the gardens of the farm. The smell of a freshly plowed field, crickets chirping, violins plucking the beat, as the family twirled around a make-shift dance floor flooded her memory.

Her daydream was interrupted by Ruth Callihan, the next-door neighbor crossing the road while calling to them.

"Olive, you have a phone call," she yelled as she approached the couple, walking up the path leading to the grapevines. "Your brother Ben is on the phone. Shall I tell him you'll be right over?"

"Yes. I'll be there promptly." Olive scrunched her nose as she looked at Tabs. "I wonder what *he* wants."

"Only one way to find out." Tabs reached for his wife's hand. "How long has it been since your last visit?"

She pulled her hand out of Tabs' reach. "I snuck up three weeks ago to visit the cemetery, but no one saw me."

Abandoning her tea, Olive crossed the cobblestone street and entered her neighbor's house through the back door. Ruth handed her the phone as Olive wiped her feet on the braided rope doormat.

Tabs and Olive chose not to install a phone. Although Olive's family owned two of the original telephones in the county, the need for such a luxury was less pressing in town. With shops, businesses, friends, and family all within walking distance, even shouting distance, and public phone boxes scattered throughout town, the Callihan's pridefully owned the only private phone on the street.

"Hello. Olive Bailey speaking."

"Olive, it's Ben. Will you come out to the farm? I'll send Benny with the car." His trembling voice sounded older than his forty-nine years.

Ben was the oldest of the Westchester children. He ran the lucrative thousand-acre farm with their brother Clyde.

Ben's sudden request made Olive suspicious. Family tension, a significant reason for Olive's departure after the birth of Esther and her marriage to Tabs, remained high. Her father and six siblings, all highly-strung prima donnas, had turned farm life into an unbearable hell for the youngest Westchester child—or was it the other way around?

"Why?" Olive answered before Ben finished speaking. "What's going on tonight that's so damn important?"

"Olive, please skip the attitude. Father is asking for you; he's dying." Ben's voice cracked and trailed off as he spoke the last words.

She rolled her upper lip, showing her top set of teeth. "Why should I care? There is nothing in this for me. He

11

made his bed; now let him die in it. Call me when he's gone."
Olive slammed the phone in the cradle and spun on her heel.
Turning to leave, she called out, "Thanks, Ruth. If Ben calls
again, tell him I'm not home. Unless the old man is dead.
Then I'll take the call."

Olive retreated to the arbor. Before she made herself
comfortable, Ruth had returned.

"Sorry Olive, Tabs. Ben called right back. He says
Henderson will not live until morning. Dr. Paulson is at the
farm already."

"For goodness' sake. I'm not going out there tonight."
Olive stood, shaking her head, and clomped back to the
phone.

"Ben, I'm not coming out this evening. I don't care if he's
asking for me. When he dies, let me know. I'll bring the
family to the funeral. Now goodnight, and leave me alone."

"Olive—" She hung up on her brother before he finished.

The night air carried the sound. Tabs, along with several
other neighbors, heard the entire conversation. As she
entered her property for the second time that evening, Olive
avoided the arbor area. Instead, she climbed the two back
porch steps and opened the screen door.

"Tabs, I'm going inside," she called. "It's too damp out
here."

"Do you want to talk about it? That man loves you, Olive.
You really should see him before he passes. You may come to
regret it if you don't. "

"No! It's settled. I'm not giving him the pleasure of one
last visit."

Olive, rubbing the front of her neck, left Tabs sitting
alone. With the children already in bed, she entered the
formal parlor, her sanctuary. Olive maintained a private hideaway here, off-limits to the family, including Tabs.

The walls of her private haven were papered in a popular

green and white pattern and lined with bookcases. A magnolia-print settee and two stuffed chairs matched the green of the walls. A leaf pattern was woven into a woolen rug, which covered the shiny buffed floors. Silver and wooden frames housing precious photographs filled the side tables. A niche in the wall displayed a crystal vase filled with fresh flowers.

Olive walked to the bookcase. Choosing *Call of the Wild*, she took the book and a photograph of herself with a young West Point cadet to her reading chair. Flipping on the torchère lamp, she tucked her legs underneath herself. She kissed the photo and opened the book, caressing the inscription. Before she began reading, she addressed the cadet.

"Henderson shall be in hell tomorrow. Please celebrate with Mother and the other angels in heaven, because I shall certainly celebrate here on earth. I miss you, darling Freddy."

A single tear dropped onto the glass. Quickly wiping it away, she set the photo on the side table. Curling into the chair, she began to read.

4

ETERNAL PEACE?

*T*wo days later, the family prepared for the trip out to the farm for Henderson Westchester's funeral. Olive deliberately avoided visiting during the wake, although every other resident of Campbell and Madison counties made an appearance.

"Esther, are you ready?" Tabs called up the staircase to his daughter.

"Yes, Papa. June and I shall be down in just a minute."

"Hurry, the bus leaves in ten minutes. We don't want to miss it and have to walk the whole way out to the farm."

Esther and June carefully ran down the stairs, not risking a tear in their *Sunday-best* clothing. Olive purchased a new mourning dress and hat for the occasion, while Tabs dressed in an outdated but custom-made suit. Placing his hat on his head, he took each girl by the hand, urging them to walk quickly.

"Mother is already at the bus stop with Alice and Alfred. Come."

"Where are we going today?" June asked shyly.

"We are going to the farm where Mama grew up."

"Really? But we are not allowed to visit there. Even if Uncle Ben sends a car." June exclaimed, remembering the one time Benny drove to town on Easter Sunday expecting to transport the Baileys to Westchester Farms.

"Today is an exception."

Tabs shooed the girls down the street as the bus pulled to a stop. Climbing aboard, Esther and June sat in front of Olive and Tabs, who each held a child.

Esther whispered to June, "Shush with the questions. Grandfather Henderson passed away. We are going to his funeral. You don't want to make Mother upset."

"No, I don't." June shook her head. "She's scary when she's mad. Did I ever meet this Grandfather?"

"Quiet. We'll talk about it before we go to sleep tonight."

The girls sat silent the rest of the ride out of town. The bus stopped at the bottom of the lane leading to the farm.

"Come on, children," urged Tabs. "We are going for a little walk."

Olive lifted Alice while June and Esther held hands and Tabs hoisted Albert onto his shoulders. They arrived to find a throng of people. Men, women, and children occupied every inch of manicured lawn and porch of the massive mansion grounds. A waft of ripening fruit infused with spicy summer blooms greeted Olive as she walked onto the porch. The windows of the original center house and symmetrical right and left wings reflected puffy white clouds. Double doors leading to the outer foyer were propped open for easy access to the spacious interior. Attendees doubled as mourners and spectators hoping to get a glimpse of the grandeur inside.

Olive sat down on a porch rocker with Alice in tow, fingering the pearls around her neck; she waited while Tabs and the other three children mingled.

"Papa," June tugged at Tabs' sleeve. "Mama grew up in *this* house? It's gigantic."

"Yes, she did, and yes, it is. Biggest house and biggest farm in the county. Wait until you see the inside of it." As Tabs spoke, Ben Westchester and his thirty-one-year-old son Benny greeted them.

"Tabs, thank you for coming." Ben reached out. Tabs shook hands. "Who do we have here?"

"This is Esther." Tabs beamed as he introduced his eldest, their only child born at the farm.

"Seems like only yesterday that she was born," said Benny. "I was terrified that we might lose Olive that day."

"Me too. She certainly gave us a scare," agreed Tabs. Pointing to June, he continued, "This is June, and this big guy on my shoulders is Albert."

The girls politely curtsied; Albert giggled.

"I see your nose is still crooked, Benny," Tabs laughed as he observed the bulges in the bridge of Benny's nose. Extending his hand to the younger man, Tabs continued, "You and Ingrid should bring the children for a visit. How many have you?"

"We have three, two girls and a baby boy." Benny smiled shyly. "Thanks for the invitation, Tabs, but I'm not sure Olive will welcome us. Your wife is a force of nature."

"Don't I know it—but a beautiful tornado, for which I am eternally grateful."

Ben interrupted the conversation as the guests moved toward the gravesite. "Come, follow."

Ben turned. Walking down the front path toward the hill, he urged Tabs and the crowd up the knoll to the family burial plot. Since the casket was already closed, the Baileys escaped seeing Henderson as a wrinkled, frail, balding, seventy-one-year-old man.

Tabs waited for Olive before joining the procession. Leaning over, he whispered in her ear, smiling. "Up to the infamous elm tree."

She responded with a swift kick to the shins and a coy grin.

"Why did Mama kick you?" asked a puzzled Esther.

"An old family secret." Tabs' response was met with another kick. "Ouch. Was that really necessary?"

Olive scowled. "The bane of my existence."

"Be kind, dear," Tabs teased.

Several elm trees provided eternal shade to the many generations of Westchesters buried in the family cemetery. Beneath them, the carved mahogany monstrosity that was Henderson's casket balanced on a pair of sawhorses. She instinctively reached for her neck and her mother's strand of pearls. A deep, gaping hole was dug next to the monument to Polly, a towering, four-sided obelisk that was already weathered with age. *The entrance to hell*, Olive thought.

Her eyes wandered to the American flag flying next to a modest rounded stone topped with a carved eagle, the symbol of West Point. It was engraved *Lieutenant Frederick Westchester 1893 – 1918*. Olive replaced a clump of dead flowers, a remnant from her last visit, with a fresh bouquet.

"I miss him too."

Olive jumped, startled by the voice. She spun around to see a pudgy, balding, but immaculately dressed Westchester, her nephew Samuel.

"Oh, Sammy!" She hugged the man, who was only eighteen months her junior. "How are you? Why do you no longer write to me?"

A stunning red-haired woman with a bulging belly and a small boy approached.

"Here are two of the reasons: my wife, Kellyrae, and my son Oliver." Samuel Westchester blushed.

"You...named your son after me?" Olive's bottom lip quivered.

"Why not? You are not only my aunt, but you were also

my childhood friend and confidant. I was angry at Mother for months for taking me away from you."

Olive hugged Samuel in appreciation.

"Tell me, Sammy, our communication stopped too soon. Did you finish your education?"

"Yes—Aunt Clare bequeathed money for me to attend Penn State. I graduated with a degree in engineering. What about you?"

"Sadly no. I never found a way. Too late now. I have four children. " Olive waved at Tabs and their brood. "They occupy my every waking moment."

Sammy looked back at Fred's grave. He said wistfully, "His funeral was the last time I visited this farm. I wanted to stay here; Mother refused. You know, she intercepted your letters and forbade me to write? I regret not being stronger."

"I understand, Sammy. Speaking of your mother, where is Ginny?" She tried to say the name without signs of anger.

Samuel pointed toward a group of middle-aged women. "With Sally, Bessie, and Tildy."

Six women of various ages clustered together. Ginny, the eldest Westchester daughter, now forty-five, shuffled from foot to foot as she conversed with her sisters and nieces. The four mature women, with graying hair, bulging waistlines, and crow's feet around their eyes, offered a glimpse into the future for their young, vibrant offspring.

Olive snickered, "My, they look like old women."

"Aunt Olive, I do believe you take too much pleasure in that. You still are a beauty. You always were the prettiest girl in the county. And look at you, even beautiful in black." Samuel lifted his son into his arms. Giving him a kiss on the cheek, he said, "They are about to begin; shall we join them?"

∞ ∞ ∞

Tabs carried sleeping Albert and Alice down the hill. Finding one of the many porch rocking chairs, he gently swayed, lulling the toddlers to dreamland. Olive remained impatiently at the cemetery. As Pastor Ashton pronounced the final *Amen*, Olive grabbed June and Esther by the hand, hoping for a hasty escape.

"Olive—not so fast," Levi called, stopping her mid-step.

"Well, if it isn't the illustrious New York lawyer." June and Esther looked at each other, then at their mother and the strange man wearing a skull cap. "Children, this is your uncle Levi, my older brother."

"Your presence is required at the reading of the Will, Olive. Say, six o'clock this evening? That will allow guests time to mingle, eat, and pay final respects."

"Levi, I do not intend to wait here all afternoon. And as far as respect goes, Henderson Westchester earned none. May he rot in..." Olive stopped, not wanting to swear in front of the girls. Esther slipped her arm around her sister, who trembled at Olive's words.

"Still no control over that tongue, even in front of your children." Levi's eyes squinted as he hissed the insult. "Then I shall send a car for you and Tobias. Will you linger long enough to introduce your children to their family?"

"No, I shall not. We are leaving immediately. The only reason I am here is because of Mother. He was her husband." Olive grabbed for her girls. She moved so quickly that their adolescent legs struggled to keep pace.

Finding Tabs on the porch, she called, "Tabs, let's go. *Now*."

Albert awoke at her shrill voice. Whimpering, he asked his father, "Why is Mama angry?"

"Shhh, Albert. Go back to sleep, dear Son. Anything 'Westchester' initiates a foul mood for your mother."

The family quickly walked down the lane leading away from the farm and back to town.

"Mama, are we going to walk the whole way back?" Esther mustered the courage to ask, her feet aching from her dress shoes.

"Yes, and don't complain." The answer was sharp and succinct.

"Olive, carry Alice; I'll take the other three." Tabs gently handed the sleeping child to her mother. "Esther, climb onto my back. June, up you go." Tabs gathered June into one muscular arm, Albert in the other, with Esther riding high on his shoulders. Ninety minutes later, four miles traversed, Tabs sought a well-deserved respite under the grapevines.

"Here, Papa," Esther said as she handed Tabs a cup of tea. "Thank you for carrying me. I should have brought my play shoes." She kissed his cheek in appreciation.

"We'll know to be prepared for next time." Tabs smiled at his firstborn, sipped his tea, and drifted into a lazy late afternoon nap.

5

THE STASH

*T*he car arrived promptly at five-thirty. The Westchester chauffeur, Jake—an employee since the days of horse and buggy—knocked, then waited.

"Hello Miss Olive," his face beamed as Olive answered the door. "You're looking as beautiful as ever."

"Oh, Jake," Olive kissed his cheek and followed him to the car. "You always were so kind to me. How are things at the madhouse?"

"I'll deny saying this, but your brothers need you to help run things. Mr. Ben and Mr. Clyde lack when it comes to money management." Jake lowered his voice. "If you ask me, Mr. Henderson allowed them too much liberty. Too many unwise decisions made since you left to marry Mr. Bailey."

"Kind of you to say so, but I do not regret leaving that caustic environment," Olive whispered back to Jake. "Although, this is not the life I had in mind either. Father, however, sealed my fate."

Reaching the car, Jake stopped short. "Miss Olive, how can you say such things? Mr. Bailey is a good man; you can tell he loves you and the children."

"Hmm." Olive opened the front passenger door and took a seat. "Perhaps, but this is all certainly below my social status."

"Are you sure you want to ride like a commoner?" Jake asked with a grin.

Olive answered with a punch to the arm. "Jake, you are one of the better things to come from that farm," she said smiling.

"Is Mr. Bailey coming?"

"No, someone has to mind the children. Besides, the Farm was never inviting to Tabs."

The trip to the farm took less than twenty minutes in a car, much faster than on foot. When they arrived, Jake opened the door, and Olive climbed out of the old Ford.

"I can't believe this machine is still running." Olive patted the fender.

She approached the dark house that now looked lonely without its guests, then entered the front vestibule. The foyer center table, always the host of a floral arrangement, overflowed with flowers, remnants of the funeral. Bouquets filled every inch and cascaded over the sides. A musky odor of wood polish used to shine the floors and mahogany paneling, mixed with the floral scents. Proceeding through the double doors, Olive instinctively turned left, heading to her father's office. Not making it that far, she found her siblings and their spouses seated in the parlor: the most festive room in the mansion. Olive briefly remembered her father during Christmas celebrations, jovially tossing gold coins in the air for all to reap. Her glimpse into the past vanished as she became aware of her family: Ben, the oldest, and his wife Bessie were followed by Clyde and his wife Sally, Ginny, Tildy and her husband, Tommy Jamison, and Levi and his wife, Sylvia. Even now, Olive felt the absence of Fred, the closest in age to her.

"Well, I see she still likes to make an entrance," Tildy snipped. "And flaunting Mother's pearls to boot!"

Olive took a seat, rolled her eyes, and clutched her necklace, without responding.

Continuing, Tildy chided, "Couldn't even stay long enough to greet our guests."

"Tildy, if you wish for me to stay, I recommend shutting your trap, *now*." Olive looked at Levi. "May we get on with this?"

"Olive, where is Tabs? This meeting is for all of Father's children, including their husbands and wives." Levi frowned, annoyed by Tabs' absence.

"I don't have the luxury of either a nursery or a governess, so Tabs is with the children." Olive looked at the faces in the room with disdain.

"The children are welcome upstairs. Tabs should be here."

"Please, Levi, let's get this over with." Olive inhaled deeply, then held her breath in contempt.

"Fine! As you all know, Father's Will stipulates for the farm to remain intact. Ben, as the oldest, inherits the property in its entirety."

Ben and Bessie failed to disguise their delight, while Tildy's neck turned bright red.

"You mean Tommy and I do not annex some of the adjoining fields?" Tildy spat her dispute.

"No, you do not, and neither do I. Tildy, don't be difficult. It's been common knowledge for years that the acreage remains in one parcel."

Second in line to the Westchester wealth, Clyde gritted his teeth as Levi confirmed both Henderson's wishes and his own disappointment.

Olive interjected, "If that's the case, why are we here?"

Levi exhaled a long sigh. "And this is the reason I stay in New York. Father owned stocks and bonds, independent of farm assets, that he wishes to be shared by all. There is also a sizable amount of cash to be distributed among the eleven of us."

"Eleven?" Ginny questioned as she counted the bodies in the room. "Am I to receive a half-share because I am not married?"

Voicing his objection, Ben stood and walked to Levi to examine the documents. "Will this distribution impact available farm funding? We have outstanding loans on an irrigation system."

"Quiet!" Olive screamed. "You greedy, selfish mongers. You haggle over money while Father is still warm in the ground. I despise the man, but I'll not squabble over his intent. Have some pride. Take what he gives you and be grateful, you bunch of spoiled, entitled—"

"Enough, Olive. I agree. You need not expand on your feelings toward the family." Levi facilitated control of the meeting. "Shall we continue?"

Heads with reddened faces nodded in agreement.

"Eleven equal shares. One for each child, each spouse. Ten shares stock each of RCA, Ford, and General Motors, plus cash equivalent of five thousand dollars, in gold and currency, is contained in each of these eleven envelopes." The group inhaled as Levi began delivery.

"Levi, I need these funds to run the farm." Relentlessly, Ben protested, wringing his hands. "Wheat prices are dropping."

"Ben, you have substantial money between you and Bessie; if you choose to use it for the benefit of the farm, that is your prerogative. This was Father and Mother's personal wealth, independent of the farm. Allocation is just, and shall be legally executed."

Olive grabbed two envelopes, one addressed to Tabs and one to her. "Thank you, Levi; this is the happiest I've ever been with Father. Now, if I may request Jake to return me to town, I shall be off."

"Just like that? You're not staying for dinner or to visit?" Clyde's wife Sally snipped.

"Yes, just like that. Sally, there is no one in this room with whom I wish to chat. The only sibling I ever cared about is dead, thanks to Father. Levi, do I need to sign anything?"

Levi pointed to several lines to which Olive wrote her name hastily.

"If there is nothing else, then I'll be gone."

Olive quickly exited the room, avoiding any retort from the family. Conjuring fleeting images of the night she saved Sinclair from freezing death, she remembered how Sally, once her friend, turned against her and how no family member could ever recall her birthday, despite it being so close to Halloween. Overwhelmed with Westchester memories, malicious and spiteful, she appreciatively greeted Jake, who stood in the foyer, awaiting her trip back to Campbellsville.

Olive arrived home to find bowls on the kitchen table. With the children already fed and asleep, Tabs had heated leftover chicken soup for supper.

Tabs kissed Olive as he took a seat. "I hope you are hungry. I waited to eat with you."

"Starving. I have waited ten years for this day. Now that it's over, I'm emotionally exhausted." Olive slurped a spoonful of the hot liquid. "Well, at least now I never have to see that bunch again."

"I invited Benny and Ingrid to bring the children for a visit." Tabs dropped his head as he confessed. "I hope that's okay with you."

"They'll never come. No harm done. I actually like Benny." Olive reached for a slice of bread. "Ben will never permit it, and Benny doesn't have the nerve to defy his father."

"What did Levi want?" Tabs looked at the large envelopes protruding from Olive's handbag. Olive glanced to see if Tabs' name was visible. She smiled; it was hidden.

"Nothing really. Father left the six of us some stocks and a bit of insignificant money." Breathing slowly to steady her nerves, Olive continued eating. "I'll sell the stocks, maybe get some money to put toward the house mortgage."

"Darling, why don't you take a few dollars and treat yourself? Cut your hair in a new bob. Short curls would be stunning for your face." Tabs grinned at his wife. "I wish I could spoil you like your father could."

"Don't speak of him, ever again." Olive clenched her hand into a fist. She waited a moment before releasing her grip. "I believe I *shall* cut my hair. I'm so tired of all these years trying to control it."

"Then it's settled. Make an appointment at a salon in Madison." Tabs ran his fingers through Olive's blonde locks, then leaned over to nuzzle her neck. "You can take the bus; I'll watch the children. Perhaps you can go on Saturday? It will give you a reason to get gussied up. Maybe even buy yourself another new dress—colorful, not a black one. Will there be enough to cover the expense?"

"If I spend wisely."

Olive fought down the redness creeping up her neck. If she was careful, he'd never know the truth. The money, she planned, would be her security for the future.

"I'm going up to change. Will you make us a cup of tea and wash up these dishes?"

Ensuring Tabs was busy in the kitchen, Olive retreated to their bedroom.

A large, carved, cedar-lined hope chest, gifted to her by her deceased brother Fred, sat at the end of the bed. Carefully stacking the contents on the floor, Olive pried up a board, exposing a false bottom. Removing the currency from her envelopes, she placed it in a candy box, scanned the contents, then restacked it on several identical containers filled with money. Next, she opened a red velvet bag and added the gold coins. The stock certificates remained out, pending sale. Before closing the lid to the chest, she dumped the contents of a second velvet bag onto her lap. Inspecting a battered dog tag, she held it close to her heart. She then removed the pearls from around her neck and prayed for the mother she never knew and the brother she loved and cherished.

6

UNDER THE BIG TOP

*T*abs swallowed his coffee and stared across the
kitchen table at Olive.

"I have an idea, Wife."

Olive glanced up from her newspaper, eyebrow raised.

"Did you see the advertisement for the circus? The train
is stopping in Madison next week." Olive laid her paper
down. "What say you to taking the children on an
adventure?"

"Take all four of them to the circus?" Olive stood, pouring
hot water into her cup; she reused her teabag. "Have you
ever been to a circus?"

"No, only local carnivals." Tabs watched Olive add sugar
to her tea, pausing before he asked, "Do we have some extra
funds to cover the bus ride and entrance fees? The cost is
fifty cents a person; we'll need an extra five dollars. It's an
expensive day." Tabs bit his lip, waiting for Olive to veto his
idea.

"Tabs, that is a splendid idea." Olive grinned. "I'd love
seeing a lion or an elephant. We'll tell the children tonight at
dinner."

∞ ∞ ∞

Olive admired her reflection, her figure still slim after birthing four children. Her short blonde curls bounced as she tied them away from her face with a blue ribbon that matched her eyes. After plucking a daisy from the bouquet on her dresser, she cut the stem and tucked it under the ribbon. *What a perfect day for an adventure.* Pulling on a pair of short white gloves, she walked down the hallway to hasten the children.

"Albert, stop fussing and let me tie your shoes," Olive growled at her fidgeting son. She then called to the girls, "Esther, grab a sweater for yourself and for Alice. June, get your own sweater. The evening may be chilly."

"Is everyone ready for a day of fun?" Tabs waited as the troops descended the front staircase. "We shall see lions, elephants, and clowns!"

Albert jumped up and down in excitement; June frowned. "I don't think I like clowns."

"Have you ever seen one?" Esther asked her sister.

"No, but I don't want to see one."

"I do," said Esther. "I want to see everything."

"So do I," added Olive. "I haven't been on an adventure since my trip to New York."

The girls stared at each other in shock.

"You've been to New York?" Esther asked, amazed.

"Tell us about New York, Mother. Please?" coaxed June.

"Maybe later. Shall we concentrate on the circus today?"

"Children, don't fret." Tabs gathered both girls around their waists. "There shall be plenty of things to see today other than clowns. Now hurry, the bus shall be here momentarily." Turning to Olive, he added, "You are as beautiful today as the day I met you."

Olive blushed and unclasped her handbag. Removing a

29

dollar, she paid the driver for two adults and four children as the family found seats near the rear of the bus. Albert squirmed next to Tabs; Olive shared a bench with Alice. June and Esther bounced in unison in anticipation of the day's events.

As the bus approached the circus area, June and Esther whistled together as they viewed the strange happenings throughout the grounds. Red-and-white striped tents littered the expansive Madison fairgrounds. Unusual-looking animals tethered to their trainers roamed between train cars, while scantily clad women and exotically dressed performers on stilts towered over the side booths. Jugglers, tumblers, and clowns flitted to and fro, hurrying to make their next show. Colorful flags indicating the main attraction flew at the top of the tallest center tent, which was the size of a football field. The bus from Campbellsville, at total capacity, stopped at the entrance. The Baileys waited as the forward riders disembarked.

"Be certain to hold each other's hands. Do not let go of each other," Olive lectured as they waited. "Look at all these people."

Turning to Tabs, she flashed a look of concern.

"Children heed your mother. Now take a hand, and we're off!" Tabs clung to Albert's hand as he carried Alice. June and Esther latched on to each other and to the back of Olive's blue and white dress. They stepped off the bus to the mixed aroma of popcorn, fried food, and animal dung.

"Oh look, Tabs," Olive pointed to a photo booth just inside the entrance. "Come, children, we're having our portrait done."

The children filed in front of their parents according to age.

"You," the photographer pointed to Esther, "Move forward. You're too short to be in the back."

Esther grumbled, taking her place between Albert and Alice. Esther resented her siblings' height. Albert and Alice were already tall for being toddlers.

The photographer hid his head under the curtain. Holding the flash in his hand, he said, "Smile on the count of three. One, two, three."

With a puff of smoke and a bright flash of blinding light, it was over.

Albert rubbed his eyes. "Papa, I can't see."

Esther added, "All I see are white stars."

Little Alice was the only excited Bailey. She giggled, jumping up and down and saying, "More, again!"

Olive smiled at the children's reaction, paid the photographer, and recorded her address for delivery.

"This will be a wonderful addition to my parlor photo collection. Now, shall we visit the side attractions before entering the Big Top?" Olive skipped along, sporting a wide ear-to-ear grin.

"Of course, Wife." Tabs beamed at his wife's delight. "Perhaps we pass by the reptile house? I don't think June and Esther will enjoy those sights."

"What's a repile?" asked Albert.

"A *reptile*. Like a snake." Tabs wiggled his hand, making a hissing noise.

"Oooh. No!" June and Esther confirmed Tabs' assessment of the display.

The next booth was the bearded lady, where all the children laughed at the odd-looking sideburns and hair growing from a woman's face. Next, the family strolled around the grounds, watching flame-throwing and sword-swallowing men perform their skills.

"Papa, a shooting contest." Esther pointed to a booth where men rivaled each other's marksmanship.

"Tabs, do try," encouraged Olive. "You're an expert shot."

"Let's give this a go." Tabs extinguished his cigarette and reached for the gun as Olive paid a nickel. Lining up the scope, Tabs fired a round. The slug landed left of the target. Leaning over, Tabs whispered to Olive, "The sights are off, but I can compensate; give them another nickel, please."

Olive placed three more coins on the counter. Tabs aimed, then adjusted. The bullet hit the target in the middle—bulls-eye. The booth manager frowned but handed Olive the prize: pink, air-spun sugar wrapped around a paper cone. Olive pulled off a piece and tasted.

"Yum, this is good, Tabs we shall require two more prizes." She licked her lips as she handed the confection to June and Esther. "For you to share."

Tabs aimed, adjusted, and struck the middle of the target two more times. The booth man handed over cones of spun sugar, and soon every member of the family was walking around with sticky pink fingers, lips, and tongues.

An hour sped by before the group arrived back at the entrance. Tabs opened his canteen. Spilling water on his handkerchief, he corralled the children to clean their faces and hands.

"Can't have you looking like street urchins." He patted Albert's backside. "Now you, Olive dear." Olive smiled and joined the line behind Albert. She planted a kiss on Tabs' cheek as he finished wiping her mouth. The children gaped in awe of their parents' public affection.

"Shall we watch the main event?" Taking Albert by the arm, Olive led the way inside.

A large circular dirt floor hosting three show areas was surrounded by bleachers filled with applauding spectators that moved in and out of their seats, rendering the audience as much a show as the circus. Apparatus suspending high wires and aerial swings towered from above. A cacophony of animals, people, and music assaulted their ears.

"Poo, it stinks." Albert held his nose as Tabs climbed the bleachers looking for six seats.

"Not too far up, Tabs; I want to be close to the action." Olive plopped down in the third row. Tabs retreated, children in tow, to join her.

"Alice, sit on my lap so you can see better." Tabs lifted his youngest, placing her on his knee.

"Me too, Papa." Albert climbed on the other knee.

"Albert, you sit beside me. You're getting heavy." Tabs patted the bench with his hand.

"I get to sit beside Papa!" June cuddled close to Albert, leaving a scowling Esther to sit next to Olive.

A food vendor roamed the tent, shouting, "Popcorn, fresh peanuts," at the top of his lungs. Olive motioned to him and purchased a bag of peanuts in the shell.

"This is for all of us," she said, handing the bag to Tabs.

"How do we eat them?" asked Albert.

Balancing Alice, Tabs began the task of shelling peanuts for his family. The children delighted as Tabs tossed empty shells on the floor.

Pursing her lips, Olive stuck her hand in front of her husband. "Shell some for me." All four children teetered.

Tabs lowered his voice before commenting, "Whole nuts add to the adventure, but shelled nuts are more practical."

"And they are also more expensive," Olive growled. "Doesn't hurt you to open them for us."

Tabs grimaced.

"Look, she's standing on top of a horse!"

June squealed as a rider stood upright on the saddle, prancing around the ring.

"Ladies and gentlemen, please turn your attention to the center ring for an acrobatic spectacle never seen before!" the master of ceremonies announced.

"Ahh. Ohh!" The crowd praised the trapeze artists as they

flew in the air upside down, turning midair somersaults and jumping from one bar to the other. Albert and Alice clapped in delight.

The crack of a whip distracted the audience's attention as a man dressed in a safari jacket, pith helmet, and leather boots opened the lion's cage. The beast roared, jaws wide open exhibiting menacing, jagged teeth as the whip snapped in front of his mane.

Olive applauded, smiling ear to ear. "That's what I call a cat."

Next up were the elephants, tromping trunk to tail in a circle, close to the spectators. As the massive creatures passed in front of the Baileys, one stopped to dump a load. Immediately, three clowns with shovels appeared, scooping and cleaning the mess. Before leaving, one frowning clown jumped into the bleachers and popped his head in front of Olive.

He squeezed his large red nose—*honk!* Then did the same to June—*honk!* Terrified, June burst into tears and vanished, crawling over the bleachers away from him.

Albert jumped up and down. Reaching over, he grabbed the clown's nose. Honk! Albert looked at the clown's sad face.

"Smile, you funny," he said.

Alice wiggled and giggled, squirming on Tabs' lap. Esther reached fearfully for her mother's hand.

Olive shooed her away. "Esther, don't be a baby. It's just a clown."

The clown pointed to a painted tear, did a backflip off the bleachers, and landed butt-first in a pile of sawdust and dung. Albert clapped wildly. The crowd howled with laughter.

"June, where are you?" Olive searched the crowd for signs of her daughter.

"I'm here." The whimpering voice came from the opposite side of Tabs. "Papa?" it pleaded.

"There, there, June, all is fine."

June crawled out from under the bleachers as Tabs wrapped his strong arm around the trembling child. Esther scooted down the bleacher behind Albert to take her place on the other side of Tabs.

"Both of you?" Tabs chuckled at his frightened older children. "Your baby sister and brother enjoyed his act."

"I think we've had enough for one day," Olive chided, sitting alone on the end of the bench. "Let's get in line for the return bus. Don't want to miss the last one home."

"No! Me stay," Albert protested, pointing to a troop of clowns juggling balls and hoops.

"Shh." Tabs quickly scooted the two older, bewildered children down and toward the exit. He carried Alice and Albert.

"Did you enjoy yourself, Olive? I do believe this was a fantastic day, one the family shall remember their entire lives."

He smiled, knowing he would especially savor the sight of a clown sitting in the muck, and the image of his family's five pink and sticky faces.

The Campbellsville bus company added extra runs for the event, minimizing the Baileys' wait to thirty minutes. The children ran in circles, playing tag and avoiding the animal droppings. Taking Tabs by the hand, Olive watched her children enjoying themselves.

"Thank you for this wonderful idea, Husband. It's been a long time since I've had such fun."

Tabs' heart fluttered, still hopelessly in love with his wife. "I'm delighted to bring you pleasure, dear," he said with a tender whisper.

Olive called, "Come now. Stop running; the bus is here," as it screeched to a halt.

Tabs took his seat as Alice, Albert, and June climbed onto his lap, with Esther sitting beside him. Olive sat alone.

Whispering to his brood, Tabs reminded them, "Thank your mother."

"Thank you, Mother," they called in unison before promptly falling asleep on top of their father. Olive sat alone, wistfully, wishing to join the seat in front of her.

7

PROGNOSTICATION

OCTOBER 1929

*O*live unfolded the morning paper as she drank a cup of tea. A long-established habit, Olive splurged on three different newspapers: the weekly *Campbellsville Herald*, the daily *Madison Gazette*, and The *New York Times*. She coughed as she read the headlines on the front financial page —*Dow Jones Industrial Average Down Almost 13 Percent*.

An astute businesswoman, having once been the accountant for Westchester Farms, Olive understood the gravity of the announcement. She frowned upon investment speculation—she saw it as an unnecessary risk, preferring to hoard money in her hope chest. She witnessed from afar the reckless (by her standards) behavior of her friends and relatives, who borrowed money at the current low interest rates for minimal collateral and invested in uncertain businesses and failing commodities.

"Tabs, have you left for work yet?" Olive called out the back door, hoping to find Tabs feeding the chickens.

"No, dear, I'm still here. Do you need something?" Tabs was washing his hands in the outside trough. "It looks like a nice day; shall I pull the tumbler and mangle outside for you?"

"No. I have errands to run this morning. But will you pull out the wagon? And keep your ears open today for talk at work. The stock market is falling. I fear our economy may be headed toward a recession. See what old man Songer has to say."

"Sure thing. Need me to do anything else?" Tabs called back as he carried the wagon down the back porch steps.

"No. I'll take care of the rest." She paused, then muttered to herself, "Here we go again."

Olive refolded the paper, reminiscing about the hardship of previous war years and dreading their potential return. She surveyed her stack of laundry and waited for June and Esther to enter the kitchen.

"Here's a hardboiled egg and a slice of toast." The girls looked at each other in disappointment; they were expecting a hot breakfast. "Your lunches are packed. You need to get yourself off today; I have things to do this morning. Eat, and don't be late for school."

Olive hurried out of the kitchen and up the stairs to her bedroom while Esther and June gazed after her, dumbfounded by their mother's departure.

Once in her bedroom, Olive opened the hope chest and extracted one hundred dollars in cash. Stashing the bills into her handbag, she slipped into the nursery.

"Alfred, Alice, wake up. Mommy needs to go downtown today. Come on, sleepyheads." She pulled the blanket off Albert.

"Ahh, Mommy, no! I want sleep," Alfred groaned as he rolled onto his other side, tugging the quilt up over his shoulder.

"I'm not playing; get up." Her voice grew deeper as the volume increased.

Startled, Alice rubbed her eyes and whimpered. Albert ignored the request by keeping his eyes closed.

"Now, Albert!" At Olive's shrill command, both children climbed out of bed and raced to the bathroom. "Brush your teeth while you're in there."

"Why is Mommy yelling?" Alice asked as she climbed onto the stepstool to reach the sink.

Alfred shrugged his shoulders, then spit.

While the children tended to their grooming, Olive fluffed her short curls and removed her apron.

Shoving a piece of bread at each toddler, she ordered, "Put on your jacket and climb into the wagon."

Olive wrapped a shawl around her shoulders. After leaving a note requesting extra cream and butter for the milkman, she picked up the cart handle and clattered down the brick-lined street, pulling the children along behind her.

"Good morning Mr. Lupinetti," Olive called to the grocery store owner as the doorbell tinkled.

"Mrs. Bailey, you're out early today. No washing?" In his thick Italian accent, Dante Lupinetti halted his inventory to greet Olive. "Did I miss something on your Friday order?"

"I need a few extra supplies." Olive recited a long list of staples, including flour, sugar, salt, canned goods, and other dry goods to the store owner. "Also, I need twenty pounds of potatoes, and carrots, onions, and garlic."

"Mrs. Bailey, you usually don't order roots until February. Did your garden not produce?" Mr. Lupinetti pursed his lips and cocked his head.

"Just getting in some extra supplies." Olive's expressionless face betrayed nothing. She concluded with an order for cured and salted meats. "Will you deliver this afternoon?"

"Certainly, Mrs. Bailey." Dante tried to hide his puzzled look. It was strange for Olive Bailey, usually a frugal spendthrift, to be so extravagant.

"And I shall settle up this month's bill today."

"I need time to tally."

"Of course. Oh, Mr. Lupinetti, add a case of root beer to that order. I'm going down the street. Shall I come back to settle or pay the delivery boy?"

"Pay me on Friday with your normal order, Mrs. Bailey. I'll send my son, Joseph, later with your stuff."

Olive's next stop was to the iceman to order an extra block of ice. Then came the feed and dry goods store. The children slumped against the tall sides of the wagon, holding each other upright as they napped.

"I'll take this fabric." Olive piled six lengths of cotton, one of linen, and two silks. "I'll also need thread and six pairs of shoes, one for each child, Tabs, and me. Alfred, give me your foot."

The boy held up his leg as he continued to sleep. Olive picked the next biggest size.

"Oh, and those hats," she continued, "and add five boxes each of shotgun and rifle ammunition, a carton of Lucky Strikes, two packs of smoking tobacco, and five packs of rolling papers."

The clerk gaped at the stack of merchandise.

"I expect delivery today," Olive finished.

She waited for the total, paid thirty dollars, then clipped out of the store, the wagon behind her.

Her last stop was the Campbellsville bakery. Having inherited a sweet tooth from her father, Olive very much enjoyed cakes, pies, and desserts. Usually, she baked simple endings for Sunday dinner, considering daily confections a splurge.

"I'll take that torte," she said, pointing to the one with layers of cream, flakey pastry, and raspberry jam. "And two— no, *three* sugar cookies. Gosh, everything in the store looks delicious this morning."

The clerk boxed the pastry and bagged the cookies. Olive laid the parcels in the wagon with the sleeping children. Before continuing, she reached into the bag and devoured one of the cookies in three bites.

On her way home, she made a quick stop at the drugstore. Walking through the merchandise, she browsed, looking for impulse buys. Nothing in the store was changed since she came here as a girl. The same booths, product lines, black and white tile floor, and soda counter; she glanced at the stall where she met Tabs so long ago and smiled.

"Doc Murphy," she called to the man behind the counter. "Please make up a box of stomach seltzers. I've been queasy all morning. Throw in a bottle of Paregoric and some mercurochrome. Later today is fine, for delivery." She turned to her children. "All right, children, we're done. Let's go home."

Neither Albert nor Alice moved, still sound asleep. She pulled the wagon past Dr. Paulson's office and the milliner as she headed back to her washing.

Passing the bank she recoiled when she noticed several men waiting outside, trying to get in.

∞ ∞ ∞

"Esther, June, no after-school playtime today. I got a late start on my washing," Olive called to the girls as they came home from school. "Help me hang this basket of wet things. They'll never have time to dry today, and the weather is turning cold tomorrow."

Esther immediately dropped her book on the porch and grabbed an armful of wet sheets. June stopped to play with Albert and Alice, who were still sitting in the wagon—its high sides created a makeshift playhouse.

"Mother, I have school lessons to complete," Esther remarked as she loaded the clothesline.

"Well, it will just have to wait. I need your help with laundry, then with supper preparation."

Esther hung her head; dropping her shoulders in submission, she reached for another wet sheet.

The water from the spilled tubs and barrel washer ran down the side street as Lupinetti's delivered Olive's order. Stepping over the puddles, the boy dumped five large cardboard boxes of supplies and a case of root beer onto the back porch. The grocery truck pulled away as the cart from the feed store approached, delivering more surprises. June and Esther gawked, open-mouthed, at each other.

"Mother, why are we getting all of this?" June curiously inspected the contents.

Before she answered, Olive ran into the house, grabbed a bucket, and vomited.

"Where is that delivery from the drugstore?" she grumbled. "Esther, has Doc Murphey stopped by yet?"

"No, Mother, I haven't seen him." Esther wrung her hands. "Are you sick?"

"My stomach is unsettled today. Perhaps I have the flu." Olive wiped her mouth on her sleeve then rinsed the bucket with laundry water. "Okay, girls, help me stack my purchases in the pantry."

The north kitchen wall had two large pantry closets. Lined with shelves, the back pantry stored Olive's harvest canning, extra dry goods, and Hoosier surplus. The front pantry held pots and pans, laundry equipment, wash tubs, tools, and various cleaning products, with a root cellar cut out beneath the back porch that stored potatoes, apples, carrots, turnips, squash, and extra jams and jellies.

"Mother, must I finish stocking before I do my lessons? I have quite a bit today," Esther pleaded.

"School is not important for girls," Olive quipped hastily. "Get on with your work."

Olive stomped out of the kitchen. When she bent over to lift a box, she grabbed her mouth and rushed to vomit in the bushes.

Tabs rounded the corner to find his wife bent over. "Happy early birthday, dear Wife." Tabs smiled broadly as he handed Olive a bouquet of flowers. "May I cook a special birthday dinner for you tonight?"

"Ugh," moaned Olive. "I would love it, but my stomach is so queasy today. Perhaps tomorrow, on my actual birthday?"

"Then tonight, I'll assemble sandwiches, and I shall cook for you on your birthday." Tabs' smile faded when he noticed the boxes. "What is all of this?"

"I bought some extras today." Olive waved her hand over the stash. "Just in case."

"A case of root beer and real cigarettes, that is a nice surprise." Tabs cocked his head to the side before asking, "In case of what?"

"You must make both last. I fear luxury will become scarce in the not-too-distant future." Olive reached for her midriff, then sat down on the porch step. "What was the gossip around the plant today?"

"Songer mentioned the stock market, but he's not concerned. He thinks Rockefeller, Morgan, and the New York big boys will move to reinforce the market."

"I think that viewpoint is short-sighted and foolish. Several indicators are saying otherwise." Olive moved to an Adirondack chair under the arbor as she continued rubbing her tummy. "I don't want to be caught unprepared."

"Can we afford all this preparation, Wife?" Taking Olive by the hands, Tabs peered into her eyes.

"Tobias Bailey, don't be a simpleton. If I buy something, we have money for it. I do not buy on credit. I may run a monthly account, but the money to cover it is always in hand." Olive spat the words at her husband.

"Dear Wife, I don't wish to upset you, especially if you are feeling peaked." Touching her forehead, Tabs continued, "Why don't you go sit in your back parlor? I'll help Esther and June with the laundry. I think you had an eventful day today."

"I can do it," she insisted, but did not move.

"Go rest, darling, and do not worry. I promised your father when I proposed marriage that I would also provide love and food for you and our family. I intend to keep that promise."

Olive stood and swooned. Grabbing for Tabs to steady herself, she ambled across the yard. Once inside, she sought refuge in her private space, lay on the couch, and fell fast asleep.

∞ ∞ ∞

"Papa, I need to do my schoolwork." Esther handed her father a tin of sardines. "May I finish stocking our shelves after I complete my assignments?"

"Of course, darling. School is important." Tabs looked at the filled crates, "Albert can hand stuff to me, can't you, big boy?"

"Yes, Papa." Albert sat on the pantry floor next to a box and began lifting out items, one at a time. "What is this, Papa?" Albert asked, handing Tabs a can of wallpaper putty.

Tabs wrinkled his forehead. "Ah, the wallpaper cleaner. It's a dough that I rub over the walls to make them clean."

While the walls were free of soot marks now, Tabs knew the coal furnace would turn the walls black before spring. But why buy the cleaner now?

With the last box empty, Tabs set about making dinner for

the children. Cutting slices of yesterday's leftover ham, Tabs smeared mustard on thick chunks of bread.

"Time to eat," he called.

The children found their designated seats around the kitchen table. Alice climbed into her highchair. Esther poured each of them a glass of milk.

"Where's Mother?"

"She's resting. I'll check on her after we clean up."

Four worried faces stared at their father. To the children, Olive was a pillar of strength and resolve—albeit a sometimes grouchy one.

"Don't fret. She's fine," comforted Tabs, hiding his own concern.

"June and I shall clean up after supper. You check on Mother," offered Esther.

"I help," Alice said as she licked the mustard off her plate.

Tabs left the children to their meal.

"Olive," he whispered quietly, entering the room. Olive lay on the davenport. Tabs covered her with a knit throw.

"Oh, Tabs, I'm sorry to be sleeping." Dazed and groggy, Olive yawned. "Do you think we might attend the Harvest Dance this weekend?"

"Splendid idea. It's been years since we last went."

"I miss that social. This is the first year since Esther's birth that the children are old enough to go and not require our full-time attention." Olive rubbed her eyes, sat up, and motioned for Tabs to sit beside her.

"Esther and June can help care for the little ones and still enjoy the events." Tabs slipped his arm around Olive. She rested her head on his muscular shoulder.

"Tabs, I think you should order another load of coal."

Tabs pulled away from Olive, staring into her blue eyes. "You are really concerned about the stock market, aren't you?" He chewed on his finger. "What worries you?"

"I have a sinking feeling we're being thrust into a big financial mess. Interest rates are low, money is cheap, and people borrow more than they can afford. Commodity prices are low, and business speculation is high. The gold standard is overinflated. It's a formula for disaster."

Tabs gawked at his wife. "Dear, I know you are brilliant, but I do not understand a word you are saying. I shall accept your analysis, however, and do whatever you suggest." He squeezed her hands. "I am terribly sorry your father refused your education. I should have been stronger, encouraged you to go to school even after Esther was born."

Olive smiled sadly. "You would not have made a difference back then. But, Husband, I've been thinking. Alice will be in school next year, so maybe now is the time to continue my studies. Would you mind that? That is, if things don't go to Hell in a handbag?"

"Dear Wife, nothing would make me happier than to see your life's dream fulfilled." Tabs paused before adding. "Perhaps you should amend your statement to Esther?"

"What are you talking about?"

He stroked her face. "Telling her that you feel school isn't important for girls when in fact you long for education."

Olive lowered her head. "Oh, perhaps later." She sighed and snuggled into Tabs' shoulder. "Finally, I shall complete my studies! I'm so happy." She took a deep breath as she fell back to sleep.

He loosened her apron, removed her shoes, and recovered her with the blanket. As he turned out the lights he wished her pleasant dreams.

8

HAPPY BIRTHDAY

OCTOBER 29, 1929

*T*he day the United States stock market crashed, Black Tuesday was the date of Olive's twenty-eighth birthday. All three newspapers printed special editions announcing the financial crisis. The market crash alone was not enough to trigger a recession or depression, but the throngs of terrified people rushing the banks to withdraw money tipped the scales. The US economy plummeted.

The foundry—once owned by Olive's late Uncle James Westchester, US congressman, and now under the management of his granddaughter's husbands—closed for the afternoon.

"Olive," Tabs called as he rounded the house.

The back door was closed, shutting out the late October chill. Inside, Olive performed her regular Tuesday chores. Tabs opened the door, expecting to find Olive in the kitchen. Instead, Esther stood at the ironing board.

"Where's your mother?" Tabs asked, placing his lunch bucket on the table. "Wait, when did you begin pressing clothes? And why are you home from school?"

"School let out early. Mother is bringing the clothes down

from the attic. I wanted to surprise her for her birthday." Esther kissed her father's cheek. "Why are you home from work?"

"Presumably for the same reason. Boy, when your mother has a hunch, she has a hunch." Tabs washed his hands and emptied his thermos bottle at the oversized, rectangular farm sink. "Esther, be careful not to burn yourself. Did your mother show you the proper way to heat the cast irons?"

Esther laughed. "Papa, it's not hard. You place the iron on the heat, remove the handle and attach it to the already heated iron, then press away."

"Well. Good." Tabs pulled a fresh loaf of bread out of a bag. "I'm cooking dinner tonight, so I'm happy to have some extra time to prepare. I'm making rabbit stew. Did I see a sweet in the icebox?"

"Yes, some sort of yummy-looking torte. Mother bought it yesterday."

"June," Tabs called out to his daughter, who was sitting in the front parlor—the family parlor. "I need your help."

"Here, Papa. How may I help?" Eight-year-old June, already taller than Esther, sauntered into the kitchen.

"Set the dining room table with the good dishes. We are having a special supper for your mother's birthday. Be careful, mind you. We don't want to break any of her precious china."

"Oh Papa, I'm afraid to handle it. Mother gets so angry if we break things," June protested, in vain.

Tabs responded with a gentle tap on her backside. "Don't forget to use a tablecloth."

Tabs headed outside to retrieve the skinned rabbit, which he snared two days ago. Green tomatoes hung from the vines, not yet subject to a hard frost. Tabs cut three larger ones to fry. Making a side trip to the root cellar, he grabbed potatoes, carrots, and onions for the entree.

Off-limits to daily life, the formal dining room walls were papered in a blue and white toile design. An oval mahogany table filled the center of the room was encircled by eight chairs, upholstered in blue, white, and yellow needlepoint. The large breakfront displayed Olive's collectibles, except for her salt and pepper shakers, which were front and center in the white storage cabinet in the kitchen. Blue cornflowers and a thin silver band patterned Olive's prized white china. It was less valuable than her mother's Haviland Limoges, but Olive nonetheless treasured it.

The Baileys owned two tablecloths, one plain white cotton, one embroidered white linen. June chose the cotton cloth and matching cotton napkins. Tabs handed her a small crystal vase filled with water to use as a centerpiece.

By the time Olive returned, savory smells had permeated the kitchen. She surveyed the activity, grabbed her stomach, then the bottle of Paregoric. Taking a swig, she said, "God, I don't know which is worse—the odor of that medicine or the bitter taste."

"Ah, there you are. Happy birthday, Wife." Tabs attempted an embrace, but Olive pushed him away.

"I need air."

Tabs followed Olive onto the back porch. "Darling, have you seen Dr. Paulson? Your stomach has given you issues all week. I hate to see you suffer so, especially with the Harvest Dance this weekend."

Olive's face went pale. Beads of sweat formed on her brow, despite the chilly October air. Concerned that she may lose her balance, Tabs reached to steady her.

"I need to sit." Olive plopped down onto the step and wiped her forehead with her apron hem. "I must have the flu. I'll see Paulson if I'm still feeling rough next week."

Tabs leaned over to stroke her hair. "You sit. I'll call you when supper is ready."

Biting his lip, Tabs turned to hide his concern. It was unlike Olive to be out of commission for an entire week.

"Children," Tabs called as he entered the house. "Tonight, we must be on our best behavior. Your mother is not feeling well."

Esther and June added the finishing touches to the table by carefully placing Olive's china and crystal. Iced tea filled the stemmed glasses for the adults while the children drank milk. Unlike in Olive's youth, alcohol, the cause of too many loose tongues or hot heads, was never served at the dinner table.

Poking his head out the door, Tabs called to Olive, "Dinner is served."

Olive slowly made her way into the dining room. Alice greeted her mother first with a bouquet of remnant fall flowers. "Happy birthday, Mama."

Keeping them away from her nose, Olive placed the flowers in the waiting vase. Albert bowed to his mother, took her arm, and escorted her to her chair, which was extended by June. Olive held her breath and they kissed her on opposite cheeks before moving to their own seats. Esther had the honor of presenting Olive with a package, wrapped in brown paper tied with twine, which Olive set aside for the time being.

Next, Tabs plated bowls of savory stew. The earthiness of marjoram, thyme, sage, onion, and garlic added to the glossy brown color of Tab's rich broth. A chunk of crusty bread was placed on each bowl rim.

"Children, what day is today?" Tabs began the birthday ritual chant.

"October twenty-nine," the children responded in unison.

"And what makes October twenty-nine special?"

"It is mother's birthday," four tiny voices cheered.

"Ready, steady, on the count of three. One, two, three,

happy birthday, Mother dear!" Tabs completed his mantra for the ninth consecutive year, fulfilling his vow that Olive's birthday would never be forgotten.

Olive smiled, eyes twinkling at her family with a rare expression of love. "Thank you. All of you. I truly appreciate being remembered."

Olive reflected sadly on her childhood birthdays, which were always overlooked by her father and siblings. In the past, birthday wishes came only from her nephew, Samuel, her brother, Fred, and her chauffeur, Jake.

Esther sat patiently for several minutes before excitedly asking, "Mother, open your present. We all made it together."

After untying the twine, Olive carefully removed the paper to find a picture frame decorated with hand-rubbed, polished stones.

"How lovely. It matches my hair comb." She ran her finger over the pebbles.

Albert bounced excitedly in his seat. "Alice and me collected rocks."

"And Papa taught June and me how to tumble and glue," added a smiling Esther. "We thought you could put our circus photograph in it."

"That's a splendid idea. This is a perfect birthday, with such a lovely gift. And children, I have a special announcement. Next year, I'm going back to school!" Olive smiled, eating slowly, consuming more bread than stew. Frequently moving her arm to her stomach, she privately fought back nausea.

"What type of school?" Esther's mouth fell. "You told me school's not important for girls!"

Olive blushed. "I'm not sure. I'll talk with the principal after Alice starts first grade to figure out how and where I begin." Olive sighed, happy despite her tummy discomfort, and grabbed Tabs' hand. "I have waited too long for this. Thank you, Husband. This is the best gift in the world."

Esther gawked at Olive, then shrugged her shoulders at June, who raised her eyebrows and said nothing.

Talk of the harvest dance dominated their remaining conversation as the family dined on Tabs' delicious bounty.

"Olive, do we have funds for you to buy yourself a new dress for the dance?" Tabs asked as he scooped another serving of stew. "Maybe Ruth will babysit on Friday and you can take the bus to Madison, visit the department stores." He gently stroked his wife's shoulder as he retook his seat.

"Perhaps I shall. I deserve a new, pretty dress." Olive ran her fingers through her short bob. "I'll ask Ruth tomorrow. Now, who's ready for birthday dessert?"

"Me!" cried five voices.

Tabs stood to retrieve yesterday's purchased torte. He began cutting and serving the confection as his family oohed and aahed. Alice sucked her finger after running it through the whipped cream.

"I haven't had such a wonderful treat since I left the farm," lamented Olive, smacking her lips together. "This is scrumptious—and I'm going back to school! What a good birthday."

∞ ∞ ∞

Every inch of the Campbellsville social hall was decorated for the harvest dance. Carved pumpkins lit with candles, bales of hay, strings of dried apples, and the smell of cinnamon and nutmeg mixed with a musky earthiness filled the ample space.

The Baileys arrived with Olive strutting in a new costume. Her top boasted a brown and beige vertical stripe above the waist and a horizontal striped below the waist—the latest fashion. It fell just below the hipline of the silk-pleated underdress. She wore matching beige gloves with a striped, full-wrist flounce and a beige cloche hat. Instead of the long strands of popular faux pearls, Olive wore her short string of genuine pearls inherited from her mother. The children wore their Sunday finery, with poor Tabs still wearing Levi's castoffs from years ago.

"You look beautiful," Tabs whispered to Olive as the family entered the hall. Holding her head high, Olive smiled. She already knew she looked good.

June gazed around in bewilderment. "Mother, does the town hold this party every year?"

Esther, as amazed as her sister, continued, "Why have we never attended before? This looks like fun!"

Albert and Alice jumped and giggled at the sights, then, grabbing hands, took off running toward the other children who were playing games.

Olive laughed as she watched her youngest make new friends. "June, Esther, go after them, please. There should be apple bobbing and lots of other games for you. Please keep an eye on both Alice and Albert. You'll find your father and me on the dance floor."

Tabs grabbed Olive's arm and led her to the registration desk. "That will be a quarter each," said the young woman handing out dance cards.

Olive opened her purse and pulled out two coins in exchange for two cards. "Price has gone up, I see."

The girl returned a puzzled look. "It's been a quarter for the last seven years."

"Come, dear, it has been far too long since our last dance." Tabs offered his hand; Olive accepted, and they waltzed around the room.

Tabs and Olive enjoyed two other waltzes, then rounded up with three other couples for a square dance.

Gasping for air as the music ended, Olive said, "I didn't realize how much I missed this. But I can't do more than four in a row without a break."

Out of breath, the couple sought the punch table. Walking the length of the hall, Olive spotted Bea Thompson, Sally's sister, Olive's old elementary school teacher.

"Tabs, who is Bea Thompson with? They look rather chummy, don't they?" Olive motioned discreetly to a couple in the corner, nuzzling each other's necks.

"My goodness. That's Edgar Kepler, the letch."

"Why do you say that?"

"He is married. His wife, Abigail, has an infant child, something like their tenth. And as you can see, he's *not* with Abigail." Tabs shook his head in disgust. "He's a cad and a womanizer. Always running around. Does it right under Abigail's nose, too." They reached the refreshment table. Tabs ladled two cups of punch and grabbed two cookies. "Shall we step to the side, out of the way?"

A man followed them across the floor. "Olive, is that you? Olive Westchester?"

Olive jumped in surprise, then turned to see a semi-balding man in his late twenties, early thirties.

"It's Olive *Bailey* now. I'm sorry, who are you?"

With a frown, the man answered, "Leonard Lewis. I work for your sister and brother-in-law. Don't you remember, we went to school together?"

"Oh yes—Leonard. Still harassing girls?" Olive quipped as Tabs quizzically observed his wife.

"Ha! You may be as attractive as ever, but I see you still haven't learned how to forgive and forget." Leonard extended his dance card. "Mr. Bailey, may I dance with your wife?"

"You may do so at your own risk," Tabs said with a chuckle. "I'll check on the children, Olive. Enjoy the dance."

Leonard and Olive danced together once. "Delightful, may I sign for a later twirl?"

Olive handed her dance card to Leonard. "As you wish. Later. Now, I must check on my children," Olive said as she scanned the crowd. Benny and Ingrid approached as Olive searched to rejoin Tabs.

"Olive! How delightful to see you out and about." Ingrid rushed to hug her husband's aunt. "How nice you look! Why do you never visit the farm?"

"I would think that is obvious. Shall we sit and talk a spell?"

The three found chairs, then waved for Tabs to join them. Leaving the youngsters safely engrossed in activities, Tabs greeted Benny.

Tabs scrutinized Benny's notched red nose. "Perhaps Kendrick should have called for Dr. Paulson instead of setting that nose himself."

Benny rubbed it. "I have pain when the weather changes; sometimes, it's hard to breathe. All in all, it works." Benny paused. "Got off easy, compared to the things we both saw overseas."

"Benny, let's change the subject." Olive glanced at the tension increasing on Ingrid's face. "Tell me—what they are saying about the money crisis?"

Tabs grasped Ingrid's arm. "I think that's our cue to dance. Shall we?" They left Olive and Benny to talk business.

"Father is genuinely concerned. The price of grain has fallen over the past several years. Actually, it's rock bottom. Clyde went to the bank yesterday to withdraw some money— a normal farm transaction. You know what? They were lined up around the corner, just trying to get into the bank."

Olive's brow furrowed. "Did he manage to get any money out? I saw the start of that line."

"No, he didn't. They closed the doors to business at noon.

He plans to return bright and early Monday, to be first in line, but both he and Father are worried."

Olive thought for a minute, analyzing what she just heard. "I read in the paper of the same occurrences in larger cities. I had hoped it would take another week or so to reach Campbellsville. Benny, this is bad. Tell Clyde to withdraw as much cash as possible."

"Do you really think we're in trouble, Olive?"

"Yes, I do, Benny. Do you remember how we prepared for the war? You need to do the same again. I could care less about Clyde, Sally, Tildy, and Tommy. By the way, where are they?" She hesitated before adding, "But I do care about you and Ingrid—and Nellie. What's she doing these days?"

"Nellie is married to Angus McKee. They live in Garland. Angus works in the mines." Benny studied Olive's face. "You didn't mention Mother and Father. Are you vexed with them?"

"Honestly, Benny, other than our adventure to New York, your father has never been overly kind to me. And your mother is somewhat *holier than thou*. Maybe it's the age difference? I suppose my feelings toward them are neutral." Olive turned her face away before adding, "Ben was never as strong or as bright as my father. I don't expect the farm to be successful under his supervision."

"Olive, you were the real brains of the operation. I didn't understand until after the war, but my God, you are smart. The place started to go downhill the minute you left. Grandfather complained daily that he needed your help. He missed you, wanted you, Tabs, and baby Esther to move back in."

Olive's shoulders tensed. "I shall not speak about Henderson Westchester! Please, Benny, I haven't been out in such a long time, don't ruin my night." Olive stood.

"Don't walk away, Olive. Shall we dance instead?"

Thus ended Olive's conversation about Henderson, the Westchester farm, and the pending crisis.

The general conversation of all attendees that evening centered not around the market crash but the bank closure. Only a few Campbellsville residents dabbled with stocks; however, most of the town's citizens maintained bank accounts, except for the Baileys. Olive and Tabs listened to the talk of the day but did not speculate the outcome. The evening ended with every Bailey family member enjoying themselves and promising to return next year.

Alice in Tab's arms and Albert on his shoulders, Olive leaned against Tabs as the family walked home.

"After tonight's exercise," he asked, "how is your stomach?"

Olive hummed her favorite song. "Today, I feel great. Thank you, Husband. This was a wonderful birthday week."

9

THE CRASH

*O*live's advice to Benny proved sound. Clyde arrived at the bank at six in the morning to find himself fifth in line. He managed to withdraw all his meager personal funds and about half of the farm's assets, after which the bank closed its doors to business and never reopened. Banks, including the one in Campbellsville, demanded early loan repayment to replenish the run-on money. Folks across Pennsylvania and the rest of the country faced premature foreclosure.

On Tuesday of the second week of November 1929, mail delivery caused a stir up and down the street. Ruth Callihan rapped urgently on Olive's door.

"Hello Ruth, come in. Do I have a phone call?" Olive asked as she looked up from the ironing board. Albert and Alice played quietly in the corner.

Ruth waved an envelope in front of Olive's face. "Did you open your mail? I can't believe this."

Olive motioned to a stack of unopened parcels lying on the table. "No. My mail's right there. Believe what?"

Ruth fought back the tears. "They are threatening to fore-

58

close on our house unless we repay our mortgage!" Ruth confessed. "I don't have money to pay off my house. Who does? Isn't that why you get a mortgage in the first place?"

Olive took the letter and read it. When she finished, she rifled through her mail, looking for a similar correspondence. She found it at the bottom of the pile. Tearing open the envelope, she read her own letter of payment request.

"Well, Ruth, it looks like the bank is sending these to everybody. I have one too." Olive pointed to a chair. "I think we need a cup of tea." Olive filled the kettle with water and placed it on the stove. "Now, shall we read the fine print? See if the bank is requiring partial or total repayment before you panic?"

By the time she reached the bottom of the letter, the kettle had whistled; Olive poured hot water into a teapot while Ruth wrung her hands in dismay.

"Ruth, read closely now," Olive said, re-reading over her own letter. "What exactly is the bank asking of you?"

Ruth stirred a teaspoon of sugar into her cup and read aloud. "It says I am required to repay the full amount of my loan within thirty days, or my house will be repossessed." Tears filled her eyes. "Oh Olive, what are we to do? I have no savings, none!"

Olive sucked on the inside of her mouth. "You have nothing? How is that possible? I thought you and Charlie were doing okay." She stirred three teaspoons of sugar into her cup.

Tears streamed down Ruth's face. "Charlie invested our money in stocks. One of his bosses gave him a hot tip, so Charlie took everything to invest. Said we would double our money in three months."

Olive reached for Ruth's hand. "I am so sorry to hear that. Speculation in stocks is exactly what the name implies: risky speculation." Olive thought for a minute. "Ruth, my advice to you is to tighten your belt. While Charlie is still making good money, cut spending everywhere. The first thing to go should be your phone."

"But Olive! N—not my phone." Ruth gasped for air. "I'm so proud of that phone."

"Seriously, Ruth, do you want pride or food?" Olive frowned; her concern was diminished by Ruth's imprudent thinking. "I'm sorry for your troubles, but you handled your money foolishly. Sit, drink your tea, but I must continue my work."

Ruth stared blankly at Olive, wondering how she could be so insensitive. "Thank you for the refreshment and advice, Olive," she said tersely. "I shall leave you to your chores."

Pushing in her chair, Ruth glanced back at her neighbor, already busy again with her ironing. She slammed the door as she left. Olive didn't bother to look up.

Esther and June arrived home from school bubbling with talk of the bank. Women living across the street from the school were quick to spread the news. Teachers and students alike buzzed over the bank closure.

"Mother, Mrs. Hammond said there is no money left in town," June blurted excitedly.

"How is that possible?" questioned Esther.

"Sit, both of you. Do your schoolwork. We'll talk about this at the supper table tonight."

Olive finished pressing the last of her items, folded the board, and hung it in the storage pantry beside a bushel basket of balls, confiscated from the neighborhood boys. Every time a ball rolled into Olive's yard, she tossed it into the basket rather than return it to its rightful owner.

"Can the bank really close?" Esther continued her questioning.

Olive sat at the table with her older girls. "Yes, the bank

can close. What is the purpose of a bank, do either of you know?"

Both girls shook their heads.

Thinking back to when she was Esther's age, Olive clicked her tongue and inhaled in disappointment. "The business of a bank is money. If a bank has no money, then there is no business. It's that simple. Do you understand?"

Eyebrows raised, and eyes widened, both girls indicated affirmatively.

"I must begin dinner, so do your work." Olive began peeling potatoes, wondering how she could beget such simple-minded children.

As promised, the dinner conversation centered around the financial crisis. Tabs anxiously reported the conversation from the foundry.

"Songer said that this may impact the entire country. Have a ripple effect on every type of business."

Olive handed him the stack of mail. "Every merchant in town is requesting immediate payment. No more carrying a monthly tab. We must pay at the time of purchase." Her eyes narrowed. "Truthfully, that is the most effective way to conduct transactions..."

"With mines and factories paying on the last Friday of the month, a tab was a courtesy to help extend a paycheck." Tabs glanced at the stack of mail and took another forkful of mashed potatoes.

The corners of Olive's mouth turned down. "Yes, Tabs, I understand. But at whose expense? We live paycheck to paycheck; we must budget and set aside money for each week's expenses. It's simple economics." The girls observed the volley of conversation. "There are some things that you and I need to discuss in private. Esther, June, clean up in here and watch the little ones. Your father and I need to talk."

Olive led Tabs to the back parlor, her private sanctuary.

The vases that held fresh flowers during the growing season sat empty. Now, front and center among the frames containing precious photographs was her circus photo in her birthday frame.

Tabs followed her with surprise. "We're talking in here?"

Olive motioned to a chair. "Sit down." Tabs obliged. "The bank is recalling payment on all loans, our mortgage included."

Tabs pursed his lips. Scrutinizing his wife, he asked, "That's serious. How much do we owe?"

Olive knew the amount, down to the last penny. "We paid a total of six thousand five hundred fifty dollars for this house—one of the more expensive houses in town, but also one of the biggest and nicest. Truthfully, Songer's house on the hill is the one I really wanted, but it wasn't on the market. I've coveted that house since I was a child."

Tabs whistled as he inhaled air through his teeth. "Songer's house. Yikes! That's a pipe dream. I only make fifteen hundred dollars a year." He shook his head, got back on task. "What do we owe, and is the bank demanding payment in full?"

Olive frowned, stuck on his earlier comment. "Songer's house is the closest building in town to the mansion in which I grew up. I deserve that house."

The house high on the hill, owned by Tabs' boss, kept guard on Campbellsville like a grand old dame scrutinizing her progeny.

"Yes, Olive dear, but you are no longer your father's ward, the privileged Olive Westchester. You are my wife, Mrs. Bailey, and we must live on my income." Tabs dabbed the perspiration forming at his temples. "Please, back to my question. I'm concerned we may forfeit our home."

"I used some of my personal savings for our down payment, about fifteen hundred dollars. Then, subtracting our monthly mortgage payments—interest is extremely low right now—we owe about three thousand five hundred seventy-five dollars." Olive's gaze latched onto Tabs' eyes.

"Oh." He let out a long heavy sigh; his breath fluttered the doily on his armchair. "Well," he asked, sighing again, "I might as well ask. How much, if anything, do we have saved?"

Olive smiled smugly at her husband. "Enough, Tobias. I have five thousand stashed upstairs. I can pay off the loan in cash."

She actually had over twenty thousand in cash stashed away in her hope chest, the equivalent of thirteen years of Tabs' salary. It consisted of the money she saved as a youngster while working as her father's accountant, Freddy's savings, and both inheritances from Henderson. She chose not to share about the money given to Tabs, opting to keep it herself and to use it as she fancied.

Tabs raised his eyebrows in astonishment. "I know you run a tight ship, but how did you manage that?"

"Remember, Father gave me a small amount when he passed." Olive reached for her neck as she lied again. "We need to be frugal, even so. You must make as much money as possible while work is available. If you can pick up extra shifts, we'll weather this crisis. Think of the children."

Tabs hugged his wife reassuringly. "I promised your father that you would never be lacking in love or in food. I shall provide for you and the children. Do not fear, darling Wife." Tabs stood, but before leaving, he asked, "I'm sorry I didn't ask earlier—we got carried away with money—but how are you feeling?"

"Totally recovered. Must have been a piece of bad meat. No more problems, other than money."

"If you're sure you're better, then I'll excuse myself." He

needed to walk, worry, and think. How was he to fulfill his promise?

Olive remained in her haven, protected in the veiled security of her future. *I've tended to me*, she thought. *The rest can fend for themselves, just like I had to do as a child.*

10

SURPRISE! SURPRISE!

JANUARY 1930

*C*hristmas 1929 was a somber event for the residents of Campbell County. Most families found little money to spare on extravagant purchases. Olive made each of the children a new outfit and gave them the shoes she purchased in October. Tabs' creative hands ensured each child received a toy from Santa.

Businesses began to falter, even close. Mr. Lupinetti, Doc Murphy, and most other establishments demanded payment at the time of purchase. The Clawson bakery posted a sign: *Going out of business.* Campbellsville Bank remained closed except for payment collection. It became the major landlord in town, already foreclosing on several houses that could not pay off their mortgage or make suitable payment arrangements. Some luckier families rented back from the bank at the outrageous rate of thirty dollars a month, avoiding a move. Typical rent was half that amount.

Snow fell in large wet flakes the morning of the second Wednesday of January. Already, several inches coated the ground. Olive sat frowning in the kitchen over her darning, with Alice and Albert at her feet giggling while playing pick-up-sticks, all three warming themselves from their early trek to see Dr. Paulson. Olive's nausea had come and gone infrequently the past several months. While Paregoric helped squelch the queasiness, her continued discomfort and craving for sugar fueled her suspicions. Olive decided to seek a medical opinion.

"Children, must you be so loud." Olive grabbed her aching head. Albert and Alice pouted at the unnecessary scolding.

"But Mama, we be quiet." Alice defended their case.

"No, you are not! Now sit there and play without talking."

Alice began to whimper; Albert grabbed his sister's hand.

"Shh," he whispered and handed her a wooden block.

"Why is Mama so mad?"

"I don't know, but we better be quiet. Okay?" The five-year-old safeguarded his little sister.

The day went on, and the snow continued to fall. When Olive looked out the window to monitor the weather, she noticed a moving truck at Ruth and Charlie Callihan's house.

"Children, stay here and don't get into trouble. I'm going out for a minute." Olive grabbed her handbag then bundled up to brave the cold.

"Ruth! Charlie!" she called as she crossed the side street. "Are you in there?"

Charlie poked his head out of the back of the truck. "Olive, what are you doing out in this weather?"

"Are you moving?"

"That's a stupid question. Yes, we are moving," Charlie moaned. "The bank foreclosed on our loan. We're moving to *Garland* to live with my brother."

Garland, a small village about ten miles away from Campbellsville, had no sidewalks, paved roads, or businesses. It

66

was simply a collection of several dozen houses and was far beneath Charlie's prideful ego.

"What are you doing with the Frigidaire? Want to sell it?" Foregoing pleasantries, Olive went straight to the point. "You just bought it last year, right? I'll give you seventy-five dollars, cash."

Charlie's face burned red; his eyes glared at her boldness. "Olive Bailey, that is highway robbery. You know damn well we paid one hundred twenty-five dollars, a whole month's salary for that machine."

Olive smirked. "That may be so, but my guess is that you need cash. Seventy-five is my offer. Take it or leave it." She waved crisp bills in front of Charlie's face.

"You are an evil woman, taking advantage like that!" Charlie spat his reply. "I'll take it." He grabbed the cash from Olive's hand.

"Have your helpers bring it over. I'll make a space for it in the kitchen." She smiled, spun on her heel, and clomped back home through the snow. *That was easy enough.*

Kicking the snow from her boots, she entered the kitchen. "Children, play in the hallway. I'm putting something in your spot." Albert and Alice looked at each other, quietly picked up their toys, and went into the front hallway.

Before long, Charlie and Ruth knocked on the door. Two men carried the refrigerator to the spot where Olive indicated.

"Please put it there, beside the icebox." She pointed to the empty space. "There is an electric plug already there."

Ruth glared at her friend. "Olive, how can you be so heartless to take gain from our troubles?" She curled her lips into a frown. "You know you undercut the value! We deserve more."

Unphased by Ruth's rebuke, Olive stared blankly. "You deserve what you reap. Had you managed your money wisely, this move would have been preventable. I'm sorry that is not the case, but do not blame me for your foolishness. Besides, you could have refused my offer!" Her hands went to her hips. She turned to face the moving men. "Now, if you will plug in my purchase, I shall like to transfer items from my icebox. Ruth, Charlie, thank you for the use of your phone. You'll be the talk of *Garland*."

Ruth Callihan grasped her husband's arm. "Come on, Charlie. We'll put all of this behind us."

As they crossed the street, Ruth whispered, "Olive sounded sinister. I never saw that side of her. Poor Tabs!"

∞ ∞ ∞

Close to a foot of snow fell by the time Tabs returned home from work. While hanging his outer clothing on the back of the door, he spotted the Frigidaire. Olive was busy making a stew for supper.

"Olive, what's that I see beside the icebox?" Tabs ran his hand over the outside of the appliance knowing the price of such a luxury. "How can we afford this extravagance? We don't know how long I'll keep my job. They are already starting to lay men off."

Olive glared at her husband, her pale blue eyes icy slits. She picked up a ladle and flung it at him. Tabs jumped to avoid being hit.

"Olive! What the heck?"

"Do you know what you've done?" Olive hissed at Tabs.

All four children peeked around the corner to see the commotion in the kitchen. Tabs shook his head, motioning for them to leave.

"Obviously, I do not, or I wouldn't be so puzzled."

When Tabs tried to approach, Olive reached for the sink

drainboard. Picking up an empty jelly jar, she flung it in his direction. It bounced off Tabs' shoulder.

"Calm down, Olive! Explain yourself."

"I'll explain myself, all right! I've missed my courses for the past two months. I went to see Dr. Paulson this morning —I'm pregnant!"

The second jar flew at Tabs' head—the flying missile missed its target. It crashed against the wall and shattered.

"Pregnant *again!*" Olive shrieked.

"My darling, how wonderful." Tabs grinned from ear to ear. "When is our bundle of joy joining us?"

"'Bundle of joy.' You're not the one who has to give birth." Both Olive's body and voice trembled. "Now, I'll never finish school. You son of a bitch! I should have known never to put stock in a pipe dream!" Another jar whizzed past Tabs' head. "Not to mention that we can't afford another mouth to feed. Do you not comprehend the financial crisis this country is facing? Well, I do!"

He cupped her face then kissed her cheek. Olive pushed away.

"My hope for school vanishes forever with another child. Damn it to hell, in another six years I'll be thirty-five—too old for a future." Olive pulled at her hair, her red face quivering in rage. "Clean up that mess." Olive pointed to the broken glass. "From now on, Tobias Bailey, you sleep in the spare room, *alone.* I never wanted a husband or a family; I'll not have child number six! Do you understand?"

Tabs cocked his neck as he caressed Olive's shoulder. She swatted his face. "Get away."

Dropping his head, Tabs retreated to the hallway to share the news of a new brother or sister with his four beloved offspring.

All four children sat on the stairsteps. Albert hugged a whimpering Alice while Esther and June held hands.

June forced back the tears. "Is Mother leaving us? Will she go away to go off to school?"

Tabs bit his lip. "Come here, all of you." He opened his arms for a group hug. "You shall never be alone. Your Mother loves you, and I am always with you."

Esther thrust forward her chest. "That's not what Mother said! She said she never wanted a family. Why does she hate us so?"

"Sweet daughter, sometimes life has plans for us other than the ones we have for ourselves. Women get—moody—when they are expecting. That's how your mother feels." Tabs kissed each of the children on the head. "Think of it; you're going to have a baby brother or sister. We have the entire winter to think of a new name!"

His enthusiasm and encouragement helped calm the children. "Upstairs, all of you. Ready yourselves for bed. With all this snow, why don't we go sledding tomorrow when I get off work?

Esther curled half her mouth into a smile. "We love you, Papa."

"And I love all of you dearly. Now scoot!"

11

IN THE GARDEN

SUMMER 1932

*T*abs welcomed a beautiful baby girl, Harriett Jane, to his family in the late spring of 1930, although he paid a heavy price. Olive made good on her promise of limiting the family to five children. Tabs' sleeping arrangement had been isolated to the fourth bedroom for two years, which he shared with seven-year-old Albert. Olive bunked two-year-old Harriett with Alice, who was now six. Thirteen-year-old Esther and eleven-year-old June remained roommates and the best of friends.

Esther was now excitedly anticipating entering Campbellsville high school in the fall. Though she was still tiny compared to June and Alice, her body had begun transforming. Her hips curved, her breasts blossomed, and her hormones exacerbated moodiness.

On a hot July afternoon, the blue sky floated puffy wisps of clouds. Esther, June, Alice, and Harriett were in the gardens helping Tabs. The financial depression that had swept across the country fostered individual resourcefulness. Tabs tripled the size of the Bailey vegetable garden to feed his families' seven mouths.

"Janie, come here, sweetie," Tabs called to his youngest, preferring to use her middle name, the same name as his mother. The toddler waddled over to her father. "Sit here. Pull these weeds with the yellow tops. Dig your fingers into the ground and try to get the root."

"I do, Papa." Harriett pushed her tiny fingers into the loose tilled garden soil.

Being small and quite petite, Harriett favored her father and oldest sister in physique. However, by age two, she exhibited cleverness and ingenuity beyond her tender age, taking after her mother in that respect.

Across the garden, Esther bent over to tie a tomato plant when June noticed a dark spot on her shorts.

"Sister, are you all right?" June asked. "I think you are bleeding. Did you scratch your leg?"

Tabs turned toward his older daughters. "June, where did you see blood?"

"On the back of Esther's shorts."

Tabs raised his eyebrows. "Esther, turn around for me to see. Darling, has your mother ever spoken to you about becoming a woman?"

"No, Papa." She touched the back of the shorts then looked at her bright red fingertips. "Papa, there is so much blood. What's happening?"

Tabs spoke gently. "Go speak with your mother now. She'll explain."

Tears filled Esther's eyes. "Papa, am I okay?"

Tabs stood and tenderly hugged his oldest. "Yes, darling, you are fine. Now go see your mother."

Alice and June looked at each other in dismay. "Papa?"

Tabs continued with his chores. "Don't worry, children, Esther is fine. Come now, we have work to finish."

Esther reappeared in less than five minutes with tears

streaming down her petite face to Tabs' surprise. She ran to her father and grabbed him around the waist.

"Have I been a bad girl, Papa?" Esther blurted.

"No darling, whatever are you talking about?" Tabs rubbed Esther's back with soothing strokes. "You are a delightful child."

"Then why did Mother tell me I was horrid?" Esther gasped for breath as she sobbed.

"Horrid, what gives you that idea?" He clenched his teeth, then Tabs kissed the top of her head. "Come, dear, let us go talk privately, under the grapevines. Children, continue your work. June, you're in charge, darling."

June nodded affirmatively as Tabs and Esther walked to the Adirondack chairs.

"Now tell me, exactly what did your mother say?" Tabs asked as he glanced at the kitchen window.

"She said that I am bleeding because that's what happens to bad girls my age. Am I a bad girl? I don't know what I did wrong. Oh, Papa, there is so much blood, and my tummy hurts." She sniffled in between words.

"I see." Tabs wrung his hands together. He glared at the house and the woman hidden behind its walls. Taking a deep breath and letting out a profound sigh, he began. "Esther darling, this would be better coming from your mother—she is a woman, after all, and knows more than I do—however, I shall tell you what I know about the subject. You, my darling daughter, are not bad. You are simply changing from a little girl into a woman."

Father and daughter sat under the grapevines talking for the next thirty minutes. Tabs retrieved some clean rags for Esther and explained to her in detail the female cycle and how to care for herself. Deciding Olive was incapable of motherly nurturing, he went on to explain human reproduction.

At the end of their talk, he hugged and kissed Esther. "My dear daughter, you have three sisters who will need this information. June's time may come sooner than yours. Please make sure that they are not surprised by the event like you were. Will you do that for me?"

Esther squeezed her father. "Of course, Papa, thank you. I love you so much."

"And I love you, darling Daughter. I love all of you more than you'll ever know."

∞ ∞ ∞

Esther and June cleared the table and began washing the supper dishes.

"Olive, may I see you outside?" Tabs growled at his wife.

The children looked at each other in alarm, disturbed by the harsh sound so infrequently heard in their father's voice.

"I have nothing to say to you." Olive quipped. "I am going outside, but you better not follow."

"Wife, we have plenty to discuss, and you shall not avoid it." Tabs grabbed Olive by the arm and dragged her out of the kitchen. His grip was so firm that Olive had no choice but to follow.

Once outside, Olive pushed Tabs away. "How dare you grip me so!"

Tabs raise his hand, thought twice, then lowered it. "How dare you tell that poor innocent child that she is a bad girl?" Tabs pursed his lips, his brow furrowed. "For God's sake, Olive, you are her mother. Act like it."

"I don't care to act like a mother. I never wanted to be a mother; I wanted to be a doctor. Remember?!" she stomped her foot, just missing Tabs.

"Would a doctor tell his patient they are bad *because they are diseased?* It is quite obvious you don't care to be motherly

74

at all by how you treated Esther today. You're smart, too smart for your own good, but you have four daughters and a son who need their mother. You better figure it out quickly." Tabs grabbed her wrist. "Do I make myself clear?"

"And how do you intend to force the issue?" Olive inhaled through clenched teeth.

Tabs contemplated his wife's words. "I've been in love with you for over fifteen years, ever since that night you lied about your age. Olive, you were and still are the most beautiful woman in the county." He paused and shook his head. "But why are you always angry? It's not just to me. It's public knowledge that you unleash your temper without being provoked."

"Just where are you getting this information, may I ask?" She thrust her nose in the air defiantly.

"I shall never name individuals. Let's just say that most of the town is of a similar opinion, due to hearing tales of your youth. I have championed you, defended your honor, and been called a fool for doing so. I'm one of your few allies, Olive. Keep it that way." Tabs slowly stood.

"I have one last thing to say on this matter." Calming herself, she glared directly at Tabs. In a soft, tranquil voice, she said, "I don't care what the fools in this town say about me. I never have. As for you, Tobias Bailey: if you threaten me, I suggest you learn to sleep with one eye open."

Tabs cupped his chin with his thumb and forefinger. His sad eyes engaged Olive for several minutes before leaving his wife sitting alone under the grapevines.

CYCLE OF LIFE

NOVEMBER 1935

*T*he United States economy continued to fail. The election of Franklin D. Roosevelt in 1933 brought about a federal government policy called the New Deal. Its purpose was to stabilize the economy and reform banking. With unemployment at over twenty-five percent, many businesses collapsed. The main street of Campbellsville impersonated a ghost town.

Industries all along the Conemaugh River from Campbellsville to Madison lost orders. Workers were furloughed or their hours were drastically cut. Close to fifty percent of the United States workforce were under or unemployed.

The local foundry suffered the same fate. Tabs schedule decreased to part-time; he spent hours in the local forests collecting firewood, harvesting mushrooms, and searching for ginseng, which he sold to an Asian merchant in Madison for much-needed cash. Hunting and trapping game produced additional food for the table and pelts to sell.

Five-year-old Harriett spent every day at her father's side. A natural athlete, when she was not carrying woodland treasures for her father, she was always swinging from grapevines, climbing trees, or swimming. She was already diving at her tender age.

The snows that November were late to make an appearance. One clear, chilly late afternoon, Harriett and Tabs returned from collecting firewood. Harriett pulled a pillowcase full of kindling, blowing breath puffs, while Tabs pulled the wagon stacked with logs, blowing cigarette smoke rings.

"Janie, pile your twigs up under the chicken coop. We want to keep them dry. Then go inside; I'll be in as soon as I finish stacking."

Harriett hugged her father then did as she was told, heading to the back door. As she entered, Esther bumped into her. Rubbing tear-filled eyes, Esther stopped.

"Harriett, where's Papa?" Her speech was labored.

"Sister, what's wrong?"

"You're too little. Just tell me what Papa's doing." Esther grabbed Harriett's arm.

Shaking loose, Harriett pointed to the top of the yard. "He's stacking wood."

Esther trudged up the slope. "Papa," she called meekly.

"Oh, hello, darling Daughter. What brings you out on this cold afternoon?" Tabs smiled as he kissed his oldest on the top of her head.

"Oh, Papa. I don't know what to say!" Esther's lip quivered.

Tabs stopped working. He looped his arm around his daughter. "Now, what has you so troubled? Come, we'll talk." Tabs led the way to the oversized chairs that remained under the arbor all year round. "Sit; tell me what is on your mind," he said as he brushed off a few dead leaves.

"Oh Papa, you can't tell Mother. She'll kill me." Esther's red eyes filled with water.

"Esther, you better just come out with whatever is bothering you."

"Papa, I think I'm pregnant." She burst into tears. "I know I'm pregnant."

Tabs bit his lower lip, then let out a long, sad sigh. Slowly and calmly, he asked, "Who is the father?"

"Darrel Cline, Papa." Esther dropped her head into her hands. Taking deep breaths, she slowly stopped crying. "We've been dating in secret for a year now."

"Is Darrel also a junior in school?" Tabs handed Esther his hankie.

"No, he graduated last year. He's lucky enough to have a job working in the mines." Esther did her best to dry her eyes. After several blows of her nose, she continued. "I told him yesterday."

Tabs stood and began pacing. "Well, what did the young man have to say about your news?"

Esther's eyes sparkled. "Papa, he is so excited. He wants to get married right away. He says that we can live with his parents. They have several acres on the edge of town. Not a large industrial farm like Grandfather Henderson's, but enough for a massive vegetable garden, a few pigs, and chickens."

She exhaled and stared into her quiet father's eyes.

"Do you love him?" Tabs reached across to touch her shoulders.

Esther grabbed his hand. Without hesitation, she answered, "Very much, Papa. I'm just so sorry to do things in the wrong order. I know that good girls get married first, then they have babies."

Tabs chuckled. "Is that what you think? Let me tell you a little story. You were almost a year old before your mother and I got married."

"Really?"

"Yes, dear. Not that I didn't want to marry Olive. She just refused. It wasn't until she could no longer tolerate living at the farm that she agreed to be married." Tabs laughed. "She is a stubborn woman. Now you must promise to never tell this story to a living soul!"

Esther rolled her head. "I promise Papa. Will she be angry with me for dropping out of school?"

"Of course." Tabs thought before adding, "Make your plans first. Have the wedding lined up before you tell her; it may lessen the blow. She's not the typical sentimental mother who plans an extravagant party, and with money so tight, she may even be…."

"Be what?" Esther cocked her head to the side.

"Never mind. Just keep me posted on your progress. I'll help however I can." Tabs embraced his daughter. "Esther, you were the delight of my life the day you were born. I love you so very much, sweetheart."

"Thank you, Papa. For being so understanding, and—for being a wonderful father."

The two linked arms as they walked to the house. Neither one of them saw tiny Harriett huddled under a rose bush, listening to their entire conversation.

∞ ∞ ∞

Two weeks later, the Bailey and Cline families met at the Justice of the Peace office for a quiet civil ceremony. Lined up on the wooden bench, waiting for their turn, Esther wore her fanciest dress, and Darrel wore his best suit. The couple held hands while gazing into each other's eyes.

"I now pronounce you man and wife! You may kiss your bride."

Darrell scooped Esther into his arms for their first married kiss.

Olive rolled her eyes, mumbling, "Fools."

No party followed. There was neither dancing nor eating. With ingredients too sparse and too hard to procure, the two families managed to pull resources for Mrs. Cline to bake a two-layer yellow cake glazed with a thin layer of sugar, the highlight of the day.

After cake, Tabs kissed his daughter goodbye. His hand lingered on her face, eyes welling with tears as he remembered the day she was born.

"Take care of my special girl," he said to Darrel.

After shaking the boy's hand, he watched Esther link arms with her new husband.

"Yes, sir!" Darrel beamed, then kissed his wife. "I shall place her on a pedestal."

The remark reminded Olive of a letter from the past, something from her brother Fred. She frowned as she and Tabs gathered the family to go. Olive looked at the newlywed couple and sneered.

"Esther," she called out, snarling. "Make sure your room is cleaned out by next week. I have rearranging to get done."

"Mother, you haven't spoken to me all week. Instead of congratulations, you demand I clean my room." Esther rested her head on Darrell's shoulder. "Of course, Mother, I'll clean out my belongings, happily."

"Don't get snippy with me, little Miss!"

"And Mother, I shall not allow you to upset me today. I am happy to be married and become a mother!"

∞ ∞ ∞

Esther packed her belongings into paper sacks while June sat on the bed, crying.

"What am I going to do without you?" June rubbed her

eyes, refusing to look at her sister. "Why did you have to go and get pregnant? You know better!"

Esther stopped collecting her clothes and asked, "Why are you so cruel? I thought you would be happy for me, marrying the love of my life?" Esther sat down beside her sister. "Remember all those nights we talked about finding our knights in shining armor? Darrel is my knight, my prince."

"How am I to manage on my own? Mother will make me do all of your work *plus* all of my work. I'll never have time to myself." June's sobs increased in volume and frequency. "Oh, Esther, it's not fair!"

"Oh. I see. You're worried about yourself." Esther stood; walking to her dresser, she resumed packing.

Hearing Esther's criticism, June wailed at the top of her lungs, "I'm sorry! Esther, *you* are more like my mother than our real mother, and you're also my best friend." June hugged her sister, laying her head on her shoulder. "I'm not as strong as you. I don't want to be the oldest; it's too much responsibility."

Esther laughed. "Being the oldest is not always fun, but you'll manage. And besides, I'm still going to be living in town."

"Well. Count on me visiting every day!"

"Who are you visiting every day?" Olive poked her head into the room. "Esther, are you about done? I want to get moving with my work."

June dried her eyes with her sleeve. "I'm going to see Esther every day!"

Olive scowled. "You'll visit no one until all your chores are done. Esther, are you finished?"

Esther winked at June. "Yes, Mother, I'm out of your hair."

Turning to June, Olive said, "June, from now on, both Alice and Harriett will be sharing your room. Albert and

Alice are getting too old to be together. Albert and your father will each get their own room."

Olive left as quickly as she entered. Esther and June stared dumbfounded at each other.

"I guess I'll have no time to get lonely," June moaned, helping Esther finish the task at hand.

13

WATER, WATER, EVERYWHERE

APRIL 1936

*R*ain pelted the valley for five consecutive days. Thunder and lightning seemed to spin in circles as the atmosphere recycled the inclement weather, dropping several inches of rain each day.

Olive's discomfort with storms and the nightmares they brought increased daily, and she woke every morning drenched in sweat as she pried the hands that haunted her dreams away from her neck.

On day three, she sequestered the family to the kitchen for all activities—eating, playing, and sleeping. The table became the center of their world. Despite continuous complaints, Tabs slept at the table with five-year-old Harriett curled up in a blanket beneath his chair as Olive paced back and forth. If she did manage to sleep, the boney, cold hands encircled around her neck. Albert and Alice found a corner and snuggled together, while June, missing her sister, hid in the roomiest pantry.

On the sixth morning of storms, Olive read one of her three soggy newspapers at the table with red, sleep-deprived eyes. She lowered it when Tabs entered unexpectedly.

"Why are you home so early?" she asked her rain-drenched husband, whose eyes were also heavy from lack of sleep. "Still coming down in torrents?"

"Yes, I'm soaked through." Tabs began removing his outer jacket. "Songer cut my hours. I'm down to fifteen hours a week." Tabs hung his head. "Though, I'll have time to hunt more game. We should eat better."

"How dare they do that to my husband? My family owns that business," Olive protested.

"Olive, the only reason I still have a job is because I am married to a Westchester. As much as you try to distance yourself from it, the name carries much weight in this county. Be thankful." Tabs poured himself a glass of water. Before drinking, he continued, "I hear some local men found work with the Public Works Department. Edgar Kepler is one of them. But he's a civil engineer when he decides to remain sober enough to work."

"He's a lousy sot. Abigail is a fool for staying with him." Olive clicked her tongue judgmentally.

"It's not that easy Olive, you should understand that." Tabs' reply was interrupted by a loud banging on the door behind him. Turning around, he opened it to a local fire volunteer.

"We have an emergency on our hands!" he warned. "One of the dams east of Madison gave way with all this rain. There is a wall of water rushing toward the south end of Madison and then on to Campbellsville. Anyone living near the river needs to evacuate to high ground. Tell your friends and relatives!" He closed the door and quickly made his way to the next home to notify the unsuspecting occupants.

"Good God!" Tabs hurriedly put on his coat. "I need to get back to the foundry to get my men out."

"Tabs, that's not your worry. Songer is in charge; let *him* risk his life."

"As the supervisor, they are my responsibility. I'm going." Tabs rushed out the door, leaving Olive again pacing the floor and Harriett whimpering under his chair.

The water was already beginning to rise when Tabs arrived at the foundry. The river churned violently, foaming white as debris rapidly accumulated in the nooks and estuaries of the Conemaugh. Watching the speed with which the water rose, Tabs knew he must act quickly. Entering the building, he found an inch of water already covering the factory floor. The river often exceeded its banks during springtime, so the men had continued working without concern.

Tabs grabbed two pipes and clanged them together to attract attention. Slowly the men recognized an alien noise and stopped to listen.

"All of you, grab your personal belongings and get out of here. Now!" He ran through the work area warning, pushing men into motion as he went. Most of the skeleton crew ignored him, not wanting to jeopardize however many precious hours they had on the clock.

"I'm not kidding! Antonio! You, Mark Antonio, move now! A dam above Madison is breached. It's only a matter of time before..."

They heard the sound of rattling brick become a rumble, then a roar, before the ten-foot wall of water rushed through the eastern side of the building, forcefully picking up men, machinery, and raw materials. It all came charging at Tabs, who bolted toward a side exit. Too slow—Tabs was swept up, along with the rest of James Westchester's factory.

The water pushed him through the side door into the less violent current outside. Tabs grabbed a desk and thrust his arm into the opening left by a missing drawer, putting aside the risk of breaking his arm. He hung on for dear life. The wood kept him afloat, but the water moved quickly and crashed into all opposing objects. Tabs tried to stay in the rear by climbing over and around the pitching desk as it sped down river.

Trees, vehicles, even boulders smashed against each other and any other object they came close to. The pillar supports to the only bridge connecting the two sides of the town were bombarded with wreckage. Tabs watched in horror as the bridge collapsed into the raging water. Within fifteen minutes, the north and south sides of Campbellsville were separated.

Not all the foundry workers were fortunate enough to find floating devices. Tabs spotted William Kepler, one of Edgar and Abigail's middle sons, bobbing lifeless, facedown in the whoosh of water. Another man, caught in the mainstream, flailed his arms as he screamed for help.

Ahead, a train trestle crossed the span of water. As Tabs approached, the corner of his desk caught on the edge of the stanchion, jarring both furniture and occupant. Tab's hat flew off with the jolt of impact. The desk split in two, and Tabs was launched into the rolling water.

His head broke the surface as he gulped for air. He was caught in a tumbling, turning wave. The hydraulics of the water took him under, spinning him around in a disorienting freefall. Every break to the surface was a surprise. Tabs instinctively raised his hand and quickly gulped air before being churned underwater again. On his fourth spin, his hand bumped into something. Tabs frantically grabbed, finally clutching the back half of his desk. The combination of man and boards was enough to break the tug of the water. They were spit out of the tumble to continue their journey downstream.

Exhausted and scared, Tabs bounced and pitched for another twenty minutes, which seemed like hours. Thunder continued booming as the sky thrust powerful bolts of electricity toward the earth. The heavens cracked, and a flash of light struck a tree on the bank. With a puff of smoke, it split in half, falling into the water. The smell of burned wood jolted Tabs to attention. His desk surged toward the downed tree. Tabs braced for impact as the desk slammed into the tree, lodging his bad leg against a branch.

He heard the crunch before he felt the pain.

The cold April rains coupled with frigid water temperatures sucked the heat out of Tabs, dulling the break. Several minutes passed before the needles shot up and down his leg. Stomach acid burned his throat as he spat out the foul, acrid liquid that was breakfast. Tabs hung to his lodged desk, trying to clear his spinning head and regain what little strength remained before he climbed onto the tree. Muscles in the strong man's abdomen burned as he carefully swung his good leg over the downed trunk, paused, then shimmied slowly toward the shoreline. Not wanting to resubmerge into the cold river, he clung to the tree and waited, and waited, and waited for his strength to return.

The water raged all day. The wind and rain pelted sharp, stinging dribs into Tabs' face. He continued to hold tight, clinging to the tree, cold, weary, and terrified, as Olive paced the kitchen, clinging to her neck. By evening, the rain finally slowed, stabilizing the river somewhat. While the water maintained its depth, it stopped increasing its breadth.

News of the foundry flood spread quickly through the close-knit community. Drenched search parties of local men, many of Olive's family members, combed up and down the river for survivors. Mr. Songer, the foreman, was safe at home when the water inundated the plant. Unaware of Tabs' return to rescue the men, he knocked on the Bailey front door shortly after suppertime. Olive reluctantly answered the door, not wanting to drench her floor.

"Mrs. Bailey, is Tabs home? I need him to come with me to the shop." Songer requested.

"He's already down there. When he heard of the danger, he ran back to get the men out of harm's way." Olive wrinkled her nose at Tabs' superior. "That was hours ago. He hasn't returned."

Songer swooned, catching himself on the doorframe. "Mrs. Bailey, may I come in and have a seat? Perhaps you should sit also."

Olive rolled her eyes and motioned to her right, showing him to the front family parlor. Songer's leg bounced nervously before he spoke. "I'm afraid a wall of water washed through the foundry, taking everything in its path. We only had a small crew, fifteen men working. But only one is accounted for. The rest are missing."

Olive inhaled as a tiny voice cried out, "Papa!" Harriett hid in the hallway, listening to the conversation.

"Harriett, hush!" Olive turned back, glaring at Songer. "Will the company be compensating the widows for their loss?"

"What? This is an act of God. Why would they?" Songer grabbed his face. "Mrs. Bailey, how do you think of money at a time like this?"

"Someone needs to think of the bigger picture!"

Songer's head shook in shock, staring at Olive. He paused a moment.

"Mrs. Bailey, it is our deepest hope to find these men downstream," Songer spoke softly but succinctly. "A search party has been assembled and is out looking already.

"You're the foreman, aren't you?" She stood, chin thrust forward, her hands slapping her hips. "You better find out because my guess is those men are gone, and you now have fifteen women without husbands! Now, if you don't mind, I have my family to look after."

Her hand gestured toward the door. Songer rose. "Mrs. Bailey, I pray your husband is found alive, for your children's sake!"

Olive locked the door as Harriett sat on the staircase, muffling her sobs. She grabbed Harriett by the shoulder. "Back into the kitchen." Swatting her backside, she scolded, "You should not spy on people's private conversations!" Then muttering, "Damn fool trying to be a hero!" she walked down the hallway.

"Mother, is Papa alright?" Harriett rubbed silent tears from her eyes.

"How should I know?" Olive filled the kettle with water. Placing it on the stove, she grabbed a cup and a used teabag. "Damn it. I wish I had some sugar."

June, Albert, and Alice poked their heads out from the pantry. "Psst. Harriett," Fifteen-year-old June whispered, waving her hand. "Grab your blanket and pillow. Come on." Harriett scooted under Tabs' chair, collected her bedding, and ran to the pantry. June quickly closed the door. "What did you hear?"

Harriett began trembling. June embraced her sister. "Calm down, little one."

"Why do I always have to be the spy?" Harriett asked in a small voice.

"Because you are so tiny; you fit into small places. Now, what did you hear?"

Harriett began crying. "It's too terrible to say."

Albert, eleven, and Alice, ten, each took one of Harriett's hands. "Who came to the door, and what did they say?" June questioned again.

"It was Papa's boss. Papa's missing. Mother says he's probably dead." Harriett burst into deep sobs. June gasped for air; Albert and Alice clung to each other.

Hearing all four children sniffling, Olive opened the pantry door. Her offspring jumped, startled by the intrusion.

"What are the four of you blubbering about?" With both hands on her hips, Olive stared down at the huddle in the pantry corner. "Harriett, if you shared my conversation with those three, and you are all crying over your father, then I suggest the four of you sleep in the pantry tonight. I don't want to hear your bawling." Olive slammed the door shut.

The children clustered together, crying and blowing their noses. The hems of their dresses filled quickly with salty tears and snot. Finally, piled on top of each other, the mass fell into a fitful sleep. Olive paced the kitchen, making a third cup of tea from the same teabag. Dawn brought a splinter of sunlight, and finally, the rain ceased. Olive eventually lay her head on the table and dozed, too afraid of her bed but too tired to dream.

∞ ∞ ∞

The flood split Campbellsville in half when it took out the bridge. The Baileys, the main business street, and the foundry were on the south side of the Conemaugh; the Kepler's and newer construction sat on the north side of the river. Tabs and his desk came to rest on the north side of the river, which was less populated and had more farmland. If they still stood, the nearest bridges were twenty miles to the east, in Madison, ten miles to the west in Garland. He was stuck.

Tabs watched the river calm down as he garnered strength. After an hour or so, he felt revived enough to drop into the shallow water between the felled tree and dry land. He cringed as his injured leg hit the ground. Using the fallen tree for support, he dragged his way to land.

The night was falling on the evergreen forest of an already

dark, gloomy, wet day. He knew he needed to protect himself and somehow recover body heat, or he may perish from hypothermia. Reaching into his pocket, he searched for his hunting knife. It was there. He crawled over to a stand of pine trees and stripped off the lowest branches to patch together a sort of roof. On hands and knees, he gathered fallen pine straw. Nothing was dry, so a fire was out of the question; however, piled together, the needles formed a barrier over the wet ground. He huddled under the trees, staying as dry as possible, conserving energy and rebuilding his strength. If he lived the night, he'd fashion a crutch and search for a farm in the morning. He allowed himself to doze.

Tabs woke to the sound of barking dogs. They were faint, coming from his east. Crawling out from under the pine branches, he called out, but his parched, weak voice did not carry through the dense humid air. He called again.

"Over here. I'm down by the river in the pine trees."

The dogs barked louder. Another five minutes passed before he saw bobbing points of light. He continued calling; the glow grew more prominent and closer. A group of six unknown men wearing hip boots and carrying lanterns approached.

Tabs pulled himself up, winced, and waved. "I've never been so happy to be seen!"

The men laughed as they inspected the area. "Who are you, mister?" asked one of the older men in charge of the animals.

"Tobias Bailey. I was in the foundry when the water hit. My leg is broken."

The word "foundry" caught the attention of a muscular young man. "You're my brother's boss. Did you happen to see him?"

"Who is your brother, Son?" Tabs was afraid to hear the answer, knowing the fate of only one man.

"Billy Kepler. He was working a short late shift today."

Tabs sighed. "I'm sorry, lad. He didn't make it."

The young man collapsed onto the wet ground. An older man bent over to console him.

"I'm Jim Rogers," said another man who approached Tabs. "Come on, Mr. Bailey, let's get you out of here and into some dry clothing. Stay at my farm tonight, and I'll try to set that leg for you. Do you think you can walk?"

Cringing in pain, Tabs tried to stand but collapsed. "Only with help."

Two men propped Tabs up and helped him walk (though, mostly he was dragged) the several miles to Jim's home. Another man braced Billy Kepler's distraught brother, leaving three volunteers to continue their search.

Jim carried Tabs into the farmhouse kitchen. "Better strip out of those wet clothes. I need a good look at your leg."

Tabs collapsed into a chair and slowly stripped out of his clothing. Shivering in only his wet long john's, he said, "Boy am I relieved you came along! I thought I was a goner."

Jim handed Tabs an old quilt to throw around his body. Tabs sat at a small table, lowered his underwear onto the stone floor, and wrapped himself.

Gently picking up the leg, Jim said, "Bailey, you're lucky; looks like it was a clean break. I'll splint it to keep it secure, but it's going to hurt like hell. Bite down on this wooden spoon."

Tabs complied. Spoon in mouth, he held his breath as Jim snapped the leg back into place. Tabs saw stars as moving bone cracked. He gagged, expelling the spoon, but did not vomit. Despite the lingering chill, Tabs wiped the sweat from his forehead as he let out a long sigh. "Yikes. That was brutal. Thank goodness it's over."

"Better eat something. I'll get you some dry clothes." Jim

offered Tabs a bowl of hot liquid and a cup of tea. "This is not a good day for Campbellsville."

Sipping a spoon of thin soup, Tabs watched six or seven Rogers children run wild around the small farmhouse. "Mr. Rogers, I appreciate your rescue and sharing your food with me. Especially when you have such a large family."

"Only Christian charity. Speaking of family, I'm sure yours is worried sick, Mr. Bailey. We have no way of contacting them tonight; the flood wiped all the telephone and telegraph lines. Men have been up and down both sides of the river all day searching for survivors."

"If it's okay with you, I'll sleep on the floor in the kitchen tonight and then head out in the morning. The water may be calm enough to cross if I can find a rowboat."

"We'll see what morning brings, Mr. Bailey. Recharge tonight." Jim shooed his children into a sleeping room. "Let's give Mr. Bailey some peace and quiet. He's had a hard day."

"Goodnight, Mr. Bailey," was recited in unison.

Tabs finished eating, then gratefully curled up in the quilt, snoring within minutes.

∞ ∞ ∞

Tabs awoke the following day disoriented. His muscles were stiff and sore, his leg throbbing from hip to toes, but it was all tolerable. The sharp, shooting pain in his calf and shin caused him to grimace until he smelled the aroma of frying bacon.

Searching his surroundings, he spotted Jim Rogers at the stove over a sizzling skillet. "Is that bacon I smell?"

"Ah, good morning, Mr. Bailey. How's the leg today?" Jim turned his attention to the kitchen guest.

"Truthfully, I ache all over, but I'll live." Tabs rubbed his shoulders. "You wouldn't happen to own a pair of crutches, would you?"

"Sorry, Mr. Bailey, no. But I did go looking for a good tree branch. Just lying there waiting for me. Should serve a purpose." Jim pointed to a freshly cut, stripped pine branch leaning in the corner.

"Oh, thank you! How splendid. Mind bringing it over?" Tabs hoisted himself up into a chair. "I need to wobble to the outhouse."

Jim helped Tabs to his feet. After a minute, Tabs finally balanced enough to begin the trek outside. The clean smell of spring washed over Tabs as he opened the door. It was as if the world had taken a bath and only the sweet smell of cleansing soap remained. Tabs inhaled deeply as he looked up.

"The system's finally moved on. Blue sky! Not a single cloud," he called back to the house.

Precariously rambling along the path, Tabs made his way to the outside latrine. Afterward, as he began the hobble back to the house, Tabs was greeted with a honking horn coming down the lane. The car stopped in front of the porch.

"Uncle Tabs. Are you okay?" the driver called out.

"Benny, is that you?" Unable to contain his smile, Tabs' entire face grinned. "How did you find me all the way out here?"

"I've been up and down this river, searching properties all night. We have men combing the riverbanks, just in case. I sure am happy to see you!" Benny put the car in park, grabbing a pair of crutches from the backseat. "Here, take these. They'll work better than a branch. You ready to go home?"

"In just one moment, son." Rebalanced on his crutches, mobility increased, Tabs walked back into the kitchen. "Jim, I seem to be rescued. My nephew is here. I can't thank you enough for your hospitality and care."

"Well, Mr. Bailey, invite him in to have breakfast." Jim stirred eggs frying in the bacon grease.

"I can't impose any more than I already have. Feed your children this feast that you have so generously prepared. I'll not take food out of their mouths!"

Jim Rogers smiled gratefully. "Thank you, Mr. Bailey. I'm sure they'll enjoy a hearty start to the day." Jim reached to shake Tabs' hand but received a strong bearhug instead.

"You are a good Christian man. I am forever in your debt."

Tabs hobbled to the car, opened the passenger door, and waved goodbye to a litany of little Rogers.

∞ ∞ ∞

Olive's nap was short-lived. She jerked her head up off the table to the sound of loud banging.

"Olive, open the door," Benny called out as he pushed it open.

Stunned and groggy, Olive gaped at her nephew. "Benny, what on earth are you doing here?" Awakened by the conversation, the children opened the pantry to hear better.

"I have a surprise for you." Benny walked back to the car. Opening the passenger door, he helped Tabs to his feet. Using crutches, Tabs walked to the porch, up the two steps, and into the house.

"Papa!" Four children rushed from their hiding spot, attacking him with glee. Giggles filled the kitchen. All color drained from Olive's face as she clutched the side of the sink, steadying herself.

"Easy, kids. Don't knock him over. Your father has a broken leg." Benny laughed and touched the bump on his nose. "After all these years, I'm glad to be able to return the rescue. Dr. Paulson will be around later to check on you.

Now get some rest." Benny slapped Tabs on the shoulder and guffawed. "Hopefully, I'll find some more ragamuffins to save today!"

Tabs limped into the family parlor and sat on the settee; the children climbed up beside him, smothering him with hugs and kisses and an unlimited supply of questions.

"Papa, shall I make you a cup of tea? How about something to eat?" June asked.

"Darling, I would love an egg and some tea." Tabs closed his eyes, trying to disguise the pain in his leg. As June made her way to the kitchen, Olive joined her family. She stood gawking at her husband.

Tabs returned her gaze. "Ahh, darling Wife. What an adventure I have to share with you. Sit, join us."

Olive tightened her lips and crossed her arms. "You had no business going back to that foundry, Tobias Bailey!"

Tabs smiled lovingly as he sunk deeper into the davenport. "Hopefully, I was able to save some men."

"What if you had drowned? I was worried sick." Her eye twitched as she scolded.

Tabs sighed. "Dear Wife, it fills my heart that you were so concerned about my wellbeing." He reached for her. "Please, sit beside me."

"Concerned for *you?* Don't be ridiculous. I was concerned for myself. I don't want to be stuck raising four brats on my own. Next time, think about that!"

She spun on her heel and left Tabs stunned and confused.

∞ ∞ ∞

Benny and Jake continued their night-long search, driving the Westchester vehicles up and down both sides of the river while Kendrick and Ben harnessed wagons for rescuing and returning as many survivors as they could find.

Five of the fifteen men working at the foundry perished that day.

The foundry was wiped out, literally and figuratively. With profits so low, no money was available to reinvest. The sixty-eight-year-old business of the deceased congressman closed its doors.

Most of Madison was spared the water's wrath. The breach was located on a tributary southeast of the central city, impacting only two suburbs. Campbellsville took the brunt of the flooding. The foundry, blacksmith, and several other small industries located along the lower street were gone. Other than Lupinetti's butcher and a few menial posts at local stores, Campbellsville no longer offered a means of livelihood. Gregor Campbell's town was reduced to a collection of half-empty houses, a grocery store, a feed store, and a pharmacy.

Receding water deposited slime and sludge in the lowlands. Dry air converted the muck into dust, which blew up and down the valley, coating the town and adjoining countryside. With each passing day, the bucolic morphed into bemired macabre.

Five days post-flood, the valley gathered for a joint memorial service. Twenty lives lost begat twenty destroyed families and fifty orphaned children. Although five foundry men perished, Tabs' quick thinking and heroic actions saved ten men and ten families from an unthinkable outcome.

Collecting in the largest sanctuary, the Presbyterian church, the valley paid tribute to all lost lives. Packed full, inside was standing-room-only, with townsfolk lining up down the block to pay respects. The church bell rang twenty times, once for each deceased, as a family member lay a flower at the altar.

Olive couldn't be bothered to attend, too busy, having overlooked her housework during the week of storms. Albert and

Alice remained at home; however, Tabs, June, and Harriett sat in the fifth row. With Tabs on crutches, the Baileys approached Edgar and Abigail Kepler and their sons, who occupied a front pew. Harriett hid behind Tabs' leg, trying to remain unnoticed.

Tabs lowered his eyes as he balanced himself, then extended his hand to Edgar. "Mr. Kepler, I am deeply sorry for your loss. I tried to save all our men. I regret my failure."

Edgar gave Tabs a once over, assessing his character; before taking his hand, Abigail dabbed her eyes then blew her nose. "So I hear Mr. Bailey. I understand you put yourself in danger to help your shift. Thank you."

"Mr. and Mrs. Kepler, may I introduce two of my girls— June, my second-born, and Harriett, my youngest." The six-year-old, always trying to be invisible, was forced out into the open.

"You know my wife, Abigail. These are my sons," Kepler said, motioning to his brood. "Earl, George, Roy, and my seven-year-old namesake, Little Edgar."

The older boys supported their mother, while little Edgar ignored the adults, choosing instead to stare at Harriett. The precocious wavy blonde-haired boy, with a beguiling smile, towered over her by three inches and outweighed her by thirty pounds, despite being only a year older.

June curtsied to Abigail. "Sorry for your loss, ma'am."

Harriett thrust her tiny hand forward. "My deepest sympathies," was uttered by the soft, innocent voice.

Edgar Kepler smiled as he kissed the child's hand. "Thank you, little one. Your Papa has raised you well."

∞ ∞ ∞

After the service, June walked Harriett home while Tabs— with his leg encased in a plaster cast—joined Mr. Songer and a few other foundry workers at the Campbellsville WWI veterans club to drink beer and discuss the ordeal.

"Hell of a loss!"

Mark Antonio slapped Tabs on the back. "You saved my life, Bailey. I'm grateful." Turning to the barkeep, he yelled, "Bailey drinks free today."

"Here, here!" responded the group.

Songer slung a dart at a cork target. "As if we haven't endured enough. There's nothing left in this town." The missile bounced and fell to the floor. "Blasted! At least I'm old, worked a lifetime, ready to retire. I made my money. What are you younger men going to do to feed your families?"

Tabs lifted his glass to drink. Swallowing slowly, he looked around the table. "Gentlemen, times are tough all over. We are alive; be thankful for that."

Several of the men grumbled. "Well, I, for one, need money. I think I'll head to the big city and look for work."

A second man added, "Maybe we can get hooked up with a work project, like Kepler? Not have to move the family, just move ourselves."

Tabs rubbed his chin. "The forests around here provide plenty of small game. Olive is a whiz at preserving and canning the garden surplus. Our only problem is finding flour, butter, and milk."

"Hell and tarnation, Tabs. How do you cook or bake without flour, butter, or milk?"

Tabs took another sip, "Well, I'll not move. My house is paid for, and I'll never find a buyer to pay a reasonable price for it. I'm forced to stay and make the best of it."

As the men shook their heads in agreement or voiced objections to Tabs' decision, old man Cline rushed in the door. The men turned toward the squeaking hinges.

"Tabs," he called out of breath. "Esther had her baby. We're both grandfathers." Cline collapsed into a chair.

Tabs broke into tears. "Good grief, man, are they well? What was it, a girl or a boy?"

Lloyd Cline heaved a deep breath. "She's well; they're both healthy. A little boy. They named him Toby, Tobias Lloyd, after you and me!"

Tabs covered his face with his hands. He took a moment to compose himself before he looked up at Lloyd. As their eyes met, both men burst into tears, rose, and embraced each other.

"Drinks all around!" yelled Tabs as he wobbled on his broken leg. To himself, he added, *Thank God they are healthy.*

"Next round's on me!" said Lloyd. "To the proud grand-fathers!"

14

CAKE

LATE SPRING 1937

*W*ith Esther married, June found herself missing her sister and often frequented the Cline household. Albert and Alice, practically twins, were now eleven and twelve and spent their days together with friends. Consequently, Harriett was often alone.

In three weeks, Harriett Jane Bailey would celebrate her seventh birthday. She loved school and was an instant scholar, like her mother—she already read at a third-grade level. Her teachers applauded her curiosity and enthusiasm.

Beyond academics, Harriett loved tumbling. She was always performing cartwheels, somersaults, and handstands up and down the alleyway. She also loved retrieving and throwing balls back to the older boys who lived in the house next door. Every stray ball that found its way into Olive's yard was confiscated by Olive and placed into a bushel basket in the pantry. Harriett made it her mission to save all wayward balls from her mother.

The town, its lifeforce shattered from the previous seven years, was ready to move forward. It anticipated a possible economic revival for a few fleeting moments when rumors of the foundry reopening circulated throughout gossip channels. However, the stories were false, unemployment remained high, and Campbellsville and the country slipped into a financial recession within the larger depression.

To feed his family, Tabs hunted squirrels, deer, and rabbits. "Poached" was a more accurate description, since his hunting was done out of season, but Tabs didn't care; his responsibility was to feed his family. Olive didn't mind, either. She benefited from her husband being one of the town's more skilled hunters. The Baileys were blessed with a catch at least twice a week.

When not in school, Harriett accompanied Tabs frequently. She knew the names of most local insects, birds, plants, and animals. She became stronger, climbing higher into the trees during their hikes. Falling often resulted in skinned knees, elbows, and bumps on the head but never deterred her from trying again.

One such afternoon, while skipping through the woods with her father, Harriett asked, "Papa, do you think Mother will bake me a cake for my birthday?" She licked her lips. "Remember the cake we had for Esther's wedding? Boy! That tasted really good."

Tabs squeezed his daughter, "Janie, if you wish really hard, perhaps your wish will come true."

Harriett squeezed her fists tight and cinched her eyes shut. "I wish, I wish, I wish!"

∞ ∞ ∞

Tabs cornered Olive in the kitchen after dinner that evening. "Wife, any chance of making Janie a birthday cake next week? The child's only taste of the confection was at Esther's wedding. She excels in school and deserves a cake this year."

Olive scowled at Tabs. "We all deserve more than we get! Our life is pitiful. Even the war wasn't this bad."

Tabs lowered his voice. Leaning in, he continued, "I know, darling. I regret not being able to give you more. Times have gone from bad to worse, but we are doing okay, aren't we? We're fed, clothed, and sheltered. We love each other. Isn't that truly all we need?"

Olive glared at her husband. "I'll not dignify that with an answer." Spinning on her heel, she stomped out of the kitchen.

∞ ∞ ∞

The morning before Harriett's birthday, Olive hiked the four miles out of town to the farm. The irregular bus schedule no longer guaranteed timely transit. Enjoying the physical exercise, she hummed as she walked up the stone lane, carefully avoiding exposed roots and wagon ruts. The graves of Fred and Polly were her usual destination when trekking this path, but this time she walked past her usual turn-off and stopped to gaze at the hilltop cemetery. The tall obelisk was now engraved with two names. It has been eight years since Henderson's death. Eight years since she last entered her childhood home.

Strolling further down the drive, Olive noticed another change: a mansion in disrepair. She rubbed her neck subconsciously. The left-wing of the grand home was overgrown by vegetation. A bird flew out of a gap in the roof, hinting to water damage inside. Olive bit her lip as she surveyed the damage. Slowly, a smile crept across her face. *Everyone gets their comeuppance.*

As she got closer, she saw how the once pristine flower gardens surrounding the front porch now boasted more weeds than blooms. Olive's smile widened. Paint flaked off the boards. A layer of dirt covered the large windows.

She was shocked when her knock was greeted by her oldest brother, Ben, not a servant.

Ben's face contorted. "Olive, what are you doing out here?"

Olive returned the dubious greeting with a wide grin. "Well, I'd also like to know what *you* are doing. This place is a dump."

"If you came to provoke an argument, you may leave directly."

Olive pushed her way into the outer foyer. It, too, was covered with a layer of dirt and grime. She looked through a smudge in the glass to view the main hallway. Mice scampered across the floor; cobwebs filled the corners. Dancing footprints left glimmers of lost luster. "My God, Ben, why is the place so filthy?"

"Are you here to criticize the housekeeping, then?" Ben motioned to the door. "Please go."

"Actually, Ben, I'm here because I need four cups of flour and one cup of milk." She thrust a container in Ben's direction. "It's Harriett's birthday. She's turning seven, and I want to bake her a cake. There is no flour to be found in town."

Ben shook his head. "I'm assuming Harriett is your youngest. I don't think I've met her." He then added, without pause, "No. I can't help you."

Olive cocked her head. Clenching her teeth, she demanded. "Ben, it's four cups of flour. Don't you still run the granary?"

"Olive, I'm sorry." Ben tried to soften his refusal. "We barely have enough to feed ourselves."

"Four cups, Ben. That's all I want. For a cake!"

Ben closed his eyes, tilting his head backward; he inhaled. "We're losing the farm, Olive! I've sold off as much as I can, at a loss. I need to come up with two thousand dollars by the end of the month, or the bank will repossess it. You help me with that, then I'll help you with the flour."

Olive smirked. "I have money, Ben. I can pay for the damn flour." Her nostrils flared. "You're a fool, Ben. Both you and Clyde are idiots. Times are tough, but there is no reason this farm should be in jeopardy."

"Well, Olive, you left—remember? Father offered you and Tabs a place to live and raise Esther. But no—you needed *freedom*." Ben sputtered, "He missed you. Dammit! Olive, he died longing for you. Father needed your guidance..."

Ben hung his head, refraining from revealing that he and Clyde also needed her help. With Olive in charge, the farm would not have failed.

Olive turned to hide her smirk. With her back to her brother, she shouted. "Oh and Ben, I have two-thousand dollars, but you'll never see one penny of it." She practically skipped off the porch and down the front sidewalk. It wasn't until she passed through the front gate that she turned to look back. Ben was still standing on the porch, tears streaming down his face. He waved goodbye.

She spun around without salutation. The journey home was light and carefree. She grinned until she reached the town, feeling like a victim for whom justice had been served.

∞ ∞ ∞

The morning of Harriett's birthday arrived with unseasonal heat and humidity. Olive was almost glad not to have to fire the coal stove to bake a cake, although, having indulged in nightly desserts as a child, she now craved the sweet more than Harriett.

Harriett was doing backflips in the alley by the chicken

coop. Suddenly, a scruffy, ragged man appeared out of nowhere, startling her.

"Come here, little girl," beckoned the tattered fellow.

His pants were mere shreds of fabric held up by a piece of rope; his collarless shirt was saturated in sweat. Weeks of body odor announced his presence. Scratching his bearded face, he snarled, moving closer to Harriett.

"No. Leave me alone! You stink," she quickly quipped, the smell of urine gagging her.

Taking offense to the insult, the vagrant moved closer to the chicken coop. He raised his voice to a menacing level. "Fetch me some eggs. Hurry!"

Terrified and sensing danger, Harriett picked up a stick. Charging the hobo, she switched his back and face with her weapon, all the time screaming at the top of her lungs. Her element of surprise caused the man to falter long enough for Tabs to hear his daughter. Tabs bounded up the yard, carrying his shotgun.

"Mister! You better back away from my little one, or I'll splatter you with buckshot." Tabs' face contorted, brows tense, lips pursed. "Janie, get over here behind me."

Quickly moving to the safety of her father, Harriett tripped over a root, landing in the middle of the coop. She was covered with mud and chicken poop. She scrambled back to her feet and ran to Tabs.

"Now, Mister," Tabs continued. "I know you're hungry, so I'm givin' you an egg. You take this egg, and you get a move on. If I see you around these parts ever again, I'll shoot you. You hear?" Tabs waited for an answer. "You hear? I'll shoot you dead on the spot."

The hobo grabbed the egg from Tabs' hand and backed away. He began a slow saunter down the alley as he looked over his shoulder.

"I said move out of here!" Tabs shot a round at his feet.

The vagrant increased his speed, trotting toward the station in hopes of catching a train out of town.

"Janie, you go to your mother. I'm following this guy to make sure he scats."

∞ ∞ ∞

"What in the name of God did you get into?" Olive screeched at the child. "Look at you. I can't possibly bake a cake now. I have no time. You require a good scrubbing."

Harriett pouted, looking at her filthy clothes and shoes. "But Mama, there was this stinky, scary man. I fought him off, and I fell. He was trying to steal our chickens."

"I don't want your silly stories. Strip down to your panties while I run a bath. No cake for you today!"

Not bothering to stoke the stove to heat a kettle, Olive filled a washbasin with chilly tap water. "In. Now!"

"Mother, it's too cold," Harriett whimpered quietly—but she complied, not wanting to upset her mother more than she already was. She shivered as she placed her foot into the tub.

"Hush!"

Olive scratched her hair and skin with unnecessary roughness. The drying process was equally painful.

Skin red from the brush and towel, Harriett mumbled, "Mother, that hurt."

"I said hush. Now get dressed. Don't you dare go back outside. No cake for you, Missy!" Olive swatted Harriett on the backside and scooted her out of the kitchen.

Harriett stared at her mother. No cake? Her tiny lips curled downward, but she refused to cry. Climbing the stairs one at a time, she sulked into her bedroom.

Tabs later returned home to find Harriett curled in the corner of the front parlor, reading a book.

"Janie, why aren't you outside enjoying this early summer day? That bad man will not return. You're safe. I followed him out of town."

"Oh, Papa." The tears began to flow freely as Harriett ran to the comfort of her father. "Mother said 'no cake' because I got dirty, and she had to stop to give me a bath. She doesn't have time to bake one now."

Tabs embraced the child. "Precious darling Daughter, don't cry." Tabs lifted Harriett, carrying her through the kitchen and outside to the Adirondack chairs.

Olive called after them, "Tobias Bailey, don't you dare let her get dirty."

Tabs flashed Olive a scowl. "We'll speak later, Wife."

Tabs sat on the big chair, scooping Harriett into his arms. Reaching into his pocket, he pulled out a package wrapped in newsprint. "Sweetie, it's not much, but here. Happy birthday, honey."

Harriett gazed at her father with wide innocent blue eyes as she tore away the paper, finding a hand-sewn rag doll with buttons for her eyes and nose.

"She's beautiful!" Giggling, Harriett kissed the toy. "What shall I name her?"

Tabs scratched his chin. "I think Mary is a good name. It was my grandmother's name. She would have loved you."

Harriett hugged her father's neck with both arms. "Oh Papa, that's a perfect name."

Squeezing the doll, she slid back down into Tabs' lap.

Tabs reached into his pocket. "I have one more surprise." Withdrawing a wrinkled piece of foil, Tabs unwrapped a square of melted chocolate. "Dip your finger into this, then lick it." He held the treat in front of Harriett.

Harriett licked her chocolate-covered finger. "Yum! Oh, Papa, this is better than cake. This is my best birthday ever!"

Tabs' heart melted with the child's unconditional love, regretting that her mother could not feel the same.

∞ ∞ ∞

The dinner conversation was mainly Albert and Alice rehashing the day's ball game. June ate at Esther's, Olive sat quietly, and Harriett hugged her doll while Tabs stewed. He waited patiently for the children to retire before he spoke.

"Olive, we need to talk."

Olive scrunched her nose. "Get it over with. You've been waiting all day to spout off."

"How dare you allow Janie to think it's her fault you didn't bake a cake?" His gaze held Olive's blue eyes.

"Well, it's true. I didn't have time to bake after cleaning her up."

Tabs slammed his hands on the table; Olive flinched. "The child feels guilty for *tripping*, all the while you had no intention of baking a cake. Didn't you? "

Olive ground her teeth together. "I walked out to the farm to get flour and milk. Ben wouldn't share. So I did try!"

Tabs shook his head. "Do you blame Ben? Why should he be generous with you?"

"I was willing to pay."

"I'm sure he'd gladly take your money." Tabs prodded, "Did you bother to tell him that you'd pay?"

Olive stood. "That is none of your business." She walked toward the door.

"Olive Bailey, you sit yourself down. I'm not finished." Tabs inhaled through his teeth. "This is my business when it involves my children."

"*Your* children? I don't remember you giving birth."

"You are a stubborn, spiteful woman. You may bully me, but I'll not allow you to bully our offspring. I advise you to bear in mind these words." Tabs exhaled a long whistling breath.

"Or you'll what? Do not threaten me, Tobias Bailey, unless you have the guts to follow through! Because I know you will not." Olive flashed daggers at her husband, leaving him sitting alone in the kitchen, arms dangling at his side. She stomped up the stairs, slammed the door, and crawled into bed.

15

DAR AND AIR GUNS

DECEMBER 1941

*C*ampbellsville, gutted and lifeless, strived to survive the devastating decade of the 1930s. The townspeople led simple lives, helping one another cope with their hardships. Neighbors and family shared what little they had, except for the Westchesters, who lost the farm to Olive's delight. Ben remained in the cottage, working a small fifty-acre plot while allowing the mansion to deteriorate, unable to afford the upkeep. Clyde and Sally moved to Pittsburgh. Tildy and Tommy fared slightly better, purchasing additional two-hundred acres from Westchester Farms at auction. Benny and Ingrid moved to Campbellsville, buying a corner house several blocks from the Baileys. The once majestic, enviable Westchester Farms, established in the late 1700s, died a slow, agonizing, ten-year death.

In September 1939, Germany invaded Poland, resuming a stance of aggression. France and Britain rallied, defending the free world from the Nazis. The United States found itself again promoting an isolation policy while supplying goods and equipment to the Allied forces. President Roosevelt preferred a slightly more involved foreign policy but acquiesced to isolation in exchange for his New Deal political support.

Manufacturing needs increased and the old foundry, like the phoenix, was reborn.

James Westchester's great-grandchildren benefited, establishing a new business that provided a much-needed lifeline to Campbellsville in the form of a spring factory. Springs were shiny coils to be used to manufacture vehicles, tanks, amphibious craft, aircraft, and various artillery, including rifles. All these were products of war. Despite the newfound industry, income and property values remained low, still not returning to the levels of the 1920s.

Tabs also benefited from a promotion to plant foreman when Mr. Songer officially retired in 1939. Although a foreman, Tabs earned only slightly more than his salary was before the flood. However, that didn't matter to Tabs; being gainfully employed kept money in Olive's pockets and a frown off her face. In turn, Tabs hired Benny as a new supervisor.

Time marched on for the Baileys, who celebrated many holidays and family birthdays (with Olive's celebration always being the most elaborate, due to Tabs' encouragement).

Summer patriotic days, with flags and parades, were family favorites. Every Decoration Day, Fourth of July, and Armistice Day, Olive lined her front steps and sidewalks with flags and swagged bunting across the porch roof, with a large American flag waving proudly above a front window. The veterans of Campbellsville paraded through the streets as residents gathered in appreciation. Sometimes a drum and fife corps joined the march, which ended with speeches from local politicians at the local Veteran's Club.

The Baileys minimally recognized the Christian holidays of Christmas and Easter by placing a single wreath on the front door. Halloween, Thanksgiving, New Year, and Epiphany were insignificant, a sharp contrast to the many elaborate festivities of Olive's youth.

∞ ∞ ∞

The morning of Saturday, December 13, 1941, Tabs and Olive sat at the kitchen table. Olive read her newspapers while Tabs rolled cigarettes.

Tabs paused for a moment to ask, "Olive, what are they saying about the attack in Hawaii?"

Olive grunted. "I don't like this one bit. I knew when those damn Germans invaded Poland that we were headed back to war. Now, thanks to Japan, we are getting involved, too."

"I agree, it's not good. Thank goodness Albert is too young to be drafted." Tabs licked the paper, struck a match on his belt buckle, and puffed.

"The only good to come out of this is you going back to work." Olive waved away the smoke. "Why do you continue to roll those weeds? You can afford to buy pre-made cigs."

Their conversation was interrupted when the back door opened. Esther, now twenty-one, waddled in, holding her protruding belly. She had her son and daughter in tow.

"Grandpapa, Grandpapa!" Five-year-old Toby and three-year-old Heddy jumped into Tabs' lap. "Happy birthday, Grandpapa!"

Esther leaned slightly to kiss her father's cheek. "Papa, you need to meet me halfway," she laughed. "I'm having trouble bending these days."

Tabs shooed the children, he stood, hugging his firstborn. "My beautiful daughter, pregnancy becomes you."

Olive harumphed. "Pregnancy does not become any woman. That is such a typical male comment."

"Mother! I'll take any compliment I can find in this condition." Esther rubbed her belly. "I see you still read three newspapers every day. Why don't you get out and make some friends?"

"Just where am I to make friends?" Olive frowned. "I don't have any desirable neighbors now that Ruth is gone."

"Mother, new people are moving back to Campbellsville all the time, now that the spring factory is open. Benny and Ingrid live only two blocks away. Why don't you join the Daughters of the American Revolution with Mrs. Cline and me? Yes, that's just what you need! You are already very patriotic."

Olive, who remained engrossed in the news article, raised her hand, signaling Esther to stop. "I'm not joining those hoity-toity women."

"How can you even say such a thing? Most of them are your relatives." Esther shook her head, gazing at her mother. "Mrs. Cline is not snobbish, and neither am I! Aunt Tildy is a member."

Olive dismissed the idea with a shake of her head. "If Tildy belongs, I'm *definitely* not joining."

Hearing different voices, Albert and Alice ran down the stairs, side by side, to join the family. Harriett followed a few steps behind, hoping to find a Christmas tree.

"Hello, Sister dear. When is June coming?" Fifteen-year-old Alice fussed with her hair as she greeted her sibling.

Right on cue, the door opened for the second time to admit twenty-year-old June Bailey Ralston.

"Happy birthday Papa, though a day late." June kissed Tabs and handed him a wrapped box.

Glancing at his second-born, he observed her glow, along with a slight bulge in the otherwise tall, slender figure. "June, are you pregnant?"

June giggled. "Yes!" She hugged Esther. "We're having babies the same year!"

Olive scowled at both girls. "Good God, not again. I endured that with my sisters. I don't care to relive the experience with my daughters."

June fidgeted. "Why is that a problem, Mother? I don't understand."

Tabs intervened. "Never mind your mother, dear. This is the most delightful news and the best birthday gift I can be given." Tabs glowed.

Alice ran to hug both girls. "I'll babysit. Will you pay me?"

"Alice, I already pay you to watch the children. Why would I stop?" asked Esther.

The family laughed as Alice blushed. "Just checking!"

Eleven-year-old Harriett hung in the background, quietly taking in the conversation.

"Well, sisters, you'll not find me making babies," Albert said. "I'll be fighting Nazis and Japs."

"Albert!" Olive objected, throwing Tabs a concerned look.

"Son, that's all well and good. But you're only sixteen. Trust me on this, you don't want to go to war unless they force you to."

"Papa's right, Albert," Esther said. "Darrel had to sign up for the draft, and we're anything but excited about it."

"So did Dave," said June about her husband. "That was peacetime draft. Now that we've declared war, I'm sure it will be expanded."

Albert thrust an air gun at the ceiling and began making shooting noises. Toby laughed, joining his attack.

"That's enough! Stop it. All of you, stop it! War is no laughing matter." Olive glared at her family, then exited for the seclusion of her parlor.

"Mother, come back. We are celebrating Papa's birthday," Albert called after her. His request was met with silence.

"Albert, sit. War is a sensitive subject for your mother. Her brother…"

"Yes, Papa, she's told us about Fred—too many times. You served; I shall serve too."

Tabs placed his hand on his son's shoulder. "Yes, Son, when and if the time comes. Until then, shall we try not to encourage your mother's anxiety?"

Harriett, sitting in the corner, spoke up. "I'm all for keeping Mother calm! Now Papa, open your gifts." She handed Tabs a basket full of plants.

Tabs picked up the vegetation. "Ginseng. Janie, where did you find this?"

Harriett smiled. "Papa, you taught me well. I pay attention to you when we hunt. I found it in November, right before the first snowfall, and I dried it under my bed. You can sell this to your man in Madison and buy yourself something special."

Tabs beamed at his protegee. "Thank you, Janie, my sweet littlest one."

Heddy spoke up, "Me littlest."

Everyone chuckled. Tabs kissed the toddler.

"Here, Papa, from Alice and me." Albert cued Alice, who handed Tabs a cotton handkerchief. "I paid; Alice sewed. It's your initial."

"Lovely stitching, darling Alice. And such fine fabric. Thank you, dear children."

"Papa, open our gift next." June insisted, pointing to the package on Tabs' lap. Tabs ripped off the wrapping to find a carton of Lucky Strikes cigarettes.

"June, so extravagant—and so close to Christmas. Thank you."

"Oh Papa, you are worth every penny. You shouldn't have

to wrap your own smokes, and your birthday shouldn't be slighted just because it's close to Christmas."

Toby, not to be outdone, jumped up and down. "Grandpapa, here's our gift." He pulled a gray, wool, herringbone cap from his back pocket. "For your head."

Tabs bent over, allowing Toby to place it over his hair. "Now I'm a Dapper Dan. A very blessed one."

Esther removed the lid from her metal cake carrier. Showing her creation to the room, she said, "It's red velvet cake. My mother-in-law's recipe. I'll cut us all a piece."

Tabs rubbed his hands together as Harriett licked her lips, having inherited her grandfather's and mother's craving for sweets.

The family, minus Olive, enjoyed Esther's creation. Despite the temptation of dessert, Olive stayed in her parlor, fondling her picture of a handsome West Point cadet in full uniform and sulking to herself.

Harriett asked as she finished her cake, "Papa, when are we cutting down our tree?"

"Sweetie, we have to wait until next week. Your mother doesn't want the mess in the house."

Heddy and Toby peered at Esther, wide eyes round with curiosity. "Is Santa coming?"

"Yes, darlings, Santa is coming soon." Esther faced her father. "Papa, will you join us for dinner on Christmas Eve?"

Alice was quick to respond. "I will! Nothing happens around here. All my friends have large family get-togethers, sing carols, and go to midnight services. Here, we just sit quietly in the front parlor and stare at each other."

Tabs frowned. "Oh darling children, I wish I could, but I must remain at home with your mother. She won't participate, and it's not right for me to leave her by herself." He searched Alice and Albert's faces, who eagerly indicated the desire to accept Esther's invitation. "You children may go; take Harriett with you. I'll stay with Olive."

Alice and Albert hugged each other as they jumped up and down. Harriett, who was again sitting out of the way, spoke up. "I don't want to go. I'll stay with you, Papa."

16

UNCLE SAM WANTS YOU

*I*t didn't take long for the December 7th attack on Pearl Harbor to affect Campbell County residents. President Roosevelt referred to it as "A date which will live in infamy," which was soon proven correct: the United States declared war on Japan on December 8th, 1941, then reciprocated a declaration of war against Germany and Italy on December 11, 1941.

June's prediction of an expanded draft became policy, resulting in too many from Campbellsville receiving notice to "Report to Uncle Sam." It spoiled many Christmases. The drafted Westchesters included Lucas Jamison—Tommy and Tildy's son—and Sammy Westchester, Olive's thirty-eight-year-old nephew from Philadelphia. Darrel Cline and David Ralston—Esther's and June's husbands—plus three Kepler boys—Earl, George, and Roy—were also summoned to report for active duty.

Earl, Roy, Darrel, and Lucas preemptively decided to control their fate by enlisting in the Navy. David, obsessed with flying, joined the US Army Air Forces, while Sammy and George waited as long as possible for their Army draft notice.

Except for the Baileys, everyone in the valley spent a somber holiday in church at prayer. Families stayed at home; Albert and Alice joined the Cline family on Christmas eve, while Harriett, Tabs, and Olive sat in silence. Jovial New Year's celebrations were postponed. The traditional toast to a fresh beginning would have to wait for the soldiers to return.

The cold January deployment morning came too soon. Once again, the Bailey family found themselves among throngs of Campbellsville citizens, waiting at the train station to say goodbye to their loved ones marching off to war.

Dave Ralston rubbed June's ever-growing belly. "Darling, don't cry; I'll be safe in the skies, dropping bombs on Jerry."

June wrapped her arms around her husband's neck. "I can't help it. I don't want to have this baby with you thousands of miles away."

Olive grunted. "Too late for that now."

"Mother!" Esther clung to both her children and her husband. "Please be more generous; everyone here is suffering."

Harriett stood to one side, hiding behind Tabs as she observed the sadness of families being separated.

Tabs trembled when the train whistle blew, announcing its arrival at the station.

Olive grumbled, "This is déjà vu. An all-too-familiar scene, which I'd like to forget."

As she spoke, she noticed Tildy and Tommy, further down the platform, hugging their son. Lucas spotted her, calling out, "Aunt Olive! See you when we defeat these bastards. Stay well!"

Olive turned her back on her sister's family. Tabs immediately responded for her: "Good luck, nephew. Where are you headed?"

"Great Lakes," Lucas called above the din.

A few other men, including Earl and Roy Kepler, and Darrel Cline, responded, "Me, too."

The youngest Kepler boy, Eddy, spotted Harriet hiding and scowled at her as he waited with his brothers.

"Who said that? Hold up your hand." Six arms went into the air as the men made mental notes of their new compatriots.

"Keep your heads down, boys—I mean literally!" Tabs sang out.

Many of those waiting chuckled; the tension lessened slightly. Clicking his heels on the wooden platform, Tabs came to attention; raising his hand to his forehead, he saluted the group.

"God keep you safe," Tabs called. "God bless America."

Other veterans from the first war followed suit, honoring the new recruits as they waited in line to board the train. "God bless America," they said to their sons, husbands, fathers, nephews, and friends, all eager to defend their families' way of life and freedom.

One by one, cigarettes were extinguished as the boys climbed the rack into the cars. Heads, hands, even entire torsos hung out the windows, waving goodbye as the train rounded that last bend out of Campbellsville.

∞ ∞ ∞

Two days later, at the breakfast table, Harriett asked, "Mother, may I join you in reading the paper? Before school? I want to keep up with the war."

Olive scolded. "You're eleven; don't you have friends to play with?"

"No, I don't have friends. Kids pick on me because I'm so little." Harriett grabbed a folded section of newsprint, opened it, and began. "Prime Minister Winston Churchill traveled to

Washington to meet with President Roosevelt. Despite the United States declaring war on Japan before Germany, the two powers agree that the defeat of Germany and Italy and the liberation of Europe is the main objective of the allies. Japan shall remain a secondary target until Germany collapses."

"Well, aren't you a little smarty pants!" Olive huffed.

"Please, Mother, there's no harm in letting me read it."

"I guess not. Just don't be getting too highfalutin, Missy." Olive threw the remaining paper at Harriett.

∞ ∞ ∞

Every morning before school, Harriett rose early to read the paper, while Alice and Albert remained under their quilts as long as possible. She began to understand how war raged as she read about Germans bombarding London and the British industrial cities daily.

Several weeks after the mass deployment, Benny knocked on the door early in the morning. Harriett carefully folded the paper for her mother, then answered the knock.

"Hi, Uncle Benny. Come in."

Benny kicked the snow from his boots before stepping inside. "Is Aunt Olive home?"

"She's still upstairs. Have a seat. Would you like a cup of tea?"

Benny removed his cap and licked his lips. "Tea sounds wonderful. We only drink coffee nowadays."

Harriett brewed a cup as Olive entered the kitchen. Benny stood, walked to his aunt, and kissed her cheek.

Olive drew away from him. "To what do we owe this honor, Benny?"

Trying to disguise the awkwardness, Benny ran his hand through his hair and sat quickly. "I'm going to Madison after extra supplies like we did the last time. Do you need me to pick up anything for you?"

Olive cocked her head, confused. "What prompted this?"

"Well, I only live down the block now. You had the entire Westchester household organized for the last war; I'm sure you already made your own list."

Olive let out a long sigh. "I have, but I swear I am so tired of hoarding for wars and depressions; when is it going to end? I just want to live a normal life!"

Harriett stared at her mother. "Define 'normal,' Mother."

"Shut up, Harriett. Don't be such a smartass."

Biting her lip, Harriett continued. "I am dead serious. What is 'normal,' if not making the best of what's thrown at you?"

"That's enough. Go to school." Olive walked to the back of the door, grabbed Harriett's coat, and threw it at her. Harriett bundled up without comment.

Benny opened the door for Harriett, "Don't fret, child; your mother is always on the edgy side of *normal*."

Harriett smiled at his choice of words. "Thanks, Uncle Benny. I'm glad you live in town. Mother needs a friend or two. So do I, even though you're my uncle."

"She never did have friends." As Harriett exited, Benny stood silently watching Olive. "Well, I'll be off," he said after a moment's silence. "Let me know if you want me to grab some items for you?"

Olive held up her hand. "Wait, Benny."

Benny stood at the door. "Yes, Olive?"

"You're correct. I do have a list. It shall save me from trekking on the bus in this weather." Olive retrieved a paper from the dining room table. Handing it to Benny, she added, "Wait just a minute, I'll grab some money."

Olive opened her purse. Turning her back to hide her

stash, she unrolled several large bills. Tucking the wad back into her bag, she turned again to Benny.

"Here. I'm sure the store requires payment upon purchase. Thanks for helping me out. I've had enough of this lifestyle. I prefer something more stable and much more affluent."

"Wouldn't we all!"

∞ ∞ ∞

Campbellsville High School Principal, Mr. Ron Wakefield, already felt the pinch of war. Many of his teachers and staff members enlisted or were scheduled to report for duty. Mr. Wakefield feared his turn was coming, so he designed a mass reorganization of the schools to minimize personnel needs.

Immediately following Christmas break, his first move was to double up all elementary schools, ending their grade level at six rather than eight. Teachers like Bea Thompson, who usually taught thirty students from grades one through eight, now taught forty students grades one through six. Middle school now held grades seven through nine and moved to the high school building, leaving high school as grades ten through twelve.

Harriett trudged several blocks through cold wind to the elementary school that early morning in February 1942. The seventh and eighth graders were already gone; she was one of the oldest students, despite being smaller than some fourth graders. Opening the side door, she was met by her teacher.

"Ah, there you are. Harriett, there have been some changes," her teacher said. "You need to go to the high school and report to the seventh-grade teacher, Mrs. Sokol."

Harriett hung her head. "Did I do something wrong?"

"Oh no, dear. I've been giving you seventh and eighth-grade work for the past several months. They are making more war changes, so I'm able to bump you up a class—put you where you will be challenged."

Harriett smiled a big toothy grin. "Thank you, I'm really excited!"

As Harriett redonned her coat and readied to leave, a few of her classmates huddled in the corner, mumbling.

"Where's Miss Goody Two Shoes going?" one asked.

Another said, "No loss here. All she does is study; she's no fun."

Standing with the group, Eddy Kepler joined the taunting. Newly moved to this elementary school as part of the reorganization, he pouted in jealousy as Harriett walked out. He really wanted to be pushed ahead as well, but for athletics, not academics. Eddy excelled in every sport—baseball, basketball, track, and football. As a sixth-grader, he already played on the junior varsity squads. A move to the high school building would afford him the chance to break into varsity sports and begin his journey to a college football scholarship, his strongest desire.

Harriett continued walking another block and neared the Campbellsville High School building, a sight she viewed almost every day of her life. Today, the approach seemed daunting. The long, expansive center staircase led up the hill to the Governor's style driveway. Looming double doors imparted the image of a mountainous climb. Like every other building in west-central Pennsylvania, the school was located on the side of a hill.

Harriett slowly climbed the staircase, holding onto the balustrades. She stood at the top and regarded where she just traveled, sighed, then, throwing open the heavy paired doors, she entered the front lobby. The ten-foot ceiling towered over the four-foot-nine-inch child. She gazed up in awe. The gymnasium was directly in front of her, whose roller-based bleachers folded up to get out of the way for non-sporting events. Four sets of double doors led into the heart of the building—two in the front, one on each side.

A row of five classrooms ran off the long hallway on either side of the gym. The hallways ended with back staircases, up to a duplicate setup on the second floor and down to a basement lunchroom. The front staircases flanked both sides of the entrance doors, also going both up and down. The cafeteria, home economics labs, woodshop, and male and female locker rooms filled the lowest floor.

Never having stepped into this hallowed sanctuary, Harriett froze, stunned and frightened. Boys and girls hurried past her, giggling and laughing. Their wide skirts and petticoats crushing into each other. All the students walking the halls were so much larger than she was. Even the shortest girls topped her by a full head. She looked and felt out of place.

Mustering her courage, she approached a woman who didn't look threatening. "Pardon me. I am looking for the seventh-grade classroom?"

The woman smiled. "You must be Harriett. I'm your homeroom teacher, Mrs. Sokol. Follow me; I'll get you set up."

Mrs. Sokol was a tall, thin woman with graying hair. Her kind face and eyes eased Harriett's anxiety as she followed her down the left-side hall to the third door. Mrs. Sokol opened the door, and the class immediately stopped talking, jumped into their seats, and sat quietly, waiting for the day to begin.

"Class, may I have your attention?" Mrs. Sokol began. "I want you to meet a new student, Harriett Bailey. She moved over from Valley Elementary." Turning to Harriett, she whispered, "Say Hello."

"Hello, class. Pleased to meet you." Harriett's shy voice was barely heard.

Grinning, Mrs. Sokol encouraged Harriett, "Speak up, child, they'll never hear your tiny voice."

One of the boys giggled, "Her voice is as little as her."

"As little as *she*," corrected Mrs. Sokol.

"That's what I said!"

Another student whispered to her neighbor, "She's supposed to be in sixth grade, not seventh. I wonder why they sent her up?"

Mrs. Sokol answered with, "Quiet class. I'm sure you all have questions and want to meet Harriett. Shall we take fifteen minutes to welcome our new classmate before the morning bell?"

Mrs. Sokol pointed to an empty desk in the front of the room. Harriett hung her coat, emptied her few school supplies into her desk, and braced for the barrage of curious classmates.

Harriett was introduced to fifty classmates before the first bell. She tried her best to remember their names, using the techniques and learning tricks she used to understand the names of plants and animals when she was off running, climbing, and jumping in the woods with Tabs. In her mind, she played the game. Bobcat Runner, the boy with pointy ears that looked like a fast bobcat, was really Bobby Renner.

The second bell rang as Mrs. Sokol concluded, "Lynette, please take Harriett with you today. Harriett is an advanced student and will be studying the same subjects as you. Thank you. Off you go, all of you, now don't be late."

Mrs. Sokol clapped her hands as she motioned toward the door, hurrying her students to first-period class. Her own tenth-grade history students already lined up to enter the room.

Lynette, a brunette wearing a snug sweater, reluctantly dragged Harriett from class to class, introducing her to each teacher, while Lynette's friends avoided the new girl. Finally, the first half of the day was over, and the lunch bell rang for the second lunch shift.

Lynette pointed to the back stairs as she ran back to homeroom, leaving Harriett alone. "Lunch is down there," she shouted, pointing to the staircase. "I'll see you right here when class begins again."

Harriett stood watching the other students rush toward the lower level. Her packed lunch was in her desk. As she reached the room, the door closed, shutting Harriett out and her lunch in. A teacher other than Mrs. Sokol stood in the front of the room and glared at the short girl standing outside.

"Mr. Callihan?" Albert, who sat in that classroom, raised his hand. "That's my little sister. I don't know why she's here, but maybe something is wrong at home. May I see what she needs?"

"Yes, Albert."

Mr. Charlie Callihan lost his job as a salesman during the depression. He took a few courses at Madison College, garnering about twenty credits. His practical knowledge, a few college classes, and the lack of better-qualified staff landed him the job of teaching civics to the upper level, current events to junior high, and woodshop to all students.

As Albert opened the door, his classmate snickered.

"Harriett, what's wrong? Why are you here?"

"I need my lunch."

"What?"

"My lunch. It's in the second desk from the front, third row. Can you get it for me?" Harriett whispered so low that Albert strained to hear.

Albert looked at Charlie Callihan, Bailey's old neighbor, shook his head, then walking straight to the aforementioned desk, excused himself, lifted the top, retrieved Harriett's lunch, and handed it to her. The class roared with laughter. Within minutes, another bell rang.

"Harriett, go; you only have ten minutes left of lunch. Go eat. We'll talk tonight about how it works. I assume you are now attending here?"

"Yes, Albert. Thank you."

Harriett, face flushed red, hurried down the hall, descending to the cafeteria. Groups of friends gathered together. Lynette was giggling with four other girls. None of them motioned for Harriett to join. She found a seat, alone in the corner, where she quickly ate her dry bologna sandwich and left before the others began to clamber up the staircase.

Harriett found the girls' restroom and the water fountain. She gulped long, refreshing mouthfuls of the cold liquid, which helped wash down her sandwich and calm her nerves. She found the appointed spot and waited, bouncing from one leg to the other, for Lynette and the second half of the day.

Harriett bravely initiated a conversation on their walk to the next class. "Lynette, do you live in Campbellsville? I don't recall seeing you before."

"Why would you see me? You don't hang out with my type." Lynette flung back her hair.

"On which street do you live?" Harriett tried again.

"Pine."

Harriett sighed and added. "Oh, I live on Maple."

"I know."

"Maybe we can study together sometime?"

"No."

Harriett decided to conclude the non-conversation. The rest of the day, Harriett followed Lynette silently to and from class, noting the schedule and that, most likely, she would need to duplicate the day's events from then on unaided.

∞ ∞ ∞

Harriett bubbled, chattering through the evening's meal.

"I have earth science, early American history, Latin, math, English grammar, and writing composition—oh! And current events." She stopped to sip her water. "Oh, Mother, guess who is teaching my current event class? Mr. Callihan. Albert said he used to live next door."

"Slow down, Janie. My, you're excited." Tabs beamed at his young daughter's enthusiasm.

Olive, only half-listening, looked up from her plate. "What did you say about Callihan?"

"Mr. Charles Callihan is my current events teacher."

Albert piped in. "He also teaches civics and woodshop."

Olive pursed her lips then cackled. "Well, if that's the caliber of teachers at that high school, I'm glad I didn't waste my time. Charlie Callihan teaching school. The man's a fool."

Alice, Albert, and Harriett stared at each other.

"I like him as a teacher. He's interesting and funny. He puts things in language that's easy to understand," Alice added her opinion.

"That's because the man doesn't understand anything but *small* words."

"He's better teaching shop than civics," said Albert

"Olive, shall we permit Janie the enjoyment of her first day of high school?" Tabs smiled at his youngest. "Go on, Janie, tell us more." Olive sulked, making no further comments about their previous neighbor.

Harriett continued her ramble. "A girl named Lynette took me around to meet my teachers. She wasn't very talkative."

Alice gaped at Harriett. "Lynette likes being the best at everything. She must feel threatened by you."

"By me?"

"Okay, enough of the school talk. Clean up the dishes, girls," Olive ordered. "I'll be in my room reading. One good thing coming out of this, Harriett will be more willing to bring home books from the library for me to read." Olive rose, flashed Alice and Harritt a scowl, then, without looking at the mess left behind, walked into her parlor, opened a book, and began her solitary evening.

Albert and Tabs carried the dirty dishes to the sink, where the girls rinsed, stacked, and readied for washing.

"Coach Ludwig is enlisting this summer," Albert added nonchalantly. "I might think about enlisting too."

"Joe Ludwig? I thought he'd miss the draft, being an educated, family man," Tabs commented. "I remember him back in the day. Talented athlete. Went on to play football for Pitt." Tabs thought a moment before adding, "I bet a few of the young men in the valley will miss his guidance. I'm sure a few of the stars are hoping to follow in his footsteps, especially since he knows the ropes."

"Young Eddy Kepler is one of those guys. For a thirteen-year-old, that kid has skills. I've watched him play junior varsity—man, the kid's fast!"

"I met that boy after the flood. Large for his age, if I remember correctly." Tabs finished wiping the table.

Harriett broke her silence. "I don't like him—Eddy Kepler. He was in my old class for about a month, and he's a big, arrogant bully. He's also scary-looking. He has a few whisker stubbles already." Her mouth turned down at the sides. "And he's not very smart."

"Well. I think he's good-looking. Too bad he's younger than me!" Alice playfully tossed soap suds at her sister.

"You think about boys too much!" Harriett giggled, snapping Alice with the tea towel.

Tabs rolled his eyes, noting Alice's exaggerated interest in the opposite sex. *How am I to deal with a boy-crazed daughter and a war-crazed son? Janie, thank goodness for Janie, my sweet wonderchild.*

17

BATTER UP

JUNE 1942

$\mathcal{T}$he war dragged on without any sign of an allied victory. Harriett finished seventh grade making all As without academic challenge, but also without making any new friends. She intimidated many of the girls and was too tiny and undeveloped for the boys to bother. Running through the forest, swinging over ravines on grapevines, climbing trees, riding Albert's bike, saving lost balls, and tumbling down the alley, she happily spent her days alone.

One sunny afternoon, Albert and Alice were heading out to play baseball when Alice yelled, "Harriett, why don't you come along. You spend too much time with books."

"That sounds like fun. Yes, I shall. I'll catch up. I need to change my shorts."

The usual gang of buddies gathered for the game. Albert and friends would enter senior year, while Alice would enter her junior year that fall. A group of sixteen- and seventeen-year-olds and a few graduates stood waiting for "The Bailey Twins." The usual captains were about to begin choosing team members when Harriett arrived.

"No little sisters," said newly graduated Harry Boring when he saw Harriett walk toward the group.

"Give her a try, Harry," Alice defended her sister. "She's tiny, but she's mighty."

Harry smiled. "Just this once, for you, Alice, and only because I see Eddy Kepler coming." Harry gave Harriett a once-over. "How old are you? I thought I saw you in school this year."

"You did. I'm twelve, but they pushed me up. I'll be in eighth grade this fall."

"Well, you must at least be clever. I'm not so sure about 'mighty.' But you can play...*today*," Harry said, speaking for the entire group. "But I want Kepler on my team."

Eddy smiled, smirking directly at Harriett, and stepped next to Harry.

Tony Lupinetti—Lupi for short—was the other captain. "At least Harriett makes the teams even today. I pick Alice."

So it went, back and forth, until only Harriett remained.

Lupi sighed, then threw Harriett a glove. "Well, one of us had to get her. Harriett, play right field. These guys usually hit center or left. You should do the least damage out there."

Lupi's team took the field as Harry's team prepared to bat. The baseball field, connected to the schoolyard, was surrounded by chain-link fencing. On the other side of the fence lay the remnants of a tennis court and track field, glories of the 1920s. Rarely did a ball go over the boundary since the town designated ample acreage to the campus.

Harry lined up his batters; he'd start off, with Albert second and Eddy following third. Harry took the plate—swing and a miss. The second throw was a ball. Pitch three, Harry hit a grounder that thudded off the turf as it spun toward the shortstop, Alice, who dropped and let the ball roll past. Harry landed safely on base.

Lupi rallied his team. "Come on, guys. Look sharp; Bailey is up."

A sneezing Harriett jumped from foot to foot in the right field amongst clumps of grass.

Albert surveyed the field, deciding he had a better chance of hitting a home run if he went the shorter distance to left field. Strike one. Ball one. Ball two, strike two.

It was Harry's turn to encourage by yelling from base, "Albert, you got this. Nice easy swing."

Albert connected with the next pitch. Whack! With the sun in the player's eyes, the ball dropped between center and left field—man on first and second.

Next up, Eddy Kepler. Eddy picked up the bat, adjusted his cap, and pointed to Harriett. The boys chuckled. "This is coming to you, Pip Squeak."

Harriett smiled as she pounded her fist into her glove. "You got this, Harriett. Just watch the ball," she said to herself.

The pitcher wound his arm and released the throw. The bat cracked as the ball flew to right field, directly at Harriett.

She never hesitated. Heart pounding, as soon as she heard the noise, she was on the ball, following it in the air, backing up as it got closer. She had to jump, but she caught the ball in flight. Kepler out. Quickly transferring the ball from her glove, she hesitated only a moment. With her teammates yelling "throw to first," she threw it the entire distance from the fence to first base. Albert did not make it back in time. The tiny girl executed a double play.

Lupi's team cheered. "I told you she was mighty," yelled Alice.

Harriett jumped up and down, grinning from ear to ear, as she tried to slow her breathing back to normal.

Harry tagged then ran, holding up at third base. Harry's

best, the next batter, was so flustered that he struck out, ending the inning with Harry stranded on base.

Lupi's team patted each other on the backs, knowing they were outmanned by Harry's team. "Okay, here's our lineup, I'll lead off —Alice, you're seventh, Harriett, eighth, pitcher ninth. On three—*go team!*"

Lupi started with a base hit, second up walked, the third batter struck out, and batter four dropped one behind the shortstop, driving in Lupi. The score was one to nothing, with one out.

"Oh, crap." Alice was fidgeting with her hair. "I hate it when we get this far down the batting order in one inning."

"Why?" Harriett cocked her head as she stretched her arms.

"Because I'm usually the one who gets the last out."

The fifth man hit a home run, scoring himself, number two, and number four. Now the score was four to nothing, with one out. The sixth hitter swung hard and missed three times.

A dejected Alice let out a huge sigh. "Oh, this is terrible. Here goes out number three."

Harriett stared straight into her sister's eyes. "Nonsense. Just watch the ball; swing nice and easy. You can do this." Harriett patted Alice on the behind, the boys laughed.

"Wish I could get away with that!" said Lupi.

"Hush. You better not try!"

Alice took a deep breath and let the first pitch go past. Strike one. The second pitch was slightly high and out. Alice followed the ball with her eyes, from the moment it left the pitcher's hand to the moment the bat made contact. Time seemed to stand still. Alice watched the bat vibrate as the ball changed direction, rolled past the pitcher, and short stop into left field.

"Run, Alice!" screamed Harriett. "Move."

Alice took off down the baseline as the boys watched her bounce to first base. Her teammates jumped and cheered.

"Way to go, Alice."

"Your first hit, Alice!"

"Alice finally connected.'"

Harriett looked at the boys. "You mean she never gets a hit?"

"No," said Lupi. "We let her play because she's so pretty, and most of us are sweet on her."

"Hmm. That's stupid." Harriett took the plate. Lupi ignored Harriett's comment. He was grinning and waving at Alice on first.

"Don't worry if you leave her on base. We're doing really, really good today," encouraged their pitcher.

Harriett took several practice swings to determine the weight and balance of the bat. She shifted her grip. Harry, the pitcher, smiled ear to ear and motioned for the outfield to move in.

He released the ball. Harriett's hawkeye kept it in sight as her little muscles coiled. She swung and connected. The whop reverberated across the field as the ball sailed toward right-center, the deepest part of the ballpark. Eddy, the right fielder who had moved to just behind first base, had to backpedal. He had the speed, reaching the fence before the ball, but he didn't have the height. Harriett hit the ball a foot above Eddy's jump.

Home run Harriett!

Alice ran the bases for the first time in her playing career as the boys watched her jiggle around the plates. Harriett raced so fast that she caught up to Alice and had to spur her on. The score was six to nothing with two outs.

The last out was a matter of three strikes to their pitcher. Lupi's team celebrated, patting both girls on the back. Harriett was elated.

"I told you she was mighty!" Alice hugged her sister.

Lupi's team won the day with a final score of ten to three, with Harriett collecting two hits and a walk with her other at-bats. A most impressive result for Lupi's team.

As the boys gathered the equipment after the game, Harry pulled Alice aside.

"Alice, this is awkward. It's not me—I'm okay with it, I guess—but, well...you see, some of the other guys don't want Harriett playing again. We need you to tell her."

"Are you kidding?" Alice frowned. "She's the reason we won. She's really good."

"Yeah, she is." Harry bit his lower lip. "The thing is, they don't like being shown up by a girl. And such a little one, at that."

"I don't believe you!"

"It's true."

"Well, what about me?"

"You? Alice, today was the first time you even hit the ball. You're not a threat...but you are very nice to look at."

"So, that's it for Harriett? And you keep me here for the view?"

"Alice, look at you. You're drop-over gorgeous. Every boy here is sweet on you. The only reason no one makes a move is because of Albert; he'd kill us if we did." Harry blushed at his confession.

Taking a long deep breath through her nose, Alice said, "Well! If Harriett doesn't play, neither do I. No more scenery for the guys! And let me tell you, Harry Boring, if anyone wants to ask me out on a date..." Alice winked. "Let them. I'll deal with Albert." Alice spun on her heels and hurried to catch up with Harriett.

∞ ∞ ∞

Albert lagged behind the girls, not wanting to be part of an awkward conversation. Alice quietly listened to Harriett giggle as she basked in the delight of hitting a home run her first time at-bat.

"I can't wait to play again!" Harriett rambled. "When is the next game?"

Alice hesitated. "Ahh, never."

"What do you mean, 'never?'" Harriett stopped dead in her tracks, blocking Alice's path. Placing her hands on her hips, she pressed, "Alice, 'never?'"

"Sorry. They are just silly, stupid boys," Alice began to explain. "They say women are sensitive, but men are much more fragile. Their feelings are so delicate."

"What are you talking about?" Harriett shook her head. "You're not making sense."

Alice continued, "The thing is, Harriett, you embarrassed them by playing so well. You're not allowed to play again."

"I'm not allowed to play. But *you're* allowed, and you can't even hit the ball! I don't understand."

Alice exhaled a long sigh. "I'm apparently just there for them to look at, so I told them I quit. If you don't play, I don't either."

Harriett gazed up at her sister. "You did that for me?" Harriett grabbed Alice around her waist.

"Yes, sweetie. Besides, if I don't play, maybe one of them will ask me out on a date. It seems Albert has been a little too much of a protective brother." Alice wrapped an arm about Harriett's shoulder. "Come on. We don't need those stupid boys to have fun."

Seeing the girls smiling, Albert jogged to join them.

"Everything okay?" he asked sheepishly.

Alice punched her brother in the arm. "No, it's not, but we'll make the best of it. And you listen to me, Albert Bailey;

if one of those boys wants to ask me out on a date, *do not interfere*."

Albert cringed. "Alice, all of them are smitten with you. Especially Lupi."

Alice batted her eyes at her brother then punched his arm. "I'm available to date! You understand?"

"Sure, Sis. Sorry. I'll put out the word. You just made every boy in town happy!"

18

CALL TO DUTY

*B*y the beginning of summer 1942, the United States was cranking out soldiers. Earl, Roy, Darrel, and Lucas, along with several other Campbellsville citizens, graduated from Navy basic training. Eager to leave the wind chill of lake Michigan, Roy Kepler headed to San Diego, California, to join the fleet and become a Machinist Mate. Darrel Cline, Esther's husband, also prepared for San Diego—but not to escape the cold weather, which he didn't mind. Instead, Darrel was lucky enough to be accepted into sonar school. Earl Kepler and Lucas Jamison stayed north in Chicago, bracing the brutal breezes. Earl decided to pursue training as a radioman, learning Morse Code and hoping for eventual security clearance to decode messages. Lucas enrolled in Corps school at the encouragement of old Doc Paulson, whose son, Ralph Jr., was Lucas's buddy.

Dave Ralston, June's husband, finished boot camp in Greensboro, North Carolina, and headed to Maxwell, Alabama, in hopes of becoming an Army Air Forces pilot.

For all those not engaged in tropical climate training, summer always seemed to pass too quickly, except during pregnancy. June's due date came and went without the addition of a baby. July in west-central Pennsylvania can be hot and humid, and July 1942 hit and broke all records. Temperatures in the mid-90s with 95 percent humidity felt like living in boiling water. The air was so saturated that sweat could not evaporate. June reached the stage of waddling rather than walking, precariously holding her back with one hand and her belly with the other. Meanwhile, Harriett terrorized the woods, exploring them alone after being banished from sports, while Alice began visiting her sister daily.

Per Alice's routine, she stopped at Lupinetti's every day on her way to June's to buy two ice cream cones. June only lived three doors down from the store. It was close, refreshing, and an excuse to see her old team captain, Lupi. On yet another hot afternoon, Alice juggled both cones in one hand. Bracing open the front screen door with her hip, she entered the Ralston house.

"June, I'm here." Alice licked the edge of the melting treats, slurping sugary runoff. "June, your ice cream is melting; where are you? I bought you chocolate."

June tottered as she walked through the door. "Oh, thank you. I can't stand this heat." Sweat trickled off her nose despite her hair being pulled away from her face with a rolled bandana.

Alice licked June's cone to prevent a drip from soiling the rug, then handed it to her. "Eat quickly," Alice commanded as her tongue coiled around the liquifying confection.

After slumping into a stuffed chair, June jerked forward, smashing her face into the ice cream.

"Goodness, that was a sharp pain." She wiped her mouth with the back of her hand as she laughed. "I got it all over my face."

Then, she felt the warm gush of liquid running down her leg. June's eyes bulged.

"Alice, oh my...it's finally time."

Alice jumped to her feet, stuffed the entire cone in her mouth as she ran to the door. "I'll...ave Lu...doct...," she mumbled, trying not to choke.

Alice raced back into Lupinetti's. "Lupi, hurry! Call Dr. Paulson. June's gone into labor."

Seven pounds and nineteen inches long, baby Susie Ralston was born three hours later.

∞ ∞ ∞

Alice stayed with June the rest of the week and readied her and the house for the grand reveal. Tabs, Olive, Albert, Harriett, and Esther—shooing Toby and Heddy and carrying little Lloly, arrived promptly at two o'clock Sunday afternoon. A bubbling Tabs headed straight to the baby.

"My newest granddaughter," he said as he cooed and rocked baby Susie, who made sucking motions with her mouth. "How I am blessed with four daughters, a son, two grandsons, and now two granddaughters?" His eyes welled with tears.

"Don't be a blubbering old fool. It's just the normal cycle of life." Olive flashed her husband a scowl. Viewing the baby over Tabs' shoulder, Olive added, "Hmmm. Average looking child, but of course, I am not that fond of babies to begin with."

Everyone, even the children, stopped talking to glare at Olive.

All four of her daughters howled in unison, "Mother!"

Toby searched his mother's eyes. "Why doesn't Grand-mother like babies?" he asked as he moved away from Olive.

Esther caressed a cowering Heddy. "How can you say such a thing? And in front of the little ones? It was bad enough when you said the same thing to us, years ago, but to tell your grandchildren. It's unforgivable!"

"Wife, will you ever learn the skill of nurturing? Or making appropriate comments?" Tabs shook his head. "Shall we change the subject? What have you girls heard from your brave husbands?"

Esther took a glass of iced tea from Alice, sipped it, then answered, "Darrel is excited to be finished with basic. He says it is so cold up there that your fingers and toes could freeze and literally drop off your body with one quick snap."

Harriett shivered. "That doesn't sound appealing. Makes me cold just thinking about it, even in this heat."

Albert sulked. "Well, I am ready to withstand the cold if it means fighting for my country!" Tabs squeezed Albert's shoulder, who ignored his father and continued. "I turn eighteen this fall, and I've decided to drop out of school and enlist."

Tabs' fingers dug into Albert. "Why must you agonize your mother with such talk? It serves no purpose, son."

Olive glared at Albert. "Do what you wish. I shall no longer object. You want to go kill yourself, then, by all means, join the others and do so. Quickly please, just get it over with!"

Alice burst into tears. Harriett scrutinized Olive's face for any indication of contriteness; there was none.

Tabs handed the baby to Harriett. Gathering his three older daughters in his arms, he attempted to comfort them. "They'll all be safe, girls. Pray for them nightly. Right now, they are learning skills vital to saving their lives." He pulled them closer, whispering, "Don't give them cause to worry about things back home. Be bright, cheery, and positive in your letters. That's what they need. Trust me on this."

Hearing their father's strength and wisdom, the girls garnered control of their sensitivities.

June was the first to speak. "Dave is on his way to Alabama to learn how to fly. What an exciting skill to learn. Think of it! He's going to fly an airplane! Maybe it will lead to a good post-war position?" She reached for Susie, who was fussing in Harriett's arms. "He said it helped to have some college credits. His father was so disappointed when Dave withdrew from Madison College. If it weren't for the war, I think he'd have maybe headed to Pitt."

Esther bounced Lloly on her knee. "I know Darrel is excited to go to California." She glanced at June. "I agree; maybe this blasted war will bring about something good. I'm not sure how, but I sure do hope sonar school gets Darrel out of the coal mines."

Harriett, who sat quietly listening to her sisters, joined the conversation. "I bet Darrel can find some other job with his new training."

Alice refilled the iced tea glasses as she watched Albert stewing in the corner. "Albert, why so quiet?"

Albert glared at his mother. "Mother, if you truly care so little for any of us, maybe you'll get your wish. Maybe I'll die."

Olive crossed her arms in front of her body and scowled at Albert. "Just go!"

"Now, Son, don't be rash. Your mother does care..."

"But that's the problem, Father! She doesn't!" Albert stormed out of the house. Heading straight to the bus stop, he traveled to Madison, searched for the Army recruitment center, lied about his age, and enlisted before the others returned home. He deployed within the week.

∞ ∞ ∞

Lost without her "twin," Alice spent her time vacillating between Esther and June. Harriett confiscated Albert's bicycle and rode for miles every day, her thin, short legs amplifying sinew as she powered over the Appalachian foothills. Summer faded to autumn as Tabs' crew at the spring factory continued to diminish.

Complaints about the staffing shortage consumed dinner conversation. "I don't know how I'm going to fill my orders." Shoulders slumped; Tabs chewed slowly as he contemplated his problem.

"Papa, why don't you hire women?" Harriett suggested.

"Women?" Tabs pondered her remark.

"I read that factories all over the country are employing women while the men are away fighting. They are working in the steel mills, the shipyards—really, any type of manufacturing."

"Hmm. Do you think Campbellsville women would do the same?"

"I'm sure they will. You still have to pay them," Harriett clarified.

"Of course." Tabs cocked his head. "Janie, you may be on to something."

Olive listened, let out a big harumph, then continued eating. Alice was quietly preoccupied.

"Papa, ask Esther and June. I bet they can use a little extra money; they have growing families and husbands away," suggested Harriett.

"They are mothers. Who would watch the children?" Tabs looked at Olive.

"Oh no! I'm not watching someone else's brats," Olive sneered. "Don't even think about it for a minute."

"Olive, they are your grandchildren."

Alice, suddenly alert, sat up straight. "I'll watch them."

"Alice, thank you, dear Daughter, but you're still in school," Tabs reminded.

"No, I'm not. I decided I'm not going back. Lupi is enlisting; he turned eighteen yesterday. He's joining the army, and we are getting married before he ships out."

"You're what?" screamed Olive. "Will none of my children have a normal wedding ceremony?"

"And that matters why? You and Papa certainly didn't have a typical wedding. At least I'm doing things in the right order—marriage, then children!"

"Do what you want; no one cares about school, so why should I?" Olive threw her hands in the air.

For the first time, Harriett mentioned her goals. "I care about school, Mother. I intend to graduate and go on to college."

"Of course *you* would, Missy." Olive snarled.

Alice sputtered. "What's your problem? You're angry if we drop out, and you're angry if we continue on. There's no pleasing you! Mother, you are impossible!" She grabbed her plate and walked to the sink.

Harriett threw a defiant glance at Olive. "Alice, I'll clean up tonight. You go see Lupi, make your plans. You don't have much time left." Harriett smiled at her sister. "And you babysit for Esther and June. Give them a chance to make some needed money; I'll cover your chores."

Alice kissed her sister on the cheek and silently closed the back door.

∞ ∞ ∞

Alice and Lupi had a small wedding ceremony at St. James Catholic Church. Olive, who refused to step foot into a Catholic building, stayed home. Harriett, Tabs, Esther, and June—the matron of honor—represented the Bailey family.

The Lupinettis celebrated the nuptials in vibrant Italian style: after the couple promenaded through town, the entire family of brothers, sisters, cousins, aunts, and uncles gathered for an elaborate feast in the Lupinettis' backyard. The music of several accordions and fiddles floated throughout town while the family danced, feasted, sang, and drank Mr. Lupinetti's homebrewed wine. Showered with gifts of items and money, Alice and Lupi amassed an abundant stash and were ready for housekeeping.

The newlywed couple spent their honeymoon night at June's apartment, with June and baby Susie bunking at Esther's. The next day, Alice and Lupi moved their gifts over to Esther's home, where Alice would live, tend to her nieces and nephews, say daily prayers for her husband, and wait for the end of the war and Lupi's return.

Not long after their wedding, the couple waited for the bus to take Lupi to Altoona, then on to Fort Indiantown Gap for boot camp.

"Lupi darling, do you prefer I call you Tony?" Alice asked as she clung to her husband.

Lupi smiled gently at his wife, kissed her lips, then answered, "Call me whatever you like. My favorite name is *Husband*." He kissed Alice again. "All those years of watching you never hit or catch a ball were so worth it! I can't believe out of all the boys in our gang, *I'm* the one to land the gorgeous Alice Bailey."

"Lupi, sweetie, you didn't 'land' me. It may have been my only catch, but I caught you! Be safe, my love."

The bus pulled to a stop. The couple kissed one last time before Lupi climbed on board and joined the multitudes of other soldiers who were ready and waiting to stop Herr Adolf.

19

LET'S JOG

FALL 1942

*O*n the first day of school, Harriett anxiously searched for familiar adult faces. Seeing none, she entered the eighth-grade homeroom.

Where were all the teachers from last year? she wondered. At least most of my classmates are the same.

Several girls, including Lynette, stared at Harriett as she walked by; her tanned skin and well-formed muscles on a tiny frame—barely tipping the five-foot mark—made her look like a miniature bodybuilder with an adolescent face.

Mrs. Sokol peeked into the room, and Harriett smiled in recognition.

"Hello, class," Mrs. Sokol said. "Your teacher, Miss Reven, is running late today."

"Where is Mr. Ludwig?" asked one of the boys.

"Mr. Ludwig enlisted; he's now in the army."

The class cheered.

"You get 'em, Mr. Ludwig!"

"Way to go, Coach! We're sure to win, now."

Hearing the noise and mention of Mr. Ludwig, several

boys from the seventh-grade homeroom poked their heads in from the hallway.

One of those boys, Eddy Kepler, asked, "Mrs. Sokol, who's taking over the athletic program?"

Mrs. Sokol turned toward the new voice and waved her arms at the boys. "Back into the room, go now. I'm sure all of your questions will be answered by the end of the day."

Murmuring and muttering commenced among the eighth graders.

"Who the heck is Miss Reven?"

"Where did she come from?"

"I wonder if this 'Miss Reven' is nice?"

They only waited ten minutes for their questions to be answered. A tall, slender woman dressed in a brown, tailored business suit and high heels approached the doorway. Miss Judith Reven of Madison strolled into the class and hung her hat on the coat rack. With her heels clicking her way to the desk, she placed an alligator bag into the bottom drawer then sat down, crossed her legs, and addressed the class.

"Good morning, class. I am Judith Reven—Miss Reven, to you. I have been hired to replace Mr. Ludwig in all aspects of his position." She rose, straightened her skirt, and wrote her name on the chalkboard. "Are there any questions?"

The students looked at each other dumbfounded. *Questions? Heck yes, there are questions!*

One brave boy raised his hand.

"I'll get to you in just a moment. I have your class schedules here; please come forward as I call your name."

One by one, the students received their curriculum for the school year 1942/ 1943.

"Okay, Son, your questions?" Judith asked.

The same boy raised his hand; this time, he was called on to speak. "Are you taking over all sports?"

"What is your name, son?" asked the perfectly coiffed and

groomed newcomer, her shapely legs once again crossed under the desk.

"Keith Boring, ma'am." Like his brother Harry, Keith Boring was athletically blessed. He was a junior varsity star, second only to Eddy Kepler.

"It's 'Miss Reven,' not 'ma'am.'" Judith's eyes locked onto Keith's. "Mr. Keith Boring, yes, I shall be taking over Mr. Ludwig's sports programs and coaching positions."

A unified groan filled the room as the second bell rang. The students quickly gathered their morning supplies and headed off to class.

Judith Reven was the talk of the day, from both students and faculty alike. Most talk evolved around Campbellsville High School athletics.

"What was Principal Wakefield thinking?"

"How can a woman possibly coach football?"

"Look at the way she dresses; she's never crawled around a sports field."

Keith found Eddy at lunchtime, keen on sharing his news. "Kepler, come here." Keith motioned to Eddy, who was sitting with his classmates. "First off, you don't sit with those kids; you sit with us jocks."

Eddy grinned, "Cool!"

Keith continued, "Secondly, did you hear that the new teacher, Miss Reven, is in charge of all sports this year?"

Keith waited for the full impact of his statement to register with Eddy.

"I did," answered Eddy. "But I didn't really believe it. Will she be able to help us get a football scholarship?"

"How should I know? It's her job, so I guess so. Why don't you ask her?"

"Nah. I'll wait. I have a couple years before all that paperwork needs to be filled out. Besides, I'm sure there are others ahead of me who want the same thing. She can learn with them, not me."

∞ ∞ ∞

Judith Reven, Madison Country Club tennis professional and math whiz, quickly found a protégé in Harriett Bailey. Quizzical, bright, and athletic, Judith saw herself in Harriett —minus seven inches in height. However, Harriett seemed to compensate for her lack of stature with ease. Harriett became Judith's favorite student, to the boys' dismay.

The football team had played and lost their first two games, an anomaly for both junior and senior varsity of Campbellsville High. The boys mulled around on Monday, the week of game three, instead of warming up before practice. Several of them were even smoking cigarettes when Coach Reven arrived, dressed in gym clothing.

Judith addressed her teams. "Why are you standing here instead of running the track? You should be warming up. There is no excuse for our loss the past two games. It's a lack of commitment." She clapped her hands together. "Come on. Move!"

No one took the field.

"What's the problem? I said, 'move.' Get your butts in gear."

"No, ma'am," Keith Boring mumbled.

"Who said that?" Judith scanned their faces.

Eddy Kepler braved an answer. "We don't want a woman coach. Women can't properly coach football."

"And what gives you that idea, Mr. Kepler?" Judith stared at her young player.

"Women don't have the strength or ability to beat a man." Kepler backed his opinion. "Which means they can't coach either."

"Is that so? Well, I have a bet for you—all of you. I'll quit coaching if any of you, junior varsity or varsity, can outlast me running." She looked at the boys for a buy-in. Having their attention, she continued. "In fact, I'll sweeten the pot and make it more equitable. Harriett Bailey can run with me, two girls against all you tough, rugged, athletic *men*. If anyone outlasts either Harriett or me, I'll go to Principal Wakefield and resign as coach and athletic director. *But*, if Harriett and I outrun all of you, then you become *my* team. What I say goes, which means you work—and work hard. Is it a deal?" Judith's eyes never left her team.

The boys smiled. "Right now? We running right now?" asked Bobby Renner, one of the team's sprinters.

"If Miss Bailey is still around, then yes, right now." Judith left the ballfield in search of Harriett, who was studying in the library. Judith approached her favorite student, "Harriett, would you care to join me in besting a few bragging boys?"

Harriett grinned. "Always. What are you thinking?"

"Are you up for a little jog? Go change into your gym clothes and shoes; we have some male egos to deflate." Judith smirked.

Harriett gathered her books and hurriedly changed clothes. As she entered the field, several boys laughed. "She's so little. She'll drop after one lap."

Judith's look was stoic but concentrated.

Another boy called out. "Oh no! That's Homerun Harriett. My older brother told me about her. She's a mighty little thing, he said."

Eddy Kepler looked at Harriett. "Let's see how mighty she is." Eddy reached out his arm and grabbed hold of the fence. Keeping his arm straight, he said, "Go ahead, Pip Squeak. Hang off me if you are so mighty."

Harriett had to jump up; her right hand was too small to encircle Eddy's muscles, so she strategically grabbed the top of his biceps. Her left hand clung to his flexors. She hung for a moment, reversed her grip, and began counting chin-ups.

One of the older boys mumbled, "She's pretty quick on those chin-ups."

Eddy kept his arm firm, not wanting to be bested by a girl. When Harriett reached ten, Eddy felt the muscle quiver. He flicked her on the nose, shooing her as if she were a tiny flea before he lost his grip.

Harriett jumped down, breathing normally; she stretched her leg muscles, first the quads, calves, hamstrings, and lastly her glutes. The boys watched the tiny girl, never looking at their coach doing the same stretching routine.

"Okay, men, line up." Six across four deep in the track, the boys lined up, giving Harriett and Judith the first row. "Begin!" Judith yelled, and they were off.

Eddy, Keith, and Bobby went out of the gate flying. They ran past Harriett and Judith, who maintained a steady leisurely pace. The rest of the boys passed the girls one by one until Eddy and the gang were ready to lap them.

"You understand, boys, I said *outlast*, not *outdistance*," Judith commented as the three front runners ran by. The boys were puffing; Judith and Harriett were not the least winded.

The race continued. Slowly but surely, the weakest of the boys dropped to the ground, bellies wrenching, some vomiting, some ready to faint, faces flushed, clutching cramping muscles. Harriett and Judith continued side by side, talking as they ran.

"Harriett, I would like to see you pursue a career in math," offered the teacher.

"I was thinking of being more practical; perhaps book-keeping," Harriett said. "Most of my brothers and sisters never finished school. I'll be the second to graduate. Don't get me wrong, I want to go on, but I think a secretarial type position is more appropriate for the likes of me."

Judith slowed her pace. "Don't you ever think that! Do not sell yourself short. No pun intended." Judith and Harriett laughed. "You can do whatever you put your mind to. Harriett, listen to me: you, my dear, are capable of getting your Ph.D. if you wish. Do you understand?" Judith squeezed Harriett's arm then added. "Are you ready to turn up the heat and beat these boys once and for all?"

"Yes I am. And—thank you, Miss Reven. I'll not sell myself short." Harriett smiled. Picking up the pace, she said, "Let them eat our dust."

The women began lapping the tiring boys. The only JVs running were a struggling Eddy Kepler and Keith Boring, along with three SV team members. Harriett remembered the older boys from the baseball game. The seven ran for another thirty minutes. Keith was the first to drop out, collapsing into a heap. Next went two of the senior boys, who leaned over the fence vomiting. One senior and Eddy remained on the track with Harriett and Judith.

"Shall we show mercy and slow down?" asked Judith.

"Never!" Harriett replied. "These boys refused to allow me to play ball because I was better than them. I say we annihilate them!"

"That sounds like a grudge. Be careful, my young protégé. You must learn forgiveness." She patted Harriett's shoulder and added, "However, today, we win."

They again revved it up a notch, increasing their speed. Eddy dropped first, holding his stomach and cramping leg calves. Finally, the last boy went down. Harriett and Judith looked at each other, slowed slightly, and continued running for another ten minutes. Eventually, they stopped in front of the pile of spent boys.

Harriett bent at the waist, gulped several deep breaths,

and began stretching again, releasing the toxins that had built up in her muscles. Slowly and smoothly, she relaxed the tension from her body. She looked totally refreshed at the end of the session.

The boys continued moaning and rolling on the ground.

"Well, men, a deal is a deal. Now get your sorry butts onto that field. We have plays to run."

Groaning objections spread across the team. "We are practicing now?"

"Keep up the complaining, and it will be a double practice. Now move it!" Judith yelled. "Thanks, Harriett; see you in math class tomorrow! Perhaps we'll play some tennis?"

"Sure thing, Miss Reven. Thanks for the jog." Harriett turned and trotted home as the boys wailed in agony.

∞ ∞ ∞

Olive was waiting for Harriett to help bring in the clothes drying on the lines.

"You're late! What took you so long?" Olive growled as Harriett came around the house. "I have to start supper. You need to get the washing in and folded. March to it!"

Harriett immediately complied, gently unpinning and tenderly folding their garments. With the basket full and the line empty, Harriett untied the rope, rolled it, and placed it under her arm.

Storing the line in the pantry, she asked, "Mother, now that Alice is gone and I am doing all the chores, is it possible for me to earn a small allowance? For my help?"

Olive stopped peeling her carrots. Looking crossly at her daughter, she asked, "Why do you need money?"

"I want to start saving for college. If I can make some money here, get summer jobs, and help Alice babysit, then maybe I can afford to continue my studies after high school."

Harriett bit the edge of her lower lip. "Mother, it's the same as your dream. I really want to go to college."

The blood crept up Olive's neck. She felt her cheeks burning. "And where did dreaming get me?" Spittle splashed onto Harriett's face. "You're no better than me, Missy. You need to end these high ideas of yours."

Wiping the back of her arm across her cheek, Harriett reiterated, "May I please be paid a small allowance for helping with all the chores?"

With a loud exhale and a harrumph, Olive agreed. "I'll give you one dollar each week. That's all, so make good use of it!" Turning on her heel, Olive continued scraping vegetables.

Dinner conversation that evening consisted of Harriett recanting the bet and race with the boys' football team. Tabs listened intently as his youngest smiled and laughed, retelling how the boys cramped and fell short of their goal. Harriett animatedly described performing chin-ups on Eddy Kepler's arm.

"Papa, I could feel his muscles start to twitch," she giggled. "He's not as strong as he thinks."

"Janie dear, that takes quite a bit of strength, even if he's only supporting the likes of you." Tabs rubbed his arm, aching in sympathy. "I might have been able to do that when I was young, but not now."

"Papa, you're fifty-one years old! You can't be expected to have the same strength as a young man."

Tabs flexed his arm; the muscle formed a firm, extended bump. Stroking his bicep, Tabs added, "That boy hasn't developed yet. He's only twelve or thirteen. I'd say it's pretty impressive."

"Okay fine. I'll agree he's strong, but I'm not impressed." Harriett continued to relive the day. "Mother has promised to give me one dollar each week for helping with all the chores."

Tabs raised his eyebrows. "Is that so? Bravo, Olive." He flashed his wife an approving smile. Olive's expression remained blank. "Olive, Janie, and I shall clean the dishes tonight. Why don't you relax, read a book?"

Olive frowned and grunted, leaving the room without comment.

Tabs waited to speak. Hearing the parlor door close, he said, "Janie, I think I can skim another dollar from my paycheck without your mother noticing. She keeps a tight rein on the money, but I'll add to your income." He patted his daughter on the back. "Are you saving for something special?"

Her eyes downcast, Harriett shyly answered. "Papa, I really want to go to college. I think Mother is upset with me, but if I start saving now, I may have enough for the first term by the time I graduate."

"Janie, your mother wanted an education in the worst kind of way. She will be jealous of you. But you stick to your dream, and I'll help any way I can." Tabs kissed Harriett's forehead. "My precious darling Daughter, I love you so."

HEROES

*F*riday night ushered in a rare evening football match-up. Campbellsville High School football field was void of stadium lighting; however, this week's game was at Madison High. Madison, a much larger school, was Campbellsville's archrival, despite being in a higher classification. Students, including Harriett, rode the bus after school to the neighboring town. Tabs joined his daughter; they sat together in the stands eating popcorn.

Coach Judith Reven led her Cougars onto the field as the announcer introduced the team over the loudspeaker. Wearing navy blue trousers and a matching suit jacket with low flat shoes, she looked more dressed for the boardroom than playing field. The team worked hard preparing for this game. Judith knew Madison as a formidable opponent; she was a Madison professional athletic community member after all.

The Junior Varsity game was to be played tomorrow afternoon; however, the entire JV team dressed in their uniforms for tonight's game. Her captains took the field for the coin toss. The Madison Mavericks won, electing to kick now and to receive the ball in the second half.

Campbellsville's offense took the field; Madison snapped the ball and kicked. The ball flew deep and Campbellsville indicated a fair catch, starting on the twenty-five-yard line. Judith quickly called a play to her quarterback as he ran onto the field.

Nerves over the rivalry and the spectators snickering at a female coach didn't bode well for Campbellsville's first possession. Three snaps and they were punting. The kick was off the sweet spot; the punt was short, leaving Madison on the fifty yard-line.

Judith rallied her defense. "Come on, boys. Concentrate! Their front line is weak on the right side. If you can break through, you can sack all day. On three—Go Cougars!"

"Come on, defense!" Tabs shouted. "You can hold them."

Harriett clapped her hands as she echoed, "Go Cougars!"

Madison snapped the ball, and the whistle blew. Campbellsville was offsides, penalty five yards, first and five. On the second snap, the quarterback gave the ball to the fullback, who easily plowed ahead for a seven-yard gain. First and ten on the thirty-eight yard line.

"Oh, crumb!" complained Harriett.

"Patience Janie, they just have the jitters. If they can hold them to three points, the nerves will settle down."

Harriett's hands went to her hips. "I don't understand all the nerves. They have a job to do. They should just do it."

Tabs laughed, "Maybe one day you'll get it. Surely you won't be good at everything, like your mother!"

"Ha. Not everything. Mother is *not* a very good cook."

Tabs almost choked as he laughed. "Don't you ever tell her that!"

Madison ran the next two plays, gaining a total of seven yards. Third down and three to go. The Campbellsville fans held their breath as if suspended underwater. Madison's quarterback stepped back, ready to throw, the Cougar defensive line broke through. The weak spot was precisely where Judith had indicated. The linebacker completed the sack; the Cougars forced Madison to punt.

Just as Tabs predicted, the players settled down. Both sides played challenging defensive games. At the end of the first half, the score was Mavericks seven, Cougars three.

At halftime, Harriett sighed. "Such a close game. Papa, may we share a cola? The popcorn is making me thirsty."

Their conversation was interrupted by the Madison marching band's drumline playing a cadence; the band took the field. Harriett commented, "Geez. Look at all those musicians. There must be fifty players!"

Tabs chuckled, "Madison is a good-sized city. Janie, stay. Watch the show. I'll get us some snacks." Tabs climbed down the bleachers and got in the concession line while Harriett, mesmerized, watched the band's routine.

By the time Tabs returned with a drink, both school mascots had run and tumbled up and down the field. The referee blew his whistle, and the teams retook their benches.

Coach Reven had laid out detailed offensive and defensive plays during halftime. The Cougars kicked the ball; the second half began.

Madison's kick returner broke loose, taking them to the fifty-yard line. Two more plays added twenty-five additional yards.

Coach Reven called a time-out. "Get your heads into this game," she told her players. "You played a smart first half. Don't blow it now! You are down four points. *Do not* allow them to score! You can still win this game."

The teams lined up. Madison's apparent throwing formation triggered the defensive line to rush. The Cougars quickly broke through, blitzing the Maverick quarterback, causing a fumble. Campbellsville recovered and went on offense.

The Cougar fullback gained eight yards on the first play but was injured during the tackle. He limped off the field, forcing Coach Reven to substitute her only spare fullback; her third man was out attending his grandfather's funeral. Calling a passing play, the quarterback threw twenty yards, making the first down and then some. The Cougars' game plan was to run on first down, using their talented fullbacks. A reverse handoff fooled the Maverick defense, allowing a flamboyant thirty-yard run as the substitute leaped, spun, and jerked to avoid being tackled.

Harriett, along with the entire Campbellsville student body, cheered as they jumped up and down.

"Papa, we're going to score; I can feel it!"

The following two plays added a meager four yards. The crowd quieted. Third down, six to go. The Cougar quarterback dropped back in the pocket, flipping the ball to his halfback, who was immediately smashed to the ground. Fourth down, four to go. The crowd inhaled, waiting to see if the new female coach was brave and trusting enough to go for it on fourth down.

They broke the huddle, and the quarterback lined up for a play. The spectators wildly screamed and clapped. Taking a clean snap, the Cougar quarterback snuck ahead. First down on the twelve-yard line!

Pandemonium broke loose. Coach stayed with her game plan, running the ball; her sub crossed the goal line as the Madison defender grabbed his leg and pulled. The pop was heard despite the cheering as the runner's knee twisted. Coach Reven called for a stretcher for the boy to be carried off the field. Cougars ten, Mavericks seven, but it came at a high price. Judith needed a fullback.

Madison returned the kick-off to their own thirty-five yard

line. Over the next fifteen minutes, Madison slowly marched down the field to score another touchdown. Cougars ten, Mavericks fourteen.

Harriett joined Campbellsville in a collective groan.

Hoping the first-string fullback recovered enough to take the field, Coach Reven was disappointed when the trainer informed her that his sprain needed rest. Her strength was in her fullback running game. The Cougars' pass completion rate, only thirty percent for the year, was predominantly due to halfback receptions. Tiny Campbellsville offered limited pickings; she had no actual receivers.

Judith surveyed her JV team. "Kepler!" she called. "You're in. Think you can play with the big boys?" She smiled at her young player. "Try to get down the field to score while running out the clock."

"Absolutely, Coach! I've been dreaming of this chance for three years." Eddy Kepler trotted onto the field, waving to the crowd.

"That kid is in junior high," someone in the crowd muttered.

"Is that little Eddy Kepler?"

The Cougars did exactly what Judith asked. First down after first down, Eddy gained ten yards for every three plays. A whistle blew, signaling the two-minute warning. The Cougars, on the ten-yard line, were second down, goal to go. Eddy got the ball and was immediately pushed back by a big defensive lineman. Outweighed, the wily youngster ducked down and pulled to the left. Losing his grip, the lineman fell forward as Eddy surged ahead. Timing his jump, Eddy leaped over a group of players, both his and theirs, crossing the goal line as the clock clicked to zero.

Both Coach Reven and Eddy Kepler proved their ability as The Campbellsville Cougars won seventeen to fourteen. Students and parents rushed to the field. The players hoisted

Eddy onto their shoulders and paraded him around the stadium, with the crowd following, chanting, "Kepler! Kepler! Kepler!"

Harriett's mouth dropped. "That sure was exciting. We may be able to pull off a winning season, after all." She gathered their trash, carrying it as they made their way off the bleachers.

"It certainly was." Tabs smiled gently at his daughter. "That Kepler boy has talent, but he seems a little cocky. This won't help his ego."

"He is arrogant and conceited. It will be hard being in the same building with him on Monday. Thank goodness I'm a grade ahead!" She turned to survey that she had gathered all her belongings when she noticed several boys kicking garbage onto the ground. "Papa," she whispered, "that's Principal Wakefield's son littering."

Tabs spun to face the juveniles. "Son, I don't think your father would approve of your actions."

The boy jumped, "How do you know my father?"

"Son, everyone knows Principal Wakefield. He wouldn't be pleased to hear about you littering."

"Are you threatening me, old man?"

Tabs placed his hand on his hips, not dropping eye contact. "Son, I suggest you crawl under the stands and pick up your trash. While you're at it, clean up some of the other trash left behind. Don't let the good people of Madison think that Campbellsville folks are ignorant country bumpkins."

None of the boys moved; Tabs stood firm, his flexed muscles visible under his shirt. After a moment's stare down, young Wakefield complied.

"All right, sir, just don't tell my dad. Okay?"

Without speaking, Tabs turned. Harriett linked her arm through her father's.

"Well done, Papa," she said, smiling proudly.

∞ ∞ ∞

Harriett and Tabs laughed, recapping the evening's events as they entered the back door. Olive sat alone at the table, frowning.

Looking up at her husband, she snipped, "You two are awfully friendly."

Harriett stopped mid-sentence, scrunched her brow, then looked at her father.

Tabs kissed his daughter's forehead. "Janie, why don't you go on upstairs and get ready for bed. Thank you for an enjoyable evening. Goodnight, dear."

Throwing her mother a questioning look, Harriett returned the kiss. "Goodnight Papa, Mother," she said, then left her parents alone in the kitchen.

Tabs sat down at the table across from Olive. "What is the meaning of that comment?"

Olive clenched her teeth. "You spend far too much time with that child. Trampling all over the woods and hills every weekend, now taking her to football games. Do you have a fondness for youngsters? Something seems amiss!" Olive's voice was low, almost a growl.

Blood flashed across Tabs' face. "Just what are you accusing me of? Foul play? With my own daughter?"

"If I recall, I was quite young when you took a fancy to me."

He placed his hands on the table. Standing slightly, he leaned toward Olive. "You're a wicked woman to think such a thing! You banished me from your bed thirteen years ago, but I remain faithful to our wedding vows. Even if I wasn't faithful, how dare you accuse me of harming our daughter? How dare you try to deprive me of the little joy I get, sharing time with our children?!"

"I only say what I see."

Tabs stood fully erect. "If you're feeling sorry for yourself, feeling left out from her love and mine, you only have yourself to blame. Those girls needed nurturing, guidance from their mother, but you were absent. I only have four years until Janie graduates from school, and I intend to make the most of them. Don't you dare try to interfere."

Tabs calmly opened the back door. "It's a mild evening; I'm going outside for a bit."

Olive sneered at the door as it closed. "Good! Go and stay away."

Tabs searched his pocket for a key as he waited on the porch, listening for her to turn the lock. He was not disappointed. Olive locked the door, turned off the lights, and went to bed.

Tabs sat in the Adirondack chairs contemplating his marriage. Long past midnight, he unlocked the door and slipped into his own bed.

21

WINNING SEASON

*M*onday morning, Harriett could see the banners flying three blocks away from the school building. The Cougar standards flew across the main entrance, flanked by homemade signs fashioned in the school's royal blue and burgundy, saying, "Eddy," "Eddy's our hero," or "Kepler-First Team."

Harriett thought to herself, *Good grief as if his head isn't big enough already!*

She climbed the stairs and entered the building to be greeted with the noise of exaggerated excitement proliferating from every crevice. She shielded her ears as she walked past the seventh-grade homeroom, where Eddy and his friends congregated in the hallway.

Eddy saw her hands move to her head. "What's the matter, Pip Squeak? Can't take a little celebration?"

Harriett ignored the conquering hero and walked into her homeroom. To her dismay, she found little relief; her own class was in an uproar, with students expounding the feats of both Coach Judith Reven and Eddy Kepler. Harriett took her seat, organized her books, and waited impatiently for the bell to ring.

Judith arrived late since Principal Wakefield and the staff had been waylaying her with congratulations in the office. As she entered the room, the students, and Harriett, stood and cheered.

"Bravo, Coach!" echoed down the hall.

Judith visibly moved, turned her back on the class to compose herself. She struggled to hold back the tears welling in her eyes. Once she gained control, her smile beamed.

"Thank you, class. It was a team effort and a grand win," she said as she turned to face them again.

"We're going to States!" yelled Keith Boring.

Judith chuckled. "That would be wonderful. However, states are a few games away. Let's take it one game at a time, shall we?"

Keith began chanting, "States and Kepler all the way!"

"States and Kepler all the way!" the class joined in.

It took only moments for the seventh graders to enter the room and join the mantra. Two of the bigger boys had hoisted Eddy onto their shoulders and began parading him around the room.

Judith pulled her coach's whistle out of the drawer and blew it. The shrill blast startled the mob. All seventy students abruptly stopped, mid-stride. "That's enough. Put Mr. Kepler down. The game is over, and the school day has begun." She inhaled, ready to blow again. "Move on; the bell shall ring any second. Friday's game is over; we must concentrate on this week's work—both academic and athletic."

The bell rang, sending a second shock through the revelers. Eddy tumbled to the floor as the seventh graders quickly gathered their books and scampered off to class.

∞ ∞ ∞

The fall semester passed rapidly. Thanksgiving 1942 was approaching next week, district football playoffs were the following week, and final exams were the week before Christmas. The Cougars managed to overcome their first two losses, accumulating a winning season of six and three. Tomorrow's homecoming, the last game before the holiday, would determine if the Cougars made the state-wide tournament.

Although Esther was scheduled to work on Saturday, June was off and offered to watch all four children so Alice could attend the game along with Tabs and Harriett. Alice would have been a senior had she remained in school and was pleased to cheer on her former classmates.

Both students' and teachers' moods were jovial. Principal Wakefield canceled after-lunch classes, replacing them with a pep rally. The entire campus, plus townsfolk, piled into the gymnasium, filling bleachers and adding chairs until it was standing room only. Thunderous clapping and cheering erupted as the team took the floor. Feet banged the risers as Coach Reven led their jog around the room. Chants of "*Cougars!*" flooded the space.

Principal Wakefield spoke first. "Welcome!" The crowd cheered again. Holding up his hands to quiet the spectators, he continued. "The war in which we find ourselves has made us reevaluate 'the norm.'"

The audience sobered at the mention of the fighting.

"Never, and I mean never, would I have considered hiring a female football coach before," he said, to room-wide laughter. "However, we live in challenging times. Women work in our factories, make our steel, build our airplanes, ships, and weapons. If women are capable of such tasks, then why should the most celebrated football coach in the district not be a woman?" Boys whistled. "I give you our illustrious coach, Miss Judith Reven!"

Ovations exploded. Coach Reven waved, but the noise did not subside. "Quiet, quiet everyone. Before I introduce our hardworking team members—" A roar went up. "—I have an announcement. This morning, I received a phone call from the state high school football commission. 'States' as we know them have been altered this year to account for gasoline rationing." A unison groan echoed throughout the room. Judith motioned again for silence. "Hush. Pennsylvania shall not hold a statewide competition. Rather, it has been decided that six regional tournaments shall be held, limiting travel distances and saving our precious petrol for our fighting forces." Several townspeople waved small flags while others clapped respectfully. "If we win tomorrow," she looked at her team, "*If we win* tomorrow, I know you'll want to travel to the next game to support our team. Come tomorrow, and please *walk* to the field; however, should we win homecoming, I must ask you to remain at home for any future games."

Cries of "Support our Cougars, support our troops!" sprung up.

Judith waited again for the noise to settle before continuing. "Now, please allow me to introduce first our junior varsity, then our varsity team, beginning with the JV captain Keith Boring."

She continued introducing her teams. Eddy Kepler's announcement as a JV player quieted the audience, who expected the young superstar to be promoted.

With JV introduced, Judith began with her varsity captain and quarterback. The crowd was on their feet. She named all her regular starters, then pronounced, "And Eddy Kepler, your young idol. Eddy, at age thirteen, is only one hundred yards away from breaking the school running record for a season."

Catcalls, girls screaming, feet stomping, and shouting

169

followed. Eddy waved, took a bow, then blew kisses to the cheerleaders.

∞ ∞ ∞

Alice, Tabs, and Harriett bundled themselves up in gloves, scarves, and hats for a blustery November day in the stands. Alice spent the day visiting old friends and roaming the grounds while Tabs and Harriett watched the game. The Campbellsville Cougars beat the Bookston Bears seventeen to three, ending their regular season with a seven and three record, more in line with Coach Ludwig's tradition.

Quarterfinal playoffs paired the Cougars against their first opponent, Weston. Overly confident, having already beaten the Cougars, the Weston Wildcats played a sloppy first half, leaving them fourteen points in the hole—a hole that could not be filled. Cougars fourteen, Wildcats zero, Campbellsville was off to the semifinals to face Madison again. Madison, whose only loss was to Campbellsville, would be ready for the Cougars' young phenom.

Too many injuries, a short bench, and a young fullback outweighed, outmuscled, and targeted by boys four and five years older ended the Cougars' season. The dejected team moped in the locker room afterward.

Judith clapped her hands once. "Listen up, all of you. I do not want anyone to be unhappy. Look at what you have accomplished this year. You came together as a team, fought hard, worked hard, and won hard games. But remember, it is just *a game*. Our brave soldiers, your brothers, fathers, uncles, cousins, are fighting the real fight so that you have the privilege and freedom to play your games. Be proud of yourselves. Teamwork will get this country through the war, and you have proven your ability for teamwork. Go home to your families, be thankful for all your blessings. Celebrate the holidays with your loved ones and pray for those who are away fighting."

Tears filled the boys' eyes. They hugged, patted each other's backsides, showered, and dressed. As they readied to leave the locker room, Judith called out, "Heads up! Be proud."

The boys were greeted by a cheering throng of Madison fans.

"You guys are a great opponent."

"Fabulous season."

"We'll be waiting for a challenge next year!"

22

NESSUN DORMA

*T*hanksgiving and the first few weeks of December 1942 found Campbellsville packing and mailing their fall labors as gifts to the fighting forces. June, Harriett, and Alice congregated at Esther's home Thanksgiving weekend, hoping to ready parcels to post. Toby, now six, and Heddy, four years old, drew holiday cards. Lloly and Susie, both less than a year old, lay in Esther's playpen.

Toby handed a card to Alice, "Auntie, will you write a note to Daddy?"

Alice smiled at her nephew as Esther looked on, waiting for her reaction to the question. "Now, Toby, you are learning your letters in school. You can write your own message. I'll help if you need it, but you must do your own writing."

Esther smiled, hearing the correct response. Although neither Esther nor Alice graduated from high school, both, like their mother, valued knowledge.

Toby pouted. "Oh, Aunt Alice! I want you to write it."

"Don't you fuss, Tobias Lloyd Cline. You'll do your own writing." Alice took the boy by the hand. "Come on, let's get started. What do you want to say?"

"I want to tell Daddy I love him and miss him." Toby moped.

Alice handed Toby a red crayon. "Start with the letter I."

June leaned in toward Esther. "She handles the children well, our Alice does. She'll make a good mother."

"Toby and Heddy love her. We're fortunate; the extra money I'm making at the plant comes in handy—not that we can buy much. But I can cover all my expenses with my salary and save anything Darrel sends home." Esther paused before adding, "And it helps Papa at the spring factory and the war effort. I'm proud to help make parts that will win the war."

June nodded in agreement. "Dave's family sends extra bits here and there. I only have one extra mouth to feed, so I save significant sums. Are we paying Alice enough?"

Esther scratched her chin, "Perhaps not. She lives rent-free with me, so I pay her less per child than you, but she is a Godsend. We'd be lost without her."

"Then it's settled; we'll each give Alice an extra two dollars each month. Is that too much for you?"

Esther fingered the air, calculating the extended expense. "If you give her one dollar a day, and I give her seventy-five cents per day plus room and board, she'll make over fifty dollars a month clear. She has no expenses other than personal, and she's very frugal. Add whatever Lupi sends home—yes—that gives her a nice nest egg to use after the war."

June added, "I can chip in some extra money to help feed this gaggle." She laughed as she waved her hand around the room.

Harriett, who was sitting alone wrapping packages in brown paper, decided to join the conversation. "Is anyone getting a tree this Christmas?"

"I am," said Esther. "Toby and Heddy are at the age where tradition is so important. Is Papa getting one?"

"No. Mother says since it's only the three of us, she doesn't want the dirt." Harriett frowned; traditions were also crucial for thirteen-year-olds.

Esther regarded her young sister. "Harriett, Alice, I have an idea. Why don't the two of you go cut down a tree for me? Today is a rare day for all of us to be off. June and I will watch the children, finish posting, then make supper. Afterward, we can decorate and sing carols. Sound good?"

Harriett's grin almost cracked the corner of her mouth. "Oh, that sounds like fun! I'll grab Papa's bow saw on the way to the woods. We'll get a splendid tree!"

Alice and Harriett rushed off on their task. June and Esther bundled the children, pushing strollers filled with babies and packages to the post office.

Esther unloaded box after box, creating a high stack on the counter. "Wait, I see one more hiding behind Lloly." She bent over, reaching past the baby to retrieve the final parcel.

"Thank you, Mrs. Cline. And you have several letters waiting for you. Oh, so does Mrs. Ralston." The postmaster handed the girls three envelopes each. "I also have a package and a letter for Alice. Do you want that too? You have to sign for it."

June gathered Alice's mail, handed over the signed form, then returned to her envelopes to survey the postmarks. "This is from Dave." She smelled the letter, then kissed it. "He hasn't written in five weeks. I've been so worried. And here's a second letter from him."

"I have three from Darrel," said Esther, who scanned her mail. "There must be something going on with the war that the mail is delayed. Gosh! I hope they get these packages before Christmas. We may have waited too long to post."

Dante Lupinetti called to the women as they passed by the store on their way home. "Ladies, Mrs. Cline! I have something for my daughter-in-law. Would you mind giving it to her?" Lupi's father handed June a chilled bundle tied with a cord.

Esther inhaled the aroma of fresh slaughter as they continued on their way. "Smells like meat. Lupi's parents are wonderful to us. We get extra cuts of meat, soup bones, and any produce that is ready to turn. Alice has become a wonderful cook, unlike Mother." Both girls snickered.

"That gives me an idea. I'll buy Alice a copy of *Joy of Cooking* for Christmas. It's a different kind of recipe collection; my mother-in-law has one," said June. "I purchased war bonds for Papa and Mother, and the Ralstons, and of course, one for Susie. But I wanted to give Alice something special, other than a pair of stockings."

Esther unlocked the door and pushed the stroller inside. "I'll take a pair of stockings! They are getting hard to find."

June followed. Lifting Susie from her buggy, she removed her pink fuzzy snowsuit. "I love this snowsuit. Thank you for sharing it with me." Then, looking at Esther, she winked. "Of course, I bought you stockings—and a surprise!"

"You know, Sis, I have a box of baby clothes in the attic waiting for Lloly and Susie to grow into. If they withstand two growing kids, you should save them for your number two—or Alice's family."

June piled Susie's outerwear in a stack. "What about another little Cline baby?"

Esther paused, she placed her hand on her cheek. "Goodness no! Well, we'll have to wait to see what Darrel says about having a fourth."

Alice and Harriett returned, dragging a seven foot, perfectly shaped tree, as the children shed their outerwear.

"We're home. Look at this beauty!" Alice puffed, catching her breath as she propped up the scotch pine to display its branches.

Esther nodded in approval. "How did you cut that so quickly?"

"Should we tell her?" asked Harriett under her breath to Alice.

"No. Let her think we can work miracles." Alice refused to share that Tabs cut it earlier in the day for his oldest daughter's family. It was waiting for them when they went to collect the saw.

Harriett lifted it, carrying the tree into the living room. "Where do you want this splendid pine?"

Esther motioned to a corner on the outside wall, between two windows. "Isn't it a spruce?—Over there."

"Scotch pine, but it doesn't matter. It's a gorgeous tree, and I can't wait to decorate it!" Harriett giggled as she placed the tree into a bucket of water provided by Alice and leaned it against the wall.

Toby and Heddy watched wide-eyed, prancing with delight as the adults proceeded to discuss the tree.

"Harriett," Esther called, "will you help me carry boxes down from upstairs? I have two boxes filled with trimmings."

Harriett followed her sister to the second floor as June handed Alice her mail. "I almost forgot; we were so taken with your tree. Mr. Lupinetti gave you this, and you got a package and a letter in the mail."

Alice took the wrapped meat. "Oh, I better put this in the fridge. I wonder what's in the box?"

"We all got mail. Perhaps we should take a moment to read it before we decorate?"

Hearing the possibility of postponement, Toby cried out, "No, Aunt June. Tree first, please!"

Alice grabbed the boy by the waist. "Come here, you little rascal." She rolled him onto his back and tickled his belly until he laughed. "We have plenty of time to decorate that tree before Santa arrives!"

Reaching for the parcel, Alice ripped off the brown paper. Inside she found another wrapped box and an envelope. With a sigh, Alice continued unwrapping the second package. She found an elaborate lidded box topped with a ribbon.

"Oh, I can use this in my hair." Alice untied the ribbon and twirled the red silk in the air.

Esther and Harriett returned carrying trimmings. "What are you two doing?" asked Esther.

"I'm opening my mail. Sit down; I'm about to find out what's in this box." Alice lifted the lid to find a small chest decorated with jewel-colored inlay. She lifted the hinged top, and the box began to play music. "Oh, how lovely. My goodness, here's yet another box."

Pulling out a tiny, cube-shaped size package, Alice opened it. Tears immediately filled her eyes as she inspected a shining ruby and diamond ring. "How magnificent." Alice placed the band on her finger, then, curving her wrist, displayed her gift.

"Wow!" Harriett gasped. "That sure is pretty. Who's it from?"

Alice tugged at her handkerchief then wiped her eyes. "Lupi. Silly." Immediately she opened the enclosed letter and began to read.

Darling Alice,

Merry Christmas, my love. I hope this reaches you in time. I haven't had much time to write. I spent the last two weeks on trains. I am now down south.

I hope you like the music box. The aria is from the Italian opera Turandot, a magnificent love song sung by a mystery man to a beautiful, perfect, but untouchable princess. You are my princess, and I am an unbelievably lucky man. Someday I'll take you to see Turandot performed. The story is a little sad, but the music is heavenly. Since we really didn't have much of an engagement, and I never bought you a proper ring, I went shopping. I knew I found the perfect ring when I saw this one. The ruby reminds me of your fiery personality. Such a deep love and passion for life. The diamonds represent your perfection, your beauty. That perfect body, with shapely...

"Maybe I better skip this part." Alice blushed. "I'll jump down a bit." Esther and June grinned at each other; Harriett sat blank-faced.

I was transferred to Louisiana to a brand-new division of the Army. It's called the 101st Airborne Division. Alice, I am so excited to be part of this new group. I am going to learn how to jump out of an airplane. Please don't tell Mom and Dad that last part. I'm writing them also, to share everything except the jumping part. I hear rumors of big things to come from our division, but everything is hush-hush, too far in the future to know details. For now, I'm learning to jump, although I haven't actually ridden in a plane yet. So far, we are jumping from a short tower into a giant air pillow. They're teaching us how to fall, can you imagine?

I can share that the general strategy of the war is to win in Europe first and then go on and win in Asia. Despite the plan, those boys in the Pacific are getting more action than we are. We are itching to get over there to show Germany the stuff of us Americans!

I have to go, it's lights out soon. When I show the guys your picture, no one believes such a beautiful girl is my wife. I am so lucky to have you, and I love you so much. Please, keep writing weekly as you do. It keeps me going. I can't wait to win this war and get back home to start my new life with you, dearest Alice.

Merry Christmas, my love. You are always in my thoughts.

XOXOXO

Lupi

All the women, including Harriett, were crying by the end of the letter.

Esther squeezed Alice's hand. "Honey, your ring is a beautiful treasure. After hearing your letter, I'm afraid to open mine. Perhaps I'll read it tonight when I am alone in bed."

"Good idea!" said June. "We are emotional enough without adding to it."

Harriett cocked her head to the side. "Sisters, Papa will be anxious for news from your husbands. I can't relay Lupi's news without him asking after both Darrel and David."

Esther ripped the top from one of her three envelopes. "I'm only reading one here, the one with the latest postmark. The other two are mine alone."

"Thank you," said Harriett.

Esther scanned the letter before sharing it with her sisters. "Finally," she flushed, "A part that won't embarrass me. Goodness, Darrel's finished with sonar school already. He says he's leaving San Diego immediately after the holidays. He's headed out into the Pacific Ocean." Esther placed the letter and her hands on her lap. Looking at her children, she began to sob.

"Now now, don't cry." Alice hugged her. "They'll all be fine. Why don't we trim the tree instead of reading letters?" Scanning the return address from her other envelope, Alice said, "Harriett, this is from Albert. I'm sure he enclosed a note for Papa. Will you take it home?"

"Sure, but why doesn't he mail it directly to him?"

"Because of Mother." Alice sucked in both cheeks.

179

"Mother is still angry with Albert. If he writes, she throws away his letters."

"*No.*" Harriett gasped. "She really wouldn't do that! Would she?"

"She most certainly would, and she does. That's why Albert sends them to me to give to Papa." Alice extracted Tabs' note and handed it to Harriett. "Don't let Mother see you give this to him!"

Bouncing Susie on her lap, June said, "Harriett, you may as well have news from David." She, too, scanned the letter. "I'll summarize. Dave was accepted into flight school, but he's not sure if he has the credentials and skills to be a pilot."

"Oh," echoed the group in unison.

"That's a disappointment."

"It's fine," June continued. "He says if he can't fly, he'll go to school to be a meteorologist. Gee, he does love science."

The big word caught Toby's attention. "What's a *matorgist*, Aunt June?"

Everyone chuckled. Harriett answered her nephew, "Toby, that's the weatherman, the guy who predicts the rain and snow."

"Hmmm. They're not very smart, are they?" asked Toby.

Esther kissed the top of her son's head. "No, sweetie, they are smart. Sometimes it's just more of a guess than a science. Now, let's get on with the tree!"

Harriett opened the box labeled "Lights" and began screwing in the bulbs. When all the bulbs were tightened, she plugged in both strands to test them. "You're lucky; they all light up. Who wants to help me put them on the tree?"

June volunteered. Alice occupied Toby and Heddy until it was time for the ornaments while Esther headed for the kitchen.

Calling back into the living room, Esther asked, "Is spaghetti okay for tonight? Mrs. Lupinetti sent over sauce and meatballs the other day." Without waiting for an answer, she placed a pot of water on the stove, lit the gas, and waited for it to boil.

The tree sparkled red, green, blue, white, and yellow as the heat from the lights permeated the scent of pine throughout the room.

"Are you ready for us?" asked Alice.

"Yes we are."

Alice, Toby, and Heddy rummaged through the second box, each looking for their favorite ornament. Toby pulled out a carved miniature teddy bear, compliments of Tabs. Heddy zeroed in on several paper angels. Harriett added the final layer, silver tinsel, saved from the previous years.

"It's beautiful," Alice said, standing admiring the tree, both arms encircling a delighted child.

"It needs a star on top," Harriett observed. "Esther, do you have a topper?"

Esther peaked into the room. "Goodness, that is a handsome tree. There should be a cornhusk angel in the box. Darrel's mother made it to top the tree."

"Oh." Harriett bit her upper lip. "It should be a star."

"Well, my dear sister, when you have your own tree, you may buy a star. Until then, I use what is given me, and that's an angel. There." Esther pointed to a box.

Harriett dug the angel out and reached it up high, but she could not reach the top of the tree even while jumping.

"Harriett, allow me to put that on the tree." Alice grabbed the angel from her.

Harriett chortled. "Fine, take it. I can't do anything about being short!"

"Dinner is ready," Esther called as Alice completed the tree.

"Oh crumb, I'm probably late." Harriett ran, grabbed her coat, and headed for the door.

"Aren't you eating with us?"

"No, Papa is expecting me home. Thanks, sisters. I had a fun day."

Harriett blew kisses, then stepped off the porch and hurried down the street for home and isolation.

23

THE BEAT GOES ON

*H*arriett spent a lonely, quiet holiday with Olive and Tabs. Most evenings, Harriett was abandoned to clean up after supper alone. Tabs spent long hours at the plant, often missing the regular dinner hour, which Olive refused to alter to accommodate him. Olive retreated nightly to her parlor, only closing the door halfway. Many evenings, Harriett glimpsed her mother sitting on the stuffed chair with a book and her silver picture frame in hand, sometimes blowing her nose or dabbing her eyes. Harriett feared asking her mother what upset her so.

As a whole, Campbellsville once again participated in a subdued Christmas, devoting the majority of time in church in prayer for their loved ones and the country's war effort. However, Esther, June, Alice, and the children still celebrated with family, fun, and frolic, enjoying their tree and each other's company.

Letters to the fighting men were sent regularly; their returns continued to trickle home sporadically. The new year, 1943, found the Navy boys—Darrel Cline, Roy Kepler, Earl Kepler, and Lucas Jamison—already active in the Pacific. Roy, stationed on a carrier and now working on planes, participated in the victory at Midway. Lucas, the only medical officer on a smaller destroyer, and Darrel, a member of a cruiser sonar team, were part of the flotilla landing troops in the ongoing battle at Guadalcanal. Earl, also stationed on a carrier, was promoted to chief radio operator and began island hopping through the Pacific as the Navy made their way to the Japanese mainland.

David Ralston, a successful graduate of Army fly school, was on his way to North Africa. Tony "Lupi" Lupinetti, matriculating to jumping out of airplanes, continued his training with the 101st Army Airborne.

Albert Bailey secured the safest and most unusual Army job when he, rather than Dave Ralston, became the meteorologist working with the Army Air Corps. Time spent outdoors with his father, absorbing Tabs' vast knowledge of nature, gave him an advantage over other recruits. He was also stationed in North Africa, working with a team to predict the weather for the planes flying bombing runs across Africa, Sicily, and Italy. Several times, he substituted for the weatherman assigned to General George S. Patton's tank division.

Having men in so many different military branches was like living the complete history of World War II for the women of Campbell County. Daily talks at the spring factory focused on the men, their challenges, and their accomplishments and often included joy along with heartbreak. The war was still ramping up, but already more than one Campbell County mother or wife had draped her front door in black.

The school year ended without excitement. Harriett ranked number one in her class. Coach Judith Reven, who rented a bedroom in town with the start of gas rationing, packed to return to Madison for the summer.

Before leaving, Judith sought out Harriett. "Harriett,

enjoy your summer holiday and practice your tennis serve. I expect you to be a formidable opponent in the fall."

"You got it, Coach."

Sugar, flour, butter, meat, coffee, tea, and many other necessities were rationed. Every person, child or adult, received a ration coupon book. Coupons were required to make most purchases. Lupinetti's continued to help Alice as much as possible, although hefty cuts of extra meat dwindled to bags of soup bones.

Tabs and Harriett enjoyed weekend hunting trips to the forests surrounding Campbellsville, killing to feed nine. All members of the Bailey family continued to enjoy meat at least once, often twice a week. Tabs still kept chickens for meat and eggs. That spring, he tilled the top half of the yard and planted a large Victory vegetable garden, which Harriett tended. Olive salvaged tubers and bulbs, storing them in sawdust in hopes of better days to come. Most of Campbellsville's flower and ornamental gardens were converted to vegetables in support of the war.

One early June morning, Harriett came in from the garden to find Olive and Uncle Benny drinking tea.

Olive complained, "Does Ingrid still keep honeybees? I'm so tired of doing without sweetener."

Benny sipped his drink. "I agree. No, she gave up the bees when we moved away from the farm, but I think she should consider keeping some here in town. No one will mind if the result is honey."

"You're right. And speaking of the farm, that's why I invited you over this morning. Will you make a run out there and ask your father if they have extra canning supplies? Considering what we used to put up every fall, the entire root cellar should be full of empty jars."

"Sure, I'll check tonight after work."

"Now Benny, if he is willing to share, let him! But, I do

have money to buy the jars. You remember what they used to cost new, don't you? Well, I'll give him half price for each dozen. I figure I need about eight dozen quarts, twelve to fourteen dozen pints, and all the jelly jars he can spare. Although, I don't know how I'll make jelly without sugar!"

"Good idea Olive. I'll get some for Ingrid, too. If she needs help this fall, will you mentor her?" Benny blushed.

"Only in exchange for honey. So you better bring back her hives." Olive grinned, pleased with her negotiation.

Harriett inhaled the fresh, dewy aroma of the salad greens then gently washed the leaves and her hands as she listened to the conversation. "Uncle Benny, are you walking out to the farm? May I walk out with you? I can help carry."

"Yes. I can't get extra gasoline for the car, so walking or riding a horse are my only options. I thought I'd pull the small cart, just in case I'm successful. If your mother allows, I'd love the company."

Olive nodded her approval.

Harriett dried her hands, wrapped the greenery in a linen towel, and hesitated before placing the leaves in the refrigerator. "Thank you. Shall I meet you at the spring factory around five? Or do you want to eat your supper first?"

"Make it five-thirty, at my house." Benny took his cup to the sink and rinsed it.

Olive watched with amusement. "I see Ingrid has you well trained."

"Even Westchesters can learn new tricks," Benny admitted.

Olive responded with a loud harumph.

∞ ∞ ∞

Harriett walked several blocks to Benny and Ingrid's corner home. Most of the larger homes in Campbellsville were occupied by Westchesters, Baileys, or their offspring. Darrel and Esther purchased a large four-bedroom, while June and David bought the three-bedroom on the opposite end of the same block, two doors down from Lupinetti's. Benny's sister Nellie and her husband Angus McKee, and Benny and Ingrid both owned three bedrooms, each two blocks opposite Olive and Tabs. Olive continued to covet the Songer house on the hill, the largest home in town, although Mr. and Mrs. Songer, both pushing their late seventies, still managed to maintain impeccable grounds.

Harriett arrived promptly at five-thirty, finding Benny waiting with a large pull cart.

"Hello, my tiny niece, shall we be off?" Benny always smiled pleasantly. "You don't look big enough to help, but I hear rumors that you are one feisty little person." He motioned to Harriett, who flexed a muscle then grabbed the handle.

The pair effortlessly pulled the cart out of town and over the hills. Harriett utilized her time alone with her uncle to pose long-burning questions conjured in her young mind.

"Uncle Benny, could you tell me about Mother when she was a girl—when she was my age?" Harriett's neck reddened as she asked.

"Oh my, that's a loaded question, Harriett. How much do you already know?"

Harriett scrunched her nose. "Actually, I know very little. Only that she had Esther before she married Papa."

Benny puckered his lips before going on. "She was bright, forceful, independent, and totally dedicated to her brother Fred." Benny paused, his mind slipping to another place and time, far away from the present.

Harriett's eyes widened. "Is that the boy in the cadet uniform? Please tell me about Fred. I think Mother still mourns for him."

Benny stopped walking. Taking Harriett by the hands, he frowned, holding back tears. "Harriett, the last war was devastating to this area; to Olive, to Grandfather, and even to me." Benny dropped her hands and sat on the edge of the cart. "I hide it now, but I suffered from shellshock when I returned. I wasn't able to talk, not to anyone, even Ingrid."

Harriett stared in disbelief. "How did you recover?"

Benny dropped his head, "That's the worst part. I didn't recover until Fred died. Olive was so stricken by his death that she shook me out of it. Seeing Olive just lying on the porch, unable to move from grief gave me the strength to comfort her and return to the world of the living." Tears filled Benny's eyes. "I feel so guilty to this day. I was cured by his death. But with another war at hand, I struggle every day to be positive and not drift into the fog of the previous war."

Harriett placed her hand on top of Benny's. "If you recovered, why has Mother not been able to do the same?"

"Oh, Harriett. Your mother blamed Grandfather Henderson for Fred's death. She never forgave him for sending Fred to West Point, so she'll never accept Fred's sacrifice." Benny picked up the cart handle. "We need to keep walking; I don't want to be returning after dark. I spent too many nights on this lane past sunset as a youth!"

The two continued on in silence as Harriett contemplated her new knowledge of her mother. She wondered how much her older sisters knew and understood about their mother's past. Curious to learn more, she vowed to ask Papa.

Olive correctly predicted a root cellar full of empty canning jars. Ben gladly sold them, happy for the extra cash. As the trio loaded the cart, Benny asked, "So, Father, are the beehives still intact?"

"There is one hive with a queen left, but no one tends it. Do you want to take it with you, Son?"

"Yes, and the extra hive boxes, if we have room. Ingrid will be delighted, and I'll certainly enjoy the honey."

"Bring me a jar now and then?"

"Sure, Father. Are you feeling okay? You look tired." Benny flashed concern as he watched his father move slowly back toward his cottage, slightly stooped over.

"I'm well enough. Just getting old." Ben instinctively rubbed his back. "Come, give your mother a kiss before you leave. Don't be a stranger." Ben smiled at Harriett. "I'm sure Bailey is a fair boss. Surely you have some time off?"

"Yes, Father. Guilty as charged. I'll bring Ingrid and the kids out before the end of the month." Benny glanced uphill at the remnants of the grand old mansion. "What's it going to cost to restore that place?"

"Ha. I don't even ponder such thoughts." Ben shook his head. "Sadly, more money than I have, son."

∞ ∞ ∞

Olive stacked the boxes of jars in her back pantry. "Good job Harriett. Did you enjoy your day with Benny? He can be a fun person when he has a mind to be."

Unaccustomed to compliments from Olive, Harriett hid her surprise. She also withheld her conversation concerning Fred. She intended to investigate further, but through Papa and her sisters. "It was a badly needed walk. I'm not exercising as much as I should this summer. Papa and I only hunt on the weekends. I need to be more active to keep my muscles."

Olive clucked her tongue. "Women do not need muscles. They need brains."

"Why can't they have both?" Harriett, stepping on a stool, lifted two cases onto the top shelf.

Olive scowled. "Both are a waste of time. Brains are more

important, but mark my words, the men of this world will squash any chance you have for success outside the home. You need brains to be able to outsmart a husband, that's all."

Harriett turned to face her mother so quickly that her stool teetered. She grabbed the shelf for support. "Why would you say that about Papa? He's so kind and loving; he adores you! I thought marriage was supposed to be a partnership."

"Well, Missy, think again. Marriage is not a romantic love story! It's a game of chance, and the winner is always the one with more brainpower."

Harriett reached for more jars. "I don't believe you. There is love and romance in this world. Just look at Alice and Lupi, and Esther and Darrel. For that matter, Dave is very devoted to June, too."

"Alice is a fool, dropping out of school. Esther is a tramp for getting pregnant, and June, well, at least she graduated."

Harriett gawked at her mother. "Well, I believe in love and romance!"

"And you're only fourteen. Mark my words, if you remain so naïve, your heart shall be broken." Olive chose to finish her work in silence.

24

HAIL THE CONQUEROR!

*J*une 1943 drifted into July. German forces in Northern Africa surrendered to the Americans, who marched into Sicily to retake Italy next. The men in the Pacific continued moving from island to island, constructing or revamping airstrips for US planes to use on their drive to Tokyo.

The war inspired the populous to have an elevated awareness of physical fitness. Thanks to Principal Wakefield, the residents and students of Campbellsville were to enjoy a new military-style obstacle course. His hope was to prepare the young students, who were soon to become young soldiers—all while providing the school's sports teams and the townsfolk a place to exercise. Construction finished on July second; highlighting that the park was the official endpoint for the July Fourth parade.

On July Fourth, Harriett and Olive sat on their Maple Street front porch, watching the various groups march past.

Tabs and other veterans from the First World War wore poppy pins to remind the spectators of the losses in Flanders fields. Women from the DAR, dressed in colonial-style costumes, carried a flag of a coiled snake that read *Don't Tread on Me*. Several girls' and boys' organizations and a baton-twirling troupe marched, proudly stepping high and waving American flags.

Harriett tried to curb her enthusiasm. "Mother, may we go to the school to listen to the speeches and try out the new obstacle course?"

Olive curtly answered. "You know I always go listen to the speeches. Of course, we'll walk down. Don't be so daft!"

Turning her head, Harriett hid her disappointment. *Why must Mother always be so brusque?* Aloud she added, "I'm excited to use this new course. I hope it helps me keep strong." She flexed an arm muscle.

"My God, stop it! You're just like your father when you do that."

Harriett smiled at the comparison. Mission accomplished.

The pair carried camping stools as they followed the parade and other townspeople to the school grounds. Unfolding their seats, they found a spot about one-third of the way from the front of the crowd. Olive, taller than most women, had a clear view. Harriett saw nothing except the capped head in front of her.

The town's mayor, the local commander of the American Legion, and the local VFW post commander took turns speaking. After thirty minutes, Principal Wakefield took the podium.

"Citizens of Campbellsville. It is with great pleasure that I present to you our very own military-grade obstacle course. Designed by World War I veteran Tobias Bailey—"

"I didn't know Papa was part of this project!" Harriett grinned with pride.

Olive leaned over. "Shush!"

"— foreman of the Campbellsville Spring Company, Tabs was wounded fighting bravely in Belgium." The crowd cheered as Tabs stood beside Mr. Wakefield and waved his hand. "This course provides an opportunity for all members of the county to maintain a higher level of physical fitness, necessary for our personal sustenance and national integrity." More clapping. "We must all prepare ourselves to win this war!" The audience roared and waved handheld flags. "Now, to open the course, I give you our Campbellsville High School football team. Boys!"

Led by their captain, the boys, dressed in their uniforms, ran onto the field as ovations filled the air. Principal Wakefield clicked his stopwatch. Wakefield stacked the race by putting the larger, slower boys first, knowing the fastest members would pass them by. One by one, the team entered the course, high-stepping through old tires, crawling under barbed wire, and swinging from ropes through the course, which finished with a scaling wall.

When Eddy Kepler entered, Harriett heard several girls giggling. "He's so handsome," someone tittered.

Another girl feigned a swoon. "Oh, to be *his* girlfriend!"

As the last player finished the course, Mr. Wakefield stopped timing. "Fifteen minutes, thirty seconds for our Cougars to complete the run! Bravo, boys." Mr. Wakefield waved his arm, acknowledging the team. "Now, I declare this course open to the public!"

Harriett tugged on Olive's sleeve. "Mother, may I try?"

"Fine, but don't get too dirty." Olive folded Harriett's camp stool, resting it against her leg; she sat waiting for Tabs to make his appearance.

Harriett queued in line, behind most of the men and boys of Campbellsville, awaiting her turn at the obstacles. Eddy Kepler, with Lynette on his arm, walked past.

"Hey Pip Squeak. That's for us men. No women allowed," Eddy scoffed. Lynette snickered.

Laying her head on Eddy's shoulder, Lynette said, "Harriett's just a plain Jane, a tomboy, not a real woman!" Harriett's eyes popped as Lynette fluttered her eyelashes, leaned up, and kissed Eddy on the cheek. Undeterred, Harriett remained in line.

"Principal Wakefield, will you time me?" Harriett asked when she finally reached the front.

"Of course, Miss Bailey. It's your father's creation; it's only proper for his offspring to have a starting time. On your mark, get set, go!"

Harriett took off; she flashed past some slower runners, quickly stepping through the tires despite her short legs. By the time she scaled the wall, she had passed everyone on the course.

Mr. Wakefield glanced down as he clicked his watch when she crossed the finish line. "My goodness Miss Bailey. That's impressive."

Harriett bent at the waist, inhaling deeply. "What was my time? I want to work to beat it before the start of school."

Mr. Wakefield shook his head. "My dear, I believe you are already close to the course record. Only the fastest on the team ran the course more quickly than you. That run was ten minutes, ten seconds. Very impressive. I must remember to inform Coach Reven of your speed when she returns in the fall."

Partially recovered, Harriett raised her head to meet the principal. "She already knows I'm fast, but thanks."

Harriett scoured the crowd, searching for Tabs. Spotting him with a group of veterans, she ran to join him.

"Papa, what a wonderful thing you've created." She gave her father a bear hug. "I finished the course in a little over ten minutes. I have work to do this summer." Still, slightly out of breath, she puffed, "My goal is seven minutes, thirty seconds. Will Army specification approve of that time?"

Tabs and the other men chuckled, looked at each other

and then at the tiny girl. "Janie darling, you already meet Army requirements."

Every day, Harriett waited for her turn to run the course. Several women made sporadic appearances, but Harriett and the football, basketball, and baseball teams ran the gauntlet daily.

∞ ∞ ∞

Harriett had shaved two minutes off of her time by the time fall arrived, although her goal remained elusive. Only three boys ran the course faster than Harriett, with Eddy Kepler holding the course record of seven minutes, forty seconds.

At the start of school, Coach Judith Reven moved back into her room in Campbellsville after a successful summer as the head tennis professional at Madison Country Club. Her tanned skin and shapely legs turned heads when she walked down the town streets or through the school halls. She enjoyed the quaint rural lifestyle of Campbellsville over the bustle and smog of Madison and was ready to start teaching.

Finally, it was Campbellsville football season again. Everyone was ready to focus on something other than the war. Despite American troops moving from Sicily into the mainland, many German strongholds still stood firm within Italy, slowing allied progress. At the same time, the lack of a French invasion frustrated soldiers and civilians alike. The town needed a diversion, and the Cougars fit the bill.

Eddy Kepler returned to school taller, more muscular, and faster than the previous year. Consistently large for his age, Eddy dwarfed the rest of his classmates. His mother holding him back from first grade didn't help. The fifteen-year-old eighth-grader looked like a man.

That fall of 1943, no one doubted Coach Reven's ability;

she had already proven herself. When the team went nine and one, securing a place again in the playoffs, the entire town gathered for a bonfire pep rally.

Judith and the players huddled in the locker room before making their grand entrance. Eddy, setting both school and district running records, was to be the first on the field.

After the Coach's pep talk, Eddy pulled Judith aside. "Coach, can I talk to you a minute?"

"What's on your mind, Mr. Kepler?" Judith smiled admiringly at the young athlete.

"I wanted to ask if you will send in the right paperwork for me to get a college scholarship." Eddy fumbled over the words.

"Mr. Kepler, I shall happily submit any paperwork. However, there is a catch, a big catch. Since this is my first football coaching position, I am not familiar with all the necessary paperwork. And sadly, between my full teaching and coaching schedule, I do not have time to research it."

"What do you mean? I can't apply?"

"No, that's not what I'm saying. I am telling you that I'll submit any and all paperwork. However, if you are truly interested in playing college ball, you need to help me procure the necessary papers. Ask the older boys to help. Ask Mr. Wakefield. I need you to do some of the legwork, understand?"

Judith placed her hand on Eddy's shoulder; he pulled away and glared at her.

"You're kidding, right? I'm a star; you should be doing this for me! *You're* the coach."

"Mr. Kepler, I just explained: you must learn to help yourself. I'll do what I can, but you must take responsibility for your future." Judith reached for the young man, he slapped away her arm. Judith inhaled slowly. "Be careful, young man. Now, they are waiting. Shall we take the field?"

Moping, Eddy sneered. "You go first. I'll catch up."

Eddy waited a good five minutes after Judith's entrance before leading the team onto the field. Looking at the team captain, Eddy ordered, "Give me a few minutes alone out there before the rest of you follow. I want to enjoy my cheers. *Understood?*"

The captain rolled his eyes at his prima donna runner. "Yes, Eddy. I got it."

The crowd went wild as Eddy trotted through the honor guard of cheerleaders—who overly admired him since he dated most of the squad (even the seniors). Roaring chants of "Kepler, Kepler!" echoed off the surrounding hills and settled over the town and valley. Eddy stopped on the fifty-yard line; raising his arms in the air like a conquering general, he flexed his muscles.

Waving pompoms high, the adoring cheerleaders followed Eddy, jumping up and down to the mantra, "Eddy, Eddy, he's our man. If he can't do it, no one can!"

Harriett stood in the spectators with Alice. As Eddy took his midfield stance, she mumbled, "What a ham! He's a good athlete, but he's dumb as a rock."

Alice laughed. "Be nice, Harriett. Not everyone can be a super-whiz like you or Mother. He may not have brains, but he does have an athletic body—and the looks to go with it."

"Alice! You're a married woman," Harriett tittered, blushing.

"Little Sister, I may be married, but I'm also alive. I'm absolutely allowed to look as long as I do not touch!" Alice giggled. "Even Lupi thinks Eddy is pretty."

The Cougars lost in the finals to Madison, last year's runner-up.

25

GOSSIP

DECEMBER 1943

A week before the Christmas holiday, the boys gathered in the locker room after gym class. Happy football season was over with basketball yet to begin, they were ready to give their bodies a break for the holiday. Jim Clawson, whose parents owned the now-defunct bakery, was the captain of the basketball squad. He was drying off after a shower.

"Hey, guys, what's the news from the war? Have you heard anything lately?" Jim asked as he pulled up his boxers. "My brother Ned writes home that they are starting to move troops in preparation for an invasion. Any of you hear that?"

Keith Boring was the first to answer. "My brother Harry is in the Marines, fighting on some Godforsaken island in the middle of the Pacific Ocean. He doesn't talk much about the Germans; he has enough to deal with when it comes to the Japs." Keith yelled over to Eddy, "Kepler, what's the news from your brothers?"

"My brothers? Why the hell do you want to hear about my brothers?" Eddy turned his attention back to dressing.

"The war, man. Don't be such a dork. What are they saying about the war?" Keith pressed on.

Eddy ticked his tongue. "George is in Italy eating spaghetti, Earl's on a boat transmitting secret messages on his decoder ring, and Roy's fixing airplanes with duct tape and bubblegum."

Jim shook his head, "Eddy, you really are a jerk. We're serious."

Eddy lobbed his towel at Jim. "Well, I don't want to talk about it, okay?"

Another team member joined in. "I heard that they are moving units into England. And Lupi, you all remember Lupi don't..."

The group replied, "Of course we know Lupi, you dunce."

"...well then, Lupi's unit, that new one that jumps out of planes, is supposed to have a major role when they finally invade."

Hearing that one of their own may be at risk quieted the group. "Geez, I wish this war would end soon."

Eddy covered his ears and buried his head in his locker.

Jim continued, "Yeah. I heard Coach Ludwig is leading some kind of special forces."

"Not real. That's just a rumor. I bet Coach Ludwig is sitting behind a desk, calling Army football plays."

"My cousin, in the Army, says they're planning something big."

"Naw, it's too soon for the *big deal*. They have to take Italy back first."

"No, they don't. And Patton is crushing the Krauts. Italy is on the edge."

"My Uncle flies airplanes, and he said they're studying new maps of Europe."

"That's bull. If they are planning a secret invasion, we wouldn't hear about it."

"How we gonna win against both the Krauts and Japs? I don't think we can."

Each of the boys took turns speculating about the war and their families' role in it, repeating what they heard from the adults at home until Eddy screamed at the top of his lungs. "Shut up! All of you just shut up, will you?"

Most mouths hung open as the boys gaped at the outburst.

Eddy grabbed each side of his head and squeezed. "Shut your lousy traps!"

"Geez Kepler, what an ass."

"I said enough!" Eddy slammed shut his locker. "I'm worried about my brothers. I already lost one brother to the flood. Okay? I'm scared!" Eddy inhaled deeply, placing his head in his hands; he bent over then counted to twenty; no one dared approach.

All waited quietly until Eddy blurted out. "Who's going to Lynette's party this weekend? She's smuggled in beer."

The boys quickly dropped all war conversation in favor of their upcoming fun.

"Yea, Lynette's parents will be gone; she has the house to herself. Kepler, you bastard, you'll probably get lucky," Jim scowled.

Eddy smirked, "I'm never unlucky!"

Towels came flying at Eddy from every direction of the room, along with calls of "Louse." "Creep." "Lucky SOB."

Eddy collected the towels and, with one throw, tossed them into the hamper. "It really has nothing to do with luck, my men. It's pure talent!" He grabbed his jacket and left the rest of the boys contemplating what it was like to be Eddy Kepler.

∞ ∞ ∞

The following day, Friday, Judith stopped Eddy in the hall. "Mr. Kepler, do you have a moment?"

Eddy, already late for his next class, stopped. "Well, if you give me a hall pass for being late, then yeah, I have a minute. What's up?"

Judith cocked her head, staring at her young star. "Have you made any progress on obtaining the paperwork to qualify for college ball? You broke every one of the school's running records this season. I'm only reminding you because you have talent, Eddy, and I don't want you to waste it."

Eddy pursed his lips, then threw his head back. "If that was the case, then you'd take care of this for me. You're the coach; it's your job."

Frowning, Judith insisted, "Eddy, you must learn responsibility. I'll happily complete and submit the forms, but I already told you that *you* must provide them. Do not take this lightly, or you'll lose your window of opportunity."

Eddy turned and raced to his next class, mumbling to himself, "Bullshit! I'm the star!"

26

OFFENSE

FEBRUARY 1944

*I*n the Pacific, the little-known island called Iwo Jima was now a household name. Over in Europe, the Allies retook Italy in February 1944, giving the green light for France. The Allied Forces were playing offense now and seemed to be finally winning. A blow in France might be enough to end the war.

Harriett continued to read the papers before leaving for school, always staying informed. This morning, one headline caught her eye.

"General Patton has been demoted," Harriett said to her mother. "I wonder why? I like him! Eisenhower is no longer his boss."

Olive rolled her eyes as she glanced at her daughter. "Patton's a bully. Who's his boss now?"

"Some guy named Bradley," Harriett said nonchalantly.

She had Olive's full attention. "Omar Bradley?"

"Yes. How do you know his first name?" Harriett handed the section to Olive.

With a chuckle, Olive answered, "Ha! I danced with him

at Fred's graduation. He tramped on my foot. Look at him now!"

Dropping the rest of the paper, a bewildered Harriett gawked at Olive. "You actually danced with General Omar Bradley?"

"Harriett, I'm not a country bumpkin. I've been to New York City." Olive smiled as she drifted into the past. "I used to have beautiful clothes, beautiful jewelry, wonderful, elegant meals that included wine and delicious sweets, all served by housemaids." Olive rose, wiped her hands on her house dress, then frowned. "I lived in luxury; now look at me. I wear tattered frocks, eat rationed meat, slave over a house and husband. Fine life I have!"

Olive met Harriett's stunned gaze and added, "And most of my demise is because of you, Missy!"

Olive poked her finger into Harriett's chest, then stomped out of the kitchen and slammed the door to her parlor, leaving Harriett dumbfounded and dazed.

∞ ∞ ∞

May 1944

Alice, Esther, and June nervously waited for any mail from their soldier husbands and brother. Weeks passed before a letter from Albert arrived. Harriett's three older sisters gathered in June's living room, drinking weak, unsweetened tea, to hear the news.

"Hurry, Alice, open it!" June paced the room with Susie toddling after her.

"Okay, already. Hold your horses." Alice ripped at the envelope and cut her finger. "Ouch," she said as she sucked blood.

"Alice, we want to hear what's going on!"

Finally, Alice removed the precious communique and began reading.

Dearest Sister,

I hope this letter finds you and the family well. I am now in the south of England. Yes, it's true, it rains here all the time. You'd think a meteorologist wouldn't mind the rain, but boy, it sure makes me anxious. I'm the one that has to tell the Brass, "yes, you can fly today," "no, you cannot fly today." Even though I have no control over the weather, they're not happy when I tell them no.

I shouldn't tell you this, I could get into real trouble, but we're getting close to the big one. The 101st is here now, too. They have been flying and jumping every day possible. From the looks of things, they'll be the first in. That's Lupi's unit, Sis. I haven't seen him yet, even though I hang out around the airfield. I'm hoping to find him before *it* starts. I'll give him a hug and kiss from you.

Alice stopped reading, letting Albert's words sink in. Lupi, at the front of the invading force. Shaking off her fear, she laughed nervously, joking, "Do you think Albert will really kiss Lupi? On the lips?"

The fleet is also arriving, at least part of it. Craft is piling up everywhere. I hope whatever they have planned works because this blasted war has dragged on too long. I'll admit, I'm homesick. I miss my twin sister, Papa, and the rest of you. Well, maybe not Mother, but don't tell her that! Is she still as cantankerous as before I left? Stupid question, I'm sure she is. I don't know how Papa tolerates her and stays such a nice, pleasant man. God, he's a real saint.

I don't have much more to say that will make it past the censors. That's if I haven't said too much already. Know that

I am well and that I think about you every day. Give Esther,
June, little Harriett, and Papa a kiss from me.

All my love,

Albert

Alice refolded the letter, placing it on her knee; she
crossed her hands in her lap. "Oh boy, I guess all the rumors
are true. There's going to be an invasion of France, and my
Lupi is going to be part of it."

Esther hugged Alice. "I have an idea. Why don't both of
you apply for membership to the DAR? I'm a member, so you
qualify also."

Alice frowned. "How will being a Daughter of the American Revolution help?"

"To start, the women are very patriotic. You know, with
that type of heritage. But they work together to support our
troops and to support each other. Many—*most* of them have
husbands or sons fighting. Those ladies are an amazing
support group." Esther moved toward the bedroom. "I have
my paperwork in here. You both can use it."

Alice fumbled, unfolding Albert's letter to reread. "I could
use some friends."

June smiled. "And what are we?"

"You know what I mean. All my friends from school
vanished as soon as I quit. Mrs. Lupinetti is a sweetheart —so are you— but you know what I mean.
Someone other than family." Alice stood and walked to
the door; she grabbed both sides of the jamb. "You are
so lucky to have children. I wish I had become pregnant
before Lupi left. I'd love having a little Lupi to take
care of."

Susie waddled over to Alice. "Auntie Alice, play?"

Alice reached down, lifted Susie into her arms; kissing her
on the forehead, she said, "Sure, sweetie." Turning to her

sisters, she continued, "I guess if I had my own child, I wouldn't have enough time for your kids."

"Well, they certainly love you, and we certainly depend on you. Don't forget, without you, Papa would be out two of his best workers!"

"Of course, you're both his favorites!" Alice grabbed a stuffed bear and threw it at Esther, who caught it one-handed.

Esther laughed, tossing the bear into the air. "Seriously, we are grateful. Will you both consider DAR?"

"Fine, start the paperwork."

∞ ∞ ∞

A majority of the families in Campbellsville received similar letters that May, hinting of bigger things to come. The month of June arrived with an air of tension and anxiety; all were on edge, waiting to hear that the end had begun.

On June 6, 1944, the wait was over; the invasion of France began after a flotilla delivered joint allied forces across the English Channel from Britain to the beaches of Normandy. Lupi Lupinetti, along with other members of the 101st Airborne, parachuted into the French countryside behind enemy lines.

Rumors about Coach Joe Ludwig were true. The coach was part of an elite group of two hundred twenty-five Army Rangers tasked to climb the steep cliffs of Pointe du Hoc. The Germans reinforced the high ground between Utah and Omaha beaches with casements and circular gun pits. Coach Ludwig's athletic prowess, a necessary criterion for the Ranger Battalion, helped him scale the heights with grappling hooks and rope ladders to take out the high-caliber guns.

Both Olive and Harriett buried themselves into the newspapers, searching for information about sons, brothers, sons-in-law, or brothers-in-law. On June 8, 1944, all three papers boasted headlines of the Normandy invasion.

Mother and daughter discussed the events of June sixth.

"It says here," Olive reported, "that the invasion was delayed one day due to weather."

Harriett looked over her reading. "I wonder if Albert was involved with predicting the weather?"

"Why Albert?" questioned Olive.

Harriett immediately blushed, realizing her disclosure. "Oh, Albert is a meteorologist."

"How do you know that? Does Albert write to you?" Olive pursed her lips, indicating an upcoming interrogation.

Stammering, Harriett muttered, "No, Mother, Albert does not communicate with me. He has written to Alice once or twice. Those two are just like twins, after all."

Satisfied, Olive continued reading. "Alice's man jumped in. I bet he's in the thick of it!"

"Yes, Mother, that's what Alice has been told."

Olive's reading stopped again. "Just how often do you go visit those sisters of yours, Missy?"

Harriett exhaled through curled lips. "Not often enough. I'm invited for holidays, but I spend them with you and Papa. I'm too much younger than they are. We have nothing in common."

"Harrumph!" Olive grunted. "Don't remind me about the age gap!" Olive folded her paper, tossing it at Harriett; she continued, "Read by yourself. I've had enough of you for today."

Harriett took a deep breath, once again confused by her mother's behavior. *I must ask Papa,* she thought.

∞ ∞ ∞

The community eagerly read the daily headlines and gathered each evening around the radio for news from France. The movie theater ran newsreels showing troop activity. The county craved information from the front.

In August 1944, June received a long-overdue letter from David. He reported that he was to participate in the second invasion of France, this one coming from the Mediterranean Sea. He would be moving north with the hopes of meeting up with the forces from Normandy. At the same time, General Patton pushed east into Germany.

>...June dearest, the tide is turning. It is possible that we may win this war before the year's end. I long to hold you, kiss you, tell you how much I love you. I have never met my little daughter. If she is half as beautiful as you, I'll need to keep her under lock and key to fend off the boys.
>
>Pray for me, darling, that I may return to you soon.
>
>My everlasting devotion and love,
>
>Dave

June kissed the letter, holding it close to her heart. "Come home soon, darling. Come home to meet your daughter."

∞ ∞ ∞

September and the start of school brought more turnover with the teaching staff. Principal Wakefield enlisted in May. Mrs. Sokol assumed the position of acting principal. All non-basic classes, such as Latin, music, advanced mathematics, chemistry, and biology, were canceled as the administration reassigned the teachers to more essential subject matter.

Judith, always a math whiz, also moved to teach history, civics, social studies, basic math, and introductory algebra. Mr. Carnahan and the other male faculty either joined the fighting or went to work in heavy industry too strenuous for women to handle.

Harriett began her sophomore year disheartened, hoping to take advantage of Judith Reven's mathematical knowledge. Instead, she was forced to enroll in home economics. The entire class mumbled complaints as they received their class schedule.

"This looks like kiddie class!" grumbled Keith Boring.

Harriett grinned. "You're right; this schedule is silly, a waste of time. But you're a jock; you're not supposed to want to learn."

"Ha. I may be a jock, but not all of us are lucky enough to be a Kepler. I'll not be going to college. May as well learn as much as I can now." Keith collected his books and shook his head as he trudged off to first period.

Harriett wrung her hands together, bit her bottom lip, then called out. "Keith, if you ever want to study together, let me know. I think it'll be fun."

"What, with you, Raggedy Anne? Sorry, don't think so!" Keith burst into laughter. "If I'm studying, it's with a *looker*, not you and your second-hand clothes."

Mortified, Harriett turned away to hide her red face. *So much for boys! I'll stick to books.*

The most significant shock of the day came at lunchtime when Judith's voice boomed from the loudspeaker. "Attention, students. I have an announcement. The Pennsylvania high school athletic association has announced the suspension of all interscholastic athletic competitions. In plain language, that means no football season this year. As decisions unfold, I shall keep you posted; however, Campbellsville high school, per Mrs. Sokol, has officially canceled football and cheerleading this fall. That is all."

Food and utensils flew across the cafeteria as disgruntled students objected to yet more changes.

Eddy Kepler screamed, "Bullshit!"

The crowd quieted down to hear more of whatever profanity might erupt from Eddy's mouth.

Mrs. Sokol entered the room at the height of Eddy's rant. Grabbing her by the shoulders, he shouted directly into her face. "How the hell am I supposed to get a football scholarship if we're not playing football?! All the other states will be playing ball; I have to keep up my skills and speed!"

"Now, Mr. Kepler, calm down and let go of me, or I'll be forced to suspend you." Mrs. Sokol backed away from Eddy's grip.

Eddy moved forward. "Then suspend me! Why the hell do I need to stay in school if I can't play ball?"

"Mr. Kepler. You are only a freshman. You have two years to complete your college ball requirements. Now calm yourself."

Eddy slammed his fist on a nearby table; food bounced with the impact. "It's all bullshit, damn fucking bullshit!"

"All right, Mr. Kepler. If a suspension is what you wish, then you may have it. Two weeks. And remember, this will be on your permanent record, the one that colleges review. Now get out!" Mrs. Sokol pointed to the basement door. Her face red with anger, she placed her hands on her hips, stuck out her chin, and yelled, "Now, Mr. Kepler. Go!"

THE BULGE

LATE 1944

*A*s the Allies pressed on through France, life in Campbellsville went from glum to dreary. Those left in town had no distraction from their everyday lives of sacrifice and toil. The children were barred from their education and the adults were barred from their entertainment.

Another Christmas approached with little to celebrate. Harriett spent her free time in the library, self-supplementing her curriculum. Fearful of more rejection from either mother or classmates, she withdrew from any attempts at making friends, male or female. Eddy spent most days skipping school, jumping rides on freight trains, and hanging out at truck stops. Following diversifying his dating pool to include girls from Garland and Madison after exhausting the Campbellsville supply, Eddy cultivated a reputation of cad that rivaled his father's.

Two days before Christmas break, Harriett sat in the library, solving extracurricular trigonometry problems for Judith. She jumped when a hand touched her shoulder.

"Harriett, sorry to disturb you." Mrs. Sokol's brow creased. "I need you to come to the office with me, please."

Sweat formed in her palms. Harriett dried her hands on the side of her skirt. "Am I in trouble? Did I do something wrong?"

"No, Harriett, but I'm afraid I have bad news."

Harriett's eye twitched, and her lip trembled as she collected her belongings. She squeaked out, "Is it Albert? Oh no, not Papa?"

"Please come, your father is waiting for you. I already have your coat." Mrs. Sokol led the way down the stairs and to the office.

Tabs stood tall, hands in his pockets, head down. Tears streaked his face.

Upon seeing Tabs, Harriett immediately ran to him. "Papa, what is it? What is wrong?" No longer able to contain herself, she burst into tears and hugged her father.

Tabs returned her embrace. "Harriett, sit down, sweetie. I have something to tell you."

"Papa, I can't stand the suspense any longer. Is it Albert? Tell me what is wrong, please!"

"As far as I know, Albert is fine...but Lupi's been killed." Tabs covered his face with his hands. "I know you've been following the war closely. He jumped into France with the 101st Airborne Division in June."

Harriett quietly sobbed, glad for Albert but distressed for Alice and the Lupinetti family. "Do you know how?" she asked, gulping air.

"He—his division, was cut off—surrounded, in the Ardennes Forest. From what I'm told, the fighting was and still is fierce. All I know is that Lupi was killed in the heat of battle." Tabs handed Harriett her coat. "We must go. Your sisters and mother are with Alice at Esther's house."

Harriett mumbled so quietly that Tabs had to strain to hear. "Mother's right. Believing in true love only breaks your heart."

Tabs stopped. "What did you just say, Janie?"

"I told Mother that I believed in romance, in true love. She told me I was a fool and would only get my heart broken." Reaching into her pocket, she pulled out her handkerchief and blew her nose. "Alice and Lupi only had one night together, but they loved each other so much. Oh, Papa!" She threw her arms around Tabs' neck. "Poor Alice. What will I even say to her?"

Tabs circled her shoulder with his arm. Pulling her close, he said, "Come, sweetie. I know you are full of sorrow, but your dear sister is heartbroken. We must put on a brave face and be strong for her."

Harriett and Tabs arrived at Esther's to find June, Esther, Alice, and the children sitting quietly in the living room. Olive, devoid of expression, sat on the sofa beside Alice, alternated wringing her hankie and twiddling her thumbs. Alice's red eyes stared blankly into space but were dry. She absentmindedly clutched her ring. At the sight of her father, Alice broke down.

Running to Tabs, she threw herself at him, tightly hugged his neck, and openly sobbed. "Oh, Papa! Lupi's gone! What if he suffered? Or worse, was alone?" Alice grabbed the back of Tabs' shirt and clung tightly, almost ripping the fabric. "I don't know anything. All they said was that he died." She gulped for a breath. "I have terrible visions of him lying alone, in the dark, in a pool of blood. Oh, poor sweet Lupi!" After several minutes of sobbing, she stopped to stare at her father. "How do I manage without him?"

"There, there. Just cry and let it out." Tabs patted her back as if comforting an infant. "Life will turn around for you; give it time. You'll find a way."

Alice stepped back and, looking directly into Tabs' eyes, asked, "What if it doesn't? Mother never moved on after Uncle Fred's death; what if I can't either?"

Olive lifted her head, hearing Fred's name. "What do you mean, I 'never moved on?'" Glaring at Alice, Olive stood, hands on her hips.

Tabs defended his daughter. "Olive, it is common knowledge that you still grieve deeply for Fred."

"And grieving for my brother should not be anyone's business but mine!" Olive stomped out of the house without her coat into the cold.

Harriett watched from the corner of the room. She approached Alice, but rather than hugging her, she whispered into her ear, "You're nothing like Mother; you only look like her. Sister, you are strong and shall muddle through this pain. You'll be happy again someday, I know it."

Tabs kissed his youngest daughter on the head. "When did you get to be so wise? Alice, Janie is right, I know it doesn't feel that way now, but the pain will be less with each passing day. But today, you need to grieve, so cry, my darling daughter, cry."

Alice sat back down on the couch, allowing her sorrow to flow freely from her eyes. After about ten minutes in the cold, Olive, shivering, rejoined the group, with Mr. and Mrs. Lupinetti following her into the house.

The older Lupinettis, mourning openly, rushed their daughter-in-law. Mr. Lupinetti spoke first. "Alice dear, you are a daughter to us. Tony loved you, and so do we." Mrs. Lupinetti sobbed more intensely upon hearing Lupi's name. "You will move into our house?"

Stunned, Alice squeezed her father-in-law. "Oh my, I love you too. It's too soon. I can't think of such things right now." Alice swooned, sitting back down; she said, "It all feels like a nightmare. It's all too much!"

June scurried into the kitchen to get water. Returning with a tray of glasses and a pitcher, she offered drinks to the family. "Here, all of you, please drink."

Tabs sat down on the couch, taking the spot vacated by Olive. He held Alice, who placed her head on his shoulder and clasped the ruby ring on her finger. Both father and daughter wept for the loss of life.

∞ ∞ ∞

A memorial service was held for Lupi at St. James Catholic Church one week later.

Alice, continuing to live with Esther, panicked the day before the service.

"Oh my God, what shall I wear?" Alice paced frantically around the living room, touching random objects as she circled. "I have nothing appropriate. Esther, do you own a black dress?"

Esther gaped at her sister. "Alice, I have a black dress, honey, but you are five inches taller and two sizes larger than me. My black dress will never fit you."

Alice burst into tears. "What will I wear? Oh no, what will I wear?"

Esther clasped Alice by the arm. "Alice calm down; I'm sure June has something appropriate. And if June doesn't, Mother will."

"Ha! Mother!" Alice stuttered. "She won't willingly share. Never has, never will."

"Okay, I take that back, but I'm sure June can help out." Esther gathered her children. "Alice, will you watch Lloly? Toby, Heddy, come with Mommy. We're going over to see Aunt June for a minute."

Holding the toddler calmed Alice. Lloly diverted her attention to playing a game.

Esther, Toby, Heddy, June, and Susie returned within fifteen minutes, carrying a complete ensemble for Alice to wear.

The next day, the elder Baileys walked solemnly to church. Tabs and Harriett entered the church together and sat down beside June, Esther and Alice. Olive followed reluctantly, hesitating before entering.

Making her way to the front pew, Olive took Alice by the hands. "Daughter, I want you to wear these today; they were my mother's." Olive handed Alice a perfectly matched string of pearls.

"Oh, Mother!" Alice's wide eyes filled with tears. "Yes, I shall wear them today in honor of my beautiful husband." She sniffed, blew her nose, then clasped the pearls around her neck.

Olive fidgeted through most of the funeral mass. A filled sanctuary of mourners went directly to the Lupinettis' home to pay their respects since there was no body, therefore foregoing the usual journey to the cemetery.

Despite rationing, Mrs. Lupinetti managed to offer her guests an extravagant meal. She draped the dining room table with a beautiful hand-crocheted tablecloth. A crystal vase, full of boughs of pine and holly from their undecorated and removed Christmas tree, was surrounded with trays of gnocchi, pasta, and biscotti.

Alice was too stunning to be a widow in June's black, fitted dress, black pumps, a little black hat, and Olive's pearls. She stoically greeted a plethora of Lupinetti relatives, all of whom handed her an envelope of cash. Olive, Tabs, June, Esther, Harriett, Benny and Ingrid Westchester, and Wyeth Bailey, Tabs' cousin, were the only mourners from her family in attendance.

Alice repeatedly voiced, "Thank you for coming." "Lupi would be honored that you traveled so far." "You are too generous; thank you for your gift." Guest after guest kissed her cheek and extended their condolences.

As the last person exited the Lupinetti home, Alice

collapsed onto the sofa, bursting into tears. "I shall never celebrate Christmas again!"

She grabbed the sides of her face and squeezed. Closing her eyes, she lay her head back and sobbed. Tabs and Dante Lupinetti sat on either side of her, giving her support while allowing her to purge her grief. The women, minus Olive, began the arduous chore of cleaning up.

Anthony Nazario "Lupi" Lupinetti's remains were buried in Luxembourg.

∞ ∞ ∞

Harriett stacked her clothes in a pile on her bed. Calling down the staircase, she asked, "Mother, may I borrow your luggage?"

Sitting in her parlor, Olive walked into the front entrance to hear more clearly. "Why are you bothering me? What do you need?"

With a sigh, Harriett repeated. "May I please borrow a piece of your luggage? I am going to stay at Esther's this week to help babysit until school starts again. Alice is still in shock, and Esther can use a hand."

Placing one hand on her hip Olive scoffed. "And what about all my chores? Who's going to help with those?"

"I'll only be gone a week. How much extra work do you have with two people?"

The blood rushed to Olive's neck. "Don't you get snippy with me, Missy. You'll not get your dollar this week!" Olive spun around. Before returning to her secluded hideaway, she called up, "Use a paper sack!"

Harriett filled two paper bags with her supplies, mostly books. Carrying one in each arm, she walked the five blocks to Esther's.

Esther was bustling around in the kitchen. "Harriett, is

that you?" she said as Harriett entered. Alice sat on the couch, despondent and staring into space.

"It's me."

"Just in time! I have to leave for work, and Alice isn't ready for this."

"May I leave my stuff in the living room since I'm sleeping on the couch?"

"Sure, put your suitcase in the corner, out of the way." Esther grabbed her coat from the hook. "Where's your suitcase?"

"Mother made me use paper sacks. It's okay. I'd rather comply than make her angrier than she already is. She's mad because I'll be gone all week."

Esther laughed. "She did the same to me when I moved out after my wedding."

Harriett tucked both bags behind a chair. Sitting down on the couch beside Alice, she hugged her sister. Alice flinched at her touch.

"How are you today, Sis?"

Alice continued staring ahead without answering.

Esther shouted last-minute instructions as she opened the door. "The children are still asleep. Toby can help with most things. Heddy will snuggle up to Alice and stay there most of the day. Lloly will be your only challenge, but he'll settle down after June drops off Susie." Esther took a deep breath. "Okay, food's in the refrig, and I'm off. Good luck!"

Harriett looked around the quiet room, wondering what trials the day would bring. Worrying, she stared at Alice, hoping that, in time, she would recover from this tragedy. Harriett pulled a blouse, needle, and thread from her bag and began darning the elbows of a hand-me-down. She stitched until she heard the children moving overhead.

"Good morning, nieces and nephews!" she called up to them. "Anyone need help?"

Toby answered, "No, Aunt Harriett. It's me and Heddy. We can dress ourselves."

"Be sure to brush your teeth."

"Yes, ma'am."

Harriett listened at the bottom of the steps. Satisfied after hearing the commode flush and the water running, she began fixing breakfast for the children and Alice.

The day passed by without incident. Eight-year-old Toby played alone, six-year-old Heddy mothered Alice, and Lloly and Susie, both in their terrible twos, managed to behave with minimal oversight while entertaining each other.

Esther returned home after five that evening to the smell of herbs and tomatoes. "Sorry I'm late," she called into the kitchen. "I picked up a few extra hours today. What smells so good? Harriett, are you cooking?"

Harriett laughed. "I can't cook. I'm worse than Mother. But I can reheat. Mrs. Lupinetti brought over a big bowl of sauce. I'm just cooking the noodles."

"She's a godsend. Poor dear woman lost her son, yet she pampers us. I thought my mother-in-law was special, but Mrs. Lupinetti takes the prize. She's a gem!"

Harriett entered the living room. "I have the dining room table set. Will June be along soon?" Walking over to Alice, Harriett stroked her hair. "Mrs. Lupinetti sat with her for a couple hours. I think being together helps comfort both women. Gosh, I hope the war ends soon."

"Me, too. Me, too." Esther greeted her children with bear hugs. "Were you good for Aunt Harriett today?"

Toby ticked his tongue. "Of course we were, Mommy."

Esther chuckled. "He's such a little man. Darrel will be so surprised with how they've grown."

Harriett motioned to the table. "We better sit down. My noodles are getting soggy!"

June appeared in time to pass the sauce. Dinner conversation was light and cheerful, an effort to prevent Alice from slipping further into depression. As they ate and talked, June noticed the patches on Harriett's sweater.

"Harriett," June said. "Your sweater is patched. Are you saving your good clothes for school?"

With a frown, Harriett glanced at her sweater. "These are my good clothes. I only have fourth-generation hand-me-downs."

"I thought I recognized that sweater. I wore it in better days," said Esther with a chuckle. "Does Mother not buy you school clothes?"

Harriett's frown deepened. "No. I've never had a new dress purchased just for me. Mother says with the depression and now the war, there are no goods to purchase and no money with which to purchase them." Speaking the words herself cut into Harriett's heart.

June and Esther looked at each other. Rolling her eyes, Esther continued, "That's a crock of crap. Mother's just a mean person, especially to you. Let me see if I have some things for you to wear to school. Well, I know they will be more hand-me-downs, but at least they won't have holes."

"Harriett, do you have sewing skills?" asked June.

Harriett giggled. "Actually, I do. I had to take home economics because we don't have real teachers this year. I'm a stitching whiz."

"Then I'll check my closet, also. You may have to alter things since you are so tiny. I'll look through Alice's clothes too. She usually gets my cast-offs. We're the same size, almost." June scowled. "Her chest is slightly larger."

All three sisters laughed. Alice sat holding Lloly on her lap while she moved her fork, playing with her food.

"That would be wonderful! I'm a little embarrassed that my clothes are so raggedy. They are clean, but most of the fabric is too worn to mend." Harriett chose not to add that the other students might not tease her so much with newer clothing.

The week passed by quickly, with the children on their best behavior. Alice became more responsive; Mrs. Lupinetti visited her every day for an hour or two. On New Year's Eve, both senior Lupinettis stopped by.

Mr. Lupinetti began. "Alice darling," he said as he sat beside his daughter-in-law. "We love you very much."

"I love you too, Papa Lupi," Alice said, throwing her arms around Mr. Lupinetti's neck.

Mr. Lupinetti took one of Alice's hands and Mrs. Lupinetti took the other.

"Darling Daughter," he continued. "You shall always have a place in our hearts and in our home, should you want to live there. But we have something vital to tell you." Alice tilted her head to the side, listening intently. "You are a lovely young woman. No wonder Tony fell head-over-heels in love with you. You were all he talked about from the time he turned fourteen." Tears filled Mr. Lupinetti's eyes. "Alice darling, we want you to move on. You are too young to live your life alone, wearing black. Mourn our Tony, briefly—I mean *briefly*—then get on with living. Find yourself another husband when this blasted war is over. Tony would want you to be happy, to find someone, so you're not a sorrowful widow."

Alice interrupted her father-in-law. "This is still too much to think about."

"I know, but with the new year coming, it has to be said. Be happy, darling Daughter, as you shall remain our daughter until we die. And we shall welcome you with a new husband and with children. Live, dear girl, live your life." The Lupinettis kissed Alice on the cheek, stood, and wiped the tears from their eyes.

Mrs. Lupinetti forced a smile. "Happy New Year, sweet

wife of my darling Tony. May 1945 bring you newfound joy." They left Esther's, blowing their noses as they walked home.

Alice sat quietly for a moment, then asked Esther, "Do you mind if I spend tonight alone in my room?"

"Absolutely not. We are not celebrating this evening, only playing with the children."

"Thank you, sisters, all of you. You are the best family in the world." Alice climbed the stairs to her room, closed her door, then spent the night looking at pictures, rereading Lupi's letters, and listening to her music box while purging herself of the pain.

I shall move on, she thought, *with Lupi's approval.*

LIFE RETURNS

1945

*S*lowly, the school year came to an end, and with it came victory in Europe. Adolf Hitler, Nazi leader and German Chancellor, committed suicide in late April. The war with Germany was over. May 8, 1945, known as Victory in Europe Day, allowed the Allies to concentrate on ending hostilities in the Pacific against Japan.

Harriett finished her sophomore year, once again first in her class. On the last day of classes, Coach Judith Reven packed her personal belongings. With Coach Ludwig set to return home soon, she was preparing to return permanently to Madison. As she packed a cardboard box, she called several students to her room.

Eddy Kepler, the first, entered without knocking. Judith turned to the boy standing beside her desk.

"Mr. Kepler, thank you for stopping by. I have a question. Did you ever request the paperwork for your college football eligibility?"

Eddy hissed. "This again? I thought we covered this. You're the coach; I'm the star. You fill out papers; I break records."

Judith straightened to her full height, then sighed.

"Mr. Kepler, shall you never learn?" She opened her attaché case and removed a file folder. Handing it to Eddy, she continued, "Here. Sadly, I knew you were incapable of acting on your own behalf; however, I don't want to be the one responsible for your waste of talent. Although you have not followed through, I have completed a set of paperwork for you. However, there is one crucial piece missing. You must write an essay and complete several pages of personal information. This must be completed by you. Mr. Kepler, I implore you to please do this immediately, then post the complete packet in the envelope provided." Judith handed Eddy the file. "You're gifted, Son, don't squander it. Dismissed."

Judith refocused on her packing as Eddy sauntered out of the room. He passed Harriett in the hall. "Hey Pip Squeak. You visiting Coach, too?" He smirked. "What, they have scholarships for women's sports too?" He doubled over, laughing at his joke.

Harriett's brows furrowed. "I wish they had such a thing as women's athletic scholarships. But, no—I'm going to college without one." She knocked on the door and waited.

Eddy guffawed. "Even if they had them, you're too little, Pip Squeak. You'd never get one." Laughing, he walked away.

"Harriett, please enter." Judith closed the lid of her box. "I'm sorry to say goodbye to you; Mr. Ludwig shall be returning in the fall." Judith handed Harriett a piece of paper. "This is my personal information. If you ever need a reference for college, work, or anything, please consider using me. You've been such a pleasure to teach. I hope you intend to continue your education."

Harriett accepted the note. Tucking it into a book, she said, "Thank you, Miss Reven. I truly appreciate this. I do intend to go on. I'm not sure how, but I'll find a way. I enjoyed our extra work." Harriett blushed. "And our runs, especially against the boys!"

Judith smiled. "Boys this age need to be tethered to reality at times. I'm happy I had a partner to help. Now—as to your education, I may also be able to help you obtain funding. Don't be shy; just reach out. Now I shall be off. Goodbye, delightful Miss Bailey!"

Judith Reven ended her teaching career at Campbellsville High. On the drive back to Madison, she reminisced over how surprisingly pleasant she found coaching, teaching, and molding young lives. Thinking to herself, she vowed, *I shall alter my future to include more instruction, other than country club tennis.*

∞ ∞ ∞

On a hot July afternoon, a vehicle pulled in front of the Bailey house. Olive, in her sanctuary, heard the car door open and shut. She stood to gaze out the window.

A soldier dressed in uniform with a duffel slung over his shoulder stood looking at the house, smiling. Albert hurdled up the front steps, taking two at a time, then barged through the front door.

Yelling at the top of his lungs, he called out, "I'm home! Anyone here? I'm finally home!"

Olive entered the foyer. "Well, if it isn't the prodigal son."

Albert forced Olive into an embrace. She stiffened, her arms hanging straight at her sides. Despite her resistance, or maybe because of it, Albert squeezed tighter, then planted a wet kiss onto her cheek.

Shaking loose, Olive protested, "Let go of me!"

Albert laughed at his mother. "Good to see you too, Mother. Is my old room still available?"

"So you intend to live here?"

Albert grinned. "Only temporarily. Don't worry. I won't stay a minute longer than I must! It's just until I find a job and get on my feet."

Olive scowled. "I expect room and board from you and some help around the house."

"I wouldn't have it any other way, Mother. You are so predictable!"

Albert grabbed his duffel and bound up the staircase and into his bedroom. He closed the door and inhaled deeply, smelling the familiar scent of home. He cradled his baseball glove, worn and grass-stained, then jumped onto his bed, closed his eyes, and slept deeply for the first time in two years.

That evening Tabs returned to find four plates at the table.

"Olive, are we expecting a visitor?"

Waiting in the dining room, Albert ran into the kitchen, lifted his father, and swung him in circles.

"My goodness, Son! Welcome home!" Tabs said as he was returned to his feet. "Let me look at you. Did you remain unscathed?"

Albert's entire face grinned. "It's kind of hard to get hurt when you're the weatherman, Papa!"

"If you give enough bad predictions, you may find a stray bullet!" Tabs clasped Albert's hands. "Look at you, all filled out, a man! I am so grateful that you have returned to us." Tabs hesitated before asking, "Did you hear about Lupi?"

Albert sobered. "Yes. Alice writes frequently. I feel so badly for her, but she is so stunning. She'll find another suitor soon enough. I'll visit her after dinner."

Olive scoffed. "She should have never married him in the first place, leaving school for the sake of a man! Such nonsense."

Albert and Tabs met eyes, then shook heads. "You see, son, everything is the same back in Campbellsville."

Harriett pulled Albert's bike onto the porch and washed her hands in the trough before going inside. Absentmindedly, she entered the kitchen, walked to the sink, and gulped a big glass of water.

"Good to see you too, little Sister."

Stunned by the voice, Harriett choked on the water, spitting half of it back into the sink. She ran to her brother, throwing herself around him. "Oh Albert, you're home! I'm so thankful you're safe."

"Me too, little girl." He gave her the once over. "Harriett, you haven't grown any taller, but my goodness, you do look older. You are one muscular, tanned specimen. How do you keep so fit?"

"Harrumph. All she does is ride your bike, traipse through the woods, and run that stupid obstacle course," Olive said, outlining Harriett's day.

"Mother, don't forget, I also read the paper, do the laundry, wash the windows, clean the house, iron the clothes, wash the dishes, and study," Harriett said, rolling her eyes at Olive.

Albert squeezed Harriett. "What grade will you be in this fall? Sorry, I can't remember, but being away did funny things with my sense of time."

Harriett beamed. "I'll be a junior. I have moved up a grade. Have you seen Alice yet? She'll be so happy to see you."

Albert fingered his chin. "Goodness, a junior! My tiny baby sister, soon to graduate. You do intend to graduate, don't you? If not, you'll have me to answer to!"

"Yes, Brother, and I'm going to college."

Olive scoffed. "Oh yes, this little Missy has *big* plans."

"Why do you discourage her, Olive? You had the same idea at her age." Tabs pursed his lips. "You should support Janie."

227

"And look where my dreams got me! I'm trying to prevent her from a lifetime of disappointment," Olive spit the answer. "Saving her from *my* miserable life!"

Tabs exhaled. "Olive, I'll not dignify you with a comment. Janie, why don't you and I join Albert tonight on his visit? We'll eat a quick dinner, clean up for your mother, then get out of her hair."

Olive glared. "Suits me just fine. I prefer being alone."

They ate egg salad sandwiches in silence. On the walk to Esther's, Harriett could no longer contain herself. "Albert, tell me about meteorology school. How did you manage to complete it without your high school diploma?"

Albert looped his arm through Harriett's. "I lucked out, little Sister. Right place, right time. Just like those poor dead bastards—oops sorry—poor dead *fellows* who were in the wrong place, wrong time." His face reddened, but he continued, "One of the Majors took an interest in me, thought I had some smarts."

"You do! Father taught us how to read the clouds, trees, and wind." Harriett giggled. "You're Mother's son too, got her brains, although she can be difficult at times!"

"You're right, there. She is brilliantly hard to stomach," Albert cracked.

Tabs scolded, "Now children, don't disparage your mother. Be respectful."

Harriett hung her head. "Sorry, Papa."

Snorting, Albert said, "Sorry, Papa, but that's going to be hard for me to do, now that I've seen what I've seen. I'll no longer tolerate her abusiveness."

"Albert, continue telling me about your schooling."

"Well, the Major suggested I get a diploma equivalent, then he endorsed me for weather school. I had an eight-month crash course and I passed all the exams with flying colors; now, I'm qualified to predict the weather. I'll be looking for a job in either Madison or Pittsburgh, though I really don't want to move that far away."

Harriett skipped, danced, and twirled down the street. Calling behind, she said, "I'm so proud of you and so happy you're back. This is a wonderful day!"

She glided to the door and knocked. Alice answered, her blue eyes wide in amazement. "Harriett, I wasn't expecting you tonight. What's going on?" Alice asked as Lloly tugged at her hem.

Harriett chuckled. "I have a surprise." She waved her arm at two men following her.

Alice screamed and ran forward. "Albert!" She flew at him, wrapping her legs around his waist, her arms around his neck, suspending herself in midair. "Oh Albert, you're home!" Kissing his cheek, she began crying.

Gently placing her feet on the ground, Albert returned her hug and her tears. "It's okay, Sis, you cry. I'm here for you now."

Harriett was first into the house. "Toby, is Mommy working tonight?"

"Yes Aunt Harriett. But Aunt June is off." Alice and Albert entered, wrapped in each other's arms, sobbing. "Why is Aunt Alice crying, and who is that man?" Toby asked, hands on his hips.

"That's your Uncle Albert. He's our brother, just come home from the war."

Taking his cue from *home from the war*, Toby ran to Albert, saluted him, and declared, "Welcome home, Uncle Albert!"

Albert returned the boy's salute. "This fine young man can't be Toby?" Albert teased the youngster.

Toby flung out his chin. "I am! I'm the man of the house until Daddy returns!" Motioning to his siblings, he continued, "this is my sister, Heddy, and my brother, Lloly."

His siblings tried to hide behind Harriett; however, there

wasn't enough Harriett to conceal them. Harriett nudged them, "Go meet your uncle, children. He won't bite."

After a moment, Lloly approached Albert. Heddy latched onto Alice.

"It's a pleasure to see you this evening." Albert shook the children's hands and was rewarded with three grinning faces.

Alice urged the family to sit. "Now that introductions are over, someone run across the street and get June and Susie. They'll want to see you. Where's Mother? Never mind, that was a stupid question."

Harriett scurried over to June's house, returning within minutes. Four of the five siblings were together, and Esther would complete the reunion within an hour. Tabs sat serenely, watching his children and grandchildren as he privately celebrated his unconditional love and devotion to family.

29

TURN THE PAGE

AUGUST 1945

*O*n August 10, 1945, Harriett stretched her muscles before her morning run. With the war nearing its end, supplies were becoming more readily available and rationing less stringent. Albert lazily read the paper and drank a cup of once-contraband coffee; Olive continued to drink tea.

Choking on his coffee, Albert sputtered. "Good God, they really did it!"

Harriett glanced at her brother. "Who did it, and what did they do?"

Albert soberly placed the paper on the table. Taking a long sip before answering, he said, "The government dropped two H-bombs on Japan. Thousands of innocent civilians died." His breathing slowed to a near stop. "Look at this picture." Albert showed Harriett a photo taken several minutes after detonating—a mushroom cloud reached high into the sky.

Harriett scanned the picture. "Heavens—literally, *heavens*. How could anyone survive something like that?"

"They couldn't." Albert tugged at his hair. "Oh, God," he exhaled. "This will certainly end the war, but at what cost?"

All of Campbellsville, including the Baileys, sat pensively around the radio on August 14, 1945, waiting to hear President Truman's address. Alice, June and Susie, huddled holding hands at Esther's house. At the Bailey home, Harriett, darning her socks, pricked her finger with the needle. Tabs, hands in pockets, paced the room. Even Olive joined her family, wringing her hankie in anticipation.

At seven o'clock, Truman announced the end of the war.

Harriett grabbed a ladle and a cooking pot, and Albert and Tabs grabbed their rifles and ran into the streets—while Olive slowly stood and walked into her parlor.

Mayhem broke out. Everyone in the county rushed out of their homes. Clanging noises and gunfire echoed off the hills and reverberated in the valley.

"I can barely hear; it's so loud!" shouted Harriett as she joined her neighbors in celebration. She put down her pot. "I'm done making noise." Harriett flipped into a handstand, turning cartwheels; she proceeded down the street among couples kissing and dancing.

Albert ran to join Alice, who was also outside but just sitting on the porch step, smiling. "Hey, Sis," he called as he neared Esther's house. "How 'bout I buy you a drink?"

Alice laughed, "Albert, neither of us are old enough to drink."

"Sweetie, they won't deny us tonight! We'll head over to the vet's club. It'll be pandemonium!"

Alice grabbed her purse. "Okay, I'll go."

"Put your money back. No man in their right mind will let a beautiful war widow pay for her own drink. Enjoy your status, because tomorrow you move on with your life. You hear me?" He wrapped his arm around Alice as they headed to one of the two veterans' clubs.

The smoke-filled bar area was wall-to-wall people. Albert

plowed his way inside, pulling Alice with him. Alice coughed, eyes burning, as she held tightly to Albert.

"Holy cow, this place is packed!" Alice yelled as they forced their way through the crowd.

Albert leaned in so she could hear, "What did you expect? The war is over!"

As "the Bailey twins" approached the bar, someone shouted, "It's Lupi's widow! Drinks on the house for Mrs. Lupi, God rest his soul."

Alice was handed one drink, then another. She steadied herself on the bar but continued drinking, toasting Lupi, toasting all the lost souls fighting for freedom, and toasting the conclusion of a dreadful war. At the end of the evening, Albert carried her home, laid her on the couch, covered her with an afghan, kissed her forehead, then stumbled home to Maple Street.

The next day the headlines read, *"Japan Surrenders."* The war was over, at least the fighting part of it. The headaches from the previous night's revelry lingered until the following day.

30

TRANSITION HOME

1945

*T*he Campbellsville High football team assembled on the field, waiting for their first practice.

"Hey, where's Coach Ludwig?" asked Keith Boring, as Principal Wakefield neared the boys.

"Gentlemen, I have some news. Coach Ludwig will miss this year's football season." Wakefield paused as a loud groan drowned out his voice. "Coach lost his leg when he stepped on a landmine." The team fell into silence. "He's in physical therapy but plans to be back before basketball season. I'm sure you all wish him well."

Many of the boys sat on the grass, thinking to themselves. They were unable to process the loss of a limb, especially for such a talented athlete.

Eddy Kepler finally broke the silence. "Will we have football this year? Who's going to coach us? Will Coach Reven be back? I need to break more records if I'm going to make it into the pros!"

"Easy, Mr. Kepler. One question at a time. I understand your concern. I shall be coaching you since Miss Reven has taken a position teaching math at Madison High. Campbellsville High shall have a football season. As for your record-breaking, that's entirely up to your effort."

The boys sat silent, plucking blades of grass, torturing an insect, drumming fingers on the ground, or staring into space.

Principal Wakefield interrupted the mood. "Gentlemen, we are here for practice. Shall we begin?"

No one moved. Clapping his hands together, Principal Wakefield raised his voice. "Come on! Get off your bottoms and start running the track. We missed last year's season, so I imagine most of you are out of shape. Now!"

Slowly, the team rose. Trotting, they began to circle the track.

Principal Wakefield jogged beside them, clapping his hands. "Pick up the speed! This isn't a Sunday stroll."

The team's attitude from the first practice carried through the season; the playoff games and a state championship went on without the Campbellsville Cougars. The season ended with a pitiful five-and-five record, despite Eddy breaking his own school records.

∞ ∞ ∞

The county prepared for extravagant Christmas celebrations with many families together again. Pilot Dave Ralston was next to return home from the war. The first week of December, Dave walked from the bus to his home on Pine Street. Wanting to surprise June, he deliberately kept his arrival a secret. Dave stood on the porch, studying the front door. Wringing his hands, Dave inhaled, imagining the toddler that was only a belly bump when he left. He hesitated several minutes before knocking.

Opening the door, June stopped midway. "Dave!" Her eyes filled with tears. "Oh, David! Thank God you're home."

Dave gently embraced his wife, kissed her passionately on the lips, then stepped back. "God, I've missed you." He smiled, "Wife, may I see my daughter?"

June's mouth popped open. "Oh, how could I forget? I was pregnant when you left. Come, come in."

Dave walked into the strange house that was now his home. He spotted the little girl hiding behind a chair.

"Susie, come here. This is your Daddy." June beckoned to the frightened child. "Sweetie, say hello to Daddy."

Dave knelt on one knee; his face beamed. "Hi Sweetie, I'm your Daddy. I sure would like a hug."

"Go ahead, Susie, it's okay. Give Daddy a kiss," June coaxed.

After several moments of consideration, Susie deemed the man safe. She walked to him, wrapped her tiny arms around his neck, and kissed his cheek. Dave returned the hug sobbing, arms trembling, his stomach doing flips. His daughter was finally in his arms.

∞ ∞ ∞

Darrel Cline and the Kepler brothers all returned from the Pacific theater before Christmas. Abigail Kepler prepared a family potluck reunion for the night of Christmas Eve, while the Lupinettis prepared a traditional Italian Christmas Eve meal of seven fishes. The following day, Esther, the new, unofficial, Bailey-family social matriarch—with the help of Alice—invited all the Clines, the Baileys, and the Ralstons for Christmas Day dinner.

Christmas morning, Harriett was the first to awaken. She pulled a shawl around her shoulders; making her way to the kitchen, she threw several pieces of wood into the stove and stoked the embers. Slipping her feet into her boots, she descended into the basement to feed the coal furnace and stoke the fire.

Back in the kitchen, the house was already warming. Retrieving a pound of bacon and fresh eggs from the refrigerator, Harriett started cooking Christmas breakfast. The kettle soon boiled and whistled.

"Hey, Sis. You're up early." Albert had snuck in without Harriett noticing. "Is that water ready to make coffee?"

"It's ready for tea, so I imagine it's ready for coffee." She handed Albert a mug. "By the way, Merry Christmas, Big Brother."

Albert smiled, leaning back into a wooden chair. He locked his arms behind his neck. "I can say it feels mighty good to be back, even if it's in Mother's house." He swung his legs onto the tabletop.

Harriett giggled as she flipped the strips of bacon. "You better move those big feet before Mother gets up."

"Tell me, Harriett: what's she been like these past two years?" Albert rubbed his chin. "Still as unyielding as before?"

Harriett frowned, then sighed. "Well—she's actually less flexible than before, if it's possible. She holds some sort of grudge against me, and I don't know why. I guess I should ask Papa."

Placing his elbows on the table, Albert leaned toward the stove. "Why don't you allow me to talk to Papa about that? I'll do it before I move next month to Madison."

"That would be a wonderful gift. How do you want your eggs?" Harriett asked as Olive entered the kitchen.

The siblings exchanged looks; Albert winked.

Olive, looking at her daughter, said, "I'll have two eggs, over easy, three slices of bacon, and two pieces of toast. It's Christmas, and I intend to eat like it's a holiday."

Harriett blushed. "Oh goodness, I forgot the toast." Flustered, she moved too quickly, touching the side of the cast iron skillet and burning her finger. "Ouch!"

"Sis, run that under water; I'll make the toast. Calm down." Albert jumped off his chair to turn on the kitchen spigot.

Harriett stuck her hand under the running water. "I'm such a clutz."

Albert whispered into her ear. "You're just nervous around her. Trust me, I get it; she used to evoke the same response from me. Took going to war to grow out of her wicked spell."

Harriett kissed Albert's cheek. "I'm so glad you're home. Even if you are only here for another two weeks."

The last to join the family, Tabs entered the kitchen yelling at the top of his lungs. "Merry Christmas, my lovely dear ones! What a wonderful Christmas this is to have my entire family here. I'm looking forward to a glorious day."

"Tabs, pipe down. You're giving me a headache," Olive grumbled as Harriett handed her a cup of tea, a new teabag, and two spoons of sugar. Olive sipped and savored. "Now *that* is a holiday treat. Be sure to reuse this teabag for your cup, Harriett. It may be Christmas, but we mustn't be wasteful."

Albert rolled his eyes as he buttered the toasted bread. "Gosh, that bacon smells good. Shall we eat? I'm famished."

Harriett handed heated dinner plates filled with eggs to each, placed a platter of bacon in the center of the table, and sat down to enjoy.

Albert added toast to the platter. "Who's going to Esther's for dinner besides me? I can't wait to eat turkey."

Harriett glanced at her father. "Papa, are you going? I should love to be with the rest of the family, but I'll not leave you alone if you're staying here."

"Olive, what do you say? Will you come with us to

Esther's?" Tabs took a sip of tea before adding. "The entire family will be there; you should really come along."

Olive harrumphed. "I'll think about it. My stomach is bothering me; I may not be able to leave the throne."

Albert scrunched his eyebrows. "What's 'the throne?'"

Snickering, Harriett answered, "Ah—toilet."

Albert and Harriett cleared the table while Olive retreated to her bedroom to lie down, feigning a Tabs-induced headache. Around one o'clock, Tabs gently nudged her arm. "Olive, it's time to leave for Esther's. Are you coming?"

Olive rolled onto her back. "What, we have to leave *now?*"

"In fifteen minutes or so."

"Good heavens, man, I don't have time to get ready in fifteen minutes. You should have got me up earlier!"

Tabs clenched his teeth. "Olive, you may have all the time you need to get dressed. Take half an hour, if you need it, though you already have on a lovely dress. I have everything ready to go. I haven't heard any flushing, so I assume your stomach is better?"

Olive seethed. Rolling back onto her side, she sneered. "Go without me! I don't have time to get ready. Go, and know this is all your fault."

Tabs slowly descended the staircase to find Albert and Harriett waiting in the front foyer, coats buttoned, packages in arms.

"Is Mother coming?" Harriett looked behind Tabs for signs of Olive.

"No. She's staying home."

"Papa, you'll come, won't you? Please?" Harriett bit her lower lip as she implored.

"Yes, Janie. I'm going with you. I've spent too many lonely holidays away from my family because of that cantankerous woman. Those days are over. If she wishes to be alone, so be it—but I shall not be punished because she's having a snit."

Harriett kissed her father. "Bravo, Papa! Bravo!"

The trio arrived at the Clines' to find utter pandemonium. A total of fourteen adults and children shared the living room with a stack of gifts and a large pine tree.

"Goodness!" Harriett said. "Where shall I place these?" She motioned to the wagonload of gifts toted by Albert.

Esther laughed. "Stack them anyplace you can find an inch. Isn't this delightful?"

Lloly, Susie, Heddy, and Toby ran uncontrollably through each room and up and down the stairs. No one stopped them. The women gathered, filling the spacious kitchen and working elbow to elbow to complete the meal. With rationing and the war over, Esther intended to celebrate.

Harriett set the table while Alice, June, and Esther plated a succulent brown turkey, stuffing, green beans, mashed potatoes, gravy, cranberry jelly, candied sweet potatoes, and creamed corn.

"Okay, everyone, gather in the dining room. Children, to the kitchen," June called as the last serving dish was placed on the table.

The family was met with the aroma of roasted meat, cinnamon, orange, and herbs.

Albert's stomach growled. "My gosh, this smells wonderful. I can't wait to dig in."

"Even after all you ate last night?" questioned Alice.

"Who ate what, last night?"

Alice grabbed her brother's hand. "Albert went with me to the Lupinettis' last night for moral support. Even though Lupi's been gone a whole year already, it was good to have my twin with me. This spread is *nothing* compared to what Mama Lupi served!"

"Sorry, Sis, but I'm hungry again. Still a growing boy." Albert pulled a chair back for Alice, then for Harriett.

"You'll be growing *out*, not up, if you keep eating at this pace all holiday."

Esther and June tended to the children, then joined the adults. Tabs surveyed the table, eyes misty. "What a wonderful blessing to have my entire family together again."

"Everyone but Mother," mused Harriett.

Albert popped a cork from a champagne bottle. "I only bought one bottle, but it's enough for a toast." He poured several ounces into each glass, some of which were jelly jars. "Merry Christmas to all!"

As Albert toasted the family, the front door opened. The family turned to see Olive, decked head to toe in a new coat, boots, dress, hat, and gloves.

She hung her coat over top of several others. "Starting without me?"

Esther quickly glanced at Tabs, who shook his head.

"Mother," Esther said. "I'm so sorry. It was my understanding that you were under the weather."

"Well, I've recovered." Olive walked to the table, waiting to be given a seat. Tabs stood, relinquishing his chair to his wife.

"Here, dear Wife, please sit."

"Father, the only seat left is this stool." Esther blushed.

Darrel took the stool, "Father Bailey, take my seat at the head of the table. After all, you are the family patriarch of this brood."

A boisterous conversation ensued. At the end of the meal, Mrs. Cline presented one of her famous red cakes for dessert. The white icing was decorated with green holly leaves dotted with red berries. Even the children oohed and aahed at the festive ending. All gathered secretly hoped for the start of normalcy without sacrifice.

Esther brewed a pot of coffee as the women packaged leftover food for the refrigerator. The men relaxed or dozed in the living room while the children continued to play, although with less energy. Finally, the time arrived for the gift exchange.

Presents were passed and paper was torn and tossed until the pile under the tree was depleted. All recipients, including Olive, who fondled a pair of leather gloves, were satisfied with their new treasures. Darrel gathered the trash, making room to walk. Susie climbed up onto Dave's knee.

Olive unexpectedly stood. "Here, little one, come here." She motioned to Lloly. The child hesitated, eyes pleading with Esther for protection.

Esther pushed him forward. "Lloly, go see your grandmother."

Reluctantly, he toddled over to Olive. She handed him a five-dollar bill. "Give this to your Mommy to save for you," Olive repeated for each person until all, children and adults alike, received a five-dollar bill. "Merry Christmas," she mumbled.

Faces feverishly fought to hide their disbelief at Olive's out-of-character attendance and generous gift; her reputation of being stingy was rooted deep.

Harriett was the first of the stunned audience to speak. "Thank you, Mother, for the gift. By the way, you look lovely today. Is that a new dress?"

"What if it is? There's no reason why I shouldn't have a new outfit after all these years of skimping, doing without."

Harriett felt the color in her neck. "Well—a—you look very nice." She turned, searching for Albert, who nodded understandingly. An awkward silence followed.

Tabs finally broke the silence. "Esther, Darrel, this has been the most delightful holiday. I am truly thankful for your return, and pray for the soul of our lost Lupi." He blew a kiss to Alice. "It's time for us to head home. God love you all, and Merry Christmas!"

Gathering their treasures, Albert loaded the wagon with gift boxes.

Tabs grabbed the handle and pulled. "Olive," he said as they began their walk home. "I'm happy you changed your mind and came to dinner." She grunted. Tabs continued, "It made the day complete, dear Wife."

"I don't know why you are all making such a fuss over me eating a meal. Drop the subject."

Tabs looked at Albert, shook his head, then asked Harriett, "Janie, what will you do with all your new clothes? I think every one of your gifts was an item of clothing. Do you have room in your closet?"

Harriett scrunched her forehead, confused by the question. "Papa, I've never had new clothes before; these are the first. I'll have plenty of room. Now I can finally throw away some of the threadbare, patched things in my wardrobe."

Tabs gaped at Harriett and squinted at Olive. "What do you mean you never had a new piece of clothing? Olive, that can't be true!"

Olive grunted. "I have three other daughters who have grown out of perfectly good clothing. Why should I spend good money on new clothes for her? She's not wearing rags today."

Harriett dropped her head. "Mother, the only reason I don't look rag-a-muffin today is that Esther, June, and Alice took pity on me and gave me some items to hold me until Christmas. I have darned and mended most everything in my closet until it barely holds together. I'll be happy to discard them. Maybe the kids at school will stop calling me Raggedy Anne."

Tabs' eyes flashed daggers at Olive. "Janie, why didn't you mention this before? The ragged clothing, the teasing?"

"Papa, I know money is tight. If we are poor, there is no shame. I get so much love from you that the material things aren't that important."

Stopping the procession home, Tabs hugged his youngest. "Janie, my dearest youngest daughter, I make good money as the spring company foreman. From now on, your mother shall provide you with new clothing." Tabs turned back to Olive. "Do you understand, Olive? Janie gets new things!"

Olive grunted.

Albert slipped his arm around Harriett. Leaning in, he whispered in her ear, "I'll get to the bottom of Mother's aversion to you, I promise."

PILGRIM DRIVE

JANUARY 1946

*A*lbert sat in his bedroom, taking a break from packing. His new position as a combined Madison-Campbell County meteorologist started in a week. The construction of a county airport required a part-time weatherman, and editors from the Madison Gazette and Campbellsville Herald collaborated with the county to create a full-time position, which Albert luckily procured.

Hoping that Harriett would be home from school soon to help, Albert listened for her return. Upon hearing the door, he ran downstairs. To his surprise, Alice stood at the bottom of the staircase.

"Alice, what are you doing here?"

Alice inhaled. "I have something to ask you. May we talk privately in your room?"

Albert cocked his head curiously. "Of course, but you better be out with it quickly; I don't like suspense." Smiling, he motioned up the steps.

The Bailey twins sat on the edge of Albert's bed. Alice kicked her legs up and down.

"If you're not still, I shall be sick." Albert grabbed her moving leg and squeezed.

"Fine. Here goes. I know you are buying a house on the outskirts of Campbellsville, close to the new airport, in that development. I was hoping that I might be able to live with you, at least for a while." Alice bit her lower lip. "Esther and Darrel are more than generous, but they need some privacy. I'm a fifth wheel."

He grinned ear to ear. "I can't think of anything I would like more. You'll add a woman's touch, help me decorate, cook, clean—"

Alice punched his arm. "Wait just a minute Brother, I'll share in the chores, but they are not all mine. And I intend to pay you rent. Now that June and Esther are no longer needed at the Spring Factory, I'll be working at Lupinetti's grocery. Business is booming. They are hiring; may as well be me."

"Okay, okay, Sis. We can share chores. But yes—absolutely, yes. You may live with me until I find a woman, or you find a man."

Alice smiled, squeezing Albert's hand. "Thanks, Brother. It will be good to get away from some of my bad memories."

The conversation stopped when they heard Harriett bounding up the stairs. Alice called out. "Hey, Little Sister, come here."

"Hi, Alice." Harriett hugged her sibling. "What brings you into the spider's web?"

"Ha. You are so right. I'm going to move in with Albert, isn't that wonderful?" Alice giggled excitedly. "By the way, Papa Lupi asked me if you'd be interested in an after-school job? Business is starting to really pick up. I'll be working the day shift, and, well—with Lupi gone, he needs some extra help."

Harriett jumped up and down. "Yes, please! That's great

news. I need to really start saving if I intend to continue with college next fall."

Nodding in approval, Alice asked, "Any chance you can start tomorrow?"

"Sure, I'll be there fifteen minutes after the last bell."

Albert began emptying drawers, "Now, with business over, both of you, help me pack! I want to get out of this house as quickly as possible."

∞ ∞ ∞

Patriot Place, a housing development of new-style, one-story ranch homes, was built adjacent to an old battlefield from the Whiskey Rebellion. Albert's modest three-bedroom home boasted fifteen hundred square feet of living space with a two-car, detached garage. Sold as "sleek, modern, and efficient," his Pilgrim Drive abode was one-third the size of his parents' Maple Street home. Alice and Albert moved into the just-finished home in mid-January 1946.

Alice placed a box in the kitchen. "Oh Albert, this place is so cute. I can't wait to unpack my wedding gifts. Geez, I haven't even looked at some of them since my wedding day."

She leaned on the white-and-yellow swirled Formica counter, fighting back the tears that always seemed to be hiding just behind her eyelids.

"Lupi and I opened our gifts, I recorded the list, then we went to bed. Next morning he was off to the bus station, leaving me to write all the thank-you cards alone." She sighed. "Seems like decades ago."

"Don't get weepy on me, Sis."

Alice inhaled. "I won't. At least, I'll try not to when I unpack everything. We're going to have to buy lots of stuff."

"Hold on. Before you start spending the money I don't

have yet, let's take inventory of what we already have, and what we really need. And I said 'need,' not 'want.'"

Alice giggled. "You talk as if you're my husband."

Albert poked his sister's arm. "Someone has to keep you in line. Come on, I'll show you the rest of the place before we unload Uncle Benny's truck."

The kitchen came with two walls of counter space and upper cabinets. The sink was under the window that faced the backyard. A short counter peninsula divided the working area from the breakfast space, large enough for a small table seating four.

As they walked through the dining room, Albert warned, "Be careful not to hit your head on that light fixture. Cool, isn't it? I had a choice of all-wood or wood with copper. I like the combination."

Only steps away, Alice commented in the living room, her voice lilting up an octave. "This is a decent size! You have room for a couch, two chairs, coffee and end tables, plus even a place for a television."

"Here she goes again. Alice, do you know how expensive televisions are? Not just yet. I'll buy a secondhand radio."

Scowling, Alice pretended to be insulted. "Fine, Brother."

The two walked down the short hallway and entered Alice's designated bedroom. "Oh, I won't be lonely in here." She chuckled, "At least it's big enough for a double bed and a dresser."

Albert gallantly waved his arms, introducing Alice to a double door. "Yes, Sister, but an armoire is not necessary." He swung open the doors. "You have a built-in closet, with enough space for even *your* clothing!"

"Oh, I do like this!" Alice glanced at the adjacent bathroom. "Are we sharing baths?"

"Au contraire." Albert urged her on and into the master en suite. "I have my own—teeny tiny—bathroom."

They could only fit one head in the doorway, but Alice eventually saw the shower, toilet, sink, vanity, and built-in medicine cabinet.

Pointing to the cubby niche, Alice asked, "Is that storage for linens?"

"Yes, for my towels. There is a small linen closet in the hallway for your stuff."

Alice plopped on the floor in the middle of Albert's bedroom. "I love it! Thank you for sharing your new space with me. You really are the best brother ever!"

∞ ∞ ∞

Pilgrim Drive became home to Alice and Albert. His new job as a meteorologist was a short bus ride east; her job in Campbellsville was a short bus ride west.

Late in April 1946, Alice was stocking shelves in her in-laws' store. The bell tinkled; a strange man entered.

"Hello. Do you carry bagged candy? I need lollipops; I've run out."

Alice turned to face the strange voice. Her eyes locked onto the gray eyes staring at her backside. She grabbed the countertop to steady herself. Inhaling, she answered, "Yes—over here." She motioned for the man to follow.

The mesmerized gaze of the blond man in his late twenties never left the shapely figure. Mr. Lupinetti smiled, watching the exchange from the back room.

Handing the stranger a bag of candy, Alice asked, "Are you new in town? Or just passing through?"

"I'm the new druggist, Teddy Jenson." Teddy thrust his hand forward.

Shaking it, Alice replied, "Hello Mr. Jenson, I'm Alice Lupinetti; this is my father-in-law's store. Welcome to Campbellsville."

Jenson's smile drooped as he heard the words father-in-law. Quickly withdrawing his hand from Alice's, he stammered. "Oh—you're Mrs. Lupinetti. A pleasure to meet another business owner." Jenson backed away from Alice, fearing he might be tempted to touch her hand again. "Doc Murphy retires on Friday. I hope to close the drugstore for just a week, do some fixing up, then open with a grand celebration. I'll send out invitations, but I would be honored if you and your husband—and family—come in support of my new enterprise."

Alice neither smiled nor frowned as she rang up Jenson's purchase. "Thank you for the kind invitation. I shall mention it to my family. I'm sure they'll happily attend."

Dante Lupinetti snuck out of the backroom and stood quietly beside Alice as she watched Jenson exit.

"My dear Daughter?"

Alice jumped at the voice. "Papa Lupi, you startled me!"

Mr. Lupinetti grinned. "Yes, I know. He's the one, isn't he?"

Alice jerked her head to look at Mr. Lupinetti. "'The one' what?"

"The one to take my Lupi's place in your heart."

Tears fell from Alice's eyes. "Don't say such things. I shall always love Lupi."

Mr. Lupinetti placed his arm around Alice's shoulder. "Of course you shall, and we shall always love you. That man is smitten with your beauty. And I think I see signs of that heart of yours healing, making room for another. Bravo, my brave girl. Bravo!" Mr. Lupinetti kissed her cheek. "And yes, we shall all attend his party, and I shall tell him that there is no longer a Mr. Lupinetti in your life."

∞ ∞ ∞

Pharmacist Theodore Jenson labored for ten days before he announced the official retirement of Doc Murphy and the closing of the Campbellsville drugstore. He scheduled the Grand Opening of the new Campbellsville Apothecary for the first week of May 1946.

Harriett opened the mail to find an engraved invitation. "Papa, goodness—look how formal."

She handed the envelope to Tabs. "Looks like this town is getting some class! I, for one, certainly shall attend. I spent my entire life in that drugstore. I want to see how this young city boy changes it."

"May I go with you?" Harriett winked at her father. "Do you think we can convince Mother to buy me a new dress to wear?"

Tabs chuckled. "Janie, I shall badger your mother until she complies with our wishes. You'll have a new dress."

Tabs, Olive, Harriett, Albert, Alice, Esther, Darrel, June, and Dave walked down Pine Street, the sweet smell of spring blossoms in the air. A large sign saying "Grand Opening" was draped over the threshold. "Campbellsville Apothecary" was carved on a gilded sign in the shape of a mortar and pestle that hung from the roof.

Harriett straightened her new skirt and re-tucked her blouse. "This is my first formal invitation to anything. I can't wait to meet our new druggist." She glanced at Alice, whose face was ghostly white. "Alice, what's the matter with you? You look like you're going to faint."

At her words, Albert hurried to Alice's side.

Placing his arm around her waist for support, Albert asked, "Sis, are you ill?" Alice stood frozen. Albert took her hand. "My God, you're ice cold. I'll get you a chair and a glass of water."

Albert entered the new apothecary and returned with a

chair and some water. "Sit, Alice. I don't understand; you felt fine this morning, even a little giddy."

Teddy Jenson joined the Bailey family within a few moments, carrying a damp washcloth. "Where's our patient?" he asked. Albert stepped aside to expose Alice.

With a discernible inhale, Jenson said, "Mrs. Lupinetti, I'm sorry that you are unwell." He placed the cloth on Alice's forehead with a trembling hand. Searching the group, Jenson asked, "Is your husband here? Perhaps he should take you home?"

Albert took Jenson by the arm. "May we speak privately?" The two moved into the street. "My sister is a widow. Her late husband, a great guy, was killed in the Ardennes toward the end of the war."

Jenson tried not to smile. "I'm so sorry for her—for your loss. She's so young and beautiful to be a widow."

Albert searched the druggist's face, seeing admiration for Alice, he went on. "Poor bastard, they only had one night together. It's been over a year now, but it's still quite a shock for her."

"She no longer wears black. Is she over her mourning period?" Jenson prodded.

Albert thought before answering. "For the most part, yes, she is ready to move on. Although, Lupi shall always have a special place in her heart."

Jenson patted Albert's shoulder. "As he should. Shame on a woman so callous that she forgets her first real love."

Albert guided Jenson further into the street. "If I may be so bold, do I detect an interest in my sister?"

Jenson gulped, turning deep red; he glanced at Alice sitting in the chair. "If I'm sincere, I was smitten with my first vision of her beauty."

Albert leaned in to whisper, "Then, you shall have my guarded blessing to pursue her. Take it slow. I'll be watching you since you are new to the county. If you act ungentle-manly, you shall have me, my father, the Lupinettis, and most of the men in Campbellsville to answer to. Understood?"

Jenson was speechless. He just nodded his head yes. It took several moments for him to recover enough to say, "I think I better join my guests. Please won't you come in?"

Jenson led the Bailey family into his new place of business. The inside sparkled. The old, carved, wooden mirror above the soda counter was cleaned and varnished. The tall wooden booths were removed and replaced with low, chrome-trimmed padded benches and matching chrome tables. The black-and-white tile floor reflected the new fluorescent lighting. Doc Murphy's secret compounding area in the back of the store was opened into a prep counter behind a low display case, allowing Jenson to appraise the activities within the establishment. No more hiding in the back, away from the public. Jenson had also installed a private consultation area, inviting the townsfolk to actively question and take a proactive role in their health.

Harriett mingled with a few of her classmates, who ignored her. Bravely she interjected, "This place is so modern looking. It's a real asset to Campbellsville."

Keith Boring sneered. "An 'asset!' What kind of comment is that?"

The others chuckled. "Harriett, always so serious."

Harriett began stammering a reply, then stopped. "Why would I expect you to understand the significance of this contribution toward the economic recovery of the county?" She ticked her tongue, shook her head, then walked away.

As she rejoined her family, she heard snickers of, "Contribution!" "Significance!" "Geez, what a brainiac."

Harriett linked arms with Tabs, then pecked his cheek with a kiss. "Thank you, Papa, for the new blouse and skirt and for taking me to this wonderful party."

June blurted, without asking Dave, "Shall we head over to our house? Relieve the babysitter and have a light dinner? Dave has an announcement." June regarded her husband's blank expression. "Sorry, darling. We are so used to making decisions on our own. Are you okay with a potluck tonight?"

Dave's face softened. "Of course, June. I'm admiring your newfound strength and independence."

"Oh, wonderful idea," Esther said. "I have several food items to contribute. Why don't I grab my food and kids? We'll see you there. Darrel has a surprise also. Let's make this one big celebration day!"

The family made its way down the block to June and Dave's house. Tabs prodded Olive along. Everyone grabbed a chair and headed to the backyard for a potluck meal. Choosing from a random collection of food items placed on an unfolded card table, they filled their plates and found a place to sit.

Olive, twirling her thumbs, pressured, "Okay, out with the news; I want to go home soon."

June rolled her eyes. "Mother, can't we celebrate something, for once, without the pressure to hurry it along?"

Olive grumbled under her breath.

"Well, I'll start," June offered. "Dave, tell them your news."

David Ralston, usually modest, beamed. "I got a job."

Olive interrupted before anyone could congratulate him. "Everyone is getting jobs at the steel mill and in the mines. Even the spring company is hiring men, now that the women are back to housekeeping. What's so special about a job?"

June frowned. "Mother, if you'd let Dave speak, he'll tell us."

Dave continued, "I'll be flying airplanes!" His leg began bouncing up and down. "And I don't have to move to Pittsburgh to do it."

Esther hugged June. "That's fantastic news. I was so afraid you'd move away from us."

June giggled. "Nope. We're staying in the house. Dave is flying out of the new, shared county airport, where Albert works. And we're buying a *car*."

"Moving up in the world. What are they paying you if you can afford a car?" Albert whistled.

Dave blushed. "Enough, Brother. Enough for us to live a good life!"

Tabs stood to shake his son-in-law's hand. "Well done. You're a good provider for my daughter and granddaughter. Congratulations." He winked at June. "And I am very pleased you shall remain in town."

Esther interrupted Tabs. "Our turn. Darrel, tell them your news."

Olive mumbled, "Yes, for God's sake, get on with it." Everyone ignored her.

Darrel grinned. "Well, something good came out of this blasted war." His neck and face flushed. "Oh, Alice, I'm so sorry. That was careless of me."

Alice smiled shyly. "Darrel, don't apologize. No one needs to walk on eggshells around me. Daytime is for the living; I'll save the dead for my prayers at night. Tell us, Darrel."

Albert sat back, thinking to himself that, yes, Alice certainly seemed ready to move on with the handsome new druggist.

Darrel showed a full face of teeth. "I'm getting out of the mines!"

Harriett was the first to comment. "Oh boy, that is marvelous! They are so dangerous."

"Don't remind me!" Esther chided.

"Where's the new job?" asked Tabs.

"I'll be working in the steel mill, but not as a laborer. I'll be using some of my skills learned in the navy for quality control. I'll inspect the product during various stages of development to ensure quality, stability, and flexibility. We'll have a whole department of inspectors, and I'm to be one of the supervisors."

Again, Tabs shook his son-in-law's hand. "Bravo, Darrel. I do have to ask, what's the pay like?"

Darrel tightened his fingers into a ball, "I'm union, so I make union wages. Higher than a skilled laborer, but lower than non-union management. Anyhow, it's a good living for a family of five."

Esther blurted out, "Family of six."

Darrell beamed.

All mouths dropped open. Tabs hugged his oldest. "I love you all so much. This is indeed a joyous day!"

Olive tugged on her sweater, mumbling as she opened the door. "Another brat! I'm leaving. Goodnight."

"Mother, don't leave yet!" Harriett interceded on Olive's behalf.

Albert's head shook back and forth. "Let her go, Harriett; she'll only ruin the evening for the rest of us if she stays."

As Olive left, Alice and June rushed to embrace Esther in congratulations. Harriett snuggled close to her father.

Slipping under his arm, Harriett whispered, "I'm sorry, Papa. Know that you are the best, most loving, gentlest father in the world—and a great husband. I love you so much."

Tabs squeezed Harriett. "No worries. I have all I need in you, in my children. I love you, too, my little Janie."

32

FLORIDA STRAWBERRIES
SUMMER 1946

*H*arriett moved from part-time to full-time at the Lupinettis' grocery store. Her winter job of pulling the delivery cart had exercised her muscles but chilled her bones. She happily enjoyed an inside job to obtain the extra income needed for college, which was only a year away.

Harriett climbed the four-rung stepladder to stock a high shelf.

"Hey Pip Squeak. When did you start working here?" Eddy Kepler asked.

Hearing the male voice, she caught herself as she teetered on the verge of falling. "I started here in January, if you must know."

"Easy there, little girl. Only asking. I haven't seen you in the store before, that's all."

Harriett regained her balance. "I usually run deliveries after school. Now that classes are over, I'm working full-time."

"Looks like we'll be work buddies." Eddy chuckled. "I'm starting tomorrow as a butcher's apprentice."

Harriett bit her lip. *I doubt that we'll ever be buddies,* she thought. "Congratulations. Are you saving for college too?"

Eddy sneered. "I'm not paying to go to college; college is paying for me to grace them on the football field."

"Lucky you." Harriett rolled her eyes then turned to continue stocking the upper shelf. "So Eddy, where are you going to school? Anyone scouting you?"

Eddy smacked his lips together. "No one has approached me yet, but I'll be recruited by both Pitt and Penn State, at least!" He looped the ties of the clean white apron twice around his thin hips. "Mr. Lupinetti, this apron will do. I'll see you tomorrow."

"Bright and early, Mr. Kepler. I expect you here at six a.m.," Mr. Lupinetti called from the back room.

"See you tomorrow, Pip Squeak." Eddy sauntered out the door to a waiting bevy of girls, all swooning over the star athlete.

Harriett rolled her eyes. *Great. Eddy Kepler, all summer!*

The next day, Harriett arrived at seven-thirty a.m., half an hour before her eight o'clock scheduled start time. As she walked in the door, Mr. Lupinetti called out. "Kepler, you're ninety minutes late."

"Sorry, Mr. Lupi, it's Harriett. I'm thirty minutes early."

"Oh hello, Harriett. You're such a good girl, just like your sister. Mr. Kepler is late."

Harriett thought to herself, *I could have told you Eddy Kepler would never show at six.* "Maybe his alarm didn't ring," she said in defense of her colleague.

Moving into the backroom, Harriett placed her handbag and sweater into her cubby, signed and clocked her timecard, put on her tiny apron, and began sorting through the delivery of produce fresh off the truck from Pittsburgh.

"Mr. Lupi, where did you find eggplant this early in the season?" Harriett called to her boss.

"It was shipped up from Georgia, on the train. We'll be getting strawberries from Florida later this week."

Harriett dreamed of strawberry shortcakes as she worked. Around eight-fifteen, the doorbell tinkled. Harriett readied herself for her first customer, but it was Eddy Kepler dragging himself through the door.

"Late night?" asked Harriett.

"Why would you say that?" Eddy quipped sharply, squinting his eyes in the light.

"Well, let's see." Harriett paused. "Untucked shirt, disheveled hair, and wrinkled trousers are my first clue. The fact that you are over two hours late might be clue number two." She giggled. "You better at least tuck in your shirt. Mr. Lupi is not happy."

Harriett strained to hear Eddy being lectured loudly in broken English mixed with Italian. *At least Eddy is getting an education in Italian swearing*, she laughed to herself.

∞ ∞ ∞

The summer of 1946 passed quickly. Working with Eddy Kepler was uneventful. Harriett stayed in the grocery-produce area of the store, while Eddy remained behind the butcher counter, developing proficiency in cutting meat. Despite a rocky start, Eddy's lust for a used sports coupe motivated him to arrive on time. Harriett maintained her rigorous physical training, although her tan suffered. Because of her day job, she was forced to run in the evenings. Principal Wakefield opened the school library to the public over the summer; Olive and Harriett read voraciously.

Senior year commenced and the world returned to normal —or, at least, a new normal. Coach Ludwig successfully rehabilitated and came home with a cane and prosthetic leg. Football and harvest season were here!

S. LEE FISHER

Eddy knocked on the coach's door one early September morning.

Coach Ludwig looked up from his desk. "Yes, Eddy, what's up?"

"Have a minute, Coach? Can I take a seat?"

"Sure, Eddy." The coach motioned to a chair in front of his desk. "Something on your mind?"

Eddy hung his head. "I wanted to know if my eligibility status for college ball was in order."

Coach Ludwig folded his hands together on the top of his desk. "Hmm. I see." Before continuing, Coach swiveled his chair toward the filing cabinet, opened a drawer, and pulled out a file folder. Opening the folder, he reviewed the contents. "Looks like Coach Reven completed all the paperwork for you, except for your personal pages. She notes that she provided you with a complete set of paperwork and an addressed envelope for submission. Did you send in your paperwork?"

Eddy's palms began sweating. He wiped his hands on the sides of his trousers. "Well—umm—you see, coach."

"Spit it out, Kepler."

"I didn't send them in because I lost the papers." Eddy hung his head. "I was hoping you could do them for me now. I really need to play college ball."

Coach Ludwig studied the young man's face. "Why do you 'need' to play college ball?"

"I—I don't want to work in the mills, like my brothers. I want to be a football star."

Coach Ludwig inhaled long and deep. "Son, it's like this. You've missed the Class A and Class B school cutoff date for eligibility for your grade level."

Eddy felt the heat crawl up his neck. "Coach, can't you fix it? Come on, for me?"

Coach Ludwig tilted his head. "Eddy, I am truly sorry; you

have real potential to make it in college ball, and maybe even the pros. But you were given one simple task to do for yourself, and you failed to follow through." Coach sighed. "You may be talented, but Son, you are not entitled to success. Coach Reven practically held your hand through the process, which is more than I would have done. This is your doing. A deadline is a deadline."

Eddy stood, pushed back his chair, then slammed his fist onto the desk. The sound echoed down the hall, causing students to stop and listen. "Dammit, Coach! Break the rules for me. You know I'm a star!"

"Son, I suggest you settle down and apologize for losing your temper. They are not my rules. And rules are made to be followed, not broken."

Eddy sucked air through his clenched teeth. Leaning in toward the Coach, face to face, he seethed. "If you're not going to help me, then screw your team. I quit!"

"If you quit, then you'll have absolutely no chance of being picked up by a class C school looking for class A and B castoffs."

"I'm not a castoff. I'm a star. You son of a bitch—win without me!" Eddy stormed out of the office, slamming the door as he left.

33

CELEBRATIONS

MAY 1947

*H*arriett fussed with her hair, taking out the bobby pins; she allowed the curls to relax before brushing. She wanted to look special today. She slipped a new sundress over her head and fastened the belt around her waist. Looking in the mirror, she admired her reflection, thinking that yellow was a good color for her. Grabbing her cap and gown, she ran down the stairs.

"Papa, I have to be there early. We need to practice our speeches. I'll have seats saved for you and Mother in the front row. Everyone else is on their own. Okay?"

Tabs replied, "See you soon. I'm proud of you, Janie, Miss Head-of-her-class!"

The Campbellsville High School graduating class of 1947 marched into the auditorium and onto the stage. Harriett wore the gold cords of valedictorian, ranking highest in her class. Tabs grinned and waved as she passed the front row. He tried but failed to camouflage the empty chair beside him, occupied by only a bouquet of flowers.

Principal Wakefield spoke first, followed by the Campbellsville mayor. Finally, it was Harriett's turn to speak.

"...And in closing," Harriett said, "I want to challenge my classmates to rise to the same heights as our brothers, uncles, and fathers, who fought and possibly died to ensure our freedom. Let us not forget their sacrifice for the gifts given us. We must seize our opportunities and enjoy, but never take for granted our freedoms: of speech, to bear arms, to vote, to education, to better ourselves, and to make our children's futures bright and prosperous without the threat of war or poverty. As we make our mark on the world, it is imperative that we leave it better than how we found it. Congratulations and best wishes."

Tabs jumped to his feet, clapping wildly. Proudly he said to all seated around him, "That's my daughter, little Janie. She is going to do great things!"

Principal Wakefield announced each graduate alphabetically, summoning them forward to accept their diploma.

"Harriett Jane Bailey." Scattered rounds of applause, mostly from her siblings and other adults, followed. The principal placed a gold medal around her neck, shaking Harriett's hand as he presented her with her diploma. Harriett beamed as Tabs whistled and cheered. There was no way for him to hide the empty chair.

The Bailey family headed to their Maple Street homestead. Gathering under the grapevine arbor, they congratulated their tiny sibling with envelopes of money.

"Where's Mother, and why didn't she come to the ceremony?" Harriett searched the yard for her missing parent.

Tabs frowned, "Janie, your mother is a fickle woman, unpredictable."

"It's okay, Papa. I had to ask, just in case she had a legitimate excuse. I understand. Well, actually, I don't understand, but I accept it."

Albert took Harriett aside. "She's jealous."

"Why, in the name of heaven, is she jealous of me?" Harriett's brow furrowed. "What have I ever done to her?"

Albert touched Harriett's shoulder. "I'm sorry, my little sister. Mother can be very selfish at times. You are everything she ever wanted to be, but never was."

"But I'm her daughter. Are mothers really capable of that kind of behavior?"

"Silly question." Albert hugged his sister. "You're supposed to be smart, Harriett. She mistreats each of us, and you worst of all; of course she's capable. I'd say she's an expert!"

"Papa told you this?"

"Yes. We spoke briefly. He didn't want to get into details, other than saying she's jealous."

Harriett tried not to allow her mother's feelings to dampen her excitement. She climbed into one of the over-sized Adirondack chairs, her legs pinned underneath, and opened her envelopes.

"My goodness, you are all so generous!" She counted a total of one hundred dollars.

Alice responded first. "Harriett, we want you to be successful. You're a real whiz when it comes to learning. Hopefully, with this, you'll have a head start on college funding." She smiled as Teddy Jenson rounded the house. "We love the idea of educating a girl! Don't we, Teddy?"

Jenson grinned as he took Alice's hand. "I'm not sure what I agreed to, but if you say so, then I agree!" Everyone chuckled.

"Typical Alice, twisting the boys around her little finger." Albert poked his sister's arm.

Jenson glanced up and down. "With that face and that body, she has the whole world on a string!"

"And you're tied the tightest?" asked Albert.

Jenson blushed. "Perhaps I am." He approached Harriett,

handing her two envelopes. "Congratulations, Harriett. Bravo on being number one. This is from Mr. Lupinetti and me."

Harriett opened her newest gifts to find another fifty dollars. Tears formed. "Oh my. One hundred fifty dollars added to what I've saved over the past two years—I should certainly be able to pay for secretarial school."

The Baileys emitted a collective moan.

"Secretarial school! What about college?"

"No, Harriett, start college in the fall."

"Don't sell yourself short!"

Harriett remained sitting on the Adirondack amidst their protests. "My dearest family, I shall never sell myself short." She laughed at the irony of her statement. "However, I am practical. If I get a job as a secretary, I'll have a steady income that can support me while I enroll in college classes."

Tabs interceded. "I trust you, Janie. Become financially independent first."

"Well, Papa, with that in mind, may I rent my bedroom from you and Mother? For a year or two?"

Tabs nodded. "If it were up to me, I'd have you live here forever, free of charge. But your mother will require room and board."

Olive, standing behind the corner post partially hidden, decided to speak. "Damn right, I require room and board. No one gets a free ride in this life, not even your precious *Janie*." Olive glared at Tabs, then at Harriett. "And I still expect help with the chores."

Harriett peered at Olive. "If I perform chores, then my rate shall be discounted."

"Harumph."

June and Esther exchanged smiles while Albert and Alice winked at each other.

"Thank you all for your generosity," Harriett said, turning

now to face the rest of them. "I deeply appreciate your kindness. By the way, I start school next week!"

∞ ∞ ∞

Harriett began an eighteen-month course in bookkeeping, typing, stenography, and general management, with an associate degree as the end goal. Homework and studies were performed during her daily bus commute to Madison. She continued to deliver Lupinetti's groceries after school, no longer encountering Eddy but ensuring income to pay for her room.

October resurrected the Harvest Dance, which had been suspended for decades. Albert and Alice discussed it at dinner, the week before the designated date.

"Alice, I assume you'll be attending the dance?" Albert asked. "Do you remember the last time we went?"

Alice raised her eyebrows. "We went to this before?"

"Yep. You were around four or five. It was so much fun; even Papa and Mother enjoyed themselves. It was one of the few times I remember Mother being calmer, happier."

"Wow. I don't think I ever remember her happy. She's always been on edge."

Albert rubbed his chin. "From what I gather, she was going to go back to school, but ended up pregnant with Harriett." Albert inhaled. "Oh my God! That's it, Alice, that's why she's so mean to Harriett. Papa said Mother was jealous of Harriett, but he wouldn't say why. Mother blames Harriett. She resents her for not having that last opportunity at school."

Alice sighed. "Poor Harriett. She's so sweet and shy. Mother truly mistreats her, even more so than the rest of us."

"We'll have to make sure we encourage Harriett to join us

at the dance. Are you meeting Teddy?" Albert teased Alice. "The two of you are spending a lot of time together lately."

Alice tipped her head. "Albert, I have a secret to tell you. But! You must not repeat it to anyone. Promise?"

"What are you up to now, Alice?"

Alice's smile spread across her face. "Teddy and I are going to elope. We intend to announce our marriage at the dance."

"My! Congratulations!" Albert hugged his sister.

"I'll be moving out soon after," Alice said. "Teddy bought a house on High Street."

"Not the Songer house?" Albert's eyes widened. "That will get Mother's goat."

"No, old man Songer is still living there, with a nurse. It's a big corner house, two blocks down." Alice giggled. "It's as big as Mother's house."

Albert hugged Alice. "What do his parents think? This is his first wedding. Aren't they Pittsburgh Country Clubbers?"

Alice ticked her tongue. "*She* wants a big to-do at their club, Allegheny. God, can you imagine Mother in Pittsburgh, at a hoity-toity country club? That is if she even went." Alice said. "Ugh. Mrs. Jenson settled on having a bridal shower, after the fact."

"So, Teddy comes from money?"

"I suppose so. His father's a bigwig at one of the steel companies."

Albert coughed. "Ah—have you spoken to the Lupinettis about this?"

She nodded her head. "At length. Mr. and Mrs. Lupi are all in favor of it. But they want me to have a big wedding, and they offered to share costs with Papa." Her eyes misted. "Albert, I can't accept their generosity. That's why we're going to elope. Keep it simple and secret."

Albert opened the kitchen cabinet and began pulling out items. "What are you doing?" asked Alice.

"Helping my twin sister pack for her new life!"

∞ ∞ ∞

The entire town came out for the Harvest celebration. Harriett joined Esther, June, Albert, and their families, arriving as the doors opened. The children scattered to all corners of the room, seeking their friends and playmates among the carved jack-o-lanterns.

Tabs and Olive appeared fashionably late; Olive, hoping to make a grand entrance, smiled, wearing a new pale blue dress and hat, as she walked through the door. Her tall, slim, forty-six-year-old figure maintained a youthful mien, although her blonde curls were frosted with strands of gray. To her dismay, heads did not turn, conversations were not interrupted; the only person taking notice was the attendance clerk who requested one dollar.

Tabs had just enough time to grab a cup of cider for Olive before the room came to a halt. The door opened, and an immediate silence followed the newcomers inside. Alice Bailey Lupinetti emerged on the arm of Theodore Jenson, wearing an orchid corsage and sporting a gigantic diamond ring and wedding band on her left hand. Her right hand was adorned with a stunning ruby-and-diamond ring.

The crowd began mumbling.

"Look at the size of that rock."

"Wonder if they are married?"

"Goodness, flaunting this in the Lupinettis' faces..."

Mr. and Mrs. Lupinetti were the first to greet the couple, with hugs and kisses.

Mr. Lupinetti shook Jenson's hand. "Son, welcome to the

family. We consider Alice our daughter; that makes you our son."

Jenson kissed Mrs. Lupinetti then approached Olive and Tabs. "Mr. and Mrs. Bailey, I promise to love, cherish and provide for your daughter."

Tabs embraced his new son-in-law; Olive grunted. A radiant Alice clung to her husband's arm.

Jenson motioned to a pre-arranged waitstaff to pour and distribute champagne to all adults, sparkling cider to the children. Clicking his glass, the town's new druggist announced. "Campbell County! You have welcomed my apothecary and me with open arms. I consider you my new home. Now, please join me in toasting my beautiful new wife, Alice Bailey Lupinetti Jenson." Jenson raised his goblet. "To the most beautiful woman in the county."

Jenson leaned over, looped his arm around Alice, and scooped her close to his body. He kissed her long and passionately.

The crowd burst into cheers, hoots, catcalls, and whistles. "To Alice and Ted Jenson!"

Harriett's mouth dropped. June and Esther hugged each other while Albert's eyes misted.

Albert mumbled softly. "I'm going to miss her."

Dante Lupinetti stood between Alice and Jenson. Taking each by the hand, he nodded to his wife. "Mrs. Lupinetti and I have a surprise for you young folks." Mrs. Lupinetti placed a large sheet cake on the refreshment table. Mr. Lupinetti continued, "It's not a tiered wedding cake, but consider this cake a token of love from all of my family as we gain a son. To my daughter and her new husband, let's eat cake!"

Olive pursed her lips. Stomping her foot, she grumbled, "How dare he? Alice is *our* daughter, not his!" Olive glared at the Lupinettis, then back at Tabs. "Why were we not part of the planning? Tabs, we're leaving now!"

She reached for Tabs' hand, but he pulled away.

Olive screamed, "Tobias Bailey! Come now, or you shall pay!"

Softly, Tabs responded, "Quiet, Wife. Go, if you wish, but I'm staying for Alice's celebration. Olive, you have never taken an interest in our children's lives; why now? As for your threat, I have been paying my entire life."

Olive gasped as smiles crossed the faces of other party-goers. Many snickered at sneered.

Tabs noticed Olive sulk as she sped across the floor. Stopping before the newlyweds, she grumbled, "Alice, you took careless actions today." Spinning on her heel, she stomped out the door.

Jenson searched Alice's face for a clue to Olive's outburst.

Alice gently kissed his cheek. "Don't worry about her, darling. She's a selfish witch, past her prime. Tonight, she's angry about being upstaged by us."

The crowd stared blankly at the exchange between the Baileys, Lupinettis, and Jensons until Mr. Lupinetti called out, "Cake for everyone! Mangia!"

34

THE FOUR MUSKETEERS
JANUARY 1948

*A*round month eight of Harriett's schooling, her coursework advanced from basic secretarial skills to managerial competencies. The Dean of Students called Harriett into his office.

Harriett knocked on the closed door and waited.

"Enter."

Opening the door, Harriett cautiously approached the bearded man sitting behind a cluttered desk.

He glanced up, "Oh, Miss Bailey, thank you for stopping in." He shuffled his paperwork, pulling a file folder from the bottom of a pile. "Miss Bailey, your work is exceptional. Your skill level in every category is outstanding. Because of your work ethic, I proposed to the Board of Deans the advancement of your completion date." He paused. When Harriett remained silent, he continued. "If you double up your coursework, you shall be able to complete all requirements for graduation by the end of April. You'll be presented your diploma, however, at the commencement ceremony in September with the rest of your class."

Harriett thought for a moment. "Then I'll have a jump on

271

the class in finding a position? Will the school's placement staff support me individually? I know you usually sponsor a job fair over the summer, which shall be of no use to me."

The Dean smiled. "And this logic is why we wish to move you forward. Yes, we shall help you find employment. In fact, you'll have the best offers."

∞ ∞ ∞

Making good on his promise, the Dean of Students arranged for a small job fair in March for his top performers. Ten of the fifty girls attended, most garbed in provocative, brightly colored, tight sweaters, form-fitting skirts, high heels, and shiny red lipstick outlining salacious smiles. Harriett wore a modest ensemble: a pleated, brown, straight skirt, a starched white blouse, brown, low-heeled pumps, and faux pearls. Her wavy, thick, brunette hair was combed away from her cosmetic-free face. It all rendered her virtually forgettable.

Five small- to medium-sized Madison companies furnished interview teams, to whom the school provided an office for privacy and the students' academic records. Each girl was scheduled fifteen minutes per company in which to make an impression.

Harriett stood outside the temporary office of Dugan & Company, one of the larger firms in attendance, waiting for her turn to meet with Thomas Roland. Chief Financial Officer Roland held double duty as personnel supervisor.

After ushering a slim, voluptuous blonde out of his office, Roland watched her wiggle to her next appointment. His eyes still on the blonde, he turned quickly. The six-foot-five Roland never saw tiny Harriett waiting. Literally plowing into her, Harriett bounced backward and landed in a sitting position on the floor.

"Oh my God! I'm so sorry." Roland reached down, extending his hand. "Please, allow me."

Harriett accepted it graciously, stood, smoothed her skirt, then thrust her hand forward for Roland to shake. "Mr. Roland, of Dugan & Co.? I'm Harriett Bailey, your next appointment." Her firm grip displayed confidence and self-assurance.

"Miss Bailey, please excuse my clumsiness. I apologize for the spill. Slightly preoccupied."

Harriett smiled as she handed Roland her resume. "Yes, it was a distracting view."

Roland blushed. "Come in. Miss Bailey."

He took his seat behind the desk and motioned for Harriett to sit. Rifling through the stack of files, he eventually pulled out the one labeled "Harriett Bailey."

"Mr. Roland, if I may—where is your appointment schedule for the day?"

Roland tilted his head curiously but handed Harriett the schedule. She quickly moved to the stack of file folders and placed the folders with names scheduled prior to her on the bottom; she then ordered his remaining folders according to his upcoming appointments.

Turning to Roland, Harriett declared, "You are now ready for the rest of the day." Finally, she sat across from his desk, ready for her interview.

Roland glanced at Harriett's file. "You're the one! Dean told me you were his brightest student, and between what I see on paper, your composure, and your initiative today, I'm convinced. You're perfect for Dugan & Co. May I offer you a job, beginning the first week of May? I believe your classes end in April?"

Harriett inhaled, thinking that getting the job was much easier than expected. "Mr. Roland, before I accept, shall we discuss my work schedule, benefits, and salary?"

Roland laughed. "Miss Bailey, you and I shall get along just fine. Yes, let's review the details before you make a decision."

∞ ∞ ∞

On Harriett's first day at work in Dugan & Company's secretarial pool, Miss Kathryn White, Thomas Roland's personal secretary, led Harriett into the center of a large room populated with about twenty desks and fifteen women. She was introduced to her colleagues, all chatty girls who extended a friendly welcome then walked away.

Kathryn pointed to a desk. "Harriett, you'll be working here. You have a personal typewriter, steno pad, pen, pencil, and letter opener. If you need additional office supplies, such as a stapler or pencil sharpener, they are centrally located to be used by all."

Harriett spent the morning filling out paperwork for the personnel office. At lunchtime, the girls gathered their purses and lunches and left the room giggling, arm in arm, abandoning Harriett to sit alone at her desk. Kathryn White, only a few years her senior, rode the elevator down two levels from the executive floors to check on Harriett.

"Oh, Miss Bailey. Deserted, I see? Why don't you join me for lunch?" Kathryn asked.

"I would be delighted, Miss White." Harriett opened her drawer and pulled out a packed sandwich.

Kathryn, noticing Harriett's bagged food, said, "First off, call me Kathryn. We—the other exec secs and I—usually buy from the cafeteria, though you may bring in your own food. Come now, we only have an hour."

Two floors below the secretary's level, a small café/break room offered soup, sandwiches, and salads for purchase. Twenty or so small round tables provided sitting space for those employees not dining in a restaurant. Middle-aged, plump, jovial Mary Payne and fashion conscience Caroline Smythe sat at a table for three and were already eating.

Kathryn pulled up a fourth chair. "Harriett, introduce yourself; I'm getting in line. Be right back."

Harriett remained standing. Extending her hand, she said, "Pleasure to meet you. I'm Harriett Bailey, new to the secretarial pool."

Mary and Caroline winked at each other and reciprocated the handshake. "Caroline Smythe. I work for Mr. Dennis, the COO."

"Mary Payne. I'm Mr. Dugan's girl Friday." Mary giggled, "So Harriett, you're the new superstar hired at the job fair?"

Harriett blushed. "I don't know about 'superstar' status, but I was hired at the job fair, and I work very hard. I shall try my best to live up to your expectations."

Caroline chewed her salad then giggled. "You already have lived up to our expectations. Look at your dress. You expect to be evaluated on office performance skills...rather than *extracurricular* activities."

The blood rushed up Harriett's neck. "Oh, my, does that sort of thing really happen?"

Both women guffawed.

Caroline placed her hand on Harriett's. "Only with the lower executives. Mr. Roland, Mr. Dugan, and Mr. Dennis are strictly business. Although, they do take notice of the landscape from time to time." Caroline smiled. "They're men, after all, but faithful men."

Kathryn returned in time to hear Caroline's reply. "Surely, dear Harriett, you noticed the other secretaries' attire. A little too tight to sit comfortably through dictation. You, on the other hand, are dressed professionally and sensibly."

Harriett's sandwich caught in her throat. "I'm afraid I don't own an extensive wardrobe. However, the pieces I do own are high quality and mix and match easily to expand my look." She sighed wistfully, "Someday, I'll afford a proper, full closet. In the meantime, I'll make the best of what I have."

"Ladies, go easy on the kid." Turning to Harriett, Kathryn said softly, "You'll be just fine wearing what you own. You may always borrow a scarf or belt from me to spice things up." Kathryn raised her glass of iced tea in a salute, "Here's to the newest member of our little elite circle."

"Why thank you!" Harriett raised her glass to meet Kathryn's. "I've never had girlfriends. This is exciting. I won't let you down!"

35

SPRINGBOARD

SUMMER 1948

*H*arriett's friendship with Kathryn, Mary, and Caroline proved quite valuable. Whenever any of the three executive secretaries needed a day off, they requested Harriett as a replacement—not only out of friendship but because of Harriett's capable skills.

The top floor friendships did not endear Harriett to the other secretaries, who talked incessantly, the sound echoing through the ample hollow space. Harriett began using cotton earplugs to block out the continuous cackling.

One day, she overheard one of the shapelier girls commenting, "Oh, he is just the dreamiest. He only just graduated from high school, but believe you me, he's a man." She waited until the tittering stopped. "Football jock—and oh, I mean jock!" Again her listeners giggled. "A little egotistic. Should have gone to college on a football scholarship, but was screwed over by that tennis bitch from Madison Country Club."

The word tennis caught Harriett's attention. She removed her earplugs and leaned in to hear more clearly.

"That country club crowd are all snobs," said one girl.

Another one retorted, "But if you landed one, you'd be happy to marry him!" More snickering.

The first secretary interrupted, "Let me tell you, this guy is muscles from head to toe. Not to mention something *else* that hangs close to his toes."

"You fiend, you didn't?" The decibel level increased.

"I did, and it was pure delight," she said with a snicker.

"Where's this dreamboat live?"

"Not here; he lives in Campbellsville. He's the all-time record holder in football rushing yards there." Shaking her head, she boasted, "It's just not fair. I could have landed a professional football star. Until I find Mr. Moneybags, I'll be happy to join Eddy for the *ride*." She made a lewd gyration with her hips, and the pool broke into roaring laughter.

They were talking about Eddy Kepler, Harriett realized. She tried not to react to the conversation, but she was surprised how they were talking about him as if he were a sex toy. She had thought only men considered women as such.

∞ ∞ ∞

Every night after her bus ride home from Madison, Harriett helped with supper preparation and clean-up, then hurriedly slipped into shorts and a sleeveless top to run to the school obstacle course. Upon three completions, she jogged the four main streets of Campbellsville, thus maintaining her muscular physique.

On weekends, she often joined other bathers at the swimming hole, a dammed section of the river. At times, she encountered some of her old schoolmates—Keith, Eddy, Jim, and Bobby always had a curvaceous beauty under their arms. Many of the other swimmers were unknown to Harriett, despite Campbellsville being a small town.

One Saturday when the weather was exceptionally warm, Harriett stumbled across a diving contest. Using a rigged springboard, the men and boys rotated turns, trying to impress their dates.

Harriett queued in line, ready to dive, with Eddy Kepler two behind.

"Hey Pip Squeak. This is for jocks only." The rest of the men chuckled.

Placing her hands on her hips, Harriett retorted, "Women are capable athletes. I'm diving."

"I have a dollar that says my dive is better than yours." The guys chimed in, placing their own side bets.

Harriett grinned. "You got a bet." Looking at the others in line, she asked, "Will all of you vote honestly for the best-executed dive? Can you be unbiased?"

"Sure."

"You got it."

"Oh, yeah."

Harriett walked to the end of the board, bounced twice, took three measured steps backward, bounced again, then sprinted forward. She flexed her knees into the board, propelling herself upwards. At the top of the apex, she spun into a somersault in midair then came out bent forward, touching her toes. She threw her legs into the air and entered the water perpendicularly, making only a tiny splash.

The crowd stood staring in awe at the perfect dive from the tiny woman.

As she surfaced, Eddy threw his hands in the air. "Hell, you win! I'm not going to try to beat that dive; I'd kill myself."

Climbing out of the water, Harriett grabbed her towel, wrapping it around her petite form.

"Kepler, I never took you for a coward," said Harriett. Hoots and whistles followed.

"I know when I'm bested. Here's your buck, Pip Squeak. Don't spend it all in one place." Eddy received back pats, arm punches, and general teasing. No one but Eddy bothered to compliment Harriett on her flawless execution.

Unphased, accustomed to being ignored, Harriett collected her money and continued diving for a while, then jumped on Albert's bicycle and rode home to prepare for Monday's work.

∞ ∞ ∞

During Monday's lunchtime with Caroline, Mary, and Kathryn, Harriett mentioned casually. "I think I'll enroll in a class this semester. I have an associate degree, but a bachelor's degree is my real goal."

Caroline passed around a bowl of plums before asking. "Why didn't you go directly for your B.A.? Why settle on an associate?"

Harriett lowered her head. "Because I need an income. Mother would never pay for my college, even if she had the money to do so. I need to support myself and pay for my education, too."

Her three companions bobbed their heads in acknowledgment. Harriett continued, "I saved all summer; I think I have enough to pay for one class."

Mary sat thinking. "Harriett, how many credits do you need?"

Harriett frowned. "Geez, I need at least sixty credits for my B.A. If I take one course each semester, year-round, it's going to take over six years to complete my degree. I need to get started now."

Mary scratched her head. "Don't hold me to this, but I may have a way to help you with tuition."

"That would be fantastic, but I won't hold you to

anything." Harriett let out a deep sigh. "I love school, but I don't want to graduate when I'm forty."

"And what's wrong with being forty?" Caroline poked Harriett's arm.

The blood rushed to Harriett's face. "Ah—I didn't..."

"I'm teasing you. How old are you, twenty?"

"I'm eighteen. But don't you dare tell anyone! They moved me ahead in school, and I finished my associate classes four months early."

A barrage of rolled-up napkins went flying at Harriett.

∞ ∞ ∞

On Wednesday, Harriett arrived at lunch to find Mary grinning, ear to ear. "Sit down Harriett, I have some news."

Harriett breathed deeply and slowly as she sat.

Mary went on, "There is a program in place for the junior executive men who wish to obtain a college degree. The company will match every dollar spent by the employee toward education, provided that employee sign a contract to continue employment with Dugan & Co. for the same number of years as those spent in school."

Harriett's leg began bouncing up and down. "Do I have a chance as a female?"

"They have never extended this program to a woman, basically because they've never had a woman interested in education. Mr. Dugan has agreed to offer you this benefit, provided you agree to the employment contract."

Harriett burst out, "Even if I'm just a secretary?"

Caroline chuckled. "Honey, you've worked for all three big wigs. They already have their eye on you for bigger and better things."

Mary nodded. "This is their way of keeping a great asset. Trust me, Dugan & Co. gets the best end of the deal."

Harriett jumped up from her seat. Hugging all three women, she said, "I think this is a win-win. I can't thank you enough."

"Maybe now you can afford to take two courses each term and finish your degree in three-plus years."

The tears streamed from Harriett's eyes.

36

MOVING UP

JUNE 1950

*H*arriett sat at her desk in the secretarial pool, earplugs inserted, typing an internal financial year-end summary. It was a favor to her friend Kathryn, who was overwhelmed with the fiscal year-end stockholder reports. Harriett was an *upstairs* regular, often working for the executive team.

The lead secretary, Miss Jones—an elderly spinster who wore round wire glasses on the end of her nose—answered the ringing phone on the main desk.

"Harriett Bailey," she called in an unsteady voice.

Engrossed in her work, Harriett ignored the summons.

"Harriett Bailey," Miss Jones called again. A tap on her shoulder finally brought Harriett to attention. "You have a phone call from the top floor."

Several of the girls rolled their eyes.

"Why does she always get called up?"

"I've been here longer than her!"

"What a suck-up!"

Harriett locked the documents in her desk drawer, arousing curiosity among several girls, then headed for the stairs. Although the building had an elevator, Harriett preferred the stairs for the extra exercise.

Knocking on Mr. Roland's door, she waited to be invited in. "Miss Bailey, enter, please. Have a seat." Roland waved his hand in the direction of an oversized chair. Harriett sat, steno pad and pen ready for whatever was in store. "How's your degree coming along, Miss Bailey?"

Harriett smiled, surprised by the question. "Quite well, Mr. Roland. I'll have my bachelor's in another two years."

Roland pursed his lips. "Are you capable of handling school, plus extra responsibility at work?"

Harriett tipped her head to the side. "Will it mean longer work hours?"

"No, still nine to five. Nothing to take home. But I would like to offer you the position of lead secretary. Miss. Jones is retiring." Roland chuckled. "I'd like you to replace her."

"I'd like that very much." Harriett extended her hand to Roland.

Laughing, Roland shook the firm grip. "You keep at this, Miss Bailey, and you'll be running this company someday." He laughed, "Don't you want to know your new rate?"

Harriett shook her head. "I'm contracted to work for Dugan & Co. I trust you'll be fair." She grinned. "And if you're not, I'll be sure to tell you."

∞ ∞ ∞

Two weeks later, the retirement of Miss Jones was announced. Kathryn organized a party for Thursday afternoon with cake, ice cream, and a monetary parting gift to be attended by the production floor, junior executives, the three senior executives, and, of course, all the secretaries. Miss Jones would pack and leave on Friday.

Mary and Caroline served cake as Mr. Dugan took the

podium. "Ladies and gentlemen, we are here today to celebrate the long and prosperous career of our beloved Miss Jones, lead secretary. Miss Jones began working at Dugan & Company in 1925..."

Caroline whispered, "Do you know who is taking her place?"

"I know who *should* get it, and I can guess who will get it. They are not always the same person."

Dugan rambled on, "...Miss Jones, we wish you a long and prosperous retirement."

Employees politely applauded their good wishes.

Dugan cleared his throat. "Now, I know all of you are anxiously awaiting the announcement of Miss Jones's replacement. I am pleased to announce that Miss Harriett Bailey shall be head of secretaries. Ladies, be on your best behavior; I'm sure Miss Bailey shall run a tight ship. Please join me in congratulating Miss Bailey on her promotion."

Kathryn, Caroline, Mary, Mr. Dugan, Mr. Dennis, and Mr. Roland applauded with enthusiasm. The junior executives and production staff clapped civilly, while the secretaries moaned and grumbled.

"She'll put an end to any non-work-related fun. She's a tightass, that one," said a junior exec.

One of the more flirtatious secretaries grumbled, "You've got to be kidding me. Goodie-two-shoes Bailey is now my boss. Isn't that just peachy!"

Mr. Roland took the podium. "Miss Bailey, well done. Would you like to say a few words?"

"Thank you, Mr. Roland. Today, I shall simply say best wishes to Miss Jones, and thank you for trusting me with this responsibility. To the secretaries, I shall outline some new policies on Monday."

∞ ∞ ∞

Harriett decided to splurge after work by going shopping. The stores in Madison remained open late on Monday and Thursday nights, with bus service running accordingly. The sky was light at five o'clock when Harriett punched out. Leaving the building, she turned left on Main Street and headed toward Gimbles, Madison's largest department store.

As if on a mission, Harriett entered the side door, marching toward linens. Her mission was interrupted as she passed a display of freshly roasted nuts. The aroma of warm, roasted cashews was too overwhelming; it delivered the expected impulse purchase. Nuts in hand, Harriett took the escalator to the fourth floor, found the bedding department, and scoured for a new spread and curtains for her bedroom. She chose a pretty yellow floral print set, made her purchase, and was home tardy by only thirty minutes.

Olive yelled as the back door opened. "Where have you been? Your sandwich is on the table."

Harriett rolled her eyes. "I went shopping after work." Holding up her new bedspread, she walked past Olive and started toward the stairs. "Mother, I work hard, I study hard, and I got a promotion today. I deserve one night off to buy myself something nice. That spread on my bed is from 1920; it's thirty years old."

Olive called after her. "Don't waste that sandwich. As for the bedspread, it's perfectly fine. Don't you dare throw it out. I'll give it to your father."

37

NOT AGAIN?

JUNE 1950

*A*bigail Kepler stirred a pot of beef stew. Earl, her oldest son, was visiting all week from Pittsburgh. He joined husband Edgar Sr. around the large pedestal table. In the past, seven men and one woman surrounded the dining room centerpiece. It seemed empty with just four.

All her boys, except Eddy and Earl, married after the war. Earl, a sworn bachelor, landed the position of lead linesman for the phone company, a direct result of his job as a radio operator in the Navy.

Filling the corner of the dining room, a large Zenith radio, gifted from Earl, reported the evening news.

The announcer finished his story "...as such, Communist North Korea has disregarded treaty agreements, and crossed over the 38th parallel into South Korea. President Truman has agreed to support United Nations measures by sending troops into Korea as retaliation for the breach."

The news caught Earl's attention. "Hey, Eddy, get in here! You need to catch the news." Earl stepped outside, calling to his brother.

A shirtless Eddy was waxing his older-model sport coupe,

his since senior year of high school. It was a rare toy for a boy his age.

Glancing briefly at Earl, he said, "I'm busy. I can't let the wax dry before I buff it out. I have a hot date with an older woman tomorrow."

Earl grumbled, observing his brother's muscles. "Well, if you're not proactive this time, it won't just be a football scholarship you'll miss out on."

Grabbing a wet sponge, Eddy threw it at Earl. "Shut the crap up about football." His arms twitched with rage.

"Eddy, I know you're making good money working in the mill, but you screwed yourself; you should be playing pro ball." Earl frowned in disgust. "You're irresponsible, my little brother."

Eddy turned red and hoisted his water bucket, throwing container and all at Earl. "Shut the fuck up, Earl!"

Abigail, hearing the outburst through open windows, appeared in the doorway. "Edgar Gregor Kepler junior, watch your mouth! Both of you inside; dinner is ready."

"I'll be in when my car's done." Eddy returned to rubbing.

"Then you'll eat cold stew." Abigail returned to her kitchen to ladle her meal.

Fifteen minutes passed before Eddy sauntered into the dining room, pulled out a chair, and sat down. "Mmm, this smells good, Mom."

"Wash your hands and remove your hat, Eddy. I've taught you better than this!" Abigail grimaced.

Freshly groomed and washed, Eddy returned and sat down to shovel spoonfuls of stew into his mouth.

Earl reiterated his initial request. "Eddy, listen to the news tonight before you go out."

"What's crawling up your ass? I'm hungry; let me eat."

Earl placed his spoon on the table. "The US is about to go

back to war. If you want to avoid the draft, I suggest you think about getting married."

Stew spewed out of Eddy's mouth. "Hell no! I'm having too much fun playing the field. I go through a new girl each week." He flushed, then wiped the table with his paper towel napkin. "What makes you think marriage will help me dodge the draft? Married men served in the last war."

"I heard my CO talking about it. He said too many children were orphaned last time, so the next draft would be single guys only." Earl resumed eating.

Eddy scratched the top of his head. "That sounds like a bunch of bullshit."

"Edgar." Abigail moaned. "Even if it's just hearsay, isn't it worth a try? I don't want another soldier son."

Eddy turned to his father. "What do you think, Dad?"

Edgar Sr. chuckled. "I like playing the field as much as any other man…"

Abigail hung her head frowning, well aware of her husband's transgressions.

"…and marriage can be a drag. But it's possible to have the best of both worlds." The senior Kepler smirked, looking directly at his wife.

Abigail held back her tears, slowly slid away her chair to retreat to the kitchen.

Earl glared at both father and brother. "Must you be so crude in front of Mom?"

"Son, the facts are the facts. She knows what I'm like. She can take it and stay, or leave."

Eddy sat thinking. "Dad, you really do upset Mom. I suppose if I did get married, the right thing is to be faithful."

"Damn right it is. A wife deserves a husband's loyalty," Earl said directly to his father, then stood. "I'll be back. I'm checking on Mom."

"But there is no girl in Campbellsville worth marrying,"

Eddy said. "If I'm going to even consider this, I don't want to marry a floozy. I want someone worth her weight in salt."

"Suit yourself, son. It's your death, either way!" Edgar Sr. roared, laughing at his own joke.

Earl returned, shaking his head. "Don't know what's so funny, Dad, but Eddy, the fact remains. You need a wife, and you need one soon. War is hell. Even distanced from the front line on a boat, I experienced it. Marriage is a small sacrifice to escape fighting." Smiling, Earl added, "And it definitely has advantages."

Eddy finished eating, leaving his dishes on the table. Mumbling to himself, he bolted out the door.

"I'm going out," he said. "If I'm forced into finding a wife, I at least intend to have a couple weeks of fun. Then I'll look for a candidate."

Speeding down Pine Street past the Apothecary and Lupinetti's grocery, Eddy spotted Harriett Bailey exiting the bakery carrying two boxes.

"Damn—there's your answer," he said aloud. "I'll start working on her tomorrow. Tonight, I party!"

∞ ∞ ∞

Harriett called out as she entered the kitchen, "Papa, Mother, they canceled my second class tonight, so I'm home early." No one answered. She placed her pastries on the table and went in search of her parents. Walking back outside, she called again, "Papa?"

Tabs answered, "Hi Janie, I'm in the garden. You're home early tonight."

Harriett walked to the top of the yard to find Tabs standing beside a pile of pulled weeds. "Papa, the bakery was open when I walked past. I bought us some pastries." Her voice lilted teasingly. "Can I convince you to have a cup of tea and a scone?"

"Did you eat your supper?"

"Yes, I ate an egg salad sandwich before my first class. Second class was canceled. How 'bout it? Tea?"

Tabs bent down to collect his weeds. "Absolutely. Allow me to tidy up, and I'll meet you under the grapevine. Oh, better call your mother. You know she has a sweet tooth."

Back in the house, Harriett put the kettle on the stove, then found Olive hiding in her private parlor. Knocking on the door, she stuck in her head. "Mother, I'm making tea and I brought home treats. Will you join Papa and me outside?"

Olive scowled at her daughter. "Bring mine in here."

She brought her mother a plate, then, carrying a tray of scones, tarts, a teapot, and cups, Harriett joined Tabs on the Adirondacks.

"Here, Papa." Harriett handed Tabs a cup.

"Thank you, Janie. Is your mother coming out?" Tabs reached for a tart. "Yum, lemon, my favorite."

Harriett furrowed her brow. "Mother is staying inside. I swear she deliberately avoids me."

Tabs sipped his tea before speaking. "No, she's spent a lifetime shunning me, as well. You just happen to always be with me, my darling daughter." Smiling at Harriett, he took her hand. "I was so in love with your mother. Geez, she was a beautiful angel, the prettiest thing I'd ever seen. More beautiful than Alice, but don't tell your sister."

Harriett squeezed her father's hand. "I know you've had your own bedroom for—well, my entire lifetime. What happened to cause that?"

Tabs bit his lip. "I'm reluctant to say."

"Please, Papa, I'm only trying to understand."

Tabs withdrew his hand. "Janie, your mother kicked me

out of her bedroom when she discovered she was pregnant with you."

Harriett gasped. "What?"

Her father nodded but stayed silent, giving her mind time to think. Several minutes passed before Harriett spoke.

"She does hate me, then, and *I'm* the cause of your unhappiness. Oh, Papa, I'm so so very sorry." The tears flowed freely, dripping into her teacup.

Tabs knelt before his daughter. "Janie, don't ever feel guilty. You are not the reason I sleep alone. That is your mother's doing. It was inevitable; her pregnancy just sped things along." Tabs hung his head. "Darling daughter Janie, you are the light of my world. You have given me so much happiness. Please forgive me for answering your question."

Harriett pressed on. "When I was a child, I overheard you tell Esther that she was born before you married Mother. Why did you wait so long to marry her?"

Tabs smiled sadly. "We were betrothed. Olive seduced me. I don't blame her. I was weak; I should have resisted. It was her first time, and she got pregnant. In her mind, she ruined any chance for higher education." Tabs paused. "She so wanted to go to college, to be a doctor. And she would have been a brilliant one."

"So she blamed you?"

Sighing deeply, Tabs confessed. "She blamed both of us. We finally married when she could no longer tolerate living with her father. Then June came, then Albert and Alice." Tabs reached for another sweet. "Olive was to return to school when Alice started first grade. But that's when we realized she was pregnant with you. It put an end to all her plans."

"I see. So all these years, she's resented me and punished you. My suspicions were correct."

"Yes, I suppose they were."

Father and daughter sat in silence, holding hands until the moon was high in the sky.

∞ ∞ ∞

Wednesday found Harriett in a melancholy mood. Rather than joining her three friends for lunch, she took her sandwich outside, sat on a wall, and ate alone. Thoughts of rectifying her father's predicament filled her every moment. *If I leave and find my own place, then he'll be able to mollify Mother. I won't be around to aggravate her, to remind her of what she lost.*

Back at her desk, Harriett searched her purse for a folded piece of paper. She dialed the number; it rang three times before a voice answered.

"Judith Reven."

Harriett sighed deeply, paused, then said, "Miss Reven, it's Harriett Bailey, from Campbellsville High School."

The voice on the line was bright and cheery. "Why, Miss Bailey, what a surprise! I'm delighted you called. May I help you with anything?"

"I'm working in Madison now. I thought, perhaps, we could meet for a cup of coffee or tea after work today?" Pausing again, Harriett added, "I only have thirty minutes before class, but I was hoping to talk. Is it possible to meet on campus?"

Madison College, known as a teacher's college, boasted an exceptional business department. Scooping a local renowned finance expert, the college offered both undergraduate and graduate degrees in business finance. The charming campus of dormitories, library, student union, classrooms, fraternity and sorority buildings spread over the west end of Madison, intertwining parks, stone walkways, and beautiful outdoor spaces for students and faculty alike.

"Yes, dear. Name the place and time. By the way, I'm delighted you are continuing your education."

Harriett chose the picnic area outside the campus student center, hoping to enjoy the warm summer evening. Judith Reven arrived promptly; she had tanned skin and was impeccably dressed. She warmly greeted Harriett.

"Since we are on a strict time frame, Harriett, what's on your mind?"

Harriett wiped her sweaty palms on her skirt. "I didn't know who else to ask. I wondered why you never got married?"

"I guess that's getting straight to it," Judith blurted out in surprise, then laughed. "I enjoy the freedom of being alone. I am self-sufficient, financially independent." She paused. "Don't misunderstand; I enjoy being around people, but I don't need to be with a crowd. Does that make sense?"

Harriett nodded. "Yes it does."

Judith took Harriett's hand. "Dear, it looks like you need to do some soul searching. My only advice to you is this: be able to support yourself financially. If you achieve that, then you can pick and choose the rest of your lifestyle. Don't ever become dependent on a man for money. It's a death trap."

Harriett glanced at her watch. "Goodness, it's time for class. I never bought you a coffee."

"I'm happy you called, my tiny friend. Please don't be a stranger. I'd love to resume our tennis games if you can find the time between work and studies! I'm proud of you, Harriett. Stay true to yourself."

Judith hugged the petite Bailey, who scampered off to class.

Harriett muddled through class preoccupied. Returning home on the late bus, she dragged herself up the street, feeling exhausted. Both Tabs and Olive sat in the kitchen drinking tea. Harriett noticed Olive's smile faded to a frown when she walked through the door.

"Janie, there are a few tarts left over from yesterday. How about some tea?" Tabs poured without an answer, handed Harriett a cup, and began rolling a cigarette.

"Sure, why not. I'll have a snack, then go up to study." She ran her hands through her hair and yawned. "I'm tired tonight."

Harriett was interrupted by a knock on the front door. The trio looked at each other.

"Who in the name of heavens is knocking on my front door this late at night?" Olive questioned her husband.

Tabs shrugged. "You two stay here. I'll get the door." Olive watched hawk-like, ensuring no loose tobacco was littered down the hallway.

"Janie," Tabs called. "You have a visitor, sweetie. Won't you come in, sir?"

Harriett looked at Olive, who snapped back, "Don't look at me; go get rid of whoever it is. I don't want strangers lurking around my house, checking out what they can steal."

Harriett smoothed her locks, then moved cautiously toward the door. Her only friends were her siblings and the three executive secretaries in Madison. A visitor at any time of the day was a surprise. She was ill-prepared for the shock of finding a male visitor standing in the foyer late at night.

"Eddy Kepler?" Harriett's mouth dropped. "How may I help you?"

Eddy grinned a charming Kepler smile. "Hi, Pip Squeak. It's been a while since I last saw you at the swimming hole. How are you?" Harriett stared back, unable to form a response. Eddy continued, "So Pip Squeak, who's Janie?"

Stammering, Harriett squinted her eyes and said, "Janie is my middle name. It's my father's pet name. Eddy, is there something I can help you with?"

She clenched one fist, inwardly regretting sharing such personal information.

Eddy took a breath, trying to calm his nerves. *Why does she make me so nervous?* "I thought maybe we'd go on a date, to the late show. Tonight?"

Harriett cocked her head. "Tonight? Absolutely not. I couldn't possibly go out tonight. I'm up early for work. My day starts at five-thirty, and I still have to study tonight."

"Did you just say *no*?" Unfamiliar with rejection, Eddy sarcastically continued, "Oh, the career woman. I forgot that you have a big important job. So sorry to impose, *Janie!*"

Harriett bit her lip, inhaled, and headed into uncharted territory. Speaking with confidence, she said, "Please, never call me 'Janie' again. You may, however, pick me up Saturday night at seven. I'll happily go to the early show. I want to be in by eleven."

Eddy glared at the petite girl, then exhaled. "Fine. It's a date. I'll pick you up Saturday." He turned quickly and rushed toward the door.

Harriett stopped him. "Eddy, please use the back door. Mother despises using the front door. I'm only permitted to receive guests through the kitchen."

Eddy exited quickly as Harriett walked into the kitchen with a blank expression on her face.

Tabs asked, "What did that young Kepler boy want with you, Janie?"

"We are going on a date, Saturday night."

Tabs sucked in his cheeks, gently placing his arms around his daughter. "Be careful, darling Janie. He's no gentleman. That boy has a reputation to rival his father. He's a ne'er-do-well that has no respect for women. I don't like the thoughts of you alone with him."

Olive cackled. "That Tomcat offspring of Abigail and Edgar Kepler asked Harriett out on a date?" She laughed heartily. "Pious Harriett, who thinks she's so much better than the rest of us, with the fancy job and her hoity-toity education? This is rich." Olive sipped her tea as Harriett stared dumbfounded. "Yes, Harriett, you go out with young Kepler, who only wants one thing. You'll end up pregnant, just like Esther. Throw it all away."

Harriett fought the blood rushing to her head. She looked at her father then glared at her mother. "You mean end up pregnant like you did? Yes, we all know you were pregnant before you were married."

Olive spit. "Why, you insolent little slut."

"Don't you dare call me a slut. You were the slut, seducing Papa, then blaming him when you ended in a *family way*. I shall date whomever I wish. And I guarantee that I shall do things in the *correct* order, marry first, then have children. You'll not catch me following in your footsteps—any of them. I'm determined to get my degree, no matter what. And I shall!" Harriett looked at Tabs. "I'm sorry, Papa, I've taken enough abuse. Now, if you'll excuse me, I have to study."

She left Tabs in the kitchen grinning at Olive, who was spewing steam.

∞ ∞ ∞

Eddy walked into the house to find Earl alone at the table. Going to the refrigerator and grabbing a beer, he flipped up the tab.

"My god Earl, I don't think marriage is worth the effort."

Earl rolled his eyes. "Please, enlighten me."

Eddy gulped a swig. "First off, she refused to go out tonight, some lame excuse about being up early for work."

"Brother, that sounds like a sensible woman."

"Then she *told* me to pick her up Saturday for the early show. She wants to be in by eleven. Christ sakes, she's twenty years old. What adult woman has to be in before midnight?"

Earl just smiled. "Perhaps she needs her beauty sleep?"

"Be serious, Earl. She's not even a looker. She's pretty, though no Greta Garbo. Tiny, has a cute butt, soft wavy brown hair, steel blue eyes, athletic—I mean real muscles..."

"For not being interested in this girl, you noticed quite a few details, Eddy."

Eddy threw his empty beer can at Earl. "Get me another one. She told me to use the back door, something about *no visitors through the front door*. Holy shit!"

Earl handed Eddy a second beer. "If you ask me, she sounds like suitable wife material. If you cast her aside, maybe I'll give her a look."

"Like hell you will. If I have to get married to escape the draft, Pip Squeak is the one for me."

Earl doubled over. "Eddy, you have a pet name? Don't you realize you already have a crush on her?"

∞ ∞ ∞

On Thursday, Harriett met her friends for lunch in the cafeteria. The three, already eating, welcomed their young understudy.

Caroline asked, without looking up, "Where were you yesterday?"

Harriett unwrapped her sandwich. "I needed to be alone to think."

"About what?"

"Family stuff. But I have some news that I may share with you. I'm going on a date Saturday night."

Kathryn stopped chewing. "What's this about a date?"

Blushing, Harriett admitted, "I've never been on a date before."

"No! Get out. A pretty little thing like you?" Caroline finally glanced up. "Who's the guy? Someone from work? What are you wearing? Are you buying a new dress?"

Kathryn chuckled. "Slow down, Caroline. It sounds like you're more excited than Harriett."

Harriett dropped her sandwich. "Do you think I need to buy a new dress?" She bit her lip. "I never gave it a thought."

"That depends. How much do you like this guy? Do you want to impress him?"

"Well, maybe not him. But he is the most popular boy in Campbellsville, maybe even in Madison, so being seen with him might encourage other boys to ask me out. I'm twenty; it's high time I find a proper beau."

Mary shook her head. "Why do you want a beau? You're making money, working on your degree; you don't need a man."

Harriett sighed. "You're right; I don't *need* a man, thank goodness for that. But—I actually *want* a man. I've thought long and hard; I don't want to grow old and be alone."

The four women smiled. Kathryn was the first to speak. "Then you need to buy a new dress. Something cute, something pretty, something not necessarily for work."

"Oh boy, I don't know if I can spend money frivolously on clothing."

"Today is payday; the stores are open late. Go get yourself something new. You deserve it, date or no date!"

Harriett grinned. "Okay, I'll do it. I don't have class tonight, so I have time to shop. Do I head to Gimbles, or is there a dress shop you recommend?"

Caroline nodded to Mary, who replied. "Start with Gimbles. I bet you find something there, and maybe even on sale. Will you consider a lipstick, too?"

"I've never worn makeup."

"We know." The three women laughed. "Try a shade of

red. Cherries in the Snow is a pretty Revlon color. I bet it brings out your eyes and will look stunning with your hair. Also, consider an eyebrow pencil."

Harriett's mouth dropped. "I need an eyebrow pencil too?"

Kathryn interjected. "Come up to see us this afternoon. There are some fashion magazines in the waiting area. We can scan them for ideas."

∞ ∞ ∞

The phone at the central secretary's desk rang around four-thirty. "Secretarial Pool, Harriett Bailey, lead secretary speaking."

"Harriett, it's Kathryn," the voice on the line said. "Wait for the elevator to go past, then come on up. Mr. Roland and Mr. Dennis are on their way out. Mr. Dugan never showed today."

Harriett watched through the window. Once the elevator cleared the fourth floor, she sprinted up two flights of stairs.

Barely breathing heavily, she greeted her friends. "I'm ready. Educate me."

The four women gathered around a stack of magazines, scanning articles and advertisements. Kathryn spotted the Revlon ad. "Look, Harriett, isn't that a nice shade?" She pointed to the lipstick on a slender model.

Harriett pondered. "You're right. My face could use some color. Now, explain to me how you use an eyebrow pencil?"

The trio of exec secs diagramed the proper arch and shading to their naïve understudy.

"How do they get their cheeks so pink?" Harriett pointed to a different photo.

Mary laughed. "My goodness, you've led a sheltered life. That's rouge, didn't your mother ever share with you?

Harriett guffawed. "Please. Don't mention my mother. She's the whole reason I need to get out of the house."

Caroline grabbed Harriett by the arm. "You never said anything about moving out. What's this about?"

Frowning, Harriett pulled back. "Never mind. Forget I said that. Now, what's the latest dress style?"

∞ ∞ ∞

Harriett punched out and headed to her bank; cashing her check, she set aside ten dollars for her indulgences. An over-powering smell of spices, musk, and floral bombarded her as she entered Gimbles' main door into the cosmetic depart-ment. She stopped at the Revlon counter, checking the lipstick prices before heading back to dresses. If she didn't have enough money, she decided she would pass on the eyebrows, but wanted to be sure to purchase a lipstick.

Never indecisive, Harriett skimmed through a rack of sleeveless cotton summer dresses. Many were bright colors and floral prints, too impractical. She kept searching for one she could wear with a cardigan to work. A navy-blue dress with large white polka dots caught her eye. It was cinched at the waist with a broad white belt. She tried it on; her tiny frame looked darling in the dress.

Harriett carried the dress to a waiting clerk. "How much, please?"

She tried to not react when the woman answered, "Eight dollars, fifty cents."

She only paused a moment. "I'll take it."

The clerk wrapped the dress and placed it into a shopping bag. Harriett bounced her way to the down escalator. She absentmindedly exited on the next floor: shoes.

"Hello Miss, may I help you find something?" Startled, Harriett turned to see a woman standing behind her. "Are you matching a dress? May I look?" Before Harriett responded, the clerk peeked into her shopping bag. Spotting the white dots, she led Harriett to a pair of low-heeled, white sandals. "These are a perfect match."

"Oh no, not white. Too impractical. Can't be worn before Memorial Day or after Labor Day. I need something that also serves as a work shoe."

The clerk frowned, looking at the low brown pumps on Harriett's feet. "Maybe a navy blue T-strap? This heel is lower, but the shoe is more stylish than the one you're wearing."

Harriett tried on the T-straps. Looking in the mirror, she decided, *Why not? I'm worth it*. "How much, please?"

"Four dollars fifty cents."

Harriett sucked on her lower lip, then dug into her wallet. Pulling out a five-dollar bill, she bought the shoes.

Her last stop was the lipstick counter. "A tube of Cherries in the Snow, please?" she asked.

"Oh, I'm so sorry, Miss, I'm sold out, but I have this shade from Elizabeth Arden that is very close to it." The cosmetician opened a tube of perfectly shaped, creamy red lipstick.

Harriett was determined not to spend over fifteen dollars total on her first date. "The price please?"

"Only two dollars twenty-five cents."

Harriett gasped. "That's thrice the price of the Revlon brand. I'm sorry, no, thank you. Where is the nearest store that I might buy Cherries in the Snow?"

The clerk scowled. "One moment, please, I'll check our back stock." She opened the cabinet door and miraculously discovered a tube of Cherries in the Snow at the price of seventy-five cents.

Harriett carried her shopping bags, skipping lightly, all the way to the bus stop. The forty-five-minute ride home sped by quickly with Harriett deep in thought about her purchases, the anticipation of a date, and the prospect of her life opening up to a male companion other than Eddy Kepler.

Finding the kitchen dark when she arrived home, she called out, "Papa. Mother. I'm home." No answer. The wall clock read ten-fifteen—too early for both to be in bed.

She climbed the stairs with less spring in her step. "Goodnight," she whispered as she passed the gentle purring noise coming through her father's closed door. Olive's door remained open; Harriett peeked inside. The bedroom was empty.

38

THE DATE

*S*aturday morning, Harriett awoke from a restless night of sleep. She slowly removed the bobby pins from her pin curls, trying not to tug on her thick hair. The girls under her charge at Dugan & Co. spoke of sleeping on hair rollers and the morning headaches they caused. Pin curls were suitable for Harriett.

Slipping on a top and pair of shorts, she made her way to the kitchen and the smell of bacon.

"Papa, good morning—and yum." She smiled at Tabs, busy with his skillet. "Why the treat?"

"Good morning, Janie darling." Tabs returned the grin. "I thought I'll placate your mother. She's been in a foul mood."

Harriett frowned. "That is most likely my fault. I'll apologize to her. Perhaps that's what she needs." She crunched on a crispy piece of meat.

Tabs laughed out loud. "You can try. I'm too much the gentleman to say what she really needs."

Olive, still in her nightgown, entered the kitchen yawning, arms above her head. "Who needs what?"

Tabs raised his eyebrows, Harriett responded without hesitation. "I need to borrow a white cardigan sweater from Esther for my date tonight." She winked at her father.

Olive grunted, grabbed several bacon pieces, poured a cup of tea, and headed for her parlor.

"Mother, before you leave...I'm sorry for yelling back at you the other night."

Olive stared blankly at Harriett, grunted, "Are you really?" then left the room.

Handing Harriett a plate of bacon, Tabs gently placed his hand on her shoulder. "Sorry, Janie. I didn't think she'd accept an apology. Goodness knows she owes you one, too."

∞ ∞ ∞

The day dragged. Harriett spent the afternoon under the grapevine, enjoying the gentle breeze and studying. She grabbed a quick sandwich before taking her bath and dressing for her date.

At seven o'clock sharp, Eddy knocked on the back door. At the sight of Harriett, Eddy inhaled. *She cleans up nicely. She's actually a doll.* Harriett wore her new blue and white dress, T-strap heels, and a white sweater draped over her shoulders, fastened with a faux pearl sweater clip.

"You look nice. Let's go."

Eddy bounded back to the car. Jumping into the driver's seat, he turned the ignition.

Harriett called her goodbyes, went to the passenger door, and stood. Looking out the window, Eddy figured she'd never ridden in a car. He pointed to the door handle, but Harriett stood firm.

What the hell? After several moments of Harriett standing still, it dawned on Eddy. *She's waiting for me to open the damn door. Good God!* Eddy dutifully got out of the running car, then opened and held Harriett's door.

"Thank you."

"What's your pleasure?" Eddy asked, ready to spout all drive-in options.

Harriett cut him off. "The seven-thirty show at the Crown Theater would be lovely."

Each month, the Crown Theater offered two viewing screens, one A movie, one B, thus promoting maximum patronage. This month's features, both headliners, were *The Big Lift*, starring Montgomery Clift and Paul Douglass, and *Annie Get Your Gun*, with Betty Hutton and Benay Venuta.

Eddy took the circuitous route to the theater, leaving Harriett wondering if he was showing off his date or building up the courage to continue. Finally, they arrived; Eddy parked the car. Jumping out, he sprinted to the box office to purchase tickets.

"Two adults for *The Big Lift*." He looked around. "That okay with—where the hell is she?"

Harriett remained sitting in the car. Eddy stared, dumbfounded. Slowly, he walked back to the car, opened the door, and presented his hand.

"Thank you," she said again.

"Are we going to do this every single time?"

Harriett smiled. "A man cannot be a gentleman if the woman is not a lady."

"I guess I've been schooled." Eddy burst out laughing. He offered Harriett his arm and led her into the doorway labeled *"The Big Lift."*

Harriett hid her disappointment in watching a war movie. Eddy excitedly admitted, "I love shoot-em-ups."

Heads turned as they entered the theater. No one in Campbellsville expected to see Eddy with Harriett Bailey on his arm. Eddy headed to the mezzanine.

Harriett tugged on Eddy's arm. "No, Eddy. Not up there, I prefer to sit on the main floor."

Leading her to a middle row, Eddy asked, "Do these seats suit your royal highness?"

"Yes, thank you." Before sitting, Harriett inspected the worn red fabric for debris that might stain her dress.

As they sat, someone called out. "Kepler, no drive-in tonight? I thought Saturdays were your hot-and-heavy, get-it-on nights."

Eddy laughed. "Not tonight; I'm here with a *lady*."

"You've got to be kidding? Where did *you* find a lady? You don't run in those circles."

The banter continued. "I'm here with Harriett Bailey. Strictly good girls for me."

"Bailey? Raggedy Anne?"

Eddy looked at Harriett before he answered. "You'd never recognize her. She's actually a looker."

"Yeah right. She's the last girl I'd be caught dead with."

"Your loss, my gain," Eddy said with bravado, imagining he defended Harriett.

Harriett sat mortified. *Slim chance of other boys asking me out now.*

"Eddy," Harriett braved after several moments of silence. "Do you mind sharing a Coca-Cola?"

Eddy moaned but acquiesced. Harriett overheard another exchange about Eddy's conversion to good girls. *That's strange*, she thought; *the comment makes no sense.* As she waited, she looked up and back, glimpsing a couple already necking in the mezzanine. "My goodness!" she said aloud.

Eddy returned with a Coca-Cola and popcorn as the projector began to hum. The heavy velvet curtains drew open to a flickering screen showing previews of upcoming movies followed by a newsreel of the trouble brewing in North Korea. The audience groaned.

Harriett watched the movie with butterflies mounting in her stomach. Careful not to drop the buttery popcorn on her dress, Harriett allowed Eddy to hold her hand. As Eddy's fingers entwined in hers, her body tingled, then he smiled at her, the infamous Eddy Kepler smile. Harriett responded with a smile, her stomach doing internal flip-flops. Eddy Kepler had scored a direct hit on Harriett Bailey's heart. Eddy leaned in for a kiss and the kill.

Harriett raised her arm. "No, Eddy," she whispered.

Backing away, he continued smiling. *She looks good in makeup. Maybe this isn't such a bad idea.*

The audience applauded at the end of the movie as folks began to exit. Eddy held Harriett's hand as they walked to the car. He opened her car door.

"Harriett, would you like to go for ice cream?"

Harriett looked at her Timex wristwatch. Nine-forty-five. "I better not," she said reluctantly.

"No? Are you kidding?" Eddy threw the car in gear. "Only kids go to bed at this hour!"

Her whole body throbbed with an unfamiliar sensation. Harriett flashed back to Olive's slanderous comment. Fearful she ruined any chance of another date, she reconsidered her response. *Now I understand! I could very easily be tempted by him,* she thought. *I better keep my distance.*

The ride home was quick and silent, with Eddy still holding her hand. He pulled up the side street beside the Bailey backyard and leaned over to try another kiss.

Harriett shook her head. "No, Eddy. Not on a first date."

She waited for him to open the door. "Thank you for a lovely evening."

Walking on wobbly knees, head spinning, Harriett headed to the house with Eddy in tow. He made a third attempt at a kiss as Harriett opened the door, but she moved away inside.

Eddy called to her, "See you again?"

Harriett's heart skipped a beat. "Yes! Next weekend?"

He agreed, and she floated into the kitchen. A second date with Eddy Kepler!

39

SHAKE, RATTLE & JUMP

JULY 1950

*H*arriett Bailey and Eddy Kepler went on an athletic second date at Harriett's suggestion. The two planned a Saturday afternoon picnic at the swimming hole. With a blanket spread on the ground and a basket of food waiting, both dove into the water. The hot July weather encouraged many swimmers—including families with children and couples on dates—to seek splashing entertainment. Eddy and Harriett paddled for a while, then swam to the dam's edge before queuing for their turn to jump off the Tarzan-esque rope swing.

Eddy swung first, legs and arms flailing as he hit the water with a splash. Harriett timed her release, gracefully diving headfirst. Spectators applauded both jumps.

Tummy growling, Eddy, first out, dried himself, wrapping a towel around his waist.

"Come on, Harriett, let's eat. I'm starving," he called.

Harriett ignored him, swimming another ten minutes before climbing the bank to dry land. As she peeled off her swim cap, she searched for her towel. "Eddy, did you see my towel?"

Eddy answered, "I haven't seen it." His mischievous grin betrayed him.

"Don't give me that! Where did you put it?" Harriett stood over Eddy and shook like a dog, spraying water in every direction.

"Hey, stop! That's cold."

"Yes, it is. Now give me my towel. I want to dry off."

Harriett reached in to cuff his shoulder; Eddy flung the towel, teasing her.

"You do have it. Give it over."

"Catch me first!" Eddy went running down the country road away from the swimming area. Harriett slipped on her pair of Keds and took off in chase, with Eddy a quarter mile ahead.

Eddy pulled a fullback move as Harriett closed the gap— he jerked to his left, jumping around the tiny woman. Then he reversed direction, heading back to the swimming hole. Reflexes tuned, Harriett reacted swiftly, changing course. She leaped onto Eddy's back, wrapping her legs around his waist as he reached their blanket—the only tackling option for a girl her size. Eddy went crashing to the ground, laughing. Harriett laughed and rolled on top of him, as the other bathers gaped in awe.

"Sneaky move, Pip Squeak!" Eddy cracked the towel at her like a whip. The snap hit her butt.

"Oh, so that's how you want to play, is it?" Harriett giggled as she ran to the water's edge. She filled her swim cap with water, then tossed. Direct hit on Eddy's face.

Eddy spun, charging at Harriett. "No rules now, Pip Squeak. You're dead."

Harriett dove back into the water. A faster swimmer than Eddy, she was across the pooled area scampering up the opposite bank before Eddy hit the halfway mark. Harriett stood laughing, hands on her hips, as Eddy began his ascent from the water.

Eddy heard the noise before Harriett. He stopped dead in his tracks, no longer laughing.

"Harriett, do not move your legs."

Harriett looked down to see the coiled rattlesnake ready to strike. "God, Eddy, how was I so careless."

"Slowly lean forward," he said. "Give me both hands."

Eddy grabbed her upper arms as his muscular legs propelled them into the air. He tossed Harriett straight up and away from the snake, which struck with a forward motion. He caught her in midair, then they both plunged back into the safety of the pool.

As the pair broke the surface of the water, Eddy screamed, "Harriett, are you okay? Did it bite you?"

Treading water, Harriett reached down to feel her feet and ankles. No swelling, no pain.

"I think I'm okay. You saved me!" She swam over to Eddy and planted a big kiss on his lips.

"Well, that's a surprise. Usually, I'm the one steeling the first kiss." Eddy chortled as he splashed water at her.

Harriett splashed him back. "I'm sure you are. That was not a romantic kiss; it was a 'thank you' kiss— for saving my life."

Although it protested her alleged motive, Harriett's heart turned cartwheels at the touch of his lips.

"I think we better eat our lunch and head home. I've had enough excitement for one day."

Eddy settled down on the blanket as Harriett rubbed her hair with her recovered towel. "Gosh, I'm going to have one frizzy head."

With an open hand, Eddy smacked her butt before she sat.

Harriett protested, "You can't touch me there!" while her insides continued their gymnastic routine.

"Seems like I just did." He grinned the charming Eddy smile and handed her a sandwich.

Neither Eddy nor Harriett paid attention to the group of swimmers gazing at the unlikely couple. A few whispers of, "When did they start dating?" and "Eddy's with Harriett Bailey?" circulated amongst the crowd.

Lunch concluded with two juicy pears that dripped sweet nectar down both chins. They ate them as they walked back to the parking lot.

"Yummy, that's a wonderful pear. Your tree?" Harriett asked as she wiped her face.

"Sure is." Eddy tossed his core into the woods. "We have a huge pear tree that is just full of fruit. If I remember correctly, it originated from a tree on your grandfather's farm."

"Which grandfather? I never knew either of them." Harriett said as she folded their blanket, placing it into the hatch of the car.

"Your grandfather Westchester, who owned Westchester Farms."

Harriett frowned. "I wish I had met him. I'll have to ask my brother and sisters if they ever met him."

"Well, whatever you do," warned Eddy, "Don't ask your mother. Rumor has it she hated him."

Harriett looked at her companion sadly. "Geez, you know more about my relatives than me."

"Don't feel bad. It's a small town. Everyone sticks their noses in other people's business." Eddy opened the door for Harriett to climb in.

∞ ∞ ∞

S. LEE FISHER

Madison College scheduled minimal course offerings during the summer. Harriett's schedule carried only three credits, giving her free time on Tuesday and Thursday evenings along with Saturday and Sunday.

Their third date occurred three days later. Eddy arrived at the Bailey house around five-thirty, Tuesday evening. Harriett was waiting, dressed in a lightweight, sleeveless frock given to her by Esther.

"Hey, Pip Squeak. You look cute in that dress," Eddy said as he opened the car door. Before closing it, he leaned in for a quick kiss.

"Geez, you're persistent! No romantic kissing." Harriett swatted his nose.

"Killjoy." Feigning a frown, Eddy bounced to the driver's side and started the car. "I thought we'd get a quick bite and then an ice cream sundae at the drugstore. Sound okay?"

"It's the apothecary, and it sounds wonderful."

Eddy rolled his eyes at the correction. "Whatever you say, Pip Squeak."

"My sister's husband is the owner and pharmacist; I'll call it by its proper name for Alice and Teddy's sake."

"Oh yeah, I forgot. You're connected." Eddy pinched her gently on the arm.

They walked arm in arm, found a booth, and looked at the menu.

Eddy quickly ordered. "Burger, medium, with onion, tomato, cheese, catsup and mustard, no pickles. French fries and a chocolate milkshake."

"Eddy," Harriett asked. "Have you ever had fried onion rings? Are they good?"

"Oh, you poor sheltered girl. Onion rings are the best; anything fried is good." Looking at the waitress, Eddy ordered for Harriett. "Burger, medium, with onion, tomato, cheese, no pickles, catsup, and mustard, fried onion rings, and a chocolate milkshake."

Harriett cocked her head. "Excuse me. No." She smiled at Eddy before correcting him. "I'll have a burger, well done, with onion and pickles—no tomato, no cheese, no catsup, no mustard. I want mayonnaise on the side. A Coca-Cola, onion rings, and a hot fudge sundae after I eat my meal." Beaming, she gazed at Eddy. "Thank you for ordering; however, I prefer to do it myself, at least until you know my preferences."

Eddy bowed with his head and hand to Harriett. "As you wish, Pip Squeak."

While they waited on their food, Harriett noticed several young folks staring at them. "Eddy, are people looking at us?" Eddy turned his head around. "Be more subtle than that, but I swear people are watching us, including Alice and Teddy."

Casually glancing at the other diners, Eddy agreed. "Yep, you're right. They're looking at us."

"Why?"

Chuckling, Eddy answered, "Really, Harriett, you have to ask? It's because you're not my typical date."

Harriett pressed her lips together. "Yes, I realize that." She paused, then added, "So, why are we dating? What was that conversation in the movie theater about *good girls, and ladies*?"

"Don't do this, Harriett. I really enjoy your company." He took her hand in his. "Yes, you are different from the others I used to date, but I've changed."

Dropping his head, he caressed the top of her hand with his thumb. After a few moments, he looked into her steel-blue eyes.

She met his gaze, causing her body to erupt in waves of tingles. Goosebumps spread up and down her arms and legs.

"Don't worry about the gawking, okay? This is our third

date, and if you are willing, I would like to make it four. How about this Sunday? I have to work Saturday." Eddy lifted her hand and kissed.

Alice and Teddy witnessed the couple until their food arrived. Whispering to Teddy, Alice said, "I think my little sister is falling in love."

"From what I hear, he's not the most savory of characters. I'll keep my eye on that boy."

Alice kissed her husband, "So shall I—and so shall Esther, June, Albert, and Papa!"

40

LEO

*S*unday, Harriett waited with Tabs under the grapevine for Eddy to arrive.

"Janie dear, you see a lot of Eddy, don't you think?" Tabs asked, concern spread across his face. "He's your first boyfriend. Don't you think you should date others?"

Harriett sucked on her top lip as she motioned at the house. "Papa, I don't see any other boys lining up to take me out."

Tabs sighed. "Janie, of course. They'll not want to compete with the infamous Eddy Kepler. He's head of the pride; no one will challenge him."

Looking nervously at her watch, Harriett remarked. "He's late; I wonder what's keeping him."

Tabs raised his eyebrows as the roar of Eddy's engine turned the corner.

"Hey, Pip Squeak. You ready for some fun?" Eddy called from the front seat.

Harriett hastily kissed her father. Running to the car, she opened her own door and jumped into the passenger side as Tabs watched, frowning.

"Where are we going?"

Eddy reached for her hand. "To Madison. They're having a carnival, with rides, and games, and the best French fries in the world. Nothing better than carnival French fries!" He squeezed her hand. "You ready?"

"Sure am." She leaned over and kissed his cheek. Tabs cringed. "Bye Papa, see you later," she called out the open window as Eddy drove away.

The carnival was delightful. Harriett and Eddy rode the Ferris wheel, merry-go-round, tilt-a-whirl, and various other attractions. They strolled hand in hand through the fairgrounds, stopping for games of chance.

"Eddy, will you win a stuffed animal for me?" Harriett pointed to a large beige lion with a fluffy mane and twisting tail.

"Holy shit, Harriett, that thing won't fit in the car!"

She tugged on his shirt as she pleaded. "Please, Eddy, I never had many toys growing up. I would love that lion."

"Whatever you wish, Pip Squeak." He linked his arm around her waist as they approached the booth advertising the lion. "Buddy, how do I win that?" Eddy pointed to the enormous prize.

"You have to knock over these bottles twenty times to win the big one. Three times gets you a small animal." He pointed to a hand-sized parrot. "If you win three parrots, you can trade up to the poodle. But you need three poodles to trade for the lion."

Harriett did a quick calculation in her head. "That's twenty-seven throws that have to hit. How much per throw?"

The booth-minder chortled, "You're actually considering this? It's three balls for fifty cents. If I were you, fellow, I'd win a parrot and go home."

"Eddy, that's four dollars and fifty cents." Her smile radiated as she looked at Eddy. "Can you afford that?"

"Well, yes, if we knock over the stack on every throw."

Harriett pulled at Eddy's sleeve. "We can take turns throwing. That way, it's only thirteen throws for me and fourteen for you."

Eddy chuckled, "I get the extra pitch?"

"Of course, don't you want to be the hero?"

"Absolutely. Set 'em up." Eddy reached into his pocket and took out a five-dollar bill.

The booth man shook his head. "You're gonna need more than that."

"No, we won't," answered Harriett.

"Okay, Pip Squeak, I'll toss first, test the waters; there is probably a catch with these carnival crooks."

"Hey, who you calling a crook?" growled the booth keeper.

"Just give me the balls." Eddy threw the first ball into the air. Whispering to Harriett, he said, "Test the balls first; they're not weighted properly. One side is heavier than the other. Can you throw a curveball, Pip Squeak?" She nodded. "Then keep the weight to the inside and throw a curve."

Following his own advice, Eddy pitched the first toss. All bottles tumbled.

"That's one," chimed Harriett. "Okay, my turn."

The carnival man looked at Eddy questioningly. "You seem to have a good arm Son; you really want to waste your money letting her throw? Why don't you give it a try yourself?

"Well, old man, there are two reasons. One, my arm will get tired, which you are counting on, and two, she's as good a throw as me."

"Suit yourself."

Harriett picked up the ball, tossed it in the air, and nodded at Eddy. Her pitch knocked over all the bottles. "That's two."

After Eddy's third toss, the booth man handed Eddy a parrot. "Keep your parrot, old man, just keep counting. When we hit twenty-seven, hand over the lion."

By the time they threw fifteen pitches, a gang of spectators had gathered to see if the couple could win the big prize.

After throw twenty, a stranger offered them a bottle of Coca-Cola to share. "Here you go buddy, I imagine you're both getting thirsty. The entertainment is worth the price of a coke!"

Eddy smiled, took a sip, then wound up; another knock over, to make twenty-one. Harriett rubbed her arm then swung it in circles.

"The little lady is getting tired," said the carnival booth owner with a grin.

"Ball, please," was all she said.

"Twenty-two, twenty-three, twenty-four," chanted the crowd as they pressed in closer to see. A tall man bumped into Harriett.

"Excuse me, all of you, please back up. You're cramming us," Harriett barked, unintimidated.

"Sorry, little lady." The man moved back, ushering several others out of the way.

"Twenty-five, twenty-six, twenty-seven!" Cheers erupted as the carnival man reluctantly climbed a ladder. Taking the lion from its hook, he handed it to Eddy.

"I must say, I never expected you to make every toss count," he said, giving Eddy fifty cents in change. "Little girl, that's quite an arm on you."

"Here's your lion, Pip Squeak." Eddy handed the animal to Harriett, who squealed with delight.

"Thank you, Eddy!" She stood on tiptoes to kiss him. He accommodated by leaning over to meet her halfway. "Do you mind carrying this thing? It's as big as me!" Harriett giggled as she stroked the mane.

Eddy leaned in for a second kiss. "I'll carry both you and this monstrosity if it means getting a kiss." The crowd laughed and clapped.

Harriett abruptly looked around. The blood rushed up to her neck into her face. "I forgot we're not alone."

"As far as I'm concerned, we are. Don't pay attention to anything but me."

Eddy grabbed her waist—pulling her close, his lips met hers. The passion and urgency of the kiss sent Harriett's head spinning.

When Eddy finally moved away, Harriett, dazed and breathless, said, "Oh, why did I ever wait on a kiss?"

"Beats me, Pip Squeak, but I aim to please." Eddy embraced Harriett with one arm and carried the lion in the other as they walked toward the parking lot.

"Wait!" Eddy stopped at the exit. "Stay here. I almost forgot our French fries."

∞ ∞ ∞

The couple became a Campbellsville *thing* with dates five, six, seven, and eight. Together, they enjoyed swimming, biking, an occasional movie, and running the obstacle course. Harriett kept pace in all events. Eddy purchased a used tennis racket and took her to the refurbished Campbellsville courts, where he learned to graciously lose.

Harriett began enjoying his old companions' nasty looks and comments when they strolled on a cool evening or shared an ice cream soda at the Apothecary.

"What does he see in her?"

"But she doesn't have any tits! Not like mine, anyway."

"She must be a witch; cast a spell on him."

"The old Eddy would never settle for plain old Harriett."

The couple only laughed in response.

Alice convinced Teddy to keep an eye open, in case Eddy showed at the Apothecary with another girl.

"I can't believe he could be that stupid," argued Teddy.

Alice rolled her eyes. "Trust me on this one. He has such an ego he'd never think about us owning the place."

Miraculously, Eddy Kepler had become a one-woman, celibate man, to the surprise of all of Harriett's loved ones keeping watch. Albert and his buddies monitored Eddy's shift schedule and all the usual haunts in Madison. Darrell listened around the steel mill for talk of wild adventures, and Tabs checked in on conversation at the veteran's clubs, but Eddy did not stray.

The pair were rarely seen apart in Campbellsville.

Eddy worked shifts at the mill. When scheduled for the "daylight" shift from seven a.m. to three p.m., Harriett took advantage by hitching a ride to Madison, although she always rode the bus home, either because of class or the difference in quitting times.

One day in late August, Harriett rode to work with him in the morning. Eddy pulled in front of Dugan & Co., and Harriett kissed him before exiting the vehicle. Thomas Roland witnessed the exchange as he entered the building. He held the elevator for Harriett.

"Good morning Miss Bailey," Roland said as he motioned for the attendant to proceed up.

"Hello, Mr. Roland. How are you this fine morning?"

"From the looks of your goodbye, it certainly is a fine morning."

Harriett blushed bright red. "Oh, you saw that. I apologize for such a public display of emotion. I'm not setting a good example, am I?"

Roland chuckled. "Don't be concerned. Actually, I'm pleased to see you dating. We were growing concerned that you might be too much of a loner."

"We?" questioned Harriett.

It was Roland's turn to blush. "Mr. Dennis, Mr. Dugan, Kathryn, Caroline, Mary, and I. The *executive* we."

Harriett smiled, nodding her head. "I have been seeing him for two months. I am shocked that I'm having so much fun, and with a boy I used to despise." The hair rose on her arms in tingles.

"Oh? Why despise?"

Harriett exhaled, then paused. "He used to be so conceited, arrogant, and full of himself. He ran around, never kept a steady girl, played the field too much." She focused on her superior's eyes. "He seems to have changed. I'm the only girl he's dated all summer." Wistfully, Harriett continued, forgetting that she was speaking to her boss. "I sure hope he's changed, because I am surprised with myself. I'm falling for him."

Roland gently touched Harriett's arm, "Miss Bailey, tread lightly, and listen to your head as well, not just your heart.

Harriett blushed. "Mr. Roland, again forgive me. I was thinking aloud. I should not say such things to you. I apologize."

When the elevator stopped on the third floor, Harriett made a quick exit before exposing more of her personal feelings to her boss.

At lunch, she joined her three friends; however, she sat quietly eating.

Kathryn asked. "No dating updates?"

Harriett shook her head, continuing to chew her sandwich without looking up.

"My goodness, you're quiet today," Caroline commented.

Harriett swallowed. "How often do the six of you upstairs talk about my love life? Or, skip the love life—how often do you talk about me, behind my back? Am I a frequent topic?"

Kathryn gazed questioningly. "Harriett, what brought on this question?"

"A conversation I had with Mr. Roland this morning." She dropped her sandwich, placing her hands on the table. "Look, I don't care to be the subject of gossip, especially my love life. From now on, I think I shall keep that to myself."

"Harriett, we never intended to offend you. The thing is, we worry about you."

Her face flushed red. "Well, you don't need to worry. Just drop it okay?"

Caroline added, "Honey, you're pretty much a loner, except for your family and us."

∞ ∞ ∞

Later that evening, Harriett stopped by Alice and Teddy's house after class. Knocking on the door, she glanced at her watch: eight-thirty. It shouldn't be too late.

Teddy opened the door. "Harriett, this is a surprise. Can I help you with something? "

"Is Alice home? I was hoping to talk to her."

"Sorry, she's at a DAR meeting with June and Esther. It's the boys' night to watch the kids. You should join DAR too, make it a true family affair."

Harriett frowned. "I'll join DAR after I graduate. No time now. Crumb! I was hoping to clear up something tonight."

Teddy motioned for Harriett to enter, she complied. "Have a seat, my sister-in-law. Maybe I can help you."

Harriett thought for a moment. "Teddy, how do you know if you're in love?"

"Oh—I see. Confused?" Teddy stood. "I'm pouring us both a glass of wine for this talk. Be right back."

Harriett twirled her thumbs together, stopping to take the goblet from Teddy. "I've never dated before. Eddy is my first boyfriend." After taking a sip, she pressed on. "Teddy, I think I'm falling in love, but how do I know for sure?"

"How do you feel around him?"

She smiled. "My insides constantly turn flip-flops, and I tingle top to bottom. He makes me laugh, and I'm relaxed around him even when we are competing in sports. I never thought I'd find a man that liked sports as much as me, but Eddy does—and he gives me a run for my money, most of the time." She chuckled.

"How often do you think about him?" Teddy questioned.

"All the time, all day, every day. I'm still able to study and concentrate on my work, but thoughts of Eddy are always in the back of my mind." She gulped more wine. "Can a person fall in love in only two months?"

Teddy sighed. "Harriett, dear, I'm a bad one to ask that question. I fell for Alice the first time I saw her. I'm talking head-over-heels in love."

"Hmm. Then can I change my opinion completely on a person *and* do the same in two months?"

"Love is a powerful emotion. It sometimes cancels out the brain. I'd say you've been struck by Cupid's arrow. Just try to keep your head in the game, sweetie, if you can."

The two sat for another ten minutes, sipping their wine and talking school and business before Harriett headed home.

∞ ∞ ∞

Harriett met her three friends at lunch the next day. Before anyone had a chance to speak, Harriett began.

"I want to apologize for my attitude yesterday."

Kathryn interrupted her, "No need..."

"Yes, there is. You've been nothing but good friends, and I behaved poorly. I'm not making excuses—well, maybe I am—

but I've never had friends before, so I'm still learning how to do it right. Yesterday, I was overly sensitive."

Caroline interjected, "Harriett, we truly are concerned about you. You're a sweet girl. We all love you."

Harriett looked at her lunch companions. "Love?"

"Yes, love." Kathryn took Harriett's hand. "We enjoy your company and appreciate your work. We truly care and only wish the best for you."

Flushed, Harriett bowed her head. "You see, I'm slightly on edge." The three women smiled. "I think I'm falling in love, but I don't know what love is."

Mary confirmed Harriett's suspicions. "Honey, think no more. Yes, you are in love. We can tell by the way your face lights up when you say his name. Or how your eyes sparkle when you relay your latest adventure. Anything *Eddy* makes you glow."

"Harriett, dear." Kathryn squeezed Harriett's arm. "Be happy! Love is a wonderful thing, a lifetime voyage for exploring and experiencing *firsts* together. My only caution is to remain true to yourself, never lose who *you* really are. Does that make sense?"

Harriett hugged her work friends. "Thank you, all of you. I appreciate your friendship. Okay, that's enough about me." For the rest of the lunch hour, they talked about work-related subjects.

CONGRATULATIONS

*T*he week before Labor Day, Eddy found a phone booth. Loaded up on dimes, he called Earl.

"Hey, Eddy, what's up? You're making a long-distance call?"

"Hi, Earl. Question for you—I want to take Harriett someplace special next weekend. Do you know a restaurant in Pittsburgh where we can go?"

Earl paused before answering. "Eddy, if you're doing what I think you're doing, be sure first. Are you ready to be faithful to just one woman?" Earl waited for an answer. Receiving none, he continued. "Harriett is a special kind of girl; she's really too good for you."

"Oh, that's nice of you. I thought I was your favorite brother," Eddy protested.

"You are, but you display too many of Dad's habits. My advice is to be certain you're capable of changing your ways."

"Earl, I've been celibate all summer. Doesn't that count?"

The operator interrupted. "Please deposit thirty cents for the next three minutes."

Three dimes clinked into the phone. With permission to

continue, Earl said, "Tambellini's on Route 51 south. But give yourself three hours to get there, with traffic lights." Earl paused only a second, "I'm serious about being sure. Harriett is an extraordinary woman."

"Will I find it on a road map?"

"Yeah, yeah. It's a Pittsburgh landmark. Call to make reservations; they are crowded on the weekends."

"Thanks, Earl. I gotta go before she drains all my coins. Appreciate it." Eddy hung the receiver in the cradle just as the operator began saying, "Please deposit…"

Click.

∞ ∞ ∞

That night, as they walked home hand in hand from the apothecary, Eddy said, "Harriett, next weekend, let's go on an adventure. I want to take you to dinner in Pittsburgh."

Harriett tilted her head to the side. "Why so far? Madison has several good restaurants."

"Earl told me about this place in Pittsburgh called Tambellini's. I thought we'd end a special summer on a special date. Do you mind wearing that pretty blue and white dress? The one you wore on our first date?"

Harriett gasped. "You remember what I wore to the movies?"

Smiling the infamous Eddy Kepler grin, Eddy casually said, "Of course I do. You looked beautiful."

Harriett's knees went weak. *What is he up to?* Hoping beyond hope, she answered, "Of course, I'll wear my blue dress."

She kissed Eddy goodnight, lingering longer than usual. Eddy seized the opportunity for a long passionate kiss. Harriett slowly opened the door, backed in, blowing Eddy a kiss as he walked away.

Tabs winced as he watched his daughter. He hated seeing her in love with a womanizing cad.

"Hello, Janie. Have a nice evening?"

Harriett jumped. "Papa, I didn't see you." She paused. "How long were you here?"

Tabs hung his head, then slipped his arm around her shoulder. "Long enough, Janie. Are you sure he's the man for you?" His eyes filled with tears. "Janie, honey, I want you to be happy. But I want you to find a good man, one deserving of your wonderful self."

"Oh, Papa." Harriett began sobbing. "God help me! I'm in love with him. I know who he was, but he's changed, really, I swear. And I love him so much." Harriett hugged her father. "Please don't tell Mother. Not yet."

Tabs nodded his head, holding his daughter, wanting to protect her from a world filled with Eddy Keplers.

∞ ∞ ∞

EDDY FINGERED the box in the pocket of his father's white sports jacket—his "Lady Killer" coat—which he had borrowed for the evening. He wore navy blue trousers, a white dress shirt, and a blue-and-white dotted tie. Standing beside Harriett's blue and white-dotted dress, the couple looked like a Vaudeville act.

Eddy beamed at Harriett. "Aren't we just the cat's meow! Let's go."

As Albert predicted, it was a clear, warm, late summer day. Eddy rolled the top down on his Coupe. Harriett tied her hair in a silk scarf borrowed from Kathryn, and they were off. The radio blasted Billboard top forty hits as they motored through all the small towns to the big city.

As they approached the eastern suburbs of Pittsburgh,

Eddy's heart raced with anticipation. His foot followed suit.

"You better slow down," warned Harriett, coughing. "Goodness, the sky is filled with soot. I'm choking. And you don't want a ticket," she said, continuing to cough.

Eddy thought, *Damn right. I don't have any money left over to pay a traffic fine. He* eased off the gas.

"Harriett, is that a rain cloud?" Eddy pointed to the western sky.

A large black thunder cloud loomed over the far edge of the horizon. "Sure looks like one to me. And it looks to be moving quickly." She withdrew a handkerchief from her handbag to blow her nose. "Eddy, we better stop to roll up the roof. I don't want to be rained on with this filthy grime," she said, holding up her black-spotted hanky for Eddy to see.

"God, you're right. I'll stop at the next intersection." He pulled over. "Dad will kill me if I ruin his jacket."

The two worked to secure the car roof. They sat down again just as the heavens unleashed a brown-black mixture of grunge on the earth.

Both scrambled to roll up their windows.

"Goodness, I'm glad I don't live here," Harriett said.

A low layer of clouds mixed with exhaust from the mill-lined rivers hung below the tops of the tallest buildings.

"Eddy, how much further? I don't want to be running through dirty rain in my best dress."

Eddy's hand went to his pocket. "Neither do I. Will you be disappointed if we head home and eat someplace along the way?" Eddy frowned. "Dammit!" He pounded the dashboard. "It's not the special evening I had planned…"

Harriett interrupted, "…but it's the practical thing to do, and I'm all about practicality."

He rested his head on the seat and exhaled. "If you're sure it okay…"

Throwing the car into gear, Eddy turned east, heading

back toward Campbellsville, holding Harriett's hand when not shifting gears. The couple outran the rain most of the way home. About thirty miles from Campbellsville, Eddy spotted a roadside diner.

"I'm hungry. Let's stop here."

She allowed her growling stomach to answer for her. Sitting down in a chrome booth, Eddy ordered the most expensive meal on the menu for both of them: stuffed pork chops, mashed potatoes, gravy, and green beans. One dollar and ninety-nine cents each. There was no wine selection and no alcoholic offerings, so they drank iced tea.

Waving to the waitress, Eddy said, "Two pieces of coconut cream pie, please."

"Oh, yummy." Harriett looked out the window. "The rain finally caught us."

"Hmm. May I have your hand?" Eddy asked as clean liquid pinged off the metal diner.

Eddy got down on one knee. Holding Harriett's hand, waiting on the pie, he pulled the box out of his pocket. Flipping open the lid with one finger displayed a small diamond, about one-eighth of a carat, surrounded by inlaid diamond chips, giving the illusion of a bigger stone.

Harriett's mouth dropped.

"Harriett Jane Bailey, Pip Squeak, will you do me the honor of being my wife?" Eddy smiled ear to ear.

Harriett gulped air. "You want to get married?"

His smile dimmed for only a moment. "Yes, I want to get married. That's what 'wife' means."

The waitress watched the proposal, holding the pie until she was sure of an acceptance.

Harriett began crying. "Oh, yes, Eddy! Yes, I'll marry you!"

The couple kissed as the grinning waitress served dessert. "Congratulations."

I DO!

OCTOBER 1950

*H*arriett awoke with a start. She had surprised herself by falling asleep. Opening the bedroom window, she inhaled the crisp autumn air. One light, fluffy cloud drifted above. Albert promised perfect weather for her wedding day. Only the morning chill reminded her that summer was over, with winter soon to follow.

"My" wedding day, she thought. *That's an oxymoron! And yet, it's today.* She stretched cat-like in her bed.

Through the open window, she heard the bustle of activity below. Her three sisters were already busy, their excited chatter filtering upward like the buzzing of bees. Hammering, followed by a litany of cursing, betrayed Albert, hard at work in the yard with Tabs.

She meticulously unpinned her bobby pin curls, allowing her hair to relax before brushing. She whispered a prayer to the hair gods: *please let it cooperate today.*

Alice, her matron of honor, appeared in the doorway with a breakfast tray as if on cue. "Good morning, my dear sister. Hungry? I have tea and a biscuit."

Harriett answered the question with a robust hug.

"Watchout! Don't make me spill this. I see someone is excited." Alice smiled at her tiny sibling. "I'm so happy that at least one of us is having a proper wedding reception!"

"Alice, I can't contain myself. Will you help me comb out my hair and get dressed?"

Laughing, Alice sat the tray down on Harriett's dresser. "Of course I shall, sweetie. But we can't have the bride fainting before she says her 'I do's,' so relax first. Enjoy your food." Alice quickly vanished, scurrying downstairs to finish her long list of chores.

When Harriett arrived in the kitchen carrying her empty tray, Alice was barking orders to June and Esther. Albert and Tabs were outside hanging a strand of lights around the grape arbor. Olive was nowhere in sight. Utterly amazed by the activity, Harriett wandered through the kitchen. The Hoosier was filled with bowls of potato salad, sliced cucumbers, tea sandwiches, fried chicken, and cookies.

Harriett squealed when she spotted the three-tier cake, topped with a porcelain couple. "A cake! A real wedding cake with figurines on top!"

Alice giggled and glanced at Harriett. "Don't you start crying. We can't have a bride with puffy eyes."

Harriett walked outside to inspect the decorations. Her father and brother were hanging electric globes around the perimeter of the grape arbor. Baskets of chrysanthemums sat on bales of hay, scattered around the yard. Garlands of tissue flowers draped the front and back porches. Even the chicken coop touted fall flowers.

"Hi, Albert. Good morning Papa." Harriett held the sides of her face. "It's so beautiful. Doesn't even look like our yard!"

"Good morning to the lovely bride," Albert said, patting

his sister's backside. "Last time I can do that without insulting another man's wife."

Tabs, dropping his hammer, beckoned to Harriett. "My little Janie, come here." He clung tightly to his daughter. "You're all grown up, and after today, you'll belong to another man."

"Oh Papa, I shall always be your little girl. No man shall ever replace you in my heart. He may reside next to you, but he could *never* replace you." She began crying.

A watchful Alice shouted, "Watch those tears! We want a clear-eyed bride." Checking the clock, Alice called for Harriett and Esther. "Come ladies, it's already eleven-thirty. Time to prepare the bride. June, do you have control of the kitchen?"

June nodded while her three sisters climbed the stairs.

Alice surveyed the contents of Harriett's room. "Grab your clothes; we're invading Mother's space today. By the way, has anyone seen her? She must be hiding in the parlor, furious at everyone assaulting her space." All three snickered.

Harriett grabbed the garment bag that contained a light blue brocade silk suit, a perfect match to her steel-blue eyes, and followed Alice into the large corner room. She slipped on the skirt, then buttoned the jacket top and pushed up the collar.

Esther fussed with the neckline, "I want this roll to lay off your shoulders. My goodness, Harriett, you still have a golden tan; let's show off your neckline."

Harriett enjoyed the attention, allowing Alice to brush out her hair. "It's time to put on your face. I brought my cosmetic bag."

Harriett smiled. "Good thing. My entire cosmetic collection consists of one red lipstick."

Alice opened her case. "Look up Harriett. Close your eyes; I'm doing your brows first." Alice combed Harriett's brow line into a perfect arch, plucked a few stray hairs, then colored the brows with a brown pencil. Next, she applied a soft blush cheek rouge, finishing with a delicate red-pink lipstick.

Esther handed Harriett her matching blue leather gloves, while Alice pinned on a simple hat with a blue band, bow, and netting in place.

"Okay, sweetie, we're done. Time to look at your beautiful self in Mother's mirror." Alice ushered Harriett to the full-length mirror of Olive's vanity. The light from the window illuminated her silhouette, giving her an angelic glow.

Gasping, Harriett exclaimed, "It doesn't look like me! Oh my, it's too pretty. This is not my face. "

"It's the face of Mrs. Edgar Kepler Jr.," Alice said softly. Standing behind her, she touched Harriett's shoulders. Both sisters giggled. "It *is* you, and you are stunning. Now go downstairs and hide in the back parlor with Mother. I need ten minutes to get dressed. Can't have your matron of honor looking like a country bumpkin."

Harriett leaned in to kiss her sisters, who both screamed together. "No, you'll mess up your lipstick!"

"Okay, okay, I'll go hide." Harriett slipped her feet into her one wedding day splurge: a pair of pale blue pumps. She then headed down for thirty minutes of eternity.

"Alice, I'll have everything ready when you return. Darrel is picking up the children and David is bringing the Clines and Ralstons. Guests should arrive around two o'clock."

"Thanks, Esther," Alice said as she slipped into her dress. "The Keplers are bringing three cars, so we are covered." Smoothing the seams of her nylons, she said, "Okay, I'm ready. Don't let the kids topple the cake while I'm gone."

"Alice, you're a hoot. They are my children; I'll control them."

Eddy was the first to arrive, wearing a new navy blue suit

and light blue-striped tie. He parked the car, top-down, on the side street. Earl and Edgar Sr. parked behind him.

Back outside, Alice continued barking orders. "Eddy, you and Harriett will go in your car. Earl, it's you and me. Papa, you, and Mother ride with Abigail and Mr. Kepler. Okay now! Let me collect Mother and Harriett from the parlor, and we're off."

Alice ran back inside the house.

"Harriett, Mother! We're ready," Alice called out. Alone, Harriett walked down the hallway, joining her sister. "Is Mother right behind you?"

Harriett shook her head. "She wasn't in the parlor."

Alice puckered her lips; looking around the yard, she said, "Never mind, you go ahead with Eddy. Mother shall ride with his parents."

Eddy whistled as Harriett walked to his side. "You look beautiful." He handed her an orchid wrist corsage.

"You're not so bad yourself." She glowed, taking his flowers and his hand. He leaned in to kiss her. "Oh no, you'll ruin my makeup. Alice worked really hard to make me beautiful. No kisses until after the ceremony."

Eddy gazed into her eyes. "You are wrong, my dear. They had easy work. You came beautiful; they only wrapped you in a bow." Extending his arm, he said, "Let's get this show on the road. I can't wait to call you Mrs. Kepler."

"Drive slowly, please, I don't want the wind to blow my hair."

∞ ∞ ∞

Eddy and Harriett waited at the courthouse, pacing, wondering why the other two cars were not behind them.

After ten minutes, Justice of the Peace Stanley asked, "Are you bringing witnesses, or shall I fetch my wife?"

Harriett looked pleadingly at Eddy, who answered. "Yes, sir, her sister, my brother, and our parents are coming. Can we wait, please?"

"Sure, son. It's your wedding." Stanley motioned to a bench. "Have a seat. I'm sure they'll be here shortly." Taking a seat on a hard wooden bench, Harriett removed her gloves. She tried to keep her fingers off the orchid. Her mouth felt like it was full of cotton balls. She swallowed so she could speak. "Eddy, where could they be? I'm worried. I knew something would happen to ruin this day."

Eddy held her hand. "Don't worry, my darling. Alice and Earl will see that everyone arrives safely." The couple sat looking at the dark-paneled walls of the courthouse, covered with portraits of Campbellsville's past dignitaries.

Fifteen minutes later, Abigail, Edgar Sr., Tabs, and Alice arrived. Eddy and Harriett exchanged glances.

"Papa, where's Mother and Earl?" Her leg began shaking up and down.

Tabs whispered in Harriett's ear. "Honey, your mother has disappeared. Earl is waiting for her."

"What do you mean, 'disappeared?'" Harriett's body trembled. "What happened to her? I don't understand."

"I don't understand either, Janie. But do not allow her to ruin your day. This is *your* day. You are a beautiful bride; pay her no mind." Tabs sat down beside Harriett. "Shall we wait for Earl?"

Harriett nodded, yes.

Ten minutes passed before Earl drove in alone. As he joined the waiting group, he shook his head.

Tabs smiled lovingly at Harriett, then turned to scrutinize Eddy. *She looks so happy*, he thought. *How can I deny her? He's wrong for her, but it's her mistake to make.*

"Sir, I believe you intend to marry my daughter today?" Tabs addressed Eddy.

Eddy chortled. "I certainly do!"

"Then please do so with both her parents' blessing."

Kissing Harriett on the cheek, knowing she would never again be his little Janie, Tabs gave her hand to Eddy.

43

WHERE'S OLIVE?

*J*une put the finishing touches on the food table as Esther greeted arriving guests. With his mother holding their toddler, Darrel herded the older children into the upper yard to avoid spilling the food or cake. The bridal couple, behind schedule, were yet to return.

Dave snuck up behind June and kissed her neck. "Honey, why is your mother walking down the street? I thought she was at the ceremony."

Spinning around to look at her husband, June asked, "What are you talking about?"

Dave pointed to Maple Street, where Olive, wearing an old, patched dress and bandana around her head, walked aimlessly in the middle of the street.

June gasped. "Oh my God! I'll be back." June ran to her mother, grabbed her by the arm, and pulled her toward the house.

Olive yanked back. "Let go of me!"

June, stronger and more determined, tugged sternly. "What on earth are you doing? You abandoned Harriett's graduation, now her wedding; you're not abandoning the reception too."

Olive leaned back, altering her center of gravity, making it harder for June to pull.

"Esther," Dave called out. "June needs help."

"Holy Hannah."

Esther ran out into the street. Taking Olive's other arm, the two sisters managed to drag her into the house and up to her bedroom, all while Olive screamed, "Leave me alone!"

Esther, standing on tiptoes, stared into her mother's eyes and growled, "You have managed to embarrass, upstage, and belittle us your entire life. It *stops* today!"

June smiled openly at Esther's scolding as Olive jerked away, squatting on her hope chest. "I'm not budging."

"Oh yes you are!" Her firstborn barked as she yanked off Olive's bandana and began brushing, tugging her tangles of hair.

June pulled off Olive's apron. Olive's arms flung wildly, slapping at her daughters. Esther clutched Olive, imparting June enough leverage to remove her ragged dress.

"Put this on, Mother." June tossed a lovely flower print at Olive, who batted it away. Not without a struggle, the sisters eventually dressed their mother. Giving up on her hair, Esther tied Olive's curls into a bun and pinned a flowered hat on top of her head.

"Good enough." Esther pinched Olive's arm. "We are taking you downstairs. You are to sit in an Adirondack chair under the grapevine, and you will not move from that spot!"

Once outside, Albert joined Esther and June, who were still holding tightly to Olive. Vowing not to tell Harriett about Olive's behavior, Albert sat Olive in a chair and stood guard.

∞ ∞ ∞

Ceremony over, Mr. and Mrs. Edgar Kepler Jr. exited the courthouse to find a "Just Married" sign on the back of Eddy's car, compliments of his brothers George and Roy.

Eddy jumped into the air. "Hot dog! We're going for a spin." Hoisting Harriett into his arms, he placed her in the passenger seat. "I'm showing my wife off," he called as he sped away, beeping his horn continuously, informing the entire population of Campbellsville that Eddy Kepler was out of circulation.

Tabs, the senior Keplers, Alice, and Earl, arrived home to find a celebration in progress. Kepler, Ralston, Cline, and Westchester families joined with Harriett's and Eddy's friends, DAR members, work acquaintances, and several relatives, including Benny and Ingrid, Tabs' cousin Wyeth, Eddy's brothers, and their extended families. The attendees filled every inch of the half-acre lot.

Spotting Olive sitting in a chair with Albert close by, Tabs shouted, "Dear Wife, aren't you just as pretty as a picture? Well worth the wait!"

Leaning down, he kissed her cheek and whispered, "If you do anything to ruin Janie's day, you wicked, selfish woman, I swear I will slit you, neck to toe, with my hunting knife and let you lay in your bed dying. And those boney, cold hands that haunt your dreams shall be *my* hands choking your neck." Tabs squeezed her arm so tightly that he left fingerprints. "Do I make myself clear, Olive?"

Olive grunted but nodded yes. Tabs sat down beside her, his body near convulsing with anger, his sad eyes mourning the loss of his precious daughter and best companion.

The honking grew louder as Eddy and Harriett returned home. Eddy lifted Harriett from the car and gently stood her in front of their oohing and aahing, clapping guests.

"May I present to you Mrs. Edgar G. Kepler Jr." Eddy

bowed as he waved his arm toward a blushing Harriett. Guests applauded.

Pharmacist and photographer looked to the sky to check the lighting. The north-facing yard was in the shadow of the three-story house. "Will you stand beside the arbor, here, in the sunlight?" Teddy posed the couple. "I want to capture your bright, beautiful faces."

Harriett giggled; Teddy clicked the shutter.

Someone yelled, "Kiss the bride!"

"Happy to oblige." Eddy swooped in and dipped Harriett backward while he kissed her passionately. Teddy snapped a candid photo.

"Oh my! I need to catch my breath after that!"

"If that's the case from just a kiss, I better bring a tank of oxygen on our honeymoon," Eddy boasted while the crowd hooted.

Earl clinked the side of his glass. "Attention, please. Attention!" Silence followed. "As best man—and I *am* the best man—" He waited on a few scattered chuckles. "—I want to wish my baby brother and his beautiful—and I mean, drop-dead *gorgeous*—wife all the happiness in the world. Raise your glasses to Mr. and Mrs. Edgar G. Kepler Jr. Cheers!"

Eddy and Harriett drank to Earl's toast, smiling. The newlyweds mingled with their guests most of the afternoon. Everyone ate and drank their fill; food disappeared as the event progressed.

After an hour or so, someone called, "Time to cut the cake."

Harriett took a knife from Alice, then hesitated. "This is too beautiful to cut."

The three-tiered cake, purchased from the Campbellsville Bakery, was a white almond cake filled with strawberry glaze. The white, interwoven frosting looked like a basket circled with yellow and red icing roses with green icing leaves. To be saved for the couple's first anniversary, the top chocolate layer was crowned with a porcelain bride and groom.

Prodding subtly, Alice moved Harriett's arm forward. With the first slice cut, Albert carried the cake into the kitchen to be carved for their guests.

The custom of feeding each other wedding cake usually resulted in icing-covered faces. Harriett delicately placed a piece of cake in Eddy's mouth, who swallowed and grinned. Non-gentlemanly, Eddy took his chunk, shoved it into Harriett's mouth, hoping for a smear. Harriett defensively opened wide, clenching her teeth together over the fork. Then with one quick swipe, she collected the cake and icing from her mouth and wiped it across Eddy's face.

Applause echoed off the hillside. "Way to go, Harriett!" yelled Kathryn.

Cleaning himself with a paper napkin, Eddy grinned. "I have a clever one here. I think I must be on guard at all times."

The guests went wild.

"It's time to open gifts," Alice whispered in Harriett's ear, knowing Eddy wanted to get on the road.

A table stacked with gifts and envelopes was placed on the back porch for safekeeping. Alice cleared two Adirondack chairs, one for Eddy and one for Harriett. After grabbing a steno pad, Alice asked Heddy and Toby to carefully bring the gifts to the couple, one at a time. Susie and Lloly, not wanting to be left out, sat at Harriett's feet, collecting bows and ribbons.

The children brought over envelopes first. Eddy's smile grew wider as the gifted dollar amount grew higher.

Upon reading, "Best wishes, Judith Reven," Eddy choked.

"Coach Reven gave us a wedding gift? Why her? She

messed up my life." Earl cleared his throat. Eddy retracted. "Okay, okay. That's not true."

Harriett smiled at her husband. "We're friends. We see each other now and then, for lunch or coffee. How do you think I learned to play tennis so well?" More laughs from their guests ensued.

Opening the last envelope, Harriett read the verse on a beautifully embossed greeting card. Inside was a crisp fifty-dollar bill.

"Oh my goodness. Fifty dollars from Mr. Roland, my boss." Harriett held back tears. She glanced at Kathryn, standing with Mary and Caroline. "This will be deposited into my—I mean our—savings account immediately."

"He gave it to me to give to you yesterday." Kathryn smiled at her coworker and friend. "You are valued by Dugan & Co."

Mary added, "Plus, you'll find something extra in your next paycheck from Mr. Dugan."

Eddy whistled through his teeth, singing, "We're in the money!"

The couple received an assortment of items including a set of sheets, towels, drinking glasses, pots and pans, and various household items. White butcher paper or brown mailing paper, tied in yarn or ribbon, was used to wrap most of the gifts. The last box, covered in shiny silver paper imprinted with white bells and tied with a silk bow, remained as the pile dwindled.

Heddy spotted the shimmering package, "Aunt Harriett, last one." After handing the gift to Harriett, she stood directly in front of her, blocking the view of the other guests.

"Heddy, sweetie," Harriett said gently. "You need to sit down. Everyone wants to know what's in this box!"

Blushing, Heddy joined Susie on the ground.

Harriett carefully removed the paper, cutting the tape to

prevent tares. Handing it to Lloly, she instructed, "Please fold this carefully, nephew. I'll reuse it." Lloly smiled in appreciation.

The box was imprinted with the words "Marshall Fields."

"Where's Marshall Fields?"

"In Chicago." The answer came from Earl.

"Chicago? How in the world...?"

Earl smiled. "Remember, many of us were there for basic and extended training. I still have connections."

Darrel whispered to Esther. "That's a real swanky store."

Harriett removed the lid and folded back the silver tissue paper to reveal a beautiful white chiffon negligee. She held up the gown for everyone to see. Its bodice was crafted of French lace and trimmed with silk ribbon atop a sheer white skirt. The matching robe was made entirely of white, thin, silk chiffon; when worn together, they would outline the body beneath without divulging detail.

"Wow, Brother. That's a stunner."

Earl's eyes twinkled. "I wanted something sexy for you, little Brother, but something to provide modesty for my sweet new sister." Earl winked at Harriett, whose face colored bright red.

"Aunt Harriett, that's all the presents," announced Toby.

"Toby, come here, Grandson," Tabs called to Esther's firstborn. "Please give this to Janie."

Toby handed Harriett an unboxed gift, wrapped in newsprint. She gently removed the paper to find a four-fox stole, the mouth of one fox biting the rump of another, the tails dangling as trim.

"Papa, did you make this for me?" Tears welled in Harriett's eyes.

"Yes, Janie dear. You are no longer my little girl, rather a married woman of the community. You must look the part. I hope you like it."

Water filled Tabs' eyes. Harriett rubbed the soft fur against her face, then ran to her father. Throwing her arms around his neck, she clung tightly. A muffled harrumph from Olive was barely heard. Tabs and Harriett embraced, lost in each other's love.

Eddy touched Harriett's elbow. "I hate to break up this party, but we need to get on the road. I have an hour's drive before I can properly introduce myself to my wife." Reaching for the negligee, Eddy added, "But be sure to pack this!"

Harriett's blush seemed to be permanent. "I'm so overwhelmed. You have all been so generous. I have a tidy nest egg and a furnished kitchen—even though I can't cook."

"I'll vouch for that," Albert chimed in, extracting chuckles.

Harriett gazed into Eddy's eyes. "This is the happiest day of my life. Thank you, thank you. I love you all."

Eddy swept her off her feet and again, placed her into the car. "Mr. and Mrs. Kepler say, 'thank you and goodbye.'" Teddy's camera clicked.

The couple waved as Eddy blew his horn.

Tabs was already gone. He had carried gifts up to Harriett's room, not wanting to see her drive away. He stacked the gifts in the corner beside the stuffed lion, then opened her closet. Pulling the blue and white dotted dress off the hanger, he rubbed it against his face, searching for a whiff of her perfume. Grabbing the lion, Tabs sat on the edge of her bed, buried his face in its mane, and wept as the sound of the horn faded into the distance.

44

THE FALLS

"Mmm," Harriett managed to moan as she snuggled closer to Eddy, content not to move in a drunken stupor of sleep and afterglow.

"Well, good morning, Mrs. Kepler." Eddy greeted her with a kiss.

Harriett purred another, "Mmm."

If Harriett doubted her love for Eddy in any part, it was dispelled with the discovery of physical intimacy. She had crossed the point of no return: she was Eddy's, heart, body, and mind, for eternity.

"Wake up, sleepyhead!" Eddy nudged her gently. "We have a five-hour drive today if we want to get to Niagara Falls before nightfall."

"I just want to stay here." She snuggled closer, kissing his chest.

Eddy chuckled. "If we hit the road now, I promise to cuddle tonight."

Harriett stretched and made her way to the bathroom. By the time she showered and dressed, the sun sat high in the sky.

"Come on, slow-poke. We'll miss check-out time and have to pay for another night if you don't hurry."

The thought of unnecessary costs spurred on frugal Harriett.

She was aglow. Alice had warned her of possible physical pain at first, but Eddy, an experienced lover, tenderly and patiently attended to his wife. The initial minimal pain gave way to physical release and a total emotional bond.

The couple drove through the Pennsylvania countryside, enjoying a sunny autumn day and the vibrant shades of oranges, reds, and yellows that ignited the hillsides with color. Harriett settled under the crook in Eddy's arm.

About thirty minutes into the drive, Harriett said, "Eddy, I'm famished. May we eat breakfast before we continue?"

Eddy roared hysterically, glancing at his tiny wife. "Yes. Although, I'm not sure why you have such an appetite...I think *I* did most of the work last night."

Harriett blushed as Eddy's stomach grumbled. "See, you are hungry too!"

They stopped for a quick breakfast at a diner, then continued top-down, arriving at the Canadian border around five p.m.

Handing the customs inspector a copy of their birth certificates and marriage license, Harriett giggled. "I'm going to a foreign country; I can't believe I'm going abroad!"

"I can't believe I'm married," Eddy answered, then leaned down to kiss Harriett.

A small room several blocks from the water awaited their arrival. Since it was less expensive than the larger honeymoon hotels on the falls, they opted for walking and saving money.

Eddy carried Harriett over the threshold for the second day in a row. She spotted a small television on the dresser top.

"Gosh, Eddy, a TV! Can we watch some tonight?"

Television had not yet overrun Campbellsville. Only about one-third of the households owned them; the Keplers and Baileys belonged to the other two-thirds.

Eddy cocked his head with a grin. "Perhaps for a little bit. I have other plans for tonight."

Harriett blushed. "First, shall we stroll down to look at the falls, then grab supper?"

They walked hand in hand down the street; the smell of brisk autumn weather stung the inside of their noses. A rumble was the first sound to be heard. It quickly turned into a roar, then a thundering reverberation. They stopped and stared in amazement at the magnificence and sheer energy of the water.

"Oh, Eddy. I never expected this. I've seen waterfalls before, but this..." Harriett, awestruck, sat down on a bench. "Sit with me?" she beckoned to her husband.

Sitting on the bench, mesmerized by the magnitude of force, they held hands as horse-drawn carriages filled with other lovers drove past. They admired the floral scents of the manicured park grounds until Eddy spotted a boat.

"It says *Maid of the Mist*." Pointing, Eddy implored, "Harriett, look over there, across the water. People are getting off; I think they offer boat rides. Do you think we can afford to take one?"

"I brought some extra cash along, just in case. That looks like fun," said Harriett claiming the purse strings for the new Kepler family. "It's our honeymoon; let's adventure."

45

BEST LAID PLANS

hree days at Niagara passed by quickly. Harriett was off work until Monday; Eddy was already back on the job. Alice helped Harriett prepare her room for the new couple, their temporary lodgings until they found a house to rent or buy.

"Here, sweetie." Alice handed Harriett a framed wedding photo. "Teddy has a small darkroom and processed them himself. You look radiant."

Taking the picture, Harriett asked, "Please order one for Mother, even though she hates me."

"Here you go." Alice handed her a copy print.

"Thanks. I'll give it to her tonight. I'll force her to add my picture to her family collection."

Alice scrunched her nose, "Don't talk about Mother. Tell me about your trip!"

"It was amazing," she said as she stacked gifts in her closet. Alice covered her mouth as she giggled. "I mean the *falls* were amazing," Harriett said, blushing. "Except when I fell. Look at the bump on my head."

"How did you do that?" Alice placed a blouse from her suitcase onto a hanger, then handed it to Harriett.

"On the Maid of the Mist. I'm usually so surefooted, but I slipped, hitting my head on a protruding rock." Harriett rubbed the red and purple contusion. "But the *other* part was pretty special too. I never realized that there could be such happiness in my life. For the first time ever, I feel whole. Is that crazy?"

"No, sweetie, it's not crazy at all. I'm so happy for you."

"Alice, when I'm in his arms, my soul is entwined with his." Harriett's radiant face glowed as she wrapped her arms around her shoulders. "In three days, the words 'till death do us part' took on a spiritual meaning. I've dedicated my life, every breath to him."

Alice hugged her sister. "I'm glad you found your soul-mate; just be careful. Stay true to yourself. It's possible to have a strong bond as a couple without losing yourself in the process."

Harriett returned the hug. "Oh Alice, thank you for a wonderful wedding. I never had any friends until I started work, June and Esther were always gone, and you were always with Albert. It's nice to finally be friends."

"Four years is a big difference in high school. Thirteen versus seventeen. Not so much now. Baileys united!" Alice's fist flew into the air. "I have some news," she said, leaning closer to her sister.

Harriett stopped her unpacking; sitting on her bed, she asked, "And what kind of news would that be?"

Alice sat beside Harriett, grabbing both her hands. Alice's grin was infectious. "I'm pregnant."

"Goodness, that's wonderful." Harriett hugged her sister. "When did you find out?"

"A week before your wedding, but I didn't want to take

away from your day, so I waited. I haven't told anyone except Albert, and of course, Teddy. He's so excited!"

"Alice, this is such good news. Now I can reciprocate by throwing you a baby shower. When are you due?" Harriett pulled a steno pad from a drawer.

"Look at you, taking notes!" Harriett responded by poking Alice's arm. "I'm due in late April, early May. Oh, I hope it's a little girl!"

They were interrupted by a voice from outside calling. "Harriett, I have mail for Eddy." Opening the window, Harriett saw Earl waving a letter.

"Earl, I'm glad to see you," Harriett called, then raced down the stairs and out of the house.

Earl fidgeted as he handed her the envelope. "You may not be so glad once I give you this."

The envelope addressed to Edgar Kepler Jr. was from the Department of Selective Services. Her knees buckled. Steadying herself on the grape arbor, she asked, "Earl, please help me back upstairs."

Harriett's face, drained of all color, alarmed Alice. "Earl, what happened?"

"I think you better stay with her until Eddy returns from work." Earl turned and left the room.

"Harriett," Alice sat on the bed beside Harriett. "What's in the letter?"

Harriett handed it to her absently. Alice glanced at the return address and sighed. She handed the unopened envelope back to her sister. "I'm so sorry, honey."

Sitting silently on the bed, holding hands, Alice listened for Eddy's car. Kissing Harriett on the forehead, she quickly left through the front entrance, without a word, when she heard the car door shut.

Eddy bound up the staircase, expecting a kiss from his bride. Instead, a pale-faced Harriett stood in their bedroom, holding the letter.

"Eddy, what does this mean?" Her voice cracked. Reaching for Eddy's hand, she squeezed.

Eddy looked at the mail; his hand trembled in hers. "This isn't supposed to happen. Did I notify them too late?"

"What does it say, Eddy?"

Eddy read, "Edgar G. Kepler Jr....you are hereby ordered to report..." Eddy flushed. "I did it for *nothing!* What a damn farce, all for nothing!"

"What are you talking about?" Harriett searched his eyes.

Feebly he answered, "Nothing. Forget it. It doesn't matter —not now."

Harriett fell into his arms. "Eddy, I'm frightened. I don't want you to go."

Grunting, he said, "I don't want to go either."

"Promise me that you'll come back to me. I need you. I couldn't bear it if I lost you." She clung to her husband, recalling his reputation only four short months ago, then remembering Lupi.

He stroked her hair, and her entire body shuddered. "Harriett, I love you. I really do."

"Eddy, be faithful, please." She leaned up, kissed his mouth as she choked back her tears.

"Harriett, I love you, really," Eddy said without promising, his colorless face betraying his words.

With one hand, he grabbed her around the waist, kissing her passionately. With his other hand held behind her back, he crushed the envelope into a crumpled mess and threw it on the floor.

∞ ∞ ∞

The next day, fall yielded to winter, bringing blowing,

freezing rain. Eddy, Harriett, Tabs, and Olive sat around the kitchen table, eating their evening meal.

Harriett handed Olive a copy of her wedding photo. "Mother, with all the chaos of Eddy's draft, I almost forgot. This is for you." She paused before asking, "Why are there no family photos with me in them?"

Olive snorted. "Because my life ended when your life began."

All three gasped at her reply.

"Olive, that's a dreadful thing to say to our child!" Tabs' eyes threw daggers at his wife. "You grow more bitter every day."

Olive continued, "And I suppose you'll be living here indefinitely now that your man is leaving."

Harriett turned white; Eddy turned red. "Mrs. Bailey, I promise you that we'll be out of your hair as soon as possible. I've only lived here a few days, and truthfully, I don't know how Harriett puts up with you!"

Olive stood. Rolling her fists into balls, she pounded the table. "And I say, good riddance to you, sir!"

She stormed out of the kitchen. Tabs muffled a laugh as she went. "I'm afraid you're on her bad side, Son."

Eddy flushed. "Harriett, I'm sorry, but she's downright wicked. Damn, I hope I haven't made things worse for you." Eddy stood, viewing the white cabinet that housed Olive's salt and pepper shaker collection. He asked, "Which are her favorites?"

Harriett sat speechlessly. Tabs pointed to a pair of cacti. "Her brother Fred gave her those."

"Well, Harriett, that's your answer. If she's mean, you kidnap the cactus!"

"I'll need to retaliate somehow. Ha! Cactus kidnapping!"

Eddy, Tabs, and Harriett laughed, despite what loomed ahead.

∞ ∞ ∞

Two weeks later, Earl parked on the side street, leaving the motor running. "Well, Brother, this is it. Say goodbye to your bride. Indian Town Gap and basic training await."

Harriett gulped air as she sobbed. "Eddy, I love you."

"Me too, Pip Squeak." Eddy kissed her,

He turned to leave; Harriett reached out with desperation. "Oh Eddy, don't leave me!" she cried.

Eddy said nothing, closed the door and sat in the passenger seat. Tabs held his daughter as she watched her husband punch Earl's arm—then both men broke into laughter. They drove away with Eddy laughing, looking straight ahead, never turning back to the house, never waving goodbye to his wife.

Olive viewed the scene from her bedroom window, smirking. "I told the twit love would break her heart. She's no different than me." She rubbed her neck with one hand, clinging to her pearls with the other.

In the doorway, Harriett buried her head in Tab's shoulder. "What shall I do, Papa? How shall I survive with him away?" She slumped to the floor.

Tabs knelt beside her, tenderly kissed her on the forehead. "You're a bright, independent woman. I'm confident you'll manage just fine, darling Janie. Just fine."

∞ ∞ ∞

The saga continues...

Coming soon- *Hill House, Divided* Book 3 in The Woman of Campbell County Series

Tabs, Harriett, Eddy, and even Olive, have a favor to ask of you...

Please leave an honest review on this book's sales page on Amazon.

Reviews help other readers find Olive, Tabs, Harriett, Eddy, and the women of Campbell County.

To leave a review, click this link to be connected automatically: Under the Grapevine

The Westchesters, Baileys, and Keplers thank you for your support. I hope you enjoy their story and continue reading until the end.

S. Lee Fisher.

Read on for a working excerpt of Chapter 1, Hill House Divided.

Heave Ho
Trieste Italy, January 1951

Crossing the Atlantic Ocean on military transport was uncomfortable for the masses of soldiers shipping off to parts unknown. However, the journey in January was brutal. There was no VIP treatment for Army grunts, stacked and racked in the bowel of the boat.

Eddy Kepler, high school athlete, svelt and chiseled from basic training, swung back and forth in his sickbay hammock, cramped in a vessel carrying hundreds of Army recruits headed east. The boat pitched, causing Eddy to grab his bucket. He wretched, gagged, passed gas, choked, then coughed. His stomach gave nothing but acrid bile.

"Damn Kepler, I don't know what's worse, the boat rocking or the noise and stench you create."

Eddy moaned, rolling over onto his side, his trousers slide down off of his hips. Seventeen days in transit, the last ten spewing his guts all over the deck did nothing to cheer his mood or maintain his physique. He was even too queasy to go up top for the magnificent view when passing through the Straights of Gibraltar.

Eddy pulled up his pants, mumbling, "When do we dock?"

"Tomorrow."

He dozed. The pitching lessened as the ship turned north, out of the Mediterranean and into the Adriatic.

He awoke to someone shaking him. "Come on, Kepler, get up. Christ, you smell."

"Huh?" Eddy instinctively reached for his bucket. "Where am I?"

"Docked, now get your ass off of the ship. It's going to take weeks to clean up after you."

He managed to sit up. Slipping out of the hammock, Eddy's knees buckled; he grabbed hold of his bed for support. "I pretty weak, doc."

"Yea, yea. Get off my boat, Kepler." The medic grumbled, continuing his rounds.

Unsteadily, Eddy dragged his duffel down the gangplank running straight into a burly sergeant. As their bodies bumped, Eddy vomited clear liquid; it landed directly between the Sergeant's eyes.

"Private, Christ Almighty!" Sergeant Hill barked. "Was that on purpose?" Hill wiped his face with his handkerchief. "What's your name, Private."

Eddy latched onto the sergeant's shoulders, keeping himself upright.

"Get off of me, you buffoon! Think you're a funny guy, do you?" Sergeant Hill pushed. Eddy tumbled backward, landing on his butt, his trousers down around his knees. "MPs! Get this clown out of my face."

Eddy managed to feebly get to his feet before the MPs arrived. Stumbling over to a waiting fleet of jeeps, he tossed his bag into the first vehicle and collapsed into the seat beside it.

"Who the hell do you think you are, private?" questioned a surly corporal behind the wheel. "This vehicle is for officers only! Noncoms queue over there for truck transport." The driver pointed to a convoy of trucks, then looked at Eddy's green face, sunken eyes circled with black rings, pants around his ankles.

The driver chuckled softly, "Okay, buddy. Let's get you over to sickbay straight away."

Unable to speak, Eddy groaned, closing his eyes trying not to puke as the jeep drove off.

"Doc, I got a ripe one just off the boat," yelled the driver.

Two corpsmen wheeling a gurney lifted the dry heaving private out of the jeep.

"Take it easy, fellow. I'll be back around to collect you in a couple hours when your head stops floating." Corporal Walter Stuart laughed as he drove away to pick up his next set of passengers.

∞ ∞ ∞

For up-to-date information about this series, and for a generational flow chart, sign up for the Campbell County/ S. Lee Fisher **newsletter** at www.sleefisher.com. Email addresses are neither sold nor shared.

AUTHOR'S NOTES

- All characters are the creation of the author. This is a work of fiction. Any similarity to actual people, living or dead, is purely coincidental.
- Any names of real people, living or dead, are done so by their request or the request of their survivors with written permission.
- In 1929, $5,000 had the spending power of $75,000 in 2020.
- The 1936 flood of this story is loosely based on a combination of the Johnstown PA floods of 1889, 1936, and 1977. The Conemaugh River flows through the narrow, steep hillsides of west-central Pennsylvania. On the dates mentioned, excessive rain along with dam failure flooded the valley. The death toll was 2,200 in 1889, 25 in 1936, and 84 in 1977.
- Decoration Day began in 1868 as a day to remember fallen soldiers of the Civil War. It later became Memorial Day in 1950. Armistice Day, celebrated on November 11, signified the end of WWI. We now call it Veterans Day.
- "Dapper Dan" was an expression used in the Roaring Twenties to mean a well-dressed man.
- The Air Force did not become a separate military branch until September 18, 1947. During WWII, the Air Force was an autonomous branch of the US Army, headed by General Henry H. Arnold.

- The reference to the summer of 1942 breaking heat records is the product of the author's imagination.
- Women all over the country worked in manufacturing jobs during WWII, filling positions vacated by deployed men. These women were collectively referred to as "Rosie the Riveter."
- The composition of the 1942 state football tournament is the author's invention. However, by June of 1942, the United States was already implementing a rationing system for rubber and gasoline. By 1943, sugar, flour, butter, coffee, meat, canned food, silk, nylons, and various other such items required rationing coupons to purchase. Household appliances, such as vacuum cleaners, refrigerators, and personal vehicles were no longer being made. Manufacturing moved to war production.
- On August 6, 1945, the plane called the Enola Gay, captained by Paul Tibbets, dropped an atomic bomb called "Little Boy" on Hiroshima, Japan. Then on August 9, 1945, the plane called Bockscar, flown by Charles Sweeney, dropped the second atomic bomb, called "Fat Man" on Nagasaki, the largest seaport in southern Japan. Both bombs killed an estimated 150,000 to 220,000 people in 1945, although it is unknown how many actually died from the aftereffects of the bombings. Japan surrendered on August 15, 1945. The United Kingdom, according to the Quebec Agreement, consented to the US use of nuclear weapons against Japan.
- The comment "worth their weight in salt" refers to salt as a precious commodity. There was a time in

history when the richest principalities and towns regulated the salt trade.

- At the end of WW2, Japan's surrender resulted in splitting the country of Korea in half at the 38th parallel; Russia administered to the North and the United States administered to the South. On June 25, 1950, the North crossed into the South, spurring the United Nations to declare the move an invasion. The conflict lasted until July 27, 1953, when an armistice, not a peace treaty, was signed, creating the DMZ. (Demilitarized Zone). Without a peace treaty, both sides are technically still at war.

ABOUT THE AUTHOR

Pharmacy to Fiction.
Award-winning writing as a second career.

S. Lee Fisher, aka Dr. "P.," a clinical pharmacist, was born and raised in "small town" Pennsylvania. After moving to Pittsburgh, she enjoyed a successful corporate career managing retrospective clinical programs for the PBM side of a Fortune 20 company.

Fisher began writing fiction as a means of channeling the pain and grief of her father's passing. In the process, she discovered that she enjoys the creativity of telling stories.

Now a full-time novelist, Fisher lives on Florida's gulf coast with her husband of 38 years, Ralph. When she's not writing or dodging hurricanes, she enjoys painting watercolors, ballroom dancing, and swimming.

Becoming Olive W., Book 1 in the Women of Campbell County Series, won four awards in 2021 and is awaiting outcomes on several other nominations.

www.sleefisher.com

Facebook: @SherriLeeFisherProgar
Twitter: @ProgarSherri
Amazon: @author/sleefisher

ALSO BY S. LEE FISHER

The Women of Campbell County: Series

(RNS Publishing)

Becoming Olive W. Book 1

Under the Grapevine Book 2

Hill House, Divided Book 3 coming early 2022

Between Two Dreams Book 4 coming summer 2022

A Mystery of Grace Newman

(Springs Publisher)

Made in the USA
Middletown, DE
14 January 2024